The Art Dealer's Wife

by

JOE HILLEY

Dunlavy + Gray
HOUSTON

Dunlavy + Gray ©2020 by Joe Hilley

Library of Congress Control Number: 2020941323
ISBN: 978-0-9997813-5-7
E-Book ISBN: 978-0-9997813-6-4

This book is a work of fiction. Names, characters, businesses, organizations, places, events, and incidents either are the product of the author's imagination or are used fictitiously. Any resemblance to actual persons—living or dead—events, or locales are entirely coincidental.

Front cover art, *Pinks*, and back cover art, *Pensive 7,* by Joy Hilley Art
Typesetting by Fitz & Hill Creative Studio

Exactitude is not truth.

Henri Matisse

Chapter 1

Jack Frazer awakened to the blare of an alarm from his phone—a seven-note riff from Coltrane that jarred him from a warm, deep sleep to the glare of early morning sunlight streaming through the window. Barely conscious, he groped awkwardly for the nightstand, felt the phone with his fingertips, and pressed a button to snooze it. With peace restored to the room, he rolled on his side toward the center of the bed, expecting to find Zoë lying beside him, feeling warm and soft and inviting. Instead, he found only the cool touch of wrinkled sheets and a recess in the pillow where she'd rested her head.

With his free arm, he drew the pillow close and pressed it against his face. He breathed deeply, filling his lungs with her musky scent. In spite of all they'd said the night before, he wanted her more than ever and the memory of her smile filled his mind, followed quickly by the thought of her body pressed against his. He should get up, he knew, and find her—seated in the kitchen or lying on the sofa or wherever she might be—and make sure things were alright between them. He would do that, he assured himself, but not right then. Not yet. Just a little longer in bed and then he'd be ready to face the day.

Frazer, a reporter for The New York Times, grew up in California, where he spent most of his teenage years bouncing from party to party and arguing with his parents. Halfway through his senior year of high school he got serious about his future and enrolled at

Wake Forest University, where his grandfather had once been an English professor. He met Zoë Maybank during freshman orientation. She was an art major. He studied journalism.

For most of that first year he thought of her as just another girl, but in an elective art class during their second semester he realized she was more than a pretty face. By the end of their sophomore year they were seldom apart and married the summer after graduation. He took a job at a newspaper in Greensboro. She went to work in the art department at Guilford College. They lived downtown in a studio apartment. Life seemed fresh and new and more alive each day than the day before.

In his second year at the paper, one of his articles caught the eye of an editor at The New York Times. Not long after that, the Times offered him a job, first with a regional bureau, then in New York. They made the move to the city and three years later, Frazer wrote an article that won a Pulitzer Prize. All at once, the world seemed to open to him in ways he'd only imagined.

More articles followed, with more awards, then things seemed to stall. The paper still published his work. He still drew interesting assignments. But his writing went…stale. Agents stopped calling with suggestions for book deals, TV anchors no longer kept him on their quote lists, and life settled into the daily rhythm of a job.

A job. The office. Deadlines. Just thinking of it made him tired. More tired than he'd felt when he'd gone to bed the night before.

With a frustrated sigh Frazer flopped onto his back and let go of the pillow. Morning light, even more glaring than when he'd first awakened, streamed through the windows and with it came the muffled sound of city traffic from the street below. He lay there a moment longer, staring up at the ceiling, listening to the city as it came to life, while the conversation from the night before played through his mind once again.

More than a discussion, not exactly a fight, it was yet another round of the running disagreement they'd had for the past two years. He loved New York. Zoë did not. He wanted to live there for the foreseeable future. She wanted to return to Charleston, where she'd grown up. But unlike the discussions and arguments they'd had in the past, this time things had reached an end. He'd been unwilling to acknowledge it, but inside he knew the inescapable truth. She'd given notice at her job, called her mother to arrange for a place to stay, and set her mind to leave.

The bedroom door was ajar and through the opening he saw the light was on in the kitchen, so he threw aside the covers, rolled from the bed, and started in that direction. As he rounded the corner from the hallway, he found Zoë seated at the breakfast table, sipping a cup of coffee. She was dressed and ready with two suitcases at her side.

"You're really doing this?" Frazer asked, pointing to the luggage.

"I'm really doing it." She glanced at him over the rim of her cup.

"You think whatever is wrong will somehow evaporate between here and Charleston?"

"I've been trying to talk to you about this for…years."

He dropped onto a chair beside her. "About leaving me?"

"Stop it," she scowled. "It's not about that and you know it. I'm not leaving you. I'm leaving New York."

A frown wrinkled his brow. "Just like that?"

"It's not just like that," she countered. "I told you. I've been telling you for the last two years. I can't do this anymore."

"Do what?"

"Live like this."

"Live like what?"

"You coming and going at odd hours." She set the cup on the table and rested her hand on his. "Both of us working day and night. Paying thousands of dollars a month for a one bedroom apartment."

"On the Upper East Side," he noted.

"It's still thousands of dollars."

He drew back his hand and leaned against the chair. "So you're just bailing?"

"I'm not bailing." Frustration gave an edge to her voice and she clinched a fist which she bounced against the top of her thigh. "Sometimes you can be so infuriating."

"Not bailing," he repeated with a catty tone. "Just moving to

Charleston?'"

"Where we can actually have a life."

"Yeah," Frazer smirked. "And spend our time reporting on how well the azaleas bloomed this year."

"This is what I'm talking about." Zoë shook her head. "You've become just like everyone else up here." She picked up her cup and stood. "If it's not from New York, you make fun of it."

"I'm not making fun of anything. I'm saying there's nothing to report on down there. Nothing."

"There's not nothing," she argued as she lifted the urn from the coffeemaker and refilled her cup.

"Then what?" he said insistently. "Your mother sends you the Charleston paper every week. What's in it?"

"Not much," she conceded as she returned to the chair at the table. "But that's not the point."

"Then what's the point?"

"I don't like New York." Her eyes bore in on him. "And ever since you won that Pulitzer you've been different."

"How?" He folded his arms across his chest in a defensive pose. "How am I different?"

"I don't know," she shrugged. "Just different. It's like 'I'm a Pulitzer winner. I have to do these great stories.'" An edge crept into her voice that was all but mocking. "Only great stories don't come along that often, so rather than write about what's at hand you go off… tilting at windmills."

"What do you want me to do?"

She looked him in the eye. "I want you to write that novel you're always talking about."

"And how am I supposed to do that and work too? When do I have time?"

"That's what I mean." Her voice was loud as she made her point, but she paused and took a breath before continuing. "If we were in Charleston," she said in a controlled tone, "you could work for the Post and Courier. Mama still owns part of the paper. She knows people. She'll tell them to hire you. You could write for the paper during the day and work on a novel at night and weekends."

He looked away. "You just want children."

Without warning, she backhanded him with a fist to the chest. "Don't you dare reduce my concerns to a sexist cliché," she hissed. "This is not about whether I want children and you know it. I just want a life." She checked her watch. "I need to get to the airport."

"Let me get dressed and I'll get the car from the deck. We can drive there together."

"No," she said. "There isn't time for that. You have to get to work. I have to catch a plane. I'll take a taxi."

He rose and took her in his arms, pulling her close as she leaned toward him. "I love you," he whispered.

"I love you, too." She kissed him lightly on the lips, then pulled away and picked up a suitcase in each hand. "But I can't stay here any longer."

"Give me those," he said, taking them from her. She glared at him unsure whether he meant to stop her. "I may be a New Yorker and all those other things you said, but I'm not letting my wife carry her own bags."

With her hands free, she took the apartment key from a table near the door and started toward the corridor. He followed with the suitcases. As they rode the elevator to the lobby, he stared up at the numbers above the door and muttered, "I can't believe I'm doing this."

"Doing what?"

"You're leaving me and I'm carrying your bags for you."

"I'm not leaving you," she sighed. "I told you, I'm just leaving New York."

When they reached the first floor the elevator doors opened and they crossed the lobby to the building entrance. She led the way. He followed a step behind. The doorman saw them coming and pushed open the door as they approached.

A blast of cold winter air rushed toward them and Frazer, clad only in cotton shorts and a t-shirt, felt a chill run through his body. He ignored it and set the luggage at the curb beside his bare feet, then turned to her. There were many things he wanted to say but instead he simply leaned forward and kissed her. "I miss you," he whispered.

"I miss you, too," she replied. Her eyes were full and she glanced away. "But I can't stay here, Jack. I just can't stay here."

The screech of the doorman's whistle was shrill as he stepped into the street to hail a cab. A moment later, a taxi came to a stop near the curb and the driver got out to open the trunk. The doorman took Zoë's luggage and Frazer opened the rear door of the car for her. He held it as she ducked onto the back seat.

"I'll be at Mother's," she said as she settled into place.

"I'll call you—" Just then, Frazer's cell phone rang. He took it from his pocket and glanced at the screen.

Zoë rolled her eyes. "That's what I'm talking about." She pointed with her index finger for emphasis. "That right there."

A scowl wrinkled his forehead. "I have no control over who calls me." He shoved the phone into his pocket.

"I know," she sighed. "But why did you even look at it. Were you really going to take a call now?"

Frazer leaned inside the car and gave her one last kiss, then stepped back and pushed the door closed. A moment later Zoë waved to him through the window as the taxi pulled away from the curb.

It was a surreal moment—him standing on the sidewalk in the cold with the traffic swirling around him, watching as his wife rode away in a cab. Then the doorman's hand on his shoulder brought him back to the moment. "You better get inside, Mr. Frazer. You'll get sick out here dressed like that." Frazer nodded in response, but his eyes were fixed on the taxi as it moved through traffic, then turned right at the next corner and disappeared.

When the car was out of sight, he took the cell phone from his pocket and checked the screen. The call he'd missed was from David Anders. With a flick of his thumb, he redialed the number and seconds later Anders answered. "We need to do lunch," he said.

"When?"

"Today."

"Okay," Frazer replied. "Where do you—" The blare of a car horn interrupted him, then a group came from the lobby, talking and laughing as they passed by.

"What's all that noise?" Anders asked.

"I'm down by the front door."

"On your way to the office already?"

"No," Frazer answered. "What time do you want to meet?"

"Noon at Minetta Tavern."

"Only if you're buying."

"Okay," Anders replied. "I'll see you there."

The call ended abruptly and Frazer lowered the phone from his ear. Still on the sidewalk, he stared into the distance and imagined again the moment the taxi disappeared from sight. Zoë was seated in back, facing forward as the car made the corner, but at the last possible moment she turned to look at him and their eyes met. At the memory of it, a sinking feeling pressed against his chest and for the first time he realized the awful loneliness of not having her with him.

Chapter 2

After a shower and a cup of coffee, Frazer came from the apartment and trekked across town to the office. He spent the morning working on a story about people who lived in the tunnels beneath the city. It was an old story—part truth, part urban legend—about the homeless who chose to live in the abandoned utility and subway tunnels that crisscrossed Manhattan. Popular lore said the underground space had become a subterranean neighborhood with carefully defined living spaces furnished with salvaged furniture and rigged with makeshift lighting. Thus far, however, no one had documented it. Frazer wanted to know if the stories were true and for a while entertained the idea of living down there long enough to see for himself.

For most of the morning Frazer read previous news articles on the topic and watched interviews from television reporters who attempted to report the story. All the while, however, his mind kept drifting to Zoë and he checked his watch repeatedly, waiting for her flight to land in Atlanta. She had a layover of several hours there before the connecting flight to Charleston, and he planned to call her while she was in the airport. Then he got busy searching for maps of the nineteenth century steam pipe system and lost track of time.

About eleven o'clock, an alarm sounded from his phone telling him it was time to leave for lunch with David Anders. He took a cab from his office on Forty-Second Street and rode to Minetta Tavern in Lower Manhattan. He was seated at a table in back when he thought of Zoë again and remembered he'd wanted to call her, but just then his phone dinged with a text message that read, "Plane is late. Still in Atlanta."

A wave of guilt swept over him as he quickly replied, "Miss you."

"There's another flight at four from LaGuardia," she responded. "You'd be at Mother's in time for a late supper."

"Meeting Dave Anders for lunch."

"Chasing another story?"

"Something like that."

Though only a few hours had passed since Zoë left, already the distance between them seemed greater than ever and right then he had the urge to do something about it. To make a reservation for the afternoon flight and catch up with her before nightfall. He'd been a jerk about the whole thing. Should have listened to her the first time she tried to talk to him about their situation. Should have done something about it then. Angry with himself for letting things get this far, he flipped the screen on the phone with his thumb to call the airline but before he could do so, Anders appeared at the table.

After graduating from Dartmouth, Anders worked briefly as a curator at The Frick, then went into business for himself as an art dealer, first with the work of emerging artists in the Village—when artists still lived there—and later uptown in the secondary market for a clientele of established painters. Now, at fifty-something, his gallery on Seventy-Ninth Street was a required stop for anyone interested in building a serious collection.

Frazer and Anders first met when Anders was liquidating an art collection owned by Edith Morgenstern's first husband. One of the paintings had been reported stolen in the 1960s and the FBI still had an open file on it. Anders' fee for his work on the entire collection hinged on resolving that open file.

Back then, Preston Cooper, the FBI agent assigned to the open case, was young, brash, and new to the bureau. Almost immediately, Cooper and Anders were at odds with each other and a lucrative sale of the collection seemed on the verge of collapsing. In an effort to get the matter moving toward resolution, Anders contacted a friend at the Times in the hope that exposure in the paper would prod Cooper in the right direction. His tip about the story arrived on a busy day and the assignment landed on Frazer's desk. Reporting on the case led to articles about the underlying art theft, one of which won the Pulitzer Prize. It also led to a resolution of the controversy in a way that preserved Anders' commission on the sale. Since then, Frazer and Anders had been friends.

Anders slid onto a seat across from Frazer. "You got here first," he grinned. "You get to buy."

"If I'm buying," Frazer replied, "we'd better find a hotdog stand."

They talked a moment longer about nothing at all and then Anders turned to the reason he called. "I know you're always on the lookout for a good story, so I was thinking maybe I have an idea for you."

"What's it about?"

"A couple of art dealers."

"Not exactly my area," Frazer said. "We have a department that covers the arts. They protect their turf rather jealously, too."

"This would be a little different from the usual arts piece your paper runs."

"What are you talking about?"

"Hasan Izmir and his brother, Ahmed. Do you know them?"

"They have a gallery in Chelsea?"

"Yes."

"I think we ran a few articles on them. Emigrated from Turkey. Made a fortune in real estate."

"That's where they got their money," Anders said. "Used it to amass a sizeable art collection, then opened the gallery in Chelsea."

"Sounds like a great American story," Frazer noted, "but it's already been done. That's what our previous articles were about."

"I'm not suggesting that story," Anders countered. "I'm suggesting a different one."

"Like what?"

"Have you ever seen them at an auction?"

"I've never seen them anywhere," Frazer replied. "And I've never been to their gallery. Never been to any art gallery, for that matter."

Anders had a skeptical expression. "You've lived in Manhattan this long and you've never been to an art gallery?"

"No."

"And you did that other story I gave you without ever attending an auction?"

"Right."

"Or going to a gallery?"

"Like I said, we have an arts department that covers that."

"You need to see an auction. One that the Izmir brothers attend."

"What do they do that's so interesting?"

"Auctions are traditionally dignified, orderly affairs."

"Right," Frazer agreed.

"These guys are loud and obnoxious. Laughing and yelling at each other the whole time. And they spend way too much money."

"Too much money?" Frazer frowned. "You're an art dealer and you're complaining that someone is spending too much money at an art auction?"

"I'm not complaining from a financial standpoint," Anders explained. "I'm just saying, when someone who's supposedly in the business throws around the kind of money they throw around, acquiring pieces at way over their value, the spending is a symptom of something else."

"Like?"

"I don't know. That's what you need to find out." Anders leaned back in his chair. "Look, I'm glad for people to spend their money on art. When people spend money, guys like me make money. That's how I make my living. That's how everyone else in the business makes a living, too. But what these guys are doing isn't right. It doesn't feel right. It doesn't sound right. It doesn't look right. I just think someone should poke around and find out what they're really up to, because it can't be art as a business. There's no way the art business is profitable for a dealer who spends that much on contemporary pieces by unknown contemporary artists. It has to be about something else."

"That's what they're buying? Contemporary art?"

"Most of it." Anders leaned forward. "Look, I'm not saying it's the next big story. I'm just saying, there's a story here and someone needs to pay attention to it."

"Maybe there is a story, but like I said, I'm not the arts correspondent. Editors don't like it when we stray too far from our assigned areas."

"But that's what I'm telling you," Anders countered. "It wouldn't have to be an article about art. Just an article about them and their gallery. An exposé of sorts."

"I don't know," Frazer said, shaking his head. "Sounds like an art story to me."

"Would you at least come to an auction and see for yourself what they're doing?"

"Maybe," Frazer shrugged. "But tell me something, David."

"What's that?"

"Why are you interested in this? You've got more money than you need. Last I heard, your business was booming. Why are you interested in this?"

"Just what I'm telling you," Anders insisted. "They've been acting like this for months. I was at an auction last night and somebody said they ought to make a movie about them. That it would be a good story. Which made me think of you. I remembered how well it worked out with that story about Mrs. Morgenstern and thought, hey, maybe a second time."

"And?"

"No," Anders demurred. "Really. I—"

"David," Frazer said, interrupting. "Tell me the rest of it."

"Okay." Anders leaned closer and lowered his voice. "I hate the bastards. They are driving me crazy. And they're ruining the business. I buy at auction to resell or to pick up something I already know a client wants. These idiots treat it like it's an amusement park.

They drive up the price, bidding against each other to see which one gets stuck with the piece. Like the whole thing is a game. And they laugh at the rest of us because they've shut us out or, worse, they've dropped a painting on one of us at a ridiculously high price."

Frazer had a knowing grin. "They outbid you last night?"

"Yes. But it's not about that." Anders was defensive. "And it's not just me. No one likes them. At least none of the other dealers. And none of the serious collectors, either. We've got to do something."

"Is it illegal to run up the price, even if you're doing it as a game?"

"No." Anders sighed. "As long as you pay, the auction house doesn't care."

"Doesn't the house sometimes have people who do that very thing on their own behalf?"

"Not like this." Anders shook his head more vigorously than before. "This isn't that. They might have people in the room to get the bidding started but they don't bid against themselves, unless they're buying a piece to protect the value or the artist's reputation."

Frazer gestured with a wave of his hand. "That's what I mean."

"Look, I'm sure in some respects the house loves it when they do this," Anders admitted. "The higher the price, the more they make. But these guys are making a mockery of the whole business. And it's gone on long enough that people are starting to talk about buying elsewhere."

"Elsewhere? Are these guys only showing up at one auction house?"

"Mostly at Mournet's, but they attend auctions all over the city."

"That's where you were last night? Mournet's?"

"Yes."

"So, when people talk about going somewhere else, where do they think they can go that the Izmirs won't be also?"

"The serious ones are talking about doing their buying in Europe or moving some of their business online."

"Europe?"

"Yes."

"They're that upset?"

"I'm telling you," Anders said. "This is a big deal. And if it keeps going like this, people will get enough of it and stop attending."

"The Izmirs must have a lot of money."

"That's their story. The story they want people to tell."

"You don't think it's true?"

"They must have money from somewhere. I mean, one or the other of them usually gets stuck with at least one of those over-priced pieces every night, but they don't seem to mind. The auction houses let them come back which means their checks to pay for the purchases haven't bounced—the house won't let you bid if that happens—so, they either have a lot of money or very good credit."

Frazer thought for a moment, then asked, "How did they go from real estate to art gallery?"

"Hasan married a smart woman."

"Oh." Frazer raised an eyebrow. "What's her name?"

"Sibel. She runs the art business."

"So, this was a rich guy setting up his wife in the art business to keep her happy?"

"I don't think so," Anders said. "I think they got into the business together, but she's the stronger of the two. Even before they set up the gallery. Listen, I think if you looked into this—I mean really investigated it—you'd find out they are up to something else besides the art business."

"You think the gallery isn't a gallery?"

"They're moving a lot of art, but my gut tells me that's not all they're doing. Like I said, they're throwing around too much money for it to be a business. They won't live long enough to see the value of the pieces they're buying catch up to the prices they're paying."

Frazer nodded. "Have you approached anyone in law enforcement with this?"

"Not really. But that's not a bad idea. Are you still friends with that FBI agent we met when we were working with Mrs. Morgenstern?"

"Preston Cooper?"

"Yeah," Anders said. "I couldn't remember his name. Are you

still friends with him?"

"I see him occasionally. Why?"

"You mentioned law enforcement. Maybe I should talk to him. The FBI would have the resources to find out what's going on. And after 9-11 they said we should call someone if we see something suspicious." Anders seemed to be thinking out loud. "That's all I'm doing with you. I'm calling someone because I see something that looks suspicious. And maybe the FBI should take a look. Just a look. That's all. I'm not accusing them of something. It just doesn't seem right and I think someone ought to take a look at it."

Frazer heard the tentativeness in Anders' voice and noted the way he seemed to cover himself, as if he didn't want to say too much and leave himself vulnerable to a claim by the Izmir brothers, though he wasn't sure what that claim could be. Still, the way Anders talked left him suspicious there was more to what Anders wanted than merely a story in the paper. "So," Frazer said. "Why don't you just call Preston yourself with this?"

Anders had a pained expression. "He and I didn't get along so well and I didn't stay in touch with him. It would feel awkward to just call him out of the blue."

"I remember you didn't like him."

"He was too arrogant for me."

"He's mellowed some."

"Some?"

"Okay. A little," Frazer conceded. "But once you get to know him, he's not so bad."

"So, you still see him?"

"Our wives are friends."

"Can you find out if he'll talk to me?"

"I don't know." Frazer was equivocal. "It's a little touchy. We're friends. We see each other occasionally. Socially. Have dinner once in a while. They come over to the apartment sometimes. We go over there. But we keep our distance professionally. I don't ask him about his work. He doesn't ask me about mine."

"I'm not asking you to vouch for me," Anders countered. "Just remind him of who I am and find out if he'll sit down with me for a few minutes. I'll take it from there."

"Okay," Frazer conceded. "I'll see what I can do."

"And in the meantime, come to an auction. Mournet's is having a contemporary sale later this week. I can get you in. Introduce you around to everyone. They'll tell you the same thing I've said, but if you come you can see it for yourself."

"I'll see," Frazer replied. "Let's eat. I'm starved."

"Good idea." Anders caught the waiter's attention and waved him over to the table.

Chapter 3

In Paris, nighttime had fallen and Marcel Kirchen watched from the van's second row seat as Rodchenko, the driver, steered them up Rue Pavée, a narrow street in the city's old Jewish Quarter. Seated next to Kirchen was Senyavin and behind them, Gennady Krylov occupied the van's third row seat.

As they passed Agoudas Hakehilos Synagogue, Kirchen tapped Rodchenko on the shoulder. "It's up there," he said, pointing to a townhouse on the left. "The one with the red door."

Rodchenko brought the van to a stop in front of the townhouse. Kirchen reached for the van's door handle. "Give me a few minutes, then come inside."

"We know the plan," Senyavin grumbled. The sound of his voice grated on Kirchen's nerves.

Very early in the project, while they still were planning it, Kirchen had come to regret hiring Senyavin for the crew. Surly and always disgruntled, he'd done his best to undermine their success at every turn. But Mogilevich had suggested him and because a suggestion from Mogilevich was never merely a suggestion, Kirchen had accepted him. But since then, Senyavin had proved his initial reluctance correct.

Rather than respond to Senyavin, Kirchen opened the door and stepped out to the pavement. He glanced warily over his shoulder, however, as he crossed the street to the sidewalk. Senyavin was not one to be trusted and as Kirchen made his way up the steps to the townhouse entrance, it seemed as though Senyavin was watching his every move. "All the more reason to eliminate him," he whispered to himself. "Once we are done."

A call box was located near the door to the townhouse and when Kirchen reached it, he pressed a button on the box, then waited. After a moment, he heard the clatter of the electronic lock, then the door opened and André Crémieux appeared.

Dressed in a dark gray suit with a pale blue shirt and red tie, Crémieux looked every bit the Paris art dealer that he claimed to be. About seventy, he was tall and lean with dark hair that had an appropriate touch of gray. His eyes were intelligent, but the kind that seemed always to be looking past everything to someone or something else. No one was certain of his earlier life, but his career in the art world began as an assistant curator at the Galeries Nationales du Grand Palais. Later, he worked for Henri Léaud before branching out on his own.

When he first opened his gallery, Crémieux sold art primarily to French clients—mostly private Parisian collectors. As his business expanded, he attracted the attention of a buyer in Luxembourg who valued anonymity. Working with him gave Crémieux access to clients in Dubai and Qatar and solidified his reputation for managing discreet transactions. Most recently, he'd been dealing with buyers from Russia and Eastern Europe who prized the secrecy he provided.

"Ah, Marcel," Crémieux said as he greeted Kirchen. "I expected you earlier."

"We were delayed," Kirchen explained as he pushed his way inside.

"No problem," Crémieux replied. "No problem at all. I knew you would come eventually." He glanced out the door, checking nervously up and down the street, then pushed it closed and fastened the lock. As he started from the entrance, he motioned for Kirchen to follow. "Come along," he said. "Let us finish our business."

Kirchen followed Crémieux from the entrance to the main

hallway, a broad corridor with oak floors and smooth plaster walls that rose to the ceiling twenty feet above. Partway down the hall, they passed a doorway on the left that opened to a parlor. Kirchen glanced inside and saw the room held three sofas and half a dozen chairs, all of which appeared to be of Rocco style, but he was not sure. That much furniture genuinely of that era would have been quite expensive.

The walls of the parlor held paintings that were mounted in heavy ornate frames. One of them—an oversized work in rich, dark colors—resembled a Vermeer. Another appeared to be a Rembrandt, but Kirchen's discerning eye quickly noted the flaws in both. Second-rate copies, he thought. Which served to confirm his suspicions about the furniture.

Beyond the parlor was a door that led to the dining room and next to the doorway was a painting that caught Kirchen's eye. He paused to admire it. Small by comparison to the others in the house, this one had bright, vivid colors with thick, bold strokes. "Woman with table and vase," he whispered.

Crémieux seemed surprised. "You know Matisse?"

"I studied art once. A long time ago." Kirchen glanced at the painting. "How much for it?"

"I'm afraid it's not for sale," Crémieux said. "This one belongs to someone else."

"Everything belongs to someone else," Kirchen mumbled, his voice barely above a whisper.

"The owner is coming tomorrow to collect it. Please," Crémieux insisted, pointing to the room across the hall. "We must get moving." He stepped in that direction. "You are prepared to consummate our transaction?"

"Yes," Kirchen answered. "Of course. You have the paintings?"

"They are over here." Crémieux gestured once more to the room across the hall.

Kirchen followed him into the second parlor and glanced around. Hundreds of paintings were propped against the wall, eight or ten deep all the way around the room.

"Yours are on the left," Crémieux directed.

Kirchen made his way slowly down that side, flipping through the paintings as he went.

"The deal was for cash," Crémieux reminded him.

"You are still comfortable with that?"

Crémieux smiled nervously. "Cash is always comfortable."

"There'll be a lot of it."

"We discussed that earlier."

"I know we discussed it earlier, but this is our first time working with you and I want to make certain you are comfortable." Kirchen glanced back at Crémieux, a hint of anger in his eyes. "It's a lot of cash."

"I am prepared for that," Crémieux assured.

"You have a place to put it?"

"Yes. I have a place to put it." Crémieux checked his watch. "Please. It is getting late and I have another client who will be here soon. We still need to make the exchange and get your paintings loaded."

Just then, the front door rattled and Crémieux went to open it. With Crémieux's attention diverted, Kirchen stepped back to the hall and stood again at the Matisse. He touched the frame with his finger and pressed against the corner just enough to make it move ever so slightly. From the weight against his fingertip and the angle of the frame's motion he knew the painting hung freely. Mounted with wooden cleats, he supposed, but without a mending plate or tether to secure it to the wall.

The heavy sound of booted footsteps caught Kirchen's attention and he looked up to see Crémieux coming toward him, accompanied by the men from the van. Each of them carried a duffel bag, stuffed and heavy, which they brought to the parlor and placed in a row near the paintings on the left side of the room.

Crémieux came behind them, stooped over the first bag, and opened it. His eyes grew wide as he saw it was filled with US currency. He unzipped the others and checked the contents, reaching with his hand all the way to the bottom. When he'd checked all of them, he turned to Kirchen, who now stood in the room. "All seems to be in order," he said.

"You are satisfied?"

"Yes." Crémieux smiled. "Very satisfied."

Kirchen nodded to the men and they began carrying paintings from the room three and four at a time. Thirty minutes later, the left side of the room was stripped bare and Kirchen was once again alone in the hall with Crémieux.

"I believe that concludes our business," Crémieux said. There was a hint of impatience in his voice.

Kirchen pointed to the Matisse. "So," he said confidently, "what was your price for this one?"

"As I said before," Crémieux responded. "It is not for sale."

"Everything is for sale, Mr. Crémieux." Kirchen drew an automatic pistol from beneath his jacket. "It's only a question of how much one is willing to pay to obtain the things one wishes to own."

Crémieux's eyes were wide with fright and he held up his hands in protest. "What are you—"

With practiced ease, Kirchen placed the muzzle of the barrel against Crémieux's skull and squeezed the trigger. The pistol made a muffled pop as the bullet struck Crémieux's forehead, just above the bridge of his nose. He stood there a moment, eyes transfixed, mouth slightly agape in a look of surprise, then a stream of blood oozed from the wound, tricked past the corner of one eye, and slowly made its way down his cheek. Seconds later, his knees buckled and he collapsed to the floor.

As Crémieux's body landed on the floor, Kirchen returned the pistol to its place beneath his jacket and carefully lifted the Matisse from the wall. He carried it across the hall to the parlor and wedged it into one of the duffel bags, then slung the strap of the bag over his shoulder. He hung a second bag from his opposite shoulder, then took the ones that remained with either hand and made his way up the hall toward the front door.

When Kirchen reached the van, the side door slid open and Senyavin stepped out to help him. Krylov, seated again on the third row, glared at him. "What is that?" he asked, pointing to the painting that protruded from the top of the duffel.

Kirchen ignored him and set the bags in the van, then climbed onto the seat behind Rodchenko, the driver. Krylov shoved the door closed and the van started forward. As they drove from the house, Kirchen took the Matisse from the bag and handed it to Krylov. "Add that to the list," he said.

Krylov took it from him. "What is it?"

"A Matisse."

"How do I describe it?"

"Woman with table and vase."

Krylov set the painting on the floor by his feet. "That wasn't part of the deal."

"We made a separate arrangement for that one."

Krylov pointed to the duffel bags. "What about those? I didn't know we were taking the money, too."

Kirchen glanced in Krylov's direction. "You ask a lot of questions."

The muscles along Krylov's jaw flexed. "Mogilevich knows about this?"

Kirchen ignored the question and turned back to the driver. "Drop me at the hotel."

Krylov slumped onto the seat and they rode several blocks without anyone saying a word, the silence broken only by the rattling of the van over the rough city streets. Finally, as the hotel came into view, Kirchen looked over at Krylov once more. "You know the contact for the shipment?"

"Yes."

"Hasan Izmir. Galerie Le Meilleur," Kirchen said. "In New York. You've got it in your notes?"

"We've been over this before," Krylov groused.

"They have another round of auctions scheduled for next month. We don't want to miss them. So, send these paintings by air."

Krylov sighed. "The paintings will be there long before the auction."

The van came to a stop at the hotel entrance. Kirchen took the duffel bags from the van just as he brought them from the townhouse—one on each shoulder, hanging by the straps, and one in each hand, holding them by the hand grips—then made his way inside the hotel lobby and disappeared.

After dropping Kirchen at the hotel with the duffel bags, Krylov and the crew rode to a warehouse on the north side of Paris. For the next two hours they packed the paintings into specially constructed wooden crates with dividers that created slots for each individual picture.

When all the paintings were in place and the crates were closed, Rodchenko opened a cooler and took out a bottle of beer. He tossed the first bottle to Krylov, then took another for himself.

"Good thing Kirchen isn't here." Senyavin groused. "He'd have your head for drinking on the job."

"Kirchen could try," Rodchenko snarked. "But he would regret it."

Senyavin lumbered to the cooler and took out a bottle. "Maybe we'll see if he can take me, too." The others laughed in response.

Krylov took a long drink from the bottle he was holding, then paused to swallow. Without looking to anyone in particular, he said, "I hate that damn German."

"Who?" Senyavin asked.

"Kirchen."

"He's from Luxembourg."

"Like I said," Krylov growled. "I hate that damn German."

Rodchenko laughed heartily. Senyavin frowned. "I thought people from Luxembourg were something else."

"Dutch, Swedes, Danes, Austrians." Krylov shrugged. "They're all Germans."

"What about the French?"

"Yeah," Krylov added. "Them, too."

"And the English?"

Krylov cut his eyes in Senyavin's direction. "You're about to get me started."

"Don't get him started," Rodchenko laughed. "We still have to get these crates to the shipper."

"Can't send them late," Senyavin added in a mocking voice. "Kirchen really wouldn't be happy then."

"It's not Kirchen we have to worry about," Rodchenko said. "If we miss that auction, we won't get paid."

"If we miss that auction," Krylov suggested, "Mogilevich will see that we never need to be paid."

Everyone laughed, but this time it was laughter tempered by the truth that Krylov was right. Mogilevich had rules and he didn't believe in second chances. Break the rules and you paid with your life.

When they finished drinking their beer, Krylov used a forklift to load the crates onto a box truck that was parked nearby. Once the crates were in place and the truck door was latched, Rodchenko got in behind the steering wheel. Krylov came around to the passenger side of the cab. As he climbed onto the seat, he called over to Senyavin. "Take the van to the hotel. We'll meet you there."

From the warehouse, Krylov and Rodchenko rode to Atlantic Air Freight, a shipping company with an office twenty blocks away. They backed the truck to a loading dock and went inside. At the counter, Krylov arranged the shipment in Kirchen's name—three crates for delivery to Hasan Izmir at Galerie Le Meilleur in New York.

When the crates were unloaded and the transfer documents signed, they walked back to the truck. Rodchenko glanced over at Krylov. "Are you sure you should have used his actual name for that?"

"Don't worry about it," Krylov smiled. "When Mogilevich finds out what he did to get that Matisse, this shipment will be the least of Kirchen's problems."

Rodchenko had a quizzical expression. "You knew about his

extra deal for that painting? Before we went in there?"

"No, but I know Kirchen and I've cleaned up after him before. And this is the last time." Krylov shook his head in disgust. "I hate that damn German."

Chapter 4

Early the following day, Jacob Edelman sat at a table in the kitchen of a Paris apartment that was owned by his cousin, Micheline Binoche. As he ate a muffin and sipped from a cup of coffee, he glanced out the window through which he had a view down the Rue de Conde all the way to Luxembourg Palace, home of the French senate. Despite all that had happened to him, to his family, to the people he knew as a child, he loved the city. The sunlight on the buildings in the morning. The sound of traffic on the street through the day. And the smells—he especially loved the smells.

Though well past eighty, Edelman was spry, active, and in remarkably good health. And despite the aches that came with age, his mind was as alert as ever. That morning, he was especially focused on the business he'd come to settle. Old business. Family business. Which he finally would put to rest, hopefully, by the week's end.

Micheline was seated across from him, reading the morning newspaper. Less than a year older than Edelman, she was thin, frail, and suffered from tremors that left her confined to the apartment. Most days she slept late, sat at the kitchen table until mid-afternoon, and returned to bed early in the evening. Edelman's visit had disrupted her schedule and even now he wondered whether she was really reading the paper or dozing.

In the years before World War II, when Edelman and Micheline were children, their fathers—Menachem and Isaac Edelman—were in business together with stores in Paris' wealthiest districts. Edelman Brothers clothing stores were very popular. Using money from the stores, the brothers filled their homes with objects of value and beauty—rare coins, collectible books, works of art, and jewelry.

After Hitler and the Nazis came to power in Germany, Menachem and Isaac took steps to protect their assets. The bulk of their coin and jewelry collection was sent to a bank in Switzerland for safekeeping. Most of the art was transferred to relatives in the United States. Rare books were sold and jewelry was secreted away, in the hope it could be used as a form of payment should normal transactions become impossible.

Their best efforts, however, proved to be not quite enough and events overtook the brothers more quickly than they had anticipated, leaving them unable to remove everything. As a result, many valuable paintings remained in Paris when the Nazis arrived. All but two of those pieces were seized by the Germans.

Isaac, Micheline's father, was sent to Auschwitz, along with her mother and two of her brothers. All of them were executed on the day they arrived at the camp. Micheline, however, caught the eye of a Catholic aid worker and spent the initial years of the war in a French internment camp. Later, she escaped to live with friends in a small village near Toulouse where she remained in hiding until France was liberated.

Unlike Micheline, however, Edelman and his parents left France, escaping only days ahead of the advancing German army. After an arduous trip across the Mediterranean to North Africa, they arrived in New York and spent the war in the safety of America. Edelman attended school in Manhattan, graduated from Columbia University with a degree in mathematics, and went to work as an actuarial with an insurance company, eventually rising to the top of his department.

Accolades and industry awards marked a professional career that saw many successes—a probability model Edelman created became the accepted standard of the business and he was known to his peers far and wide as an expert in risk assessment. But at night, when he returned home, Edelman laid aside his professional identity and turned to the project by which he defined himself and his life. The endeavor from which he obtained the deepest meaning and significance. The quest for the artworks that had been seized from his family by the Nazis.

Working in his spare time, Edelman gradually assembled letters and receipts documenting the original purchases, most of it taken from the papers of family members. He also gathered photographs from family and friends that showed the pieces hanging in his parent's home or in the home of his uncle. As he assimilated the information, he located archival photos that showed many of those same pieces in Nazi hands.

Using vacation time at first, then later in retirement, Edelman traveled the world relentlessly, doggedly, determinedly, locating each of the missing items, acquiring them, and bringing them back to his Manhattan apartment. Now, after a lifetime of work, only three paintings remained yet to be found. One of those was a work by Matisse entitled *Woman With Table and Vase*.

Thought by art historians to have been destroyed near the end of the war in a fire at Hermann Göring's country residence, Edelman spotted *Woman With Table and Vase* listed under a different name in an auction catalog from a small Vienna gallery. Using a combination of threats and bribery, Edelman obtained the gallery's records for the painting and traced it to a collector in Antwerp. However, by the time he located the owner, the piece had been sold to a Paris collector and eventually transferred to André Crémieux. On the morning when he sat at the table in Micheline's kitchen, Edelman had been in Paris for two weeks negotiating with Crémieux for the painting's return.

As Edelman sipped coffee, he looked across the table at Micheline and thought about all that had happened in their lives, the places they'd been, the things they'd been forced to endure, and how different their lives had been. His challenges had been primarily personal. Growing up in America gave him a life of privilege compared to the circumstances Micheline had endured. She had suffered many of the horrors that defined the war and bore the marks of it in her body to that day, while he'd lived a life of comparative ease, concerned only about the mundane issues of an urban existence.

Now, he was only hours away from holding in his hands an item that connected them both to a past that seemed always with them. Perhaps Micheline should have this painting, he thought. Perhaps she should have half the paintings that hung in his apartment back in New York, too. He'd reacquired many of them with his own money, but they had been purchased originally with money from the business that their fathers co-owned. Some of them had even hung on the walls of Micheline's childhood home.

And it was only art. He enjoyed it immensely but as time passed, he'd come to see that his father was right when he said, "Buy pieces you enjoy and you will receive a return on your investment every time you look at them." Micheline had children and grandchildren. They might enjoy a painting with ties to their family's history, too. After all, that was what really mattered, having the pieces back in the family.

Edelman thought about all of that as he took another sip of coffee, then looked over at Micheline once more. "When you were in the camp at Struthof, did you ever think—"

"Oh my," Micheline gasped, interrupting him. She lowered the paper and stared at him, eyes wide open, her hand to her mouth in a look of desperation.

"What is it?" Edelman set his cup aside. "What's the matter?" At her age, it could have been anything and instantly he feared the worst.

"This." She turned the paper so he could see and pointed to an article. "It's about André Crémieux."

Edelman took the paper from her and tilted it toward the light that came through the window. He quickly scanned the article, mumbling to himself as he read it. "He was found in his townhouse yesterday by his housekeeper...a single gunshot to the forehead." He studied the article more closely. "It doesn't say..."

"Doesn't say what?"

"It doesn't say…"

Micheline reached across the table and rested her hand on his forearm. "What doesn't it say, Jacob? Stop reading and tell me."

Edelman laid the newspaper on the table and stood. "It doesn't say anything about the Matisse." In three quick strides, he crossed the room to the telephone, lifted the receiver, and entered a number.

Micheline turned toward him "Who are you calling?"

"Jean-Louis Ferro," Edelman replied.

Ferro worked with the French Ministry of Culture where he supervised a special group assigned to assist French citizens in recovering property stolen by the Nazis. Edelman had collaborated with him many times in the past and the two had become good friends.

After two rings, Edelman reached an assistant and explained the reason for the call. A moment later, Ferro came on the line. "Where have you been?" he asked. "I've been calling you since yesterday."

"My phone stopped working," Edelman replied. It was true. His cell phone stopped working the day before and he'd been unable to reach his voicemail. "Did they find the Matisse?"

"I don't want to discuss this now." Ferro was curt in his response. "Meet me at Crémieux's townhouse."

Edelman ended the call abruptly, then dressed quickly and took a taxi from the apartment. He arrived at the townhouse to find Ferro waiting on the steps outside. Though Crémieux had been found dead the night before, a policeman remained posted at the entrance and investigators continued to process the scene. Ferro flashed his badge and the guard let them inside. Robert Nouvel, a detective with the French police, greeted them in the entryway.

"Is anything missing?" Edelman asked.

"We are not sure yet," Nouvel replied. "We've been here since yesterday and we're still going through the inventory."

"I was supposed to pick up a painting from him today." Edelman explained. "Could I—"

"I'm sorry," Nouvel said, cutting him off. "We must maintain the premises precisely as they are until we have completed our investigation."

"I'm not asking to take anything," Edelman explained. "I just want to see if the painting is here."

"A contemporary piece?"

"No. Historic. Quite valuable."

"I'm afraid thus far," Nouvel said, "all we have found are contemporary pieces. Our experts have recognized nothing of classic value."

"Maybe if we just had a look?" Ferro said with a smile. "Just a look."

Nouvel stared at them a moment, as if considering the request. "I suppose a look wouldn't hurt," he said at last. "But only look. Do not touch anything without asking me first."

Nouvel turned to lead them up the hall but Edelman rushed past. "It was right here," he shouted, pointing to a vacant spot on the wall beside the dining room door. "Right in this spot." He tapped the empty space with his finger.

"What was there?" Nouvel asked.

"A painting. By Matisse. *Woman With Table and Vase*. It was right there."

"When?"

"Two days ago."

"You were here two days ago?"

"Yes. And the painting was right there on the wall." Edelman looked around as if searching, then pointed to the second parlor. "There were paintings in that room, too." He stepped to the doorway. "Lots of them. Propped against the wall. Maybe seven or eight paintings deep. All the way around the room." He made a sweeping gesture as he spoke.

"We have these over here," Nouvel said, pointing to the right side of the room.

"But they were over here, too." Edelman indicated to the left. "When I saw them the rows of paintings went all the way around the room."

"We have only found these," Nouvel explained. "And no record for them."

"But you have records for some?" Ferro asked.

"No. We have found no records at all," Nouvel replied. "At least, none for the artwork."

"And none for the Matisse?"

"No. None for it or anything like it."

"Someone took it," Edelman offered. "Whoever killed Crémieux, took the painting. I know it."

"Perhaps," Nouvel smiled politely. "But so far we have found no proof of a theft."

"Not exactly," Ferro said.

Nouvel looked puzzled. "What do you mean?"

"He has given you a statement just now," Ferro said, gesturing to Edelman. "And you have a dead body?"

"Yes." Nouvel nodded. "We have Crémieux's body."

Edelman spoke up. "How did he die?"

"He was killed by a single gunshot," Nouvel said. "We know that much for certain."

"Which makes it murder."

"Most likely." Nouvel turned to the doorway. "But we are still investigating." He looked over at Edelman. "Do you know anyone who might wish to do him harm?"

"No." Edelman shook his head. "I hardly knew him at all."

"Perhaps someone else who was interested in the painting?"

"No." Edelman shook his head more vigorously. "He purchased the painting from a collector in Antwerp. But that is all I know about it."

"What was that collector's name?"

"Fabre. Roman Fabre."

"You have his address?"

"Not with me."

"Well, perhaps you can get it to me later," Nouvel said indulgently. He gestured toward the hallway. "Now, gentlemen, I'm afraid I must ask you to leave. This is a crime scene and we have work to do. We will let you know if we come across anything that might be of interest to you."

Edelman was reluctant to leave. "I can't believe it's gone." He looked over at Ferro. "I was this close." He indicated with his fingers. "And now it is gone again."

"Come on." Ferro took him by the arm. "I'll give you a ride back to the apartment."

"It was right there," Edelman protested, pointing again to the wall by the dining room doorway. "And whoever killed Crémieux took it."

"We'll talk about it in the car," Ferro said. "Please. We must go."

Reluctantly, Edelman started up the hallway and continued out the door to Ferro's car. As they drove away, he turned to look out the window. "I don't like it when people do that."

"Do what?"

"Talk to me like I'm an old man."

"You thought he was talking to you with disrespect?"

"No," Edelman replied. "I thought he was merely indulging me. He didn't believe a word I said. And worse than that, he didn't take me seriously." He looked over at Ferro. "I'm telling you, the Matisse was on the wall and there was twice as much art in that second room."

"Two days ago?"

"Yes."

"Many things could happen in two days. Perhaps he sold the paintings from the room."

"But no one would have killed him for them."

"They weren't that good?"

"They were all painted by contemporary artists. Some with a growing reputation, perhaps. But nothing important enough to steal, let alone murder to acquire."

"If Crémieux sold them, perhaps he had records. And if he did, the investigators will find them. Nouvel is a good man and an excellent detective."

"But you and I both know they won't find a single transaction record. The art world is notorious for its anonymity. Which means little or no paper. And in a business known for its discreet transactions, Crémieux was the most discreet. That Matisse could be lost forever."

"I have more faith in you than that." Ferro smiled at Edelman. "You found the painting once. You can find it again."

"Not if it was stolen." Edelman made no attempt to hide the disappointment in his voice. "If it was stolen, it's gone."

"Stolen. Purchased." Ferro's voice had a lighter tone. "It will turn up. People who buy art cannot resist displaying it. Someone will see it. Word will get around. It will turn up."

"Before, perhaps," Edelman sighed. "But not now."

"Why should this be any different?"

"Look at me." Edelman gestured to himself. "I'm not as young as I used to be. I'm treated like an old man for good reason. Time is no longer in my favor. At my age, things don't just turn up."

"Listen," Ferro soothed. "Go back to the apartment. Take your cousin out for a nice dinner. Drink some wonderful French wine. Have some of our delicious desserts. And let me see what I can find out." He patted Edelman on the shoulder. "These things have a way of working out."

For the next several blocks they rode in silence with Edelman staring out the window, then a thought came to him. "What if they shipped it?"

"Maybe," Ferro shrugged. "But I am not so sure someone would ship a painting that valuable. At least, not through a common carrier."

"What if the person who killed Crémieux was there for the other paintings, the ones that were in that second parlor? Maybe they had a dispute. Crémieux was shot. And the person who killed him took the Matisse because…it was there. Anyone who knows anything about art would recognize the style and know it was far more valuable than anything we just saw in that room."

"Maybe. I suppose it is possible."

"If they took the other paintings from the room, and they shipped them all together, you could track it. You can track a shipment that large, can't you? It would be several crates of art. There would be a record, wouldn't there?"

"How many paintings do you think there were?"

"Maybe…" Edelman thought. "A hundred. I don't know. Maybe more. And some of them were quite large. They could stick the Matisse in with them and it might get through without being noticed by customs."

"I thought you said it was noticeably different?"

"It is, but maybe not to an untrained eye. Or to an overworked inspector."

"Most of our customs agents are well-trained in spotting significant works of art. Your own government has people here to pre-clear many of the shipments. Most of them are trained at least as well as our own. I'm not sure something like this would get past them."

"If they saw it," Edelman noted.

"True," Ferro admitted. "We could probably locate shipments of the size you suggest," he added. "But we might have trouble finding records for a single painting included within that shipment."

"But shipments that leave the country are cleared by customs."

"We would know if a shipment left the country. All I am saying is, depending on how it was shipped, and the kind of information collected by the shipper, it might be a challenge to identify from the records every single item included in a particular box or crate. And that's only if they went through a legitimate shipping company. If they put it in a truck and drove it to Berlin or Madrid themselves, we would never know about it."

"You could check the records to see?"

"Yes, my friend," Ferro chuckled. "I could check the records."

"Will you do that for me?"

"Certainly. But don't get your hopes up. Our agency is a small group at a very large Ministry and before this case is finished, it will likely entangle many agencies with greater priority than ours. But I will see what I can find out for you."

Chapter 5

Three nights later, David Anders arrived at Mournet's, an auction house on East Seventy-Fifth Street in Manhattan, for the second night of a contemporary art sale. He was running late and by the time he arrived, the usual crowd of dealers, collectors, and onlookers was already there, gathered in clusters about the room as they waited for the sale to begin.

Anders threaded his way past knots of chatty colleagues, avoiding two disgruntled clients and an auction house employee who wanted to ask him for a job. Near the back of the room, he took his place among a gaggle of dealers standing along the wall. Catalog in hand, he opened to a page describing the evening's first lot, folded back the cover, and clipped a pen on the side to hold his place, then scanned the room, mentally taking attendance.

From the corner of his eye, Anders saw the auctioneer, Brice Whitman, pass by a doorway on the right. Others in the room caught a glimpse of him, too, and news of Whitman's arrival spread quickly through the room. Everyone started toward their seats and as they did, Anders again took note of the collectors who were present and those who were missing.

Just then, Hasan Izmir entered the room, accompanied by his wife, Sibel, and brother, Ahmed. Anders rolled his eyes. "Send in the clowns," he quipped to no one in particular. "And I was so hoping we could have a night without them."

Lloyd Davis, a dealer standing to the left, turned to look. "Ha," he cackled when he saw them. "More like the Chelsea buffoons."

A dealer on the far side of Davis glanced over. "They're purveyors of second-rate European art," he opined. "And this is an American contemporary auction. That ought to tell you something right there."

"They may sell second-rate art," another countered, "but they make a ton of money doing it."

Alex Rollins, standing in the corner, chimed in. "Chelsea is the perfect location for it. People go down there to plunder through lesser-known galleries in search of a deal and have no idea what they're looking for or looking at. Then they find Galerie Le Meilleur, see paintings by people with European names that sound important, and they snap up the art at outlandish prices—all the while thinking they've found a bargain."

"And legitimate collectors hear about the sales, think the market is thriving, and drive up the prices here for legitimate contemporary artists," someone suggested.

"Is that such a problem?" another asked. "I mean, don't we want someone to drive up the prices?"

"It's certainly good for sellers."

"But it kills the artist in the long term," someone added. "The prices are artificial. The appreciation nonexistent. There's no real demand, just these two brothers playing a game. And it ruins the artist's reputation when the market for his work collapses."

"Exactly," Rollins continued. "And then there's the stupid stuff they do at the auction."

"They drive the prices so high with their stupidity no one can get a bargain."

"Like I've been saying," someone rejoined. "They deal in second-rate art and they're amateur collectors but they're making a killing at it."

"Maybe we should think about getting in the market," Jenkins said.

Just then, Whitman appeared at a doorway near the front of the room, ready to take the podium, and the room fell silent. Anders leaned around, scanning the room once more, his forehead wrinkled in a frown. Davis glanced over at him. "Something wrong?"

"I don't see Charlotte Snider." He was really looking for Jack Frazer, but he didn't want to tell Davis that. At least, not yet.

"You got a thing for her?" someone snickered.

"She buys a lot of art and she loves de Kooning," Anders explained. "They added two of his pieces to this sale."

"I thought this was a contemporary sale."

"It is."

"But he's an abstract expressionist."

"It's an auction house. Don't confuse them with the details."

"Maybe Charlotte didn't know about the de Koonings. I'm not sure I did."

"Neither did I."

"She knew about them," Anders assured. He looked down the line to someone three people away. "And, yes," he added. "I like Charlotte."

"Maybe she saw the de Koonings earlier today and didn't care for them."

"I doubt it."

Tony Slidell, standing to Anders' right, spoke up. "Several galleries have showings tonight. Some of them looked rather tempting. She's probably doing that instead of coming here. I thought about going myself."

With long, confident strides befitting his tall, slender frame, Whitman came from the doorway to the podium and looked out over the audience. A few friendly faces on the first row caught his attention and he smiled at them, then he looked across the room. "Good evening, ladies and gentlemen." He spoke in a pleasant but professional voice. "Welcome to the second night of Mournet's American contemporary auction. Our first lot is a nice work by Alexander Gorman. Who'll start the bidding?"

In spite of Anders' misgivings about Hasan Izmir and his brother, the auction went smoothly at first, but as the evening wore on, Hasan grew loud, talking to Ahmed as if they were the only people in the room. Then he began driving up the prices, typically jumping in at the last minute—a move that infuriated serious collectors—only to drop out when the bidding reached its peak, leaving the original bidder with the painting but at an exorbitant price.

As usual, the tactic became a game, with the brothers taking turns to see how high they could bid up the price and still avoid getting stuck with the painting. All the while, they continued to laugh among themselves. Anders and the other dealers gestured to the auctioneer to do something but received only a shrug in response.

When the auction ended, Anders gathered with Slidell, Davis, and a handful of collectors for drinks at Johnny Galento's, a restaurant just down the street from the auction house. They sat at a small table in the corner, discussing the evening's event. After a second martini, Anders said, "Well, I've had enough." He paused a moment for effect, then continued. "This thing with the Izmirs has been going on too long. First, they were loud. Then they were loud and obnoxious. Now they've turned the orderly sale of art into a sideshow." He shook his head. "This can't go on."

"But what can we do?" someone asked. "If Whitman and the folks at Mournet's won't do anything, we can't just take over the sale and start throwing people out."

"It's not just Mournet's," Davis said. "They did the same thing last month at Immendorff's."

"And for me it's bigger even than what they do at the auctions," Anders continued. "I just don't see how they can do what they claim to do with their business and make any money."

"What do you mean?"

"Supposedly," Anders explained, "they're selling art from up-and-coming European artists who haven't become known yet in the US. That's a version of what I tried thirty years ago with artists from the Village. And I'm telling you, it is very difficult to survive with that business model. I tried it and it just wouldn't work as a legitimate business. I lost far more money than I made and I'm better at this than they are. I don't mean that arrogantly. I'm just saying, I don't think their business model will work. Not legitimately. They must be doing something else. There must be something to it that we don't know about."

"Well," Slidell said sarcastically, "I suppose murder as a solution is out of the question."

"Yes," Davis chuckled, "although I'm not sure I would be sad if Hasan were dead."

Tom Fisher, a collector who'd joined them, seemed appalled by the comment. "That's a rather harsh thing to say."

"I know," Davis admitted. "But honestly, I think that's how I feel right now."

"We could hire a private investigator," Slidell suggested. "See what he can find. Some of those guys are pretty good."

"That seems rather tawdry and sleazy," Fisher responded. "Aren't we above that?"

"With murder not an option," Slidell said sarcastically, "I might not be as averse to sleaze as some of you."

"What about the district attorney?" Davis looked over at Anders. "You know him, don't you?"

Anders demurred. "I'm not sure he's right for this."

"Not right for it?" Slidell's voice had a note of incredulity. "Investigating people is his job."

"But DAs are elected," Anders explained, "which means they have to raise campaign funds, which means they are beholden to donors. The Izmirs move in the kind of circles that fund DA campaigns. If we took this to the DA, there's a good chance Hasan would find out about it."

"We move in those circles, too," Slidell countered.

"We are those circles," Fisher added.

"I was thinking of something more subtle," Anders said. "Something a little less overt."

"Yes," Davis nodded. "Maybe something not so readily connected to us, too."

"Nothing like a good smear campaign."

"Only thing you need for that is a little gossip," someone added.

"But if it backfires," Slidell cautioned, "it might work to Hasan's advantage."

"His advantage?"

"Add to his mystique. Make him the victim. Turn him into a sympathetic character."

"And give them even more press coverage than they're already getting."

Davis turned back to Anders. "What exactly were you thinking about?"

"I'm thinking maybe this is a job for a journalist."

"Good idea," someone said. "Get a reporter to do your digging and you get the information plus the notoriety of an article."

"In this case, maybe more than one article."

Anders grinned. "I'll see what I can come up with." He'd expected Frazer to be at the sale that night and since he wasn't, Anders felt free to give his story idea to someone else. He was friends with more reporters than a single writer for The New York Times. Anders felt a sense of satisfaction as he glanced at his friends. They all wanted someone to solve the auction problem, but they were too weak to do it themselves. He would do it for them. Jack Frazer or no Jack Frazer, he would find a way to silence Hasan and his brother, and everyone seated at the table would be in his debt.

"Well," Fisher sighed as he drained the bottom of his glass, "now that we've solved that problem, I'll have another drink. Anyone care to join me?"

Chapter 6

While Anders and the others attended the auction at Mournet's, Truman Slater stood in the corner at Beers, Lambert & Wyatt, a gallery in Chelsea. Out of the way and unnoticed, he watched as patron after patron cast an unemotional, disinterested glance at his paintings before drifting through the doorway to the rooms in back where an animated crowd gathered around the work of others included in the show. The event, Slater's third appearance in the gallery's Emerging Artists series, had proved an excruciatingly painful one for him. While the work of others sold at a brisk pace, his remained largely overlooked, an experience that left him wondering whether he should give up the dream of painting and get a job.

Born in Montana, Slater grew up along the eastern slope of the Big Belt Mountains in a region that was home to some of the nation's most striking scenery. From an early age he'd been captivated by the majesty of the mountains and the serenity of the fields that formed the family ranch. As a child he learned the value of hard work, rising before sunup to labor with the hired hands before heading off to school, then returning in the afternoon to another four hours of backbreaking labor, always with the landscape before him, its majesty and glory on full display.

At the age of ten he began sketching the things he saw—the bluff above the creek with the meadow below, the imposing rock cliffs near the high range pasture, and the mountain peaks that never lost their snow. By the age of twelve he'd moved from sketches to paintings, teaching himself the use of acrylics and oils, sometimes capturing scenes from the window of his upstairs bedroom or sneaking away to the field with an easel.

In high school, he eschewed sports, opting instead to spend an hour after class taking art lessons from Esther Delaney—an artist who'd known both Jackson Pollock and Willem de Kooning. She lived at the curve on Fort Logan Road just outside White Sulphur Springs. Under Delaney's watchful eye, Slater moved beyond painting the landscape of the countryside to painting the landscape of his mind and then to the use of color with little form or structure at all.

After high school, Hank, Slater's father, wanted him to obtain a business degree and take over the ranch. "Painting could be a hobby," he suggested. "Something to do when the real work's done." But Slater clung tenaciously to the dream of art school in New York and Hank could see that ranching was never going to satisfy his son. Finally, reluctantly, he funded the two-thousand-mile trek eastward and Slater enrolled at Parson's School of Design in Manhattan.

Slater did well at Parson's, finishing near the top of his class, but his work was an eclectic mixture of landscapes and abstract riffs on patterns and forms—something an instructor once referred to as reminiscent of Diebenkorn with a Rothko feel. As a result, his work was dubbed unique but not captivating and ignored by critics, dealers, and collectors.

Rather than return immediately to Montana, Slater convinced his father to give him a year to get established. He rented an apartment in Williamsburg, across the river from Manhattan, where he painted full time, selling most of his pieces at street fairs and temporary one-man shows he arranged in nearby vacant commercial space. After a year with little artistic success, he took a part time job at Beers, Lambert & Wyatt where he prepared paintings for shipment, hung pieces for display, and performed other non-sales tasks. While working there he convinced Wyatt to look at his paintings. Wyatt found the work ambivalent, as had others, but agreed to include several paintings in the gallery's Emerging Artist shows—a series of six showings that emphasized new artists of talent whose work had never been sold at auction.

At the first showing one piece sold and Slater had been greatly encouraged. A second piece sold the following month and he'd been ecstatic, but Wyatt had expected more and now in the third event not a single painting had been purchased. The one bright spot in the evening came from Charlotte Snider.

Known to everyone in the art world, Charlotte was an astute collector with a reputation for buying from artists before the market noticed them. Her personal wealth allowed her to do so in large volume and, with a keen eye for the things others would value next, she'd amassed a collection that was worth a fortune. That evening, she'd spent twenty minutes examining two of Slater's paintings, then returned again to look at two more. He'd hoped she would buy them, but she disappeared without a word and now that the show was ending, she was nowhere in sight.

As the crowd from earlier in the evening dwindled to only a handful, Raymond Wyatt came from the back room of the gallery where he'd been talking with Rico Yunkers who'd sold four paintings during the first hour of the show. Slowly and deliberately Wyatt worked his way across the room, stopping first to speak to a couple admiring a piece from an established artist, then pausing to straighten a painting on the wall and retrieve a stray scrap of paper from the floor. Then, as he finally turned his full attention to Slater for what they both knew was an inevitable conversation, Charlotte Snider appeared from the back. Slater felt his heart skip a beat at the sight of her only to see her turn aside to a collection twenty feet away.

By then, Wyatt was standing nearby. "Slow night for you," he observed.

"Yeah," Slater replied. "Slow."

"Well," Wyatt sighed, "maybe it's time for us to face the fact that this place isn't the right location for your work."

"Seemed right last time," Slater countered. "And the time before that."

"Truman," Wyatt said coldly, "you sold one painting at each of those shows. Everyone else sold at least three."

"So now you're throwing me out?"

"I'm suggesting," Wyatt said with a stiff jaw, "that perhaps you should find another place for your art."

"And where would that be?"

"Look, Truman, I've tried to help. I'm your friend and I've tried to help. I really have. I gave you a chance, but my clients don't seem to appreciate your work."

"I can—"

Wyatt cut him off with a wave of his hand. "You've been around here long enough to know that space is important to me."

"That's what you tell us."

"And I tell you that because it's right. This is expensive real estate. Every square foot of this place needs to make money. I know we're friends, but the bottom line is this is a business, which means I need pieces in here that I can sell. If your work isn't selling, then I need to move it out and get something else in here that will." He paused to take a deep breath and glanced away. "I'm sorry. But it's just that simple."

Slater glanced down at his shoes. "I suppose I can always go back to doing street fairs."

"I don't know." Wyatt had a look of frustration and he shook his head slowly from side to side as he spoke. "Maybe I can carry you for one more show, but after that you'll need to find somewhere else to display your work."

They stood there a moment, neither one saying a word, then a woman came to ask Wyatt a question and he drifted away. As he did, Charlotte Snider turned from the pictures she'd been viewing and started toward the door. As she made her way in that direction, she glanced over at Slater and gave him a knowing smile. Slater responded with a nod as he tried desperately to think of something clever to say but before he could utter a word, she was out the door and gone.

Twenty minutes later, the gallery closed and Slater walked up the street to a corner bar. He sat alone at a table in back and sipped a rum and Coke. The bar was crowded with college students, the party crowd who'd stopped by for drinks to get the night started. Only a few years earlier Slater would have been among them, ready to hit any of a dozen pop-up clubs that occupied temporary space behind unassuming storefronts a few blocks north of Canal Street, but not anymore, and certainly not that night.

As he sipped on his drink, he relived in his mind the disappointing three hours he'd just endured. Being ignored was the worst part, he concluded. He'd given himself to the process of creating art. Given everything. And to go unnoticed.... Hardly any of his work had sold and very few of those to serious collectors.

Maybe his father was right. Maybe he should have stayed in Montana, worked the ranch, and relegated art to a hobby. But when he imagined doing that, a sense of sadness swept over him, as if by giving up and going home he'd be giving up on more than a dream. He tipped up the glass he'd been holding, drained the last drops from the bottom, and looked up to catch a waiter's eye. Maybe with enough alcohol he could wash the evening from his memory.

Chapter 7

Frazer had meant to attend the auction with Anders, and he had meant to talk with Anders afterward, but when he arrived at the apartment after work, he phoned Zoë and that led to a long, rambling conversation. Not an argument. Just a long, conversation. The kind of conversation they had when they first met. Talking for hours on end about everything. About nothing. Enjoying each other's presence. Immersed in the moment.

The phone call with Zoë lasted until almost ten and ended with Frazer lying on the bed, thinking of her, imagining her, remembering her, before drifting off to sleep. He awakened the next morning, still on the bed, fully clothed.

After a leisurely plate of fried eggs, home fries, and bacon at a diner on the corner, Frazer rode the bus to the office at the Times and spent the morning at his cubicle, researching ideas for the story he hoped to write about people who supposedly lived in the tunnels beneath the city. Thus far, he'd had little success finding a theme or an arc that would carry a feature article, much less a series.

While he worked, Frazer's mind returned again and again to the art auction he missed the night before and the story Anders wanted him to write about the Izmir brothers and the gallery they operated. Frazer wasn't sure there was a story in what he'd heard thus far and had hoped to find out more the night before. Having missed the auction, he expected to receive a call from Anders any moment and braced himself for the scathing comments he anticipated receiving in their conversation. "I need something positive to say when that call comes," he mumbled to himself. "Something that shows I'm interested but puts him off a little longer." Anders could be quite persistent at times. Doggedly so. Rudely so, when it suited him. But if Frazer was going to write the article, he'd need a way to finesse the topic past the arts editor. From what he'd seen of her, that wouldn't be an easy task.

As he thought about Anders and what to do next, Frazer remembered Preston Cooper, the FBI agent who worked on the Edith Morgenstern case. He knew Cooper far better than he'd led Anders to believe, but it was a sensitive relationship. They were acquainted because of the friendship that developed between their wives. Both husbands had been careful not to allow their professional occupations to intrude on their private interaction for fear their differences might disrupt their wives' relationship. But with Zoë no longer in New York, that might not be much of a concern anymore.

Near mid-morning, Frazer remembered that Cooper played racquetball at the Manhattan Athletic Club every day at lunchtime. The club, popular with midtown attorneys and executives, was far too expensive for Frazer but his friend, Rogers Ellerby, allowed Frazer to sign in on his membership as a guest. Preston Cooper did the same through a government connection. Frazer was sure he'd find Cooper there. They could talk, perhaps play a game of racquetball, and somewhere in the discussion he could mention Anders and the situation with the Izmir brothers. Maybe find out if Cooper was interested in a meeting with Anders.

Shortly before noon, Frazer left his desk and walked down the hall toward the elevator on his way to find Cooper at the gym. As he headed in that direction, he continued to wonder about Anders, the story he told about the brothers, and their art gallery. Each time he considered the details, a sense of uneasiness came over him. This was an article about art and the arts business. It really should be a project with the arts editor, not features. Nuancing it past that distinction was risky, but he wasn't getting anywhere with the article he wanted to write about life in the tunnels beneath the city. He might as well follow the lead from Anders and see what he found. And besides, he wasn't writing anything yet. Just looking and talking.

When he reached the elevator, he pressed the button and waited for the car to arrive. While he waited, he thought of Zoë and the conversation they had the night before. She seemed relaxed. Comfortable. No longer angry or combative. As if she was waiting for him to arrive in Charleston, fully expecting him to be there soon. And maybe she was right. Maybe he would join her, but not yet. He had worked hard to get to New York and wasn't ready to give up on it just yet.

When the elevator doors opened, Frazer saw Gina Wilkins inside. As senior correspondent for the Arts Section, Gina was known for taking her role at the paper seriously. She wouldn't like that he'd been talking to someone about a story that encroached on her area of responsibility and Frazer knew it. He pushed the thought aside, telling himself he'd done nothing wrong, yet. Anders called and they had lunch. That was as far as it had gone for now, though he knew that was about to change.

"Hello, Gina." Frazer gave her a polite smile hoping she hadn't noticed his uneasiness.

"Jack," she replied casually. The doors closed and they stood facing forward, staring up at the floor numbers. "Are you still working on that story about people living in the tunnels beneath the city?"

He glanced over at her. "You heard?"

"It's impossible to keep anything secret around here."

"Yeah," he chuckled. "That's the truth." And he wondered if she already knew about his conversation with Anders.

"I have a guy in the city records office that might be helpful," she said.

"That would be great," Frazer replied. And it really would be helpful. After several promising interviews, the story had gone cold, but he was unwilling to ask for help for fear others at the paper might think he'd lost his touch.

The bell dinged for the next floor as the elevator came to a stop and the door opened. As Gina stepped forward to exit, she glanced over her shoulder. "I'll send you an email with his contact information."

"Thanks," he called, but she was several steps away and he wasn't sure she heard. The elevator door closed, and he continued on his way to the lobby.

On the street, Frazer hailed a taxi and rode across town to the Manhattan Athletic Club. After changing into gym clothes, he trolled the handball courts, staring through the plexiglass wall that faced the corridor, searching for Cooper. As expected, he found him on a court, engaged in a hotly contested game. Frazer took a seat on a bench in the corridor outside and waited while they finished. From the sound of the ball hitting the wall, it was a hard-fought contest.

Before long, the game ended and Cooper emerged from the court, winded and soaked with sweat. He took a seat next to Frazer and patted his face with a towel. "Are you looking for me or just resting?"

"Do you play like that all the time?" Frazer asked.

"You mean that hard?"

"Yeah."

"That was a guy from one of the banks," Cooper said. "We investigated one of his clients for fraud and he doesn't like me for it. He also thinks it's terrible that I'm allowed in here. You know, government employee and all. He can't hit me with his fist, so he does his best to whack me with the ball."

Frazer smiled. "How does that work out on the court?"

Cooper grinned. "I do my best to whack him first."

"So why play him? Play someone else."

"Nah," Cooper said shaking his head. "I like the challenge." He gave his face another pat with the towel. "But you didn't answer my question."

"Which was?"

"What brings you in here?"

"I have a friend who wants to talk to you," Frazer replied.

"Oh? And what does this friend want to talk about?"

"He's an art dealer. Thinks maybe one of the galleries is using its business as a front for something."

"Something illegal, I suppose?"

"Maybe," Frazer said. "He doesn't know yet. He's seen the owners at art auctions lately and noticed how much money they're throwing around. Thinks someone should look into it."

"I thought spending too much for art was the gallery business model."

"He doesn't think they could make money with the prices they pay."

"Unrealistic acquisition costs."

"Is that what you call it?"

"Something like that. Which gallery are we talking about?"

"I think it would be better if he told you the details." Frazer glanced over at him. "Are you interested in talking to him?"

"Maybe," Cooper said. "Not much to lose from just talking. Do you think there's anything to what he has observed?"

"I have no idea," Frazer sighed. "He calls me when he thinks he's has a tip about something that would make a good story."

"Any of his suggestions ever work out for you?"

"I got a Pulitzer off one of them and a couple of good articles from some of the others."

Cooper had a look of realization. "This is that guy we dealt with before, isn't it?"

Frazer was defensive. "Look, I know we've gone out of the way to keep our professional lives separate, and I'm not vouching for the guy. He just asked me to ask you."

"Anders or Anderson or something like that. Right?"

"Anders," Frazer acknowledged.

"He didn't like me very much, as I recall."

"And you didn't like him, either."

Cooper grinned. "You owe him a favor or something?"

"Yeah," Frazer nodded. "I guess I do. Look, I don't know if what he's saying is true or not. I don't know any more about the situation than what I've told you. But it sounds like it might be a good story and that usually means someone's up to something."

"Are you gonna write about it? I mean, assuming there's something to write about."

"Probably," Frazer said. "I was planning to look into it, but he wants to talk about more than a story. So, can I tell him you're interested?"

"I'll be glad to talk to him." Cooper laid the towel on the bench. "Tell him to give me a call. But I'm not making any promises other than to listen."

"Okay." Frazer stood to leave.

Cooper looked up at him. "You aren't going to work out?"

"Nah. I just came by to see you."

"My wife tried to call your wife a couple of times this week. Left a message, never got a call back. Is everything okay?"

"Yeah." Frazer looked away. "It's…okay."

"Anything you need to talk about?"

"Not right now." Frazer gestured toward the handball court. "Got time for a game?" Anything to avoid talking about that topic.

"I thought you were leaving."

"I can stick around long enough to beat you."

"Ha," Cooper laughed. He stood and started toward the door to the court. "You're on but get ready to lose."

When the game was over and Frazer dutifully lost, he sent Anders a text message, informing Anders of the discussion he'd had with Cooper and giving him Cooper's phone number.

"Will he pursue it?" Anders asked.

"He'll talk to you," Frazer replied. "And that's a start."

"Why don't you deal with him?"

The response aggravated Frazer. "If you want the FBI involved," he replied, "give him a call." Surely, he thought, Anders would understand he needed to do at least that much.

Chapter 8

Meanwhile in Paris, Gennady Krylov sat in the front seat of an Audi parked outside the Hotel Ritz. A few days earlier, the crew had been staying there, but after they shipped the paintings, a Paris official notified them of heightened security measures put in place by the ministry of justice following the discovery of André Crémieux's body. Rather than risk detection, Kirchen decided the crew should remain in France until things calmed down. He suggested they split up, too, sending them to live in separate hotels, to avoid attracting attention. Only Kirchen remained at the Ritz.

None of the other crew members seemed concerned about Kirchen's tactics, but Krylov was suspicious and arranged for an informant on the hotel staff to notify him if Kirchen attempted to check out. The informant notified him that morning. Kirchen was on the move. Krylov was certain he would have the money with him.

They were supposed to leave the money with Crémieux, get the art, and leave without causing trouble. No one was supposed to die. Kirchen couldn't return the money to Mogilevich without explaining what he did, which would cause trouble. Deadly trouble. Mogilevich hated operatives who deviated from the plan. "The weasel has it," Krylov groused. "I know he does. And I want it."

With his eyes focused on the hotel entrance, Krylov gripped the neck of a Vodka bottle and took a swig. "I don't care what anybody says," he mumbled to himself. "Kirchen is an idiot." He paused to take another drink. "And I hate that damn German."

Talking to himself was a habit Krylov developed as a young man. Something he'd picked up from watching mob movies. The main character in one of them talked to himself as a way to supposedly avoid talking in his sleep. "Gets everything off my mind," he'd said. It sounded good to Krylov and when he gave it a try, he found that he enjoyed the sound of his own voice, so he adopted it as a practice.

While he waited, Krylov glanced at a newspaper that lay on the seat beside him. An article on the front page gave details about the investigation into Crémieux's murder. "The police are asking way too many questions," Krylov groused. "Watching the airports. Train stations. It's impossible to get out of here without them finding us." He took another drink from the bottle. "That damn German will get us all killed."

In a few minutes, Kirchen came from the hotel lugging the four duffel bags that held the cash. "There's the little son of a bitch," Krylov fumed. "Look at him. Thinks he's a real Bratva, but he's carrying his own luggage. Ain't nothing but an art expert with connections and not a very good expert at that."

As Kirchen got into a taxi, Krylov put the Audi in gear and steered it away from the curb to follow. All the while, he continued to mumble to himself. "Murdering people like it doesn't matter. And when it catches up with him, we'll be the ones to pay."

The taxi turned the corner and Krylov slowed, putting distance between them. "This is the third time he's done this. Someone ought to teach him a lesson." He caught a glimpse of the taxi working its way through traffic and sped up to narrow the distance between them. "Someone has to show the ass that being from Luxembourg means only that you're just another stupid German."

With Krylov following in the Audi, the taxi made its way across town to the Gare du Nord, one of Paris' primary train stations. The car came to a stop outside the terminal and Kirchen stepped out carrying the duffel bags. He glanced over his shoulder once as he pushed the car door closed, then made his way quickly inside the building.

Krylov parked the car in an open space at the curb nearby and followed on foot. He reached the terminal entrance within minutes and watched from just inside the door while Kirchen approached a ticket agent.

A few minutes later, with ticket in hand, Kirchen moved away from the counter. As he continued toward the train platforms, Krylov stepped up to the same agent. He did not know for certain what Kirchen's destination might be, but he took a calculated risk and said, "I'm supposed to be on the train to Luxembourg. Do you have room for one more?"

"Certainly," the ticket agent replied.

Kirchen still was visible as he made his way across the lobby and Krylov pointed to him. "I know that guy. The one with the duffel bags. Any chance I could sit beside him?"

The clerk checked a computer screen, then shook his head. "No. I'm sorry. We have no more seats in that car."

"Well," Krylov smiled, "at least get us on the same train. Maybe I can catch a word with him on the way."

While the clerk entered the ticket information, Krylov glanced to the left in time to see Kirchen disappear down a corridor that led to the tracks. The clerk interrupted him with the ticket price and Krylov paid, then dashed off to catch up.

When Krylov arrived at the departure point, Kirchen was standing at the far end of the platform with the duffel bags still firmly in his grasp. Krylov lingered out of sight behind a column, hoping to go unnoticed. When the train arrived, he waited until Kirchen was aboard, then, at the last moment, stepped inside the assigned car and took a seat.

Two hours later, the train arrived at the station in Luxembourg. Krylov followed Kirchen as he came from the railcar, stepped onto the platform, and started toward the corridor in the main terminal building. He followed Kirchen through the building, then down to an underground parking garage.

While Kirchen got into his car, Krylov searched the opposite end of the deck for an unlocked car. He found a blue Volvo, an older model, parked in a space near the corner. It was locked but a little checking produced a spare key from a magnetic container tucked in a slot behind the rear bumper. Using the key, he unlocked the driver's door and slipped inside just as Kirchen drove past. As Kirchen continued toward the garage exit, Krylov backed the Volvo from the space and followed.

Across town, Kirchen came to a stop outside a red brick apartment building. Krylov found an empty space up the street and pulled over. From that position, he had an unobstructed view of the apartment door in the side mirror of the car. He watched while Kirchen entered the building, then waited to see if he remained there.

In a few minutes, the door to the apartment building opened and Kirchen appeared carrying four duffel bags. Krylov smiled. "Such an idiot." He chuckled to himself. "This will be easier than I thought."

Kirchen returned to his car and drove a few blocks through traffic to a row of storage buildings in a commercial section of the city. Krylov followed at a discrete distance and watched as Kirchen brought his car to a stop in front of a building marked with the number 127. A padlock secured the door and it took a moment for him to open it, then he disappeared inside. After a few minutes, Kirchen came from the building empty-handed, locked the door behind him, and returned to the car.

Krylov waited until Kirchen was out of sight, then pulled up in front of the storage building. The door was locked but he found a tire tool in the trunk of the Volvo. He wedged one end of it behind the hasp that held the padlock and, with a snap of his wrist, popped the hasp free. The door swung open and he stepped inside.

The duffel bags sat atop a scuffed dresser that stood along the wall to the right. Krylov took them by the shoulder straps, two in each hand, and carried them out to the car. He tossed them onto the back seat and leaned inside to unzip the first one. "You are so predictable," he muttered with glee. "So stupidly predictable." As he unzipped the bag, he found it was stuffed with newspaper and at the bottom was a dusty old brick to give the bag weight.

Krylov pounded his fist against the door in frustration.

Two days later, Patrick Depardieu, a security agent with Grand Port Maritime in Le Havre, France, sat at his workstation reading an email from his girlfriend. Suddenly, a warning tone sounded from the computer.

With two clicks of the mouse, Depardieu flipped the image on the screen from the email tab to the port's security program and saw the system had flagged a shipment of artwork bound for London. A check of the details showed that the shipment, comprised of three crates, left Le Havre the previous day for Plymouth, England, where it was scheduled for transfer to rail that morning for delivery to a shipping company in London. Depardieu was perplexed by the nature of the alarm and notified his supervisor, Jean-Louis Aumont.

Fifteen minutes later, Aumont arrived at Depardieu's workstation. As Depardieu explained the situation, Aumont stood behind him, reading the screen over Depardieu's shoulder. A frown wrinkled his forehead. "Why was I not alerted about this before now?"

Depardieu shrugged. "I do not know. The alarm sounded. I called as soon as it rang."

Aumont continued reading and after a moment he pointed and said, "Scroll down the screen a little farther."

Depardieu did as he was instructed and Aumont pointed to a tiny box next to the cargo description. "Click on the tab." Depardieu moved the cursor to that spot on the screen and a page appeared with details of the shipment's history. "That's the reason right there," Aumont said.

"What?"

Aumont leaned over and tapped a place on the message with his index finger. "The hold request came from Jean Ferro with the Ministry of Culture."

"What difference does that make?"

"The Ministry of Culture is not a law enforcement unit,"

Aumont explained. "They do not have priority in the system."

"You mean, the system delays their request?"

"The system has limited capacity. When it has more to do than it can manage, it delays processing non-law enforcement requests until it has completed other matters of a higher priority."

"So, what do we do about this alert? Aren't we required to notify someone?"

"I'll call Ferro," Aumont replied. He stepped away from the workstation and took a seat at a nearby desk.

Ferro was in his office when the phone rang. "You flagged a shipment," Aumont said. "Three crates of art."

"Yes," Ferro replied. "You found them?"

"Our system just now alerted us."

"Great. Where are they?"

"In London." Aumont's voice was downcast.

Ferro was perplexed. "I don't understand."

"The shipment left for London yesterday," Aumont explained.

Ferro's mood shifted to one of frustration. "I wanted to know before it left." His voice was tense. His tone was terse.

"I realize that." Aumont sounded sympathetic but offered no apology. "This is a busy port. We do our best to respond timely to all requests, but we have many demands on our security system. Requests from the Ministry of Culture are not Priority Requests."

"Why not?"

"As I said, we are very busy. Our system has only so much capacity. This is the best I can do. The crates left Le Havre yesterday. Headed to Plymouth for transfer to London."

"By what means?"

"Ship from here. Rail from Plymouth."

"And the final destination is London?"

"From our details, yes."

"What does that mean?"

"It means, that is as far as our tracking information shows."

"You have details for the shipment?"

"Yes."

"Email it to me."

"Okay."

"Now, please."

"All right, all right." Aumont's voice was tense. "It's on the way."

Ferro ended the call and opened his email account to find a message from Aumont with an attachment. He read the attachment and learned the shipment was going to Adair Transshipment Company in London. Moments later, he sent an email to a contact at Scotland Yard asking for assistance. After a dozen messages and three heated phone calls, Scotland Yard agreed to investigate the matter.

Chapter 9

By the time Scotland Yard agreed to investigate the shipment of art, Jacob Edelman was on a return flight to New York City. He'd argued with Ferro and with Robert Nouvel, the detective working the Crémieux case, and with anyone else who would listen, trying to convince them that Crémieux had been murdered, that the painting by Matisse had been stolen, and that they needed to focus on the art if they ever wanted to solve the murder. But all of it had been to no avail.

Seven hours after leaving Paris, Edelman's flight landed at JFK Airport on Long Island. He took a taxi to his apartment on the Upper East Side and collapsed in bed. The following morning, he awakened feeling tired and groggy but more determined than ever to continue his pursuit of the missing painting.

After a trip to the bathroom, Edelman put on a robe and placed his feet in his favorite house slippers. He picked up his cell phone from the nightstand, dropped it into the pocket of the robe, and started toward the door to the hall. When he reached the kitchen, Edelman found hot coffee waiting in an urn. He poured himself a cup and took a seat at the table. The morning newspaper lay near his place and he scanned the front page, but his mind was already focused on the painting and the places he might look for information about it. "I was so close," he whispered. "So close."

Just then, Edelman's cell phone rang. He took it from the pocket of his robe and glanced at the screen. The call was from Ferro at the Ministry of Culture in France. Edelman pressed a button to accept it and placed the device to his ear.

"I wanted to inform you," Ferro began, "that a shipment of art comprised of three crates departed France for London, just as you suspected it might."

Edelman felt himself growing tense. "It already left?"

"Yes," Ferro replied. "It is in London now, awaiting shipment to New York."

"New York?" Edelman was surprised by the destination and it was obvious in the tone of his voice. "Where in New York?"

"Something called Galerie Le Meilleur," Ferro said. "Do you know it?"

"Never heard of it," Edelman replied. "But I assure you, by nightfall I will know everything there is to know about it."

"I am certain you will."

"Do you think it's the art from Crémieux's townhouse?"

"We have no way of knowing until we look inside."

"Your people couldn't find it before it left the country?" In his heart, Edelman was certain the Matisse was in one of the containers. He would have preferred Ferro search the crates, rather than someone in London or New York whom he did not know.

"We placed an alert for three crates containing works of art. And even without specific information, the system should have caught it, but they say our requests are not a priority for them. As a result—"

"Not a priority? Why not?"

"We are not a law enforcement agency."

"But you're working to return stolen property."

"That is true, but we are with the Ministry of Culture."

"So, they just ignore your requests?"

"No. They do not ignore our requests. They simply process them at a more convenient time. Which is never in a timely manner. Something about computer capacity and national security."

"Sounds like government bureaucracy," Edelman grumbled.

"This is what I mentioned to you when we were in the car,"

Ferro said. "These things have a way of becoming entangled in the affairs of multiple agencies."

Edelman wasn't concerned about interagency politics. He wanted to find the painting. "Can you get the authorities in London to hold the shipment?"

"I am trying," Ferro replied. "But I can make no guarantees."

"You can identify the shipment, right?"

"Yes. I have the information for it."

"Then why can't the police in London just go get it and hold onto it until we find out what's inside?"

"The detective working the Crémieux case still says there is no evidence linking the crime at the townhouse to anyone, much less to three crates of artwork. Without him to press the matter with London authorities, it has been difficult to get their attention."

"But regardless of evidence linking Crémieux's death to a suspect, they do think he was murdered, don't they?"

"Yes."

"Isn't that enough for your department to step in and demand that London hold the freight?"

"My supervisor is reluctant to press the matter on his own for fear authorities in Paris will think he is interfering with an ongoing police investigation."

"He's afraid."

"He is focused on finding art stolen by the Nazis."

Edelman was skeptical. "You mean, he wants to find the pieces that are easily recoverable. The ones hanging in a gallery and that sort of thing. Not the ones he has to work to locate and retrieve."

"He doesn't want to become embroiled in a turf war with the police over something that, in the end, may not be within his jurisdiction."

"I'm not trying to interfere with the murder case," Edelman said. He was becoming resigned to the situation and to the possibility that he would not be able to resolve the matter until the crates arrived in the US. "I just want my family's art returned to us. Art that was stolen by the Nazis. Doesn't that count for something?"

"I understand your frustration and I sympathize with you completely," Ferro said. "But I am having difficulty getting people here to see that distinction. Recovery of art versus meddling in a murder investigation is a confusing set of circumstances for them."

"Aren't the crates coming from Crémieux's gallery?"

"No," Ferro answered. "They were shipped by a private individual."

"Do you have a name?"

Edelman heard the rustling of papers, then Ferro said, "It appears they were sent by...someone named...Marcel Kirchen. At least, that's how it appears on the form in my file. The contact at the gallery in New York is Hasan Izmir. Do either of those names mean anything to you?"

"No," Edelman replied. "I've never heard of either."

"Apparently, neither have we. Our files have nothing on either of them. Nor does Interpol, I'm afraid."

"So, what do we do?"

"We wait and see if London will detain the shipment."

"Do you think they will?"

"I don't know yet," Ferro said. "I will get back to you as soon as I hear something."

Edelman ended the call and laid the phone on the table. As he sat, staring blankly at the kitchen cabinets, his mind replayed the conversation. Three crates had been found. Containing artwork. Leaving France for London, then New York. The gallery—

Just then, Anne Meltzer, his granddaughter, entered the room. The child of Edelman's daughter, Anne lived with him while attending Columbia University. She seemed to notice the look on Edelman's face as she moved past him toward the toaster. "Papa, who were you talking to?"

"A friend," Edelman replied.

"You look worried."

"I'm not worried."

"Don't get anxious, Papa. You know what happens when you get anxious."

"You sound like your mother."

"Please." Anne rolled her eyes. "Don't tell me that."

"Are we seeing her this week?"

"Yes." Anne placed two slices of bread in the toaster and took a plate from the cabinet. "I think we're having lunch with her on Wednesday. If she doesn't have an appointment that day."

"Appointments." Edelman shook his head. "How did she turn out to be such a pain."

"It wasn't all her fault. She had some help, you know."

"Not from me."

Anne poured a cup of coffee from the urn. "Maybe not, but three husbands are enough to ruin anyone."

"Well, if it's not my fault, why does she live in Queens and never come to see me?"

"It's not Queens, Papa," Anne said patiently.

"No?"

"She lives on Staten Island. You know that."

"Yeah," he chuckled. "I know. But that's even more to the point."

Anne propped against the counter. "What do you mean?"

"She's just a ferry ride away."

"Well… She's busy, I suppose."

"She was nicer when she lived in Queens."

"I think she doesn't come to see you often because when she gets here, all you do is fight."

"That's because all she ever talks about is money."

"She's never been good with it."

"You noticed?"

"How could I miss it? I was the one who had to deal with the consequence."

Edelman sighed. "I'm sorry."

"It's okay." The toaster dinged and she took the slices from it. "Was that call about your trip to Paris?"

"Yes."

"Good news?"

Edelman shook his head. "No," he said.

"Are you sure you haven't reached the end of this quest?" She spoke while she buttered the toast, then took a bite that made a crunching sound.

"Now you really sound like your mother," Edelman replied. "Always telling me I should give up my obsession with finding the art. Our art. Art the Nazis stole from us."

"She doesn't understand it, that's all."

"Well, it might help if she came around more often so we could talk about it. And talk, not argue. Have a conversation with each other for once. Like real people."

"She's not much on the give and take of a conversation."

"Would also help if she went to temple once in a while."

"She's not very interested in religion, either."

"It's not religion," Edelman countered.

"No?"

"No."

"Then what is it?"

"It's about understanding who we are and where we came from. Who she is. Who I am. Who you are. Part of her problem is, she doesn't know who she is. She's like a wandering soul with no place to light."

Anne took a sip from her coffee cup, then set it on the counter and kissed him on the head. "I have to go now. Are you okay here by yourself?"

"I'm fine." He looked up at her and smiled. "Don't worry about me. I have plenty to keep me obsessed."

"You mean busy."

"Yes," he said. "That, too."

When Anne was gone, Edelman came from the kitchen and made his way up the hall to an extra bedroom he used as an office. Coffee cup in hand, he took a seat at a desk near the window, raised the lid on a laptop that sat there, and pressed the power button. Instantly, the screen came to life.

After a sip of coffee, he clicked on the icon for his web browser and entered the names he'd learned from Ferro—Galerie Le Meilleur,

Hasan Izmir, Marcel Kirchen—then initiated a search. Moments later, the results appeared on the screen and Edelman began to read.

Chapter 10

After eluding Krylov in Luxembourg, Kirchen traveled across Europe to Moldova. Formerly part of the Soviet Union, Moldova was a landlocked republic wedged between Romania and Ukraine. Having endured a long history of domination, first by the Ottoman Empire, then by the Russian Empire, and finally by the Soviet Union, Moldova emerged in 1990 as a free republic but with one of the poorest economies on the continent. That made it a place ripe for the likes of Sergei Mogilevich—the man Kirchen came to see.

Mogilevich was born in the republic of Georgia at a time when it, too, was part of the Soviet Union. At the age of twelve, his parents moved to Moscow where his father worked as a driver for a low-level Soviet official. Soon after the move, his parents separated and Mogilevich was left to care for himself.

With no one at home to guide him, he became a member of a gang and began breaking into homes and stealing cars. A drug dealer took a liking to him and taught him the business. At the age of seventeen, Mogilevich moved into distribution. Gambling, loan sharking, and extortion followed. Then money laundering and murder, some of it at the behest of Russian intelligence operatives.

All was going well for him until 2001, when Viktor Zubkov was elected Russian president with a mandate for ridding the government of corruption and severing its ties with organized crime.

Arrests followed with dozens of Bratva leaders either incarcerated or killed. Thanks to the help of contacts in the intelligence community, Mogilevich was able to negotiate his way out of the country under the guise of an official exile that allowed Zubkov to claim victory over a major organized crime figure, while permitting Mogilevich to transfer most of his assets and criminal network to a location of his own choosing. He chose Moldova as his new home.

Ousting Mogilevich from Russia was supposed to curtail his criminal activities. However, once in Chisinau—Moldova's capital and largest city—Mogilevich quickly established control over the city's drug trade, then used the money and manpower generated by it to exert control over drug dealers throughout the country, becoming Moldova's most powerful distributor and most formidable mob boss. Even now, after Zubkov was long gone from office and the way was clear for Mogilevich's return to Russia, he remained in Moldova, where his extensive criminal enterprise gave him influence throughout Europe and even to the United States.

After crossing the border at Cobani, Kirchen took a bus to Chisinau, then hired a taxi to take him to the house, perched atop a hill overlooking the city, where Mogilevich lived. The driver, however, refused to go any farther than the main gate and Kirchen was forced to walk the last hundred yards.

When Kirchen reached the house, a butler greeted him at the door and escorted him to a room in back where Mogilevich was waiting. A bevy of young women lounged there but when Kirchen arrived, they quickly disappeared.

The hour was late. Mogilevich was dressed in silk pajamas with matching robe. He stood with his back to the room, staring out a large window that afforded a panoramic view of the city below. Lights shimmered in the distance and as Kirchen stood, waiting, Mogilevich refilled the glass in his hand. He glanced over at Kirchen and poured a drink for him, then handed it to him. "Your trip to Paris was successful?"

"Yes," Kirchen replied.

"Everything went well?"

"Yes." Kirchen nodded. "All went well."

"I understand the items were shipped as planned."

"Yes."

"Krylov tells me there was an extra painting in the lot."

Kirchen seethed at the comment, wondering how much Krylov had told him. "It was a gift," he said.

"From you?"

"From the Paris dealer."

Mogilevich caught his eye with a cold stare, as if to say he knew the details of what occurred. "Remind me to thank him."

"That won't be necessary," Kirchen said. "I took care of it."

Mogilevich looked away and took a sip from his glass. "Crémieux was a good man."

"He had served his purpose."

Mogilevich glanced over his shoulder once more in Kirchen's direction. "Meaning?"

"Meaning the only way to keep our business secret is by dealing with the same person for a limited number of times. In this case, once was enough."

Mogilevich turned back to the window. "You can always simply move on to someone new."

"And it is better if the one you leave behind is in no position to talk after you are gone."

"I see."

Kirchen caught the tone in Mogilevich's voice. "You object?"

"You killed a man in Prague three months ago over the price of two paintings. Before that, a collector in Venice. Now this." Mogilevich sighed. "Killing is expensive."

"This one didn't cost you anything."

"Killing always comes at a price."

"That is the cost of doing business."

"Yes," Mogilevich acknowledged. "But we normally reserve that practice for business."

"What we did in Paris was not business?" Kirchen's voice had a hint of incredulity.

"It was not my business."

"You think I will use it against you?"

Mogilevich turned in Kirchen's direction once more, an eyebrow arched as if he found the remark offensive. "I am not worried about what you might attempt to do to me."

"Then what is the issue?" Kirchen was growing frustrated. "Crémieux is dead."

"For our plan to work, we need an art dealer who will do business with us. When they learn of your tactics, that will become increasingly difficult."

Kirchen gave a dismissive gesture. "Europe is full of art dealers."

"You are leaving quite a trail behind you. The police in Prague have a murder to account for. As do the police in Venice. And now the authorities in Paris."

"Parisian police are idiots."

"Maybe so." Mogilevich shrugged. "But we sent the paintings to New York. If the FBI connects the murder in Paris to the paintings in those crates, they will have more than enough excuse to investigate our operations."

"The FBI won't touch us," Kirchen scoffed. "They are too busy looking for Islamic terrorists. Paris can't stop tripping over itself to explain away the shooting. And Prague is still thinking of their case as a lover's quarrel gone bad. We will be fine."

"I am sure of that," Mogilevich said. "But I can only hope for your sake that painting you added to the list is worth the four million in those duffle bags you took." Kirchen seemed taken aback. Mogilevich noticed. "Yeah," he said. "I know all about that, too. And I want it back."

Kirchen felt his heart sink. "Surely you do not think that I would steal from you."

"And surely you do not think that I don't know when you are lying." Mogilevich pointed. "You will return the money and be glad to accept only the amount you are paid for your services, or you are through with me."

Without waiting for a response, Mogilevich turned away and left the room. A moment later, the butler appeared and escorted Kirchen from the house. As Kirchen stepped outside, the door closed behind him. Suddenly, he felt more alone than ever before.

That same night, Gennady Krylov was asleep in a hotel in Luxembourg when the cellphone on the nightstand beside his bed dinged with an alarm indicating a message had arrived. He checked the screen and saw the note read simply, "Kirchen arrived."

"Good," Krylov growled. "He's in Moldova. Now I can find out what he did with that money."

Despite the lateness of the hour, Krylov dressed quickly and drove from the hotel to Kirchen's apartment. Using the tire tool from the trunk of the car, he forced his way inside with little regard for the marks he left on the door frame or the condition of the latch that he broke in the process.

Once inside, Krylov searched the closets for the duffel bags, then looked beneath the bed and behind the sofa. Frustrated when he found nothing, he checked the crawl space above the ceiling, then turned to the furniture and plundered through the drawers, searching for anything that might offer a clue as to the whereabouts of the four duffel bags or the money that was inside them.

After two hours turning the apartment upside down, Krylov was about to give up when, in anger, he jerked a drawer from a desk in the bedroom and noticed a key taped to the end of it. Krylov grinned as he peeled away the tape that held it in place. "Sneaky little bastard," he said.

The key had a rubber cover over one end with a number imprinted on it. Krylov studied it a moment and felt certain it was the key to a locker. But where?

As he sat at the desk, he recounted the route Kirchen had followed from the hotel in Paris. He'd come to the taxi with the four duffel bags and rode to the train station. Krylov followed close enough to know that the taxi did not stop until it reached the station.

At the station, Kirchen exited the taxi and made his way to the ticket counter, then walked down the corridor toward the train platforms. By the time Krylov reached the counter and purchased a ticket, Kirchen was out of sight. He found Kirchen at the platform, but during the intervening time—perhaps as much as ten minutes—Kirchen had been out of Krylov's sight. He'd been out of Krylov's sight during the ride to Luxembourg, too, but the train didn't stop and Kirchen still had the bags with him when he exited from the railcar.

If the bags were not in the apartment, and if they weren't in the storage building he'd seen Kirchen enter earlier...

"Then they must be at the station in Paris," Krylov said to himself.

Convinced he was correct, Krylov left the apartment, walked out to the car, and started toward Paris. A few hours later, he entered the city and drove to the train station on the north side. Sunup was still several hours away, which meant traffic was light. He had no trouble finding a parking space near the entrance and went inside.

After retracing his steps from the ticket counter, Krylov came to a set of passenger lockers just off the corridor that led to the platform where they caught the train. He checked the number on the key against the numbers on the lockers but didn't find a match.

A little farther down, though, he came to a second group of lockers. There, he located a large one with a number that matched the number on the key. His heart beat faster as he inserted the key in the lock and gave it a turn. To his surprise, the door swung open revealing the four duffel bags stuffed inside.

Krylov laughed as he pulled out the first bag. He set it on the floor at his feet and unzipped it part way. Through the gap in the zipper he saw the bag was filled with US currency.

"Yes!" he exclaimed in a whisper. "I knew he left it here." He closed the bag and removed the others from the locker. When they all were out, he slung the straps of two over his shoulders, one on each side, then took the others, one in each hand, and started up the corridor toward the exit.

Krylov had come in search of the money with the vague notion of returning it to Mogilevich. He'd be thankful to have it back and would see Krylov as someone he could count on, no matter what. Kirchen, on the other hand, would face the full measure of Mogilevich's vengeance. If he managed to escape, he would live the remainder of his life on the run. And he would blame Krylov for it. He considered that as he made his way through the station and by the time he reached the exit, he wondered, "Perhaps I should use the money to simply disappear."

Early the next morning, Sibel Izmir arrived at Galerie Le Meilleur. Located in the Chelsea section of New York City, near the corner of Tenth Avenue and West Twenty-Fourth Street, establishing the gallery and becoming an art dealer had been her idea. Her husband, Hasan, had a knack for making money. He also had a penchant for frittering it away. The gallery was a way to invest in something other than Hasan's predilection for racehorses at Aqueduct or the roulette wheel in Atlantic City.

At first, the gallery seemed exactly as Hasan and everyone else thought—a hobby to keep Sibel out of the way. But her contacts in Europe had proven more than helpful and her shrewdness in matters of serious business became obvious. Sooner than anyone expected, the gallery turned a profit and had continued to do so each year.

That morning, Sibel parked her car in back, entered the building through a door near the loading dock, and walked to her office. She deposited her purse in a desk drawer, then started toward the breakroom for a cup of coffee. Before she reached it, she was met by Jamie Wright, one of her young assistants.

Jamie was a recent graduate of Wellesley College where she'd obtained a degree in art history. Smart, alert, and perceptive, she had come to the gallery to gain firsthand experience before opening her own gallery. "The truck is on its way," she said.

Sibel looked dissatisfied. "It should have been here by now." She spoke with the precision of one for whom English was a second language. Correct and fluent, but learned from a book.

"Customs took longer than expected."

"You have the list of the shipment?"

"Yes."

"Make certain it's all there."

"Yes, ma'am."

Twenty minutes later, a transfer truck backed up to the gallery's loading dock. Sibel was waiting as the truck came to a stop. She watched while the driver came from the cab and raised the rear door. As the door went up, three wooden crates appeared. Each one affixed to a pallet.

Workmen from the gallery came with an electric forklift and in a matter of minutes removed the crates from the truck and set them inside the gallery's receiving room. The driver handed Sibel documents that accompanied the crates and she signed a receipt for the shipment.

As the truck drove away, Sibel turned to Jamie. "Check each crate." She handed Jamie the documents. "Make certain everything on the list is in one of the boxes."

"Yes, ma'am."

"And enter all of it in our system."

Jamie, suspicious of why they hadn't checked the shipment before the truck was allowed to leave, opened her mouth to speak, but Sibel cut her off. "Get to work," she snapped. "We need the art ready for the floor as soon as possible."

As Sibel disappeared down the hall, Jamie directed one of the workmen to open the first crate and began sorting through its contents. An hour later, she reached the second crate where she caught sight of a painting unlike any of the others in the shipment. She glanced at the inventory list. "*Woman With Table and Vase*," she whispered. "This is a Matisse. Where did they get it?"

For a moment, Jamie considered discussing the painting with Sibel. Explaining its significance. It was so unlike anything else they had received, Sibel might not know its value. Besides which, the painting might have been included in the shipment by mistake. Well … there wasn't much chance of that. Not really. But it could have happened and Sibel ought to know about it. Ought to be aware in case someone asked about it. Then she remembered the encounter with Sibel just an hour earlier and decided to keep quiet.

Sibel was smart and decisive, but things Jamie had seen since coming to work there led her to wonder how legitimate the business really was. "Better to mind my own business," she whispered. "At least for now, the less I know about what's going on here, the better it will be for me."

When Jamie finished receiving the items in the shipment, she placed the artwork in the gallery's secure room and walked down the hall to her office. Using her personal cell phone, as instructed, she sent a text to an international number that read, "Items arrived. No damage. One of the pieces is particularly nice."

Chapter 11

Around mid-morning, David Anders telephoned Preston Cooper and arranged to meet him for lunch at a vendor's cart on the corner near Cooper's office. They bought a hot dog and sat on a bench while they ate. After acknowledging their past association Anders said, "Did Jack tell you what this is about?"

"Something about art," Cooper replied. "Trouble at an auction."

"Yeah," Anders said. "Trouble is a good way to put it."

Being careful not to overstate the situation, Anders told Cooper about Hasan and Ahmed Izmir. How they made a fortune in the real estate development business, then opened a gallery. He described the way they conducted themselves at art auctions, the prices they paid, and the difficulty one would encounter in attempting to operate an art gallery in the manner they seemed to operate.

"I don't have hard evidence of anything criminal," Anders said, doing his best to avoid a claim of slander from the Izmirs, or a perjury charge with the Feds. "But I know what I have seen, and I think something's not right. They spend too much money. They do it flagrantly. They overpay on everything. It's just too much to be legitimate."

Cooper smiled. "Auction houses don't mind them overpaying, do they?" It was an obvious question, but one any prosecutor would feel compelled to ask, if for no other reason than to get it out of the way.

Anders recognized that but it left him feeling defensive.

"Look." Anders said. "We're all about making money. But that's just it. The auction houses don't care. Many of the galleries don't care, either. As long as they get their fee and their cut of a deal, they're glad for the business. But that doesn't mean that what the Izmirs are doing is legitimate."

"Sounds like they get on your nerves."

"They yell and shout when they buy." Anders gestured with his hands as he talked. "They yell and shout when they sell. They yell and shout in between. It's like we're at a ballgame, not an art auction."

"So, what do you want me to do about this?"

"Can't you take a look at them? See if they're doing something wrong?"

Cooper shook his head. "I'm not a private investigator."

"I know, but after 9-11 you guys said we should report suspicious activity. So, that's what I'm doing. I'm just doing what you said I should do."

"And you think the Izmirs are acting suspiciously."

"It looks suspicious to me," Anders responded. "Someone with authority ought to check them out."

Cooper grinned. "Did they outbid you?"

This was the same question Frazer asked and it aggravated Anders to hear it again. "Look." His voice had an edge. "I'm raising these questions for me. I'm not asking you to check them out and tell me what you find. I'm just saying—"

"So," Cooper needled, "they really did outbid you."

"Yes." Anders said. "They outbid me on several occasions. And they have forced me to pay far more for a piece than I wanted to pay. But that's not what this is about." He had an insistent tone.

"You said the Izmirs have a gallery."

"Yes," Anders acknowledged. "Hasan has one in Chelsea. His wife runs it."

"What kind of art do they sell?"

"They claim to deal in art from emerging artists and they have works from a few American artists that probably fit that category, but most of what they sell comes from Europe. Artists who are unknown in the US. And most of them are barely known in Europe."

"And you think it's not possible for them to make money doing that?"

"I've been in that business and it's impossible to make the kind of money they seem to be making by selling artwork from unknown artists. The market just isn't that deep. And they pay way too much for the things they buy at auction to then resell them in their gallery at a profit."

"Maybe they have buyers who don't care?"

"That might be so. It's possible."

"But you still think they're doing something illegal?"

"I don't see how they could avoid it."

"Have you observed them doing something you know for a fact is illegal?"

"No."

"Ever see them break any laws?"

"No. But I know they're spending a lot of money and they can't be making it back from that gallery they operate."

"They don't do that kind of business?"

"No."

"How did they get into the art business?"

"That's another thing," Anders noted. "They were in the real estate development business. Apparently, they were pretty good at it. But how did they come to be expert enough to deal in art?"

"That's a good question. Anything else you can tell me about them?"

"Nothing specific. But one thing I've thought about is this. Most transactions in the art world are handled privately. No records. No regulations. No reports. I've seen very expensive pieces by artists whose names you would recognize sell with only a handshake."

"But a dealer would have to report a cash transaction," Cooper noted. "They aren't exempt from that."

"A dealer in the United States would, but not every country

is that concerned about cash transactions. Authorities in Russia, China, and most European countries don't care. In China, they prefer cash. In some places, they have people buying cars for cash. Takes a truckload of currency to do it, but they do it."

"So, what are you saying?"

"I'm saying, if a person bought a painting in another country for cash and brought it to the United States, they could sell it at a legitimate auction house or through a legitimate dealer and turn that cash into a legitimate check that could be deposited in an account at any bank in the country."

Cooper raised an eyebrow. "Money laundering?"

"Yes," Anders said. "A drug dealer, for instance, could use art transactions to move vast amounts of wealth from Europe to the United States, and it would go virtually undetected."

"Are you accusing the Izmirs of dealing in drugs?"

"No." Anders shook his head. "Not at all. I'm just saying, the art business is ripe for exploitation. And something about the way the Izmir brothers conduct their business isn't right. They can't buy paintings and resell them at the prices they pay. Everyone else is trying to pay the least. The Izmirs seem to be trying to pay the most. That kind of thing isn't sustainable as a legitimate business model."

Okay." Cooper wadded the wrapper from his hotdog, tossed it into a nearby trashcan, and stood. "I'll take a look at it, but I'm not promising anything."

Anders stood as well. "Good. I appreciate it."

"But remember," Cooper added. "I'm not working for you. You understand that?"

"I understand," Anders replied.

Preston Cooper returned to the FBI building and called one of the office's young agents, Scott Davenport, to his office. In the briefest of terms, he told Davenport about his lunch with David Anders and described the concerns Anders raised over the Izmir brothers.

"They operate Galerie Le Meilleur in Chelsea," Cooper said. "Do you know anything about them?"

"Not really," Davenport said. "I read an article about them in the paper not too long ago. Rather flamboyant, as I recall. But that's about it."

"David Anders thinks they're a little too flamboyant," Cooper said. "He thinks we should take a closer look at them."

Davenport frowned. "Are you sure you want to get into this?"

"Why not?"

"Sounds like one art dealer jealous of another."

"Maybe." Cooper nodded. "But Anders is an influential guy and we rely on the cooperation of people like him for help, especially with our art theft cases. His tip gives us grounds to have a look. Never know what you'll find, once you get into it."

"Maybe," Davenport conceded. "But it seems a little thin."

"Just take a look," Cooper said. "That's all we need to do right now. Might be something. Might be nothing. Just poke around some and see what's there."

"Might be a waste of time, too."

"Listen," Cooper said firmly. "Anders is a credible person. If we ignore this and it turns out to be something big, it won't be good for either of us. So, look into it. I'll take the heat from upstairs for the time you spend on it."

"Okay." Davenport seemed agreeable. "Any place in particular you want me to begin?"

"Check their criminal record first. Then ask around. See what you can learn."

"I think the article I read mentioned they had immigrated from somewhere," Davenport said. "Do we know if they are US citizens?"

"I don't know," Cooper replied. "That's a good place to check, too. ICE probably has a file on them. See what they have to offer." As Davenport turned to leave, Cooper spoke up. "But do it without interviewing the Izmirs," he cautioned. "We don't want to raise their suspicion just yet."

Chapter 12

Meanwhile, Truman Slater was across the river at his apartment, a musty one-room efficiency in the Williamsburg section of Brooklyn. A canvas was spread on the floor, tacked in place at the corners. It was large, covering the space between the door and the bed with just enough room on the sides for him to make his way around it. Music played, louder than was comfortable, as Slater jumped from side to side, paint brush in one hand, can of paint in the other, alternately dribbling and splashing paint on the canvas, then stooping to add swatches and swoops in looping patterns.

A coffee cup sat on the counter in the corner, beside a two-burner cooktop. Empty energy drink cans sat near it and lay scattered about on the floor near the edges of the painting. He'd been up all night on a manic binge powered by caffeine, sugar, and whatever was in the energy drinks. Now, after more than twenty-four hours of frantic work, he was wired, nervous, and jittery.

In the midst of that frenetic activity, Slater paused to admire his work and an acrid smell caught his attention. He glanced to the left to see that the coffee pot had boiled dry. As he crossed the room to take care of it, a knock at the door interrupted him. He hurried back and opened it to find Charlotte Snider standing in the hall. Caught off-guard by her unexpected appearance, he could only stand and stare.

"Do you remember me?" she asked finally.

"Yes," he replied. "You were at the showing last night."

"Night before last," she said, correcting him.

"Oh." He smiled awkwardly. "I lost track of time."

She craned her neck to see past him. "Aren't you going to invite me inside?" Slater glanced over his shoulder in the direction she was looking and for the first time noticed the canvas, the paint cans, and the clutter. "Or, maybe I should come back another time," she added.

"No, no." He moved aside quickly. "It's fine. Please. Come in." He held open the door and gestured for her to enter.

Charlotte stepped through the doorway while Slater moved to the counter and turned off the radio. As the room fell silent, she made her way down a narrow space between the canvas on the floor and the sofa that sat against the wall. Paintings stood on the sofa, propped in rows against the back and she flipped through them as she went. "This is rather interesting," she said, holding one up for a better view. "But it seems you haven't quite found your style."

Slater didn't care for the comment. "What do you mean?" he asked.

"The strokes are bold and authoritative, but your use of color and structure is unsettled. You can't decide whether you're Jackson Pollock or Roy Lichtenstein. How did you get out of art school without answering that question?"

A frown wrinkled Slater's forehead. "Do what?"

She glanced over at him. "One critique class would have straightened you out."

"We didn't get into that at Parsons."

"No?" She seemed skeptical.

"We stayed away from thinking too much," he said. "And concentrated on doing."

"That's too bad."

"Hey." He shrugged. "Pollock and Lichtenstein were great artists. I'll take that comparison."

"They were great artists," she acknowledged. "But they didn't study at Parsons. And they were true to themselves."

"What does that mean?"

"They painted from who they were," she explained. "As an expression of something deep inside. All artists do. The good ones, at least."

"And I'm not?"

"Not yet." She looked him over. "How long has it been since you slept?" While she waited for an answer she turned back to the paintings and continued to cull through his work. "You look like you've been on a three-day binge."

"Not that long."

"Alcohol?"

"No," he replied. "Not this time."

"Then what?"

"Caffeine, mostly. I think. I came back from that show so jacked, I wanted to do something. So, I painted."

"And you've been painting since then?"

"Mostly. Working out my frustration." He glanced away. "I had a lot of frustration after that."

"Good." She smiled. "That's good."

"Good that I'm frustrated?"

"Good that you painted from it." She pointed to the canvas on the floor. "That's better than anything I've seen from you so far."

"Thanks," he replied. She continued slowly around the room and he watched her, bent over, flipping through the canvasses, her skirt pulled tight against her hips. His mind began to wander, and he was about to let it wander even further but something inside told him that was an indulgence he could not afford and so he said finally, "You've looked through most of my work. Which one am I? Pollock or Lichtenstein?"

"I think you're neither."

Slater felt deflated. "Then who am I?"

She pointed in his direction. "That is a question only you can answer."

Slater shoved his hands in the pockets of his pants. "I've gone about as far as I can go in searching for it."

"Well," she said with a coy smile. "Perhaps I can help."

"How's that?"

"I own a house in Springs."

Slater was puzzled. "Springs?"

"Long Island."

A look of realization came to him. "That's rather far out on the island, isn't it?"

"Not far from where your mentor lived."

He frowned. "My mentor?"

"Jackson Pollock."

A look of pride turned up the corners of his mouth. "You think Jackson Pollock is my mentor?"

"You're both from the west. Both love big spaces." She gestured to the canvas on the floor. "Both trying to express something you can't quite grasp."

He frowned. "How do you know where I'm from?"

She gave him a dismissive expression. "Mr. Slater, I collect art for a living, for a hobby, for entertainment, but I don't buy anything on a whim." She turned again to face the paintings that lined the room. "So, I have a house in Springs. And, yes. It's pretty far out. You'd be alone most of the time. But you would be free of distractions and you could paint anything you like. Are you interested?"

He was very interested, but also conflicted. Her assistance would be of immense help to his career. With Charlotte Snider on his side, there could be no limit to what he might achieve. But if he accepted, he would be in her debt. "I'm committed on the lease for this apartment for another six months." He said it not as a refusal, but as a way of testing her offer. If she was serious, his commitment on the lease would be of no concern to her.

She glanced around and as Slater expected, said simply, "I'll take care of that."

Still, he pressed the matter. "What would I owe you?"

"You can stay at my house for free," she said.

"Is there any work out there?" He was certain she had a solution for his living expenses, too, but he thought he should raise the issue.

If he was out there, he wouldn't be in Manhattan with his job at the gallery.

"You won't need it," she said.

"I won't?"

"I'll give you a thousand dollars a month." She gathered three pieces from their place along the wall and leaned them against her leg. "And I'll buy these to get you started. A thousand dollars apiece sound right?"

He was taken aback and unsure what to say. "Well…"

She cut her eyes in his direction. "You have a better offer for them?"

"No." He smiled, resigned to the inevitable. "A thousand apiece would be great."

Charlotte took a checkbook from her purse, filled out a check for the amount, then handed it to him. "You can use the entire place," she said. "There's a house and a barn. You could use the barn as a studio. I'll let you live there for free and pay you a thousand dollars a month to help you eat. You won't be able to work for Wyatt. Whatever paintings you sell, you get the proceeds. Whatever you don't sell by the end of each year, belong to me. Fair enough?"

"Where am I going to sell my work? You were at the gallery the other night. You heard what Wyatt said. He doesn't really want me back."

She had a confident smile. "Let me worry about Wyatt. Okay?"

"Okay."

"Now get packed." She touched one of the paintings as if to lift it, then reconsidered. "Do you have a car?"

"Yes."

"Will it get you out to the end of Long Island?"

"Yes ma'am," he replied. "It got me here from Montana."

"Well," she said, "let's hope it has a few more miles left in it. Hand me something to write on and I'll give you the address." He offered her a notepad and she scribbled the address on it, then returned it to him. "The key to the front door is under the mat." She picked up one of the pieces, then gestured to the others. "Help me get these to my car."

Slater took the paintings, one in each hand, and followed her downstairs to her car. As he placed the art on the backseat, he looked over at her. "Can I ask you something?"

"Certainly."

"Why are you doing this?"

The question seemed to touch something inside her. "I love the arts," she said. "And I know what a challenge it is to find yourself as a painter ... or as anything." She had a kindly smile. "My husband left me plenty of money and I like using it to help people find their way." She opened the front door and took a seat behind the steering wheel, then glanced up at him. "And, I heard what Raymond Wyatt said to you."

"That didn't destroy your opinion of me?"

"I've found some of my best pieces of art from the artists he throws out of his gallery." She reached for the door to close it and smiled. "But don't tell him I said that."

Chapter 13

Two days later Jacob Edelman was in the living room of his apartment when his cell phone rang. The call was from Jean Ferro. "I was able to obtain an order from British authorities holding the shipment at the transit company in London," he said.

"Great," Edelman replied. "When can you inspect it?"

"Sadly," Ferro explained, "the crates were gone from the shipping agent by the time the order could be served."

Edelman was beside himself with frustration. "This is a comedy of errors," he fumed.

"Yes," Ferro replied. "We are always one step behind."

Edelman took a deep breath and forced himself to relax. "So, where are the paintings now?"

"The crates departed London by air cargo yesterday, which means they would have arrived in New York the same day."

"And they are on their way to Galerie Le Meilleur?"

"Yes," Ferro said. "But first they must pass through customs."

"They were not pre-cleared in London?"

"I do not think so."

"Then they could still be in Customs, here in New York."

"It is possible," Ferro said. "But I suspect they already have been delivered to the gallery. These things do not take so long." He sighed. "Jacob, I am so sorry we have not been able to help as you wished. I thought I could stop the crates before they departed France. And then I was hopeful we could interdict them in London, but that was not possible."

Edelman knew Ferro had done all he could, given the limitations of the governments with which he dealt. "Can you get the FBI involved from your end?"

"I asked my supervisor about that already," Ferro replied. "He is not sure he has the authority to request FBI assistance."

"What about the detective? The one you introduced me to in Paris?"

"He says they have a delicate relationship with the FBI, and he does not want to contact them with a request for assistance unless there is something substantive to support the inquiry. Right now, they say they still are not sure they have that."

"What do you mean?" Edelman made no attempt to hide the incredulity in his voice. "They have a murder to solve! The murder of an art dealer whose most expensive piece is missing. Isn't that substance enough to ask for help from every international agency?"

"Perhaps," Ferro said. "But they feel they still have not made a conclusive connection between the artwork and the murder."

"I'm the connection!" Edelman screamed into the phone. "I'm telling you, it was there. The Matisse was there. André Crémieux knew it was mine. We were negotiating for its return."

"I know but—"

"It was there the day before he was killed," Edelman shouted. "Now it's gone. And all the other artwork, too. How can they say the murder and the missing artwork are not connected?"

"Apparently those other pieces were part of a legitimate transaction."

Edelman exhaled slowly and lowered his voice. "I don't understand."

"I know." Ferro spoke with a sympathetic tone. "And I don't always understand their reasoning, either. I think, from their perspective, they are concerned about appearing to be helping a private individual from a foreign country recover personal property with a suspicious provenance."

"Suspicious provenance? The Nazis stole it. We want it back. What's suspicious about that?"

"Those are their words, not mine. I am trying to help you, and many others like you, to recover these lost items."

"What if I call the detective in Paris myself?"

"You are welcome to try if you think it would help," Ferro said. "But if I insinuate myself into his investigation much further, I will be in trouble."

"Can your system tell us whether the shipment has cleared customs here in New York?"

"We have access to the US system for tracking shipments, but it does not always update accurately. And even when it does, it doesn't always show us every detail. Let me check and I'll call you back."

"You will call me back this morning?"

"It's not morning here," Ferro said, "but yes. It will only take a minute."

Edelman ended the call and stood before the window, staring out at the city below. A moment later, Anne, his granddaughter, appeared at the doorway. "I heard you shouting, Papa."

"Stupid French government."

"Is everything okay?"

"They can't even investigate a murder without creating an international incident."

"Let me get you some more coffee."

"I've already had three cups."

"Then tea, perhaps?"

"Okay." He glanced over his shoulder toward her. "Tea would be fine."

While Anne went to the kitchen to put on water for tea, Edelman remained in the living room and took a seat in a chair near the window. He hadn't been there long when the cell phone rang. The call was from Ferro. "What did you find out?" Edelman asked.

"It was just as I suspected."

"What?"

"The crates were delivered to the gallery on the day they arrived in New York."

"To Galerie Le Meilleur?"

"Yes."

"Who signed for them?"

"Sibel Izmir. Do you know her?"

"We've never met but I know who she is."

"I am sorry I could not do more."

"That's okay," Edelman replied. "You have done more to help than anyone."

What Edelman said was true. In all the years he'd been attempting to recover the family's art collection, Ferro had been more helpful than anyone Edelman had encountered. Still Edelman was frustrated. He'd gotten so close—just hours away from having the Matisse—only for it to vanish once more.

Edelman ended the call, slipped the cell phone into the pocket of his pants, and stood. In quick strides, he crossed the room to a closet and opened it, then reached inside for his jacket. As he took it from a hanger, Anne appeared with a cup of tea. "Here you go—" She stopped short when she realized he was going out. "Where are you going?"

"I have to see someone about something."

She had a knowing look. "This is about that phone call, isn't it?"

"I won't be long."

"And that phone call was from that guy in France, wasn't it? About the Matisse."

"The crates were delivered already. Probably two days ago, if I counted right."

Anne had a questioning look. "The crates?"

"The art shipment. With the paintings from Crémieux's gallery in Paris. If I'm right, the Matisse is in one of those boxes." He turned away to take his hat from a shelf in the closet. "No telling what they did with it by now."

"You think they could dispose of it that quickly?"

"It's a Matisse," Edelman said. "It's worth a lot of money."

"Where was it delivered?"

"Galerie Le Meilleur," he replied. "In Chelsea."

Anne sat the teacup on a table nearby. "You can't go by yourself."

"Well, you can't go with me," he responded.

"Why not?"

"You have class."

"I can miss——"

"No," he snapped. "You can't miss class every time I have an errand. Go to class. And hurry up, you'll be late." He put on his hat and turned toward the door.

"But what about lunch?" she asked.

"I'm only going to Chelsea." He reached for the door. "I'll be back before noon and if not, I can get something on the corner."

She touched his arm. "Did you forget?"

He gave her a blank expression. "Forget what?"

"Mom."

A knowing realization came over him. "Oh," he said. His shoulders sagged as he remembered. "We're supposed to meet your mother."

"And Uncle Michael is joining us," Anne added. "We're supposed to meet them both."

"Right."

"You can't be late. You know how Mom is when——"

"Listen to me." Edelman's voice was terse and he knew from the look on her face, but he could not restrain himself. "The art is all that I have left of them. All of them are gone. Snatched away in the night, kicking and screaming. Some of them worked to death. Most of them slaughtered in the camps. The pictures are all that is left, and I am this close." There was a look of pain on his face as he gestured with his fingers. "This close to getting them all back together with me." He turned away and snatched open the door to the hall. "Get a table. I'll be there before you start." And with that, he was gone.

After leaving Truman Slater's apartment, Charlotte Snider called Sibel Izmir and arranged for them to have lunch. They knew each other from a longstanding business relationship. Charlotte bought from Sibel's unknown artists, gambling that a few of them would one day become popular among collectors. Sibel took on the promising artists Charlotte found. The male artists. The young, attractive ones.

They met at The Red Cat, a restaurant on Tenth Avenue less than a block from the gallery. Over a luncheon salad they talked about art and the most recent round of sales at the auction houses. Sibel shook her head at the mention of it. "I hate going to the auctions."

"Why is that?" Charlotte was certain she knew the answer, but she asked anyway.

"Hasan and Ahmed act like such children. They've become a spectacle, I think. And I have become one by reason of my association with them."

Charlotte had a sympathetic smile. "They do put on quite a show."

"None of the dealers respect them."

"They respect you."

"Me?" Sibel sounded surprised. Charlotte was sure it was feigned. Sibel wasn't that naïve.

"You're the one who makes Galerie Le Meilleur work and they all know it."

The corners of Sibel's mouth turned down in a sarcastic smirk. "What do you want?"

Charlotte grinned. "Why do you say that?"

"You're giving me compliments. You must want something. What is it?"

"It's true," Charlotte responded. "The other dealers know you actually make the gallery successful and without you it would have failed by the second day."

Sibel raised an eyebrow in a good-natured way. "And ..."

"Okay," Charlotte conceded. "I do have something to ask you."

"I assumed as much. What is it?"

Charlotte dabbed the corners of her mouth with a napkin, then said, "I met an artist whom I think will produce a large body of work. Good work that should retain its value."

Sibel looked skeptical. "Beyond the life of a post-auction dinner party?"

"Yes," Charlotte laughed. "I think it will last much longer than anything you've shown this year."

"And you want me to show his work."

"Yes," Charlotte said. "I think you should consider doing a show and taking him on as a client."

"I don't know." Sibel rested her fork on the edge of the plate. "We're not really a primary market gallery for American art and we're already obligated to several artists."

"I know that."

"We deal in the secondary market for American art. European art is our major area."

"But you occasionally handle new American artists," Charlotte countered. "You just said so."

"If you can call them that." Sibel rolled her eyes.

Charlotte looked concerned. "There's a problem?" She knew the problem already but didn't want Sibel to know.

Sibel had a sheepish grin. "Neither of these most recent ones has any interest in anything other than art."

"Oh. They prefer to work and not play?"

"They prefer each other, I think."

Charlotte couldn't avoid a grin. She'd heard the rumors but hearing it from Sibel herself was particularly humorous. "Is their art selling?" She knew it wasn't but guiding the conversation toward her goal required her to play along.

"Not as well as I'd hoped," Sibel replied. "And with no ...

"Side benefits?"

Sibel scowled. "You're enjoying this way too much."

"I think I can help."

"With this new artist of yours?"

"I brought you Robert Capriati, didn't I? You did well with him."

Sibel had a satisfied look. "I did very well with him for a while." Her face went cold. "And then he ran off with that merchandiser from Saks."

"But he's still painting, and his art is holding its value."

"True. The business side was even better than the bed."

"And from what you said before, the bed with him was rather exciting."

"Yes." Sibel had a longing expression. "We had a wonderful time when we were together." They sat in silence a moment, Sibel apparently remembering her experience with Capriati. Charlotte refusing to speak for fear of losing the deal.

Finally, Sibel said. "So who is this new artist?"

"Truman Slater."

"And you are helping him?"

"He just moved into my house in Springs."

"I suppose it wouldn't hurt to meet him."

"I need to go out there to check on him," Charlotte said. "Why don't you ride along with me?"

"When?"

"We could go today."

Sibel shook her head. "Not today. I have too much to do."

"Then later this week. Or next, if that's better."

"He's young?"

"Yes." Charlotte nodded. "He's young."

Sibel smiled. "Then I should take a look at him."

"At the art.

"That, too," Sibel said. "But just a look. No promises."

Chapter 14

Meanwhile, Jack Frazer rode the bus to the lower end of Manhattan and walked over to the city's Department of Records to meet with Todd Mitchell, the contact in city government Gina Wilkins told him about. He liked riding the bus when he had the time. The big windows on either side allowed him to watch as the city went by. The tall buildings and the people. Office workers walking with a determined gate, head forward and tilted slightly down, striding purposefully on an important mission. Tourists from the Midwest ambling at a casual pace, gawking at how high the buildings rose. Shoppers, their hands clutching the handles of oversized bags that bore the labels of the right places, filled with the latest things that promised purpose and meaning for their lives.

After a few blocks, the rattle and hum of the bus over took the images outside. People on the sidewalk receded from view and Frazer's thoughts turned to Zoë. He remembered again how small she felt in his arms, the warmth of her flesh pressed against his, the softness of her body beneath his weight. For the first time that day, he longed to talk to her but the bus was noisy and he didn't want to talk to her in public, so he sent her a text message. A note about how much he missed her. No sooner had he sent it than she replied, "Nothing a twelve-hour ride wouldn't remedy," and he felt aggravated by it.

Coming to New York had been his idea. An opportunity to do it.

To be a journalist, not merely to talk about it or pretend or write soft stories for an obscure weekly paper. He wanted to do something. To amount to something. A thing of substance. A thing of worth. To be a person of substance and a person who made a difference.

That reminded him of Richard, a friend from high school, who went to the Grand Canyon for a great adventure reminiscent of the explorers who conquered the West. Yet when he got there, he stood at the railing and stared down at the thin silvery strip of river that ran at the bottom, then visited the gift shop, and returned to California with nothing but stories of how it looked from the safety of the top. Never hiked down the trail through the narrow spots and feared for his life. Never floated the river rapids and felt the spray of water in his face.

Afterwards, when Richard came home and told them what he'd done, the hollowness of it had been obvious to Frazer and the obviousness of it to him must have been obvious to Richard because his countenance dropped at Frazer's reaction. And Frazer felt hollow for not reacting better. At not being as good a friend to Richard as Richard had been to him.

In truth, though, Frazer didn't think of friendship in the same way he thought of other things. Never thought of doing it in terms of being a solid friend. Or even simply of being, but only in terms of doing. And then only in terms of himself and what experience he could have that would reach the depth of his need to be the kind of person who did it. A person of substance derived solely from accomplishment.

That's the way Frazer had been and the way he always was. He wanted to *do* it. Whatever it was. To be totally immersed in the thing. Consumed by it. Genuinely, authentically engaged. For an aspiring journalist, that could mean only one thing. New York City. Zoë was content with the tourist view, the shopper's view, which she could have in Charlotte or Birmingham or Charleston. Not Frazer. He had to plumb the thing. And that's what they did. They came to New York so he could be a journalist. A real journalist. A journalist of substance. A journalist who did it. It was a grand adventure for him and he thought he was finally doing it. No matter how important or unimportant the world out there might think of a story or a person or a topic, it meant something to him because he was finding it and doing it in New York.

Only now, with Zoë in Charleston and him in the city by himself, talking to someone in the city records department didn't seem like such a grand adventure. It seemed small and meaningless and insignificant. Like the hollowness when Richard returned with his account of standing at the rim of the Grand Canyon, but never going to the bottom.

That day, sitting on the bus, he came to think that maybe the meaning and purpose he'd found wasn't really tied to the place but to her. To Zoë. As if nothing meant anything unless he shared it with her. And he wondered if he'd been doing the things he'd done only to prove to her that he was somebody. That he was a man who could do it. And all she wanted was him.

Just then, the bus lurched to a halt and the doors opened. Frazer glanced around, thinking he might have gone too far, but he hadn't, and he waited two more stops until they reached Chambers Street, then got off and walked over to the building where Mitchell worked.

Mitchell was waiting when Frazer arrived. "Gina told me you might be coming by," he said. "You want to do a story about life in the abandoned tunnels."

"I know it has been done a few times," Frazer responded. "But I thought I might find a new twist."

"It's a story that comes and goes," Mitchell said. "What did you want to know?"

"Whatever you can tell me. Do you know anyone who's ever been down there?"

"Yes." Mitchell had a knowing look. "Me."

Frazer was surprised. "You?"

"I don't look the type?"

"It's not that. I just never thought I would meet an urban spelunker in the city records department."

"Well," Mitchell said with a grin. "At least you got the name right."

Frazer shrugged. "Cave in the mountain. Tunnel in the city."

"Right."

"So," Frazer said, moving on. "Do you have any maps or photographs?"

"We have both. But we have some rules about the maps."

"Oh?"

"You can look at them all you want," Mitchell explained. "But you can't make copies."

Frazer seemed hesitant. "Okay."

"And that includes taking pictures of them with your phone."

"Not even the historic ones?"

"You can make copies of surface maps all you want. But not the ones for the underground tunnels. And you can't make drawings of them, either."

"Not even a line drawing?"

Mitchell shook his head. "Not even. And I'm serious. Those are the rules."

"Okay. But why the rules?"

"The tunnels are a security risk."

"Oh."

"After 9-11, everybody went all Dick Cheney on everything," Mitchell said. "Started seeing trouble everywhere. 'Might be an attack from here. Might be an attack from there.' In the follow-up to all of that, they tightened security for everything."

Frazer nodded. "I suppose it's possible. Someone could move around beneath the city and never be noticed."

"You can go in at the Bronx and come up in lower Manhattan." Mitchell had a satisfied look. "I've done it."

Frazer raised an eyebrow. "You've gone into a tunnel in the Bronx and come out in Manhattan?"

"Yes."

"Just for fun?"

"The first time."

Frazer was even more curious than before. "You've done it more

THE ART DEALER'S WIFE

than once?"

"First time, I did it because I was curious. Then we had one of those 'what if" sessions with all the city leaders and officials and experts. They asked us about what we thought might be points of weakness in the city's security. I said the abandoned tunnels were a problem. Everyone knew they existed, but no one in the meeting took me seriously. It seemed obvious to me we had a problem. I mean, there's an abandoned subway station right under city hall."

"I didn't know that."

"Not many people do," Mitchell said. "So, I decided to show them the tunnels were a potential problem. Went into a tunnel near the Bronx Zoo, came up inside Police Plaza." A grin made his cheeks glow. "I was sitting in the police commissioner's chair when he came in."

"And you came straight to his office from the tunnels?"

Mitchell laughed. "I was a mess. Stunk the whole place up. But the commissioner had been in the meeting where everyone blew me off and he remembered what I'd said. Saw my point about the tunnels right away."

"And I'm guessing he did something about it right away, too."

"Right away."

"Interesting story."

"Yeah," Mitchell acknowledged. "But you can't write a single word about it."

"Why not?"

"For the same reason you can't make copies of the underground maps."

"Security."

"Right. And if you try to write about it anyway, your editor will get a call before the story gets out of your laptop. And we'll all get called in to somebody's office. So, don't do it."

"Okay."

Frazer spent most of the morning talking to Mitchell and examining city maps. The space beneath Manhattan was a honeycomb of tunnels, passageways, and connections. Subway tunnels, steam tunnels, utility tunnels in layer up layer, along with abandoned subway stations, abandoned rolling stock, and an assortment of carts, trucks, and heavy equipment.

After finishing at the records office, Frazer walked over to Foley Square and bought a hot dog from a vendor. He sat on a bench across from the courthouse and ate while he thought about what he'd learned that morning. Doing an article about life in the underground tunnel wasn't big enough. Wasn't unique enough. Wasn't good enough. He'd already logged the story with his editor and it would be a hassle to get out of it, so he'd have to do it. But doing that article wasn't doing it. He needed something else.

Writing about Mitchell and security measures taken by the city after 9-11 was more intriguing, but he wasn't sure anyone would be interested in the topic now. It certainly didn't seem like a prize-winner. And then he considered again the story Anders wanted him to write about the Izmir brothers. That article seemed much better than his idea about the city's underground life, but it would infringe on the newspaper's arts department. Wilkins wouldn't like it and as a senior correspondent in that department, she could make lots of trouble for him.

Still, it was an intriguing story with the potential to break wide open. If he was in it first, he might be able to finesse his way around her. At least keep a piece of the story for himself. If he did most of the work before she found out about it, she would be unable to cut him out of a byline, even if he was forced to involve her. The paper had encountered that issue before and there were rules in place to prevent it from happening again.

Frazer wanted another Pulitzer. One wasn't enough. One of anything was never enough. One never filled the hollow place inside that always cried out for more. To go deeper. To reach further. Always to do it at a more meaningful level. But if he was going to write Anders' story; if that was the bigger, better story with substance and heft and gravitas; if that was the story that defined doing it, then he had to get moving. Wilkins wasn't his only challenge. Anders seemed serious about the matter and he wasn't the type to wait long on things that concerned him. He'd give the story to someone else, maybe Wilkins herself, even if he was the one who set up Anders with Preston Cooper and the FBI.

That reminded Frazer that he hadn't heard how the meeting went, so he sent Anders a text message right then. Anders responded almost immediately, "We talked but I haven't heard anymore from him." That wasn't much, but Frazer was sure it meant that Anders hadn't shopped the story to anyone else. Didn't it? Surely, he wouldn't do that if he was waiting for the FBI to respond on a connection Frazer had arranged.

Frazer checked his watch. It was a little past noon. He needed to do some research on the Izmirs. To review the articles on them that were already in publication. The paper had files and files of that stuff back at the office. He could go back to his desk and do the work there, but if he did, and someone saw him, they might wonder why he was working on an art story and then word would get out. Gina was right about that. Nothing stayed secret at the office for very long. He had to hold this one close until the article was ready. Or almost ready. He needed a place to work that wouldn't give him away. And that's when he thought of the public library.

"It's perfect," he whispered. Access to any file in the world, and it came with the excuse and justification all in one. If anyone saw him, they would assume he was there doing research. If anyone at the office asked where he'd been, he could tell them he'd been at the library doing research. And the library was so big, just being there wouldn't tip anyone's hand to his topic.

Satisfied he had the bases covered, Frazer rose from his place on the bench, tossed the hot dog wrapper in the trash, and started toward the corner. A few minutes later, he was on the bus headed to his favorite branch of the library.

Chapter 15

After lunch, Sibel returned to the gallery. As she entered the building, she saw Jamie Wright standing out front, near some of the best paintings. With her was a man who looked to be in his eighties. Tall and slender, he wore a dark suit with a white shirt and muted tie. He had olive skin, dark hair, and a look in his eyes that she found enticing.

Sibel sized him up, as she did every man she saw, and wondered if he was what she had to look forward to in the future. No more young boys she could draw to herself. Just older men, drawn to her. She would be the hunted, the target. But could a man like this give her the satisfaction, the release, her body craved? The confirmation that she craved? The sense that she still had it?

Just as her mind was moving from question to fantasy, from supposition to testing an answer through her imagination, Sibel caught the tone of the man's voice. It was sharp and demanding and from the expression on his face she could see that he was upset. Whatever it was that made him that way, she didn't like it. Not from a man. The very idea that a man would come into her gallery and take advantage of an employee, a woman, a woman like Jamie. Young and untried. Still finding her way. She had berated Jamie herself, but that was different. She was the boss. Jamie was her employee. But not this man. Not this man with his business suit and his tie and that look. Who did he think he was? He was no one. He was nothing.

Certainly nothing to her and certainly no one to talk to one of her employees like that.

Sibel thought all of those things in the length of time it took to open the door and step inside the gallery and when she realized what the man was doing, she charged straight for him. "What is the meaning of this?" she demanded.

Jamie turned to her with a calm and collected smile. "This gentleman was telling me about—"

"I don't care," Sibel snapped, cutting her off. "I don't care what he was telling you." She stepped closer, her eyes boring in on him, summoning the force of her personality, her inner power and strength, to make her point unmistakably clear. "You cannot come in here and act like this to my staff." She jabbed at him with her index finger to make certain he understood.

"I'm only—"

"This is a place of business," she said, cutting him off again. "And when you come into my gallery, to my place of business, you will treat my employees with respect. And if you can't do that, you can at least treat them professionally. And if you can't do that, you can get the hell out of here." She delivered the last line while pointing to the street, then she took a breath. "Now," she said when she'd recovered, "why are you so upset?"

"As I was telling Ms. Wright, you received a shipment of art this week. Three containers that originated in Paris."

"We receive shipments regularly," Sibel said. "There is nothing unusual about that, except that you know about them. How do you know about our shipments?"

The man ignored her question. "The crates left France through the port at Le Havre and went to London and now they are here at your gallery. I want to see a list of the paintings in that shipment."

Sibel was so astounded she hardly know how to respond. "I can't possibly—"

"Yes, you can," the man insisted. "And I would like to see them now."

The tone of his voice and the directness of his demand both

offended and intrigued her. Here before her very eyes was the confidence that tempted her mind with the fantasies she'd entertained just moments earlier. That he might be the kind of man she would attract in the future and what would it be like to be with him and would it be enough to satisfy her. Yet, now she encountered in him a strength she had not considered possible. She wanted to explore the possibilities with him, to expand the fantasy beyond its earlier border and perhaps extend it to a present reality, to experience for a sample of the future she sensed was not too far ahead of her, but she did not. Instead, she said in a tone as demanding as his, "Who are you?"

As if on command, the man squared his shoulders and they seemed to her as broad and strong as a football player. "I am Jacob Edelman," he said proudly.

Sibel felt a smile nudge the corners of her mouth but she suppressed it. He offered so many possibilities. So many options. And she would delight in exploring those with him, but they were in the gallery and it was her business, her domain, and no one breached her sovereignty over it. "Why have you come in here demanding to know the details of my business?"

Edelman's jaw flexed and he seemed to force himself under control. "One of the paintings in that shipment," he said slowly, "belongs to me."

Just then, Hasan Izmir appeared from the hallway, a look of concern on his face. "What's all this noise about?" He crossed the room at a stalky kind of gait the way a man does when he intends to assert himself. "I'm trying to work back here in the office and there's so much commotion out here I can't think."

Sibel turned in his direction. "This is Mr. Edelman." She had a tone in her voice and a look in her eye that suggested the name should mean more to Hasan than merely a label. "He wants to see the inventory from our recent shipment."

Hasan came closer, his eyes focused on Edelman. "How is it that you people know anything at all about any shipment we might have received?"

"You people" was code with Hasan for anyone not of Turkic

descent. In this case, Jewish.

"These things are a matter of record," Edelman said.

"Yes, but those records are private. This is my business, not yours. And I—"

Edelman was not cowered by Hasan's presence. "The painting I am looking for was stolen from my family by the Nazis during World War II. Stolen from the front room of my father's apartment. The painting is mine and I want it back."

"I've afraid I can't help you." Hasan gestured toward the door. "You should leave now."

"Look," Edelman replied. "You can deal with me or you can deal with my attorney."

The comment angered Hasan and he leaned closer, his nose almost touching Edelman's. "I'll deal with you with my fist if you don't leave." Edelman refused to back away and just as they were coming to blows, Sibel wedged herself between them. She faced Edelman and her breasts brushed against him. A rush of energy swept through her body and her eyes looked into his. She wanted to feel his lips against hers, even if only for a moment. That would be enough. That would be the glimpse she wanted. She would know from that if the future would be as kind to her, as satisfying for her, as the past had been. But there was no time for that right then and she said, with her eyes still fixed on Edelman. "Gentlemen, there is no need for violence." She took Edelman by the arm. "He was just leaving."

As deftly as if they were dancing, Sibel turned Edelman toward the door. She tightened her grip on his arm and leaned against him with his elbow buried in her breast. He looked over at her. "That painting belongs to me and I intend to get it back."

"And which painting is that?" she asked softly, her mind absorbed in the press of his forearm against her.

"A Matisse," he said. "It's better than anything in your store. Obviously better." At the mention of it she looked up at him and he caught the glimmer in her eyes. "You know exactly what I'm talking about. I want that painting."

By then they were at the door and she pulled it open for him to leave. "I cannot help you with that," she said. "Neither can my husband." She nudged him through the door and Edelman stepped out to the sidewalk. "It is out of our hands."

With Edelman outside, Sibel retreated inside the gallery, pulled the door quickly closed, and locked it. Hasan came to her side and glared through the front window at him. "Those damn Jews and their art. Can you imagine the nerve?"

"If it was stolen," Sibel replied, "I can understand why he would be upset." Her eyes were focused on Edelman as she spoke and followed him as he walked away.

"But he wants to steal it from us," Hasan countered. "And how does he know about our business?"

She shrugged. "I don't know, but I think he must have connections."

"We must let them know about this." Hasan reached into his pocket for his cell phone and began entering a text message but Sibel snatched the phone from his hand. "That is not such a good idea," she said.

He frowned and reached for the phone to take it from her. "Why not? Give that to me."

Sibel moved her hand away, avoiding his outstretched fingers, and leaned near him, her lips brushing his ear as she whispered, "André Crémieux is dead."

Hasan's eyes opened wide. "You know this for certain?"

"Yes," she replied. "Someone called me about it this morning. And I am sure it was a member of Mogilevich's crew who killed him."

Hasan paused, as if considering, then shrugged. "That is bad but what does it have to do with us?"

"Death is the way Mogilevich and his men solve their problems."

"Yes." Hasan was impatient. "We have discussed that before. So what?"

"If they find out that old man is asking questions—that old Jewish man—if we tell them questions have arisen about the provenance of one of their paintings, we will become as much of a problem for them as he." A look of realization came over Hasan as she continued. "Then they will send someone here to solve that problem and it will be very bad for us."

Hasan pointed. "It would be very bad for him."

"And equally bad for us." She smiled in an arrogant way. "Better to let it go for now."

"I don't—"

"Trust me," she interrupted. "Let it go."

Just then, Hasan's cell phone rang. He snatched the phone from Sibel and took the call, but his eyes were troubled when he heard the voice. "Not now," he snapped and ended the call.

Sibel glared at him. He mimicked an innocent expression. "What? Why are you looking at me like that?"

Sibel jabbed him in the chest with her index finger. "That call was from one of your girlfriends."

He backed away. "What are you talking about?"

She stepped toward him and continued to jab him in the chest, backing him across the room. "You tell your girlfriends," she snarled. "And your whores. And all those other women. Tell them not to call during working hours."

"Who said—" He tried to protest but she cut him off. "I don't want them calling when I'm around." She leaned even closer and shouted. "Do you understand me?"

He jumped at the sound of her voice, then an amused look came over him. "How would anyone know if you're around when they call?"

"You figure that part out." Sibel gave him a shove with both hands. "I don't want them calling here. Or anywhere else when I'm around."

He smirked. "Or what?"

Sibel lowered her voice. "You need to remember one thing."

"What's that?"

"Everything you know, I know."

Hasan seemed troubled by the remark. "What does that mean?"

She had a sinister smile. "You know exactly what it means."

Hasan shoved the phone into his pocket and walked toward the hall that led to the offices. Sibel watched until he was gone, then turned to Jamie, who had been standing on the far side of the room the entire time. "If that man ..."

"Mr. Edelman?"

"If he comes back, send him to me. And if I'm not here, tell him to call for an appointment."

"Yes, ma'am."

"Do not show him any records. And do not tell him anything about those paintings. Understand?"

"Yes, ma'am."

"I don't care how many times he returns, or who he brings with him next time. No one sees those records unless I say so."

Chapter 16

When Sibel pushed him from the gallery, Edelman was determined to force his way inside again, unwilling to let the matter drop even for a moment. But as he started in that direction, he heard the lock click and realized that she had shut him out. Resigned to fighting for the picture a different way, Edelman started up the street, head down, shoulders hunched, hands in his pockets.

Despite his resolute demeanor, Edelman had been rattled by the confrontation with Sibel and Hasan—and not merely by their response in throwing him out of the gallery. Finding the painting, negotiating with Crémieux, brought the painting close. Crémieux's murder seemed to plunge the painting into obscurity again, but shipment of it to New York placed it within blocks of Edelman's home. Yet it remained beyond his reach. "How could it come to this?" he muttered to himself. "After all I've done and all I've been through. All we've been through."

Edelman methodically, numbly placed one foot in front of the other, slowly making his way uptown. He had a vague recollection of the restaurant where he was to meet Anne and the others for lunch, but right then he really wasn't interested in that. Seeing them meant engaging in small talk—the meaningless, boring, unproductive exchange of words that did nothing but fill the void that lay between them. He wanted that painting and getting it was foremost on his mind.

As he continued walking, the sense of anger and dejection ebbed but his thoughts remained on the Matisse. In his mind he saw it, as he often did, hanging on the wall in the Paris apartment where they lived when he was a child. It had hung there for as long as he could remember. Right up to the day the French police came to the neighborhood with the German soldiers and began forcing everyone from their homes. "Pack only one suitcase!" they shouted. "One suitcase per person. Take only what you can carry in one suitcase!"

Edelman's father, Menachem, was on the corner when they arrived and heard them while they were still a few blocks away. He hurried home to get Edelman and his mother. "We must leave now," he insisted. When his mother hesitated, his father took her by the arm. "We have to run," he said. "There is no time to wait now."

"But what about our things?" his mother protested. "We need time to pack. We can't leave it all behind."

Menachem snatched a small box from the table where it sat and picked up his mother's purse from a chair. He opened it and dumped the contents of the box—gold and silver jewelry—into it, then handed the purse to her. "That is all you can take," he said. "We must go."

Edelman's mother still did not seem to grasp the seriousness of the moment, so Menachem took her with one hand, grabbed Edelman with the other, and pulled them toward the door. As they stumbled toward the door, Edelman lost his balance and started to fall. His father held onto him but kept going.

When they reached the door, his father jerked it open without missing a step. Jacob, still trying to regain his balance, collided with the door and spun around in the opposite direction. In that moment, he caught a glimpse of the Matisse hanging on the wall near the piano. His mother loved to play the piano and he loved to sit and listen, often staring at the painting, absorbing every brushstroke, every nuance of color and hue, while the notes from the piano filled the air.

Pain from the collision with the door shot through Edelman's shoulder and he cried out, "What is happening to us?"

"They are taking everyone to the stadium," his father replied as he pushed Edelman through the doorway and into the hall.

The stadium was the Velodrome, site of many famous sporting events. News that others were being taken there seemed exciting. "Can we go?" Edelman asked.

"It is not for a game," his father said, and from the tone of his voice Edelman knew they faced grave danger. "It's a selection," his father continued.

"Selection for what?"

"The camps."

"What camps?"

Menachem, still holding them firmly in his grasp, led the way down the hall toward the stairway. "Women with women. Men with men. Children with children."

"What for?"

"They are sending everyone away. Those who can work will be worked to death. Those who cannot work will be killed immediately."

Suddenly, young Edelman felt very much afraid. "I don't want to die." His voice quivered as he spoke.

"That is why we must hurry," his father said.

While they made their way downstairs Edelman heard others scurrying about the building. Their voices were muffled but the sound of panic was unmistakable. For the first time he sensed the raw energy of it and it made him angry. "I hate the Germans," he growled.

Without warning, his father stopped abruptly and leaned down to look him in the eye. "You cannot hate them."

"But I do."

"Then you must forgive them."

"Why?"

"Because if you hate them, you will become like them and then they will win." His father had a serious but not unpleasant look which struck Edelman as oddly out of place with their circumstances, but which he recalled in vivid detail for the rest of his life. "You must not let them win," his father continued. "You must forgive them and rise above their hatred and become the man you were created by God to be."

Edelman's mother interrupted. "We must hurry," she urged, finally attuned to the predicament they faced. "Before we lose the opportunity to flee."

Menachem took Edelman by the hand and they continued down the steps and out the back door that led to an alley behind the building. Walking as quickly as possible, they hurried to the corner, then slowed to collect themselves before turning left into the cross street.

At the next corner, they came to a truck that was parked at the curb. It had sides on the back for hauling cargo with a canvas top, but the top was open. People were climbing in the back and as Edelman and his parents approached, someone took hold of him and hoisted him up with the others. For an instant, Edelman thought that he was being separated from his parents and he opened his mouth to protest, but before he could cry out, his parents climbed up after him and pushed him into a space along the side of the cargo bed.

More people joined them, wedging themselves tightly into every space. Then, in a few minutes, someone threw a canvas tarp over the top and tied it in place After that, the truck started forward and Edelman closed his eyes, hoping not to get sick from the rocking motion that followed.

The truck made its way slowly through the city and into the countryside. All day, they drove and by nightfall, they were in the open country with farms. Houses were few and far between. When darkness was complete, they came to a stop and everyone climbed out to relieve themselves. Edelman did so, too, near a tree at the edge of the road.

After a brief rest, they returned to the truck and continued driving through the night until they reached Saint-Nazaire on the Atlantic coast. Once there, he learned the plan had been to take a ship to England but the men who were helping them were unable to arrange passage. "No one is crossing to England now," they said. "It is too dangerous. The Germans are sinking everything that sails the Channel."

Instead, they boarded a Brazilian freighter bound for Alexandria, Egypt, and set sail down the coast. As the ship plowed through open water, Edelman and his father spent long hours standing at the rail watching the waves slip past or lying on the deck staring up at the night sky. The air was cool but not unpleasant and no one seemed to mind. In the years that followed, Edelman recalled that time as one of his best experiences with his father and he remembered it whenever he was sad.

To entertain themselves, or perhaps because of the uncertainty they faced, his father talked to him as never before. Nor, indeed, as he ever would again. "You are young and your whole life lies before you," his father said. "But to live it you must win against everyone who hates us. You can't let them beat you with their hatred. You must not let them win."

"I must forgive them?"

His father nodded. "You must forgive them. Can you do that?"

"I won't let them win," Edelman said. "I won't let them win."

Somewhere in the memory of that, as he plodded his way up the street, one step at a time, toward the restaurant to the lunch he didn't want to eat, Edelman heard a familiar voice call to him and when he looked up he saw Anne, his granddaughter, coming toward him. She looked worried as she rushed to his side and took him by the arm. "Where have you been?"

"I went to the gallery to see about my painting," Edelman replied.

"Everyone is inside. They're all worried about you."

"I had to find out about the painting."

"Is it there?"

"They wouldn't tell me."

Edelman was sweaty and disheveled, and Anne looked more concerned than before. "You're a mess," she said.

"You've been waiting all this time?"

"Yes. For more than an hour."

"Why didn't you start without me?"

"Uncle Michael said we should wait."

Edelman smiled faintly. "Michael. Always the polite one. I'm sure your mother is in a state."

"She's not happy."

"Missed her bridge game?"

"That's in the mornings."

"Oh. Right. In the afternoon it's a trip to the spa." He looked over at her. "Do they have spas on Staten Island?"

"Papa." Anne couldn't help but grin. "Don't be like this with her. She's been waiting longer than normal for her."

"I know. I should have been here earlier, but I couldn't let them win," he said. "I won't let them win."

Anne seemed to understand. "No," she responded. "They won't win. I'll help you find a way to get the painting back. Now come inside." She led him into the restaurant, which was just a short distance from them. It was winter and the heat was on inside. Edelman was glad he had her to guide him.

As they approached the table where the others were seated, Michael pushed back his chair and stood. "Papa, are you okay? You don't look well." He came to help with the chair while Edelman dropped onto it.

Edelman did not respond but reached for a glass of water that sat near his place. He emptied it in a single, long drink. Diane, his daughter and Anne's mother, looked over at him. "Are you sure you're okay?"

"I'm fine," Edelman said. "Just thirsty."

"Where were you?"

"I went to Galerie Le Meilleur?"

"By yourself?"

"I'm capable of handling my own affairs."

"I don't think so." Diane gestured in his direction. "Look at you."

"Mama," Anne replied. "He walked all the way back."

Diane's eyes widened. "You walked all the way up here from Chelsea?"

"Yes," Edelman replied. "It's a simple process. One foot in front of the other."

"But why?" Diane railed. "You could have taken a taxi."

Edelman avoided her gaze. "I needed to rid myself of hatred."

Diane frowned. "Hatred? For what?"

Edelman looked at her now. "Do you really want to know?"

Diane shook her head in disgust. "When will you ever let it go?"

"They have my painting," he seethed.

"Your painting?" Diane tipped her head at a condescending angle. "Which one is it this time?"

"The Matisse," he said.

"Matisse? That man and woman thing you talk about?"

"*Woman With Table and Vase.*"

Her eyes betrayed a glimmer of interest. "You found it?"

"Yes," he said. "I found it."

"Here in New York?"

"It is now."

A waiter appeared and refilled Edelman's glass. He guzzled it as quickly as the first. Anne placed a piece of bread on a plate and slid it to him. "Here," she said. "Eat this." Edelman smiled at her as he took a bite.

Michael spoke up. "That gallery has the painting?"

"Galerie Le Meilleur," Diane explained.

"Hasan Izmir?"

"And his wife, Sibel," Edelman noted.

"And you're sure they have it?"

"Certain," Edelman said.

"How do you know this?"

"I have connections. They tell me things."

"These connections, are they reliable?"

"Someone from the Ministry of Culture in France told me it was delivered there. It was part of a larger shipment of artwork that came from a gallery in Paris."

"Paris?" Diane's eyes lit up again. "Is that why you went to Paris?"

"Does it matter why I was there?"

"You told me you were going to visit Micheline."

"I did," Edelman said. "I stayed with her."

"And while you were there you just happened to stumble across the Matisse?" There was a biting tone to Diane's voice.

"No," Edelman said. "I didn't happen to stumble across it. I knew where it was."

"So, if it was there, why didn't you just pick it up then?"

"I had every intention of doing that," Edelman replied. "But the art dealer who had it was murdered, and the painting was stolen, before I could get to it."

"And it was shipped over here?"

"The Matisse was included with pieces from another transaction. Those pieces were shipped to Galerie Le Meilleur."

"You know this for a fact?"

"I am certain the Matisse is among them."

Michael spoke up again. "What did they say about it at the gallery?"

"They said they didn't have it. When I insisted on seeing a list of the pieces they'd received, they threw me out."

"Threw you out?"

Diane shot a look at Anne. "And you let him go down there by himself?"

Edelman intervened. "It wasn't her idea. I insisted on it."

Diane's tone was combative. "I only let her stay with you because I thought she could look after you."

"You let her stay with me," Edelman said, "because I told you I would cut you out of my will if you didn't. And now that she's no longer a minor, she can do as she pleases. She wanted to go to the gallery with me. I insisted she go to class."

"So," Michael asked, "what do you plan to do next?"

"I don't know." Edelman shrugged. "I'm still thinking about it."

"I suppose there's always the FBI," Michael suggested.

Edelman's eyes opened wide. "I hadn't thought of them." He scooted his chair away from the table and stood. Diane was startled. "What are you doing?"

"I'm going to the FBI," Edelman said.

Michael spoke up. "Do you know anyone there?"

"No."

"Wouldn't it be better if you did?"

"Maybe."

"Stay and have lunch," Michael suggested. "Then I'll go back to the apartment with you and we can make some calls."

Edelman shook his head. "They have a special unit that deals with art theft. I'll talk to them." He wiped his mouth on a napkin and dropped it onto the table. "I should have thought of them earlier."

Diane, still seated, was livid. "You'll just show up? Just like that? Jacob Edelman will show up and the federal government will take note?"

"Yes," Edelman replied. "I am a citizen of this country and a taxpayer. Agents from the FBI work for me. When I explain to them why I have come to their office, someone will meet with me."

"Sit down," Diane spoke with a maternal tone. "You can go down there when we've eaten."

"You eat," Edelman retorted. "I'm going to the FBI."

Anne stood quickly. "I'm going with you," she announced as she hooked her arm in his. "Come on. We'll get a cab out front."

Chapter 17

With Anne accompanying him, Edelman came from the restaurant and hailed a taxi, then they rode together to the FBI Building at the southern tip of Manhattan. After checking through security at the front entrance, they rode the elevator to the fifth floor where they encountered a receptionist. Anne did the talking and explained why they were there. An office assistant led them to a conference room where they met with Dennis Morgan, a Special Agent.

"They said you wanted to talk to someone about a piece of art," Morgan said.

"Yes," Edelman replied. "A piece of art that was stolen from my family."

Morgan looked concerned. "When did this theft take place?"

For the next few minutes, Edelman recounted the story about the Matisse. How it had been stolen from his family by the Nazis during World War II and his efforts to locate it. "I was working with a dealer in Paris who had the painting in his possession, but before I could conclude my business with him, he was murdered."

"Murdered?"

"Yes."

"Recently?"

"Just a week or two ago."

"That sounds like a matter for the Paris police. Why do you think we can help?"

"Shortly after the dealer was murdered, the painting was shipped to a gallery here."

Morgan raised an eyebrow. "In New York?"

"Yes. In Chelsea. It's at—"

Morgan interrupted with a wave of his hand. "Wait just a minute," he said. "We have an agent who handles art theft cases. He's in the office today." Morgan stood. "Let me see if he can join us and hear this from you firsthand."

A few minutes later, Morgan returned with Preston Cooper. After a brief introduction, Edelman repeated his account of the painting. When he finished, Cooper asked, "How did you confirm the painting was shipped to Galerie Le Meilleur?"

"A friend, Jean Ferro, at the French Ministry of Culture, told me the art was shipped from France to London and from London to the US. Three crates from Marcel Kirchen in Paris to Galerie Le Meilleur here in New York."

"And Mr. Ferro confirmed it for you from his end? He confirmed that it actually arrived here and was delivered to the gallery?"

"Yes. According to him, Galerie Le Meilleur received the shipment. I'm certain my Matisse is among them. The Ministry of Culture has a task force. Ferro is part of that.

"They have been working to identify and return property that was stolen during the war," Cooper acknowledged. "And doing a good job, from what I hear."

"They found many pieces in their own museums."

"Did any of yours turn up there?"

"One or two. Most of it I tracked down myself from private collectors. The French government wasn't very helpful at first."

"But Ferro is?"

"Yes."

"After the war, Europe was in disarray, as was the French government. They had no way of finding the true owners for much of the art they received. That's why it ended up in their museums."

"Well, they should give it back," Edelman said.

"And now they have the means to find the rightful owners and they are doing just that. Did Ferro provide you with any documents for this shipment you were telling me about?"

"I have this." Edelman reached into the inside pocket of his jacket and produced copies of documents showing shipping information for the three crates.

Cooper glanced over the documents. "Have you tried talking to anyone at Galerie Le Meilleur?"

"Yes. I went down there today and tried to talk to them, but they refused to cooperate."

"What did they say? Anything in particular about it, or did they just refuse?"

"They were concerned about how I knew they received the shipment. And they told me it was none of my business and then they threw me out."

Cooper frowned. "They threw you out?"

"Yes."

"Who were you talking to?"

"A woman. I don't know her name. But she said she was the owner of the gallery. And then a man came out and joined the argument. He was quite angry."

"He threw you out?"

"No." Edelman shook his head. "She did. He was about to hit me, but she intervened to stop him, then escorted me to the door and before I knew it, I was outside. Once I was outside, she closed the door and locked it."

"That would be Sibel Izmir," Morgan offered.

"Perhaps," Edelman said. "She never told me her name."

"And the man was probably her husband, Hasan."

"Mr. Edelman," Cooper said. "I don't know how much we can do for you, but we will look into the matter and find out what's going on with the painting."

After Edelman and Anne left the FBI office, Cooper had an assistant track down Scott Davenport, the agent he had assigned to investigate the Izmirs after his meeting with David Anders. He and Davenport met in a conference room on the fourth floor. "Did you look into Hasan Izmir and Galerie Le Meilleur?"

"Yes," Davenport said.

"Anything interesting?"

"Sort of."

"What does that mean?"

"Hasan and his wife are US citizens. As is Hasan's brother, Ahmed. They emigrated here from Turkey together about ten or fifteen years ago. Made a fortune in real estate, then Hasan and his wife started collecting art. Got into the business as art dealers. The gallery they operate is owned by Hasan but Sibel, the wife, runs the day-to-day business."

"Anything suspicious about them?"

"They live a rather open lifestyle." Davenport grinned and shook his head. "I'm not sure that counts as suspicious, but my wife and I would kill each other if we did what they do."

Cooper arched an eyebrow. "For instance?"

"He likes women," Davenport explained. "She likes young men. Apparently, Hasan has connections to some of the highest paid call girls in the city. Sibel uses the gallery to attract male artists. Nothing criminal that I could find. At least not at first glance. None of them has a record, including the brother. They're just immoral."

"Anything in our system on them?"

Davenport glanced at his notes. "We have files that were opened on each of them when they applied for citizenship, but nothing remarkable. According to updates from the State Department, Hasan and Sibel have traveled outside the US four times. All four trips were to European countries."

Cooper nodded. "Which countries?"

"France, Germany, the Czech Republic, and Italy."

"What about the brother, Ahmed?"

"Nothing on him other than the application for citizenship. He has a New York driver's license. Rents an apartment on Fourteenth Street. Nothing else."

"No travel records?"

"No. Apparently he came here, found the good life, and never went anywhere else."

Cooper thought for a moment. "Anything from Customs?"

"Yes. Customs records indicate Galerie Le Meilleur received four shipments of art last year. Two originated from Prague and two from Venice. Thus far this year, they've received two more. All of the shipments contained artwork."

"The documents confirm that?"

"Yes."

"Paperwork shows it was artwork?"

"Yes."

Cooper looked concerned. "Did anyone actually verify the contents? Were the crates opened and inspected before delivery?"

"Not by our people," Davenport replied. "But, according to the records, Customs officers opened and inspected all of the shipments."

"Have they received a shipment recently?"

"Yeah," Davenport said. "Their most recent shipment originated in France. It was delivered—"

"A couple of days ago?" Cooper said, finishing the sentence.

Davenport appeared surprised. "How did you know that?"

"I had a visitor."

"Who?"

"Jacob Edelman. He thinks one of the paintings in that latest shipment belongs to him."

"You talked to him?"

"Yes."

"When?"

"Today," Copper said. "Just now."

"Edelman." Davenport frowned. "He's Jewish?"

"A Holocaust survivor."

"And he's claiming some of their art was stolen?"

"That's his claim," Cooper replied.

For the next ten minutes, Cooper told Davenport about the missing Matisse and gave him details from his conversation with Edelman. "He says the art dealer he was working with in Paris was murdered and the missing Matisse was in one of those crates that was recently delivered to Sibel and Hasan's gallery."

"This sounds like a novel."

Cooper leaned forward. "What do we know about their latest shipment?"

"Like I said," Davenport noted. "It originated in Paris. Was shipped from there to London, then to New York. Arrived here by air cargo."

"Was there a name associated with that shipment? Or a phone number?"

Davenport checked the file. "The shipment was initiated by someone using the name of Marcel Kirchen."

"Have you checked on him?"

"No, but I'll run that name and see what I can find."

"And see if you can get the Izmirs' financial history. All three of them. And run a check on the business, too."

"Already requested it," Davenport said. "Just waiting for a response."

"We also need to talk to the French police," Cooper continued. "We need to find out what they have on the art dealer Edelman says was murdered and any information they have on the Izmirs and the other name. Marcel…"

"Marcel Kirchen."

"Right. Edelman has a friend with the Ministry of Culture. Someone named Jean Ferro. Edelman says he works for a French task force that's trying to reclaim stolen art. Call him and find out what he has to say about this." Cooper handed Davenport the documents he received from Edelman. "These might help."

Davenport placed the documents in the file, then checked his watch. "They've probably gone home by now at the French agencies. I'll call them early tomorrow."

Chapter 18

By the following weekend, Truman Slater had completed the move from his apartment in Brooklyn to Charlotte Snider's house on Long Island. As she suggested, he converted the barn into a studio. It wasn't really a barn, though. More like a shop with a wooden floor. The floor was rotten on one end but only near the wall and the damage did nothing to detract from the usable space. He swept it clean and deposited paints and brushes on a small table that he took from the attic and positioned over the rotten section.

With room in the building to spare, he turned to larger canvases, unrolling them on the floor and painting them unstretched in true Jackson Pollock style. He also increased the pace of his work, painting faster and quicker even than when he had worked in a neurotic frenzy at the apartment. The additional space and additional energy made larger brushes a necessity, too, and with them he switched from artists paint, which came in tubes, to liquid paint that came in cans. House paint, actually. Before long, his brush strokes became bolder, more expressive, and less precise. He applied more and more paint to the canvas, too, which produced abstract paintings with rich colors and large shapes. They captured mood and feeling more vividly than before, but at the expense of precision and detail.

After a week at the house, Slater had created three works that were, if not complete, at least as far as he could go at the time. He tacked the canvases to the wall of the studio to dry while he considered whether they needed more attention, then went to work on a fourth painting. Somewhere in the creative process that followed, he heard the sound of an automobile as it came to a stop at the end of the driveway. He set aside the brush that he'd been using and pushed open the door to see who it was.

As the door swung open, a bright mid-morning glare caught him by surprise. He hadn't realized it was already the next day. Instinctively, he put a hand to his brow to shield against the sunlight and that's when he saw the car was Charlotte's. While he watched, the driver's door opened, and she emerged with a wave and a smile. "You look surprised," she called.

"I didn't realize it was morning," he replied.

While they talked, the passenger door opened and a woman stepped out. Slater turned in that direction, squinting even tighter, unsure at first who it might be, just that it was a female form. As she came around the open door and moved past the fender of the car, he saw she was Sibel Izmir. He knew her only by sight and reputation. She came to the gallery several times when he worked for Raymond Wyatt. A couple of times to attend exhibitions and once or twice to talk business with Wyatt and his partners.

Sibel was tall for a woman, about five-ten or eleven, and brunette, which Slater liked. Approaching middle age, she had the body of a woman, full and rounded, which he liked, too. Far better to him than the fresh suppleness of the college students he'd encountered at the bar down the street from the apartment. Sibel had shape and form. Substance, sophistication, confidence. All of which he found alluring, even irresistible, and that morning he found it difficult to keep his eyes from roaming over her. From the way she looked, he wondered if she might be thinking the same about him.

Charlotte noticed the connection between them and positioned herself in front of the car, at a spot between them, as if to separate them and take control of the moment. "Do you two know each other?" she asked.

"We've seen each other around," Sibel said. "But I did not know this was the person you were talking about."

After a moment to get acquainted, which Slater did not mind, Charlotte said to him, "I see you have made the barn a studio. Perhaps you could show us around."

"Sure," he replied, and he led them into the building.

There wasn't much to see but Sibel seemed intrigued by the pieces that hung on the wall. "You did these recently," she noted. "They do not appear to be fully dry."

"Yes," he replied. "I couldn't decide if they were finished so I hung them there while I thought about it."

Sibel leaned closer. "Is that house paint?"

"It works better on larger canvases," Slater said. "And it's cheaper, too."

Charlotte nodded approvingly. "You seem to be finding yourself."

"It feels good," Slater replied.

Charlotte pointed to the art on the wall. "Those pieces have a cohesiveness in style and texture that the others seemed to lack. They look like they were done by someone in particular and not by a committee."

"And that's an improvement for me."

"Very much so," she agreed.

While they talked, Sibel continued studying the canvases that hung on the wall, moving slowly from one to the other, then back again, lingering over them and nodding approvingly. Slater wondered what she thought of them, but he didn't dare ask for fear he would break the mood of the moment.

After a while, Charlotte asked about his earlier work. "I have it in the house," Slater said. "In that room that I think is supposed to be the dining room." She suggested they take a look at it and Slater led them in that direction.

Inside the house, Slater's earlier paintings were propped against each other—three and four canvases deep—along the walls of the dining room. Charlotte had seen them before and made quick work of reviewing them. Sibel took her time, moving slowly past each stack, methodically flipping through the paintings. Looking, studying, considering. Several times, she lifted one and held it at arm's length, then moved near the window watching the light as it reflected off the surface.

Charlotte took a seat in a straight-backed chair near the doorway to the living room. Slater stood near her and leaned against the door frame. Both of them watching, waiting, wondering what Sibel would say.

After almost an hour in the room, Sibel went back to a painting she had seen earlier. She held it up once more, then turned to Slater. "I will give you a thousand dollars for this one."

"Okay." Slater said. "I'll take it." He was delighted to have the money but even more that she liked his art.

She smiled playfully. "You're easy."

"Only with the paintings," he noted.

Sibel's smile became a grin. "Perhaps we shall see about that."

The sexual tension between them was obvious. Charlotte seemed uneasy with it. "Think you could do a show for him?" Her tone was all business and her eyes fixed on Sibel.

"I will consider it," Sibel responded. "Now that I've seen what he can do." She glanced at Slater. "But I must warn you, we're not like Wyatt's gallery. We deal primarily in the secondary market for American art. We handle very few emerging contemporary artists. We do shows for the ones we represent but we deal mostly with previously owned pieces, not the artists."

"I understand."

"For us," she continued, "art with a proven record, even if it's not the better-known pieces, is easier to handle and the core of our business model."

Slater was impressed by the way she talked. As if she understood the art world and had a sense of how to conduct business in a profitable manner. He found her assertiveness quite stimulating and wondered what might happen if Charlotte was not present. "I know about your gallery," he said. "You came to see Wyatt a few times."

"Yes," she said. "Raymond and I are old friends."

They continued to talk while Sibel wrote a check for the painting but when their business was concluded, Charlotte glanced over at Slater and said, "You made a sale. Where are you taking us to lunch?"

Despite his misgivings about the story Anders wanted him to write, Frazer had read everything in print about the Izmirs. At the office and at home, he sorted through all of it again and again, just to be sure, and then he said to himself, "This is it. Either I am doing this article, or I'm not, but I can't go on like this, waffling in between."

In the past, he would turn to Zoë and ask her opinion. They had a litany for it. Sit together at the kitchen table with his notes. Her pumping him for details, him chattering endlessly. After they'd read everything and said everything, they would stumble into the bedroom and make love.

Later, in the afterglow of the moment, with him on his back and her lying beside him, their bodies damp, the musky scent of sex hanging in the air, she would give her answer. "Maybe you should do the story." Or sometimes she might say, "I don't think this one is right for you." Then they would get dressed and walk to the diner on the corner to eat while he considered her response. Most of the time, Frazer rejected the stories Zoë approved and approved the ones she rejected. Nevertheless, the process served to clarify the project for him.

This time, however, Zoë was in Charleston and the only way to discuss the story with her was to call her on the phone. But since she left, she had turned every conversation to the question of when he was coming Charleston. Frazer didn't want to discuss the story that way, so he made the decision on his own. "I'm doing it," he said to himself in a whisper. "And if someone doesn't like it, they can let me know."

The answer sounded good at first but as the words came from his lips, doubt rushed in and questions destroyed his confidence. He'd never met the Izmirs. Never seen them in action for himself. Who was he kidding? He'd never even been to their gallery. Not even as a casual observer having a look around. Wouldn't it be helpful to see the place, get a feel for it, maybe meet some of the people who worked there, before launching into yet one more story?

Yes. It would. And that was a good idea. Go down there and see the place. He would do that right then.

From his cubicle at the office, Frazer rode the elevator to the lobby, hoping upon hope that he didn't run into Gina. He made it without incident and hurried out to the street where he took a taxi to Galerie Le Meilleur in Chelsea. On the ride down there, he castigated himself for being so weak. For the inability to make up his mind on the matter. For always needing to consult someone else first. Gather one more piece of information. Consider one more point of view. Starting, but never finishing, story after story. This one made three at some stage of completion. One about the tunnels. This one that Anders tried to give him. And a third about the original survey of Manhattan, an elaborate project he hadn't touched in weeks.

Maybe Zoë's right. Maybe I've had enough of this place, too. But even that struck him as weakness. Choosing to run instead of buckling down to the hard work at hand. Because that was the crux of his problem and he knew it. Had known it for a long time. The stories needed work and he had been unable, or unwilling, to concentrate long enough to get them done.

When the cab came to a stop at the curb outside the gallery, Frazer paid the driver and got out, but rather than going inside immediately he gazed through the front window. Hasan and Sibel were standing inside. He recognized them from photos in the articles he'd read and from images on the gallery website. They seemed to be engaged in an intense conversation. He thought of waiting until they were finished but decided against it, pushed open the door, and stepped inside.

To the left of the window was an easel with a painting propped on it. He studied it a moment, then moved to the wall, admiring the paintings that hung there as if he were keenly interested. His mind and ears, however, were focused on the conversation taking place on the opposite side of the room. Hasan and Sibel seemed to be speaking a foreign language. Turkic, he surmised, though he was not certain he could distinguish it from Arabic or Hebrew or any other language from the distant end of the Mediterranean.

After a few minutes, Hasan and Sibel disappeared down a hallway in back. Frazer still could hear their voices but was unable to catch what they said, though he strained to listen. As the sound of their footsteps faded, a young woman came to his side and introduced herself. She was Jamie Wright. "May I help you?" she asked.

"I'm just looking," Frazer said. Voices from the hall grew louder and he glanced in that direction, then over to Jamie. "Are they having a fight?"

"Not really," she said. "That's just the way they communicate."

"Strange way to do it."

"I think they make it work for them." She gestured to the art as she backed away. "Let me know if I can be of assistance."

A few minutes later, Hasan and Sibel entered the room, this time speaking English. "It's a waste of time," Hasan argued.

"Why?"

"Because no one has ever heard of Truman Slater." Hasan's voice was loud. Frazer had little difficulty hearing their conversation. "Ask anyone and they'll say, 'Who is that?' Do you even know anything about him?" He glanced over at Frazer. "Ask this gentleman. He will not know."

"Slater is an artist," Sibel replied. "What's there to know?"

"See, even you don't know who he is. He's just someone you met."

"What does that mean?"

"It means you are always meeting someone you think is better than the one you had before."

She shot him an angry look. "What are you saying to me, Hasan?"

"All I'm saying is, I was against these emerging artist events from the beginning. And I'm against them now."

"Why?"

"Because there's no money in it. I've been saying the same thing to you for an hour now. If we're selling American art, it is better to re-sell existing, established artists with a track record. Artists whose work has proven value. Or at least a name people think they recognize."

"We need to look like a gallery."

"We look like a gallery." Hasan was insistent. "Look around for yourself. We have millions of dollars of paintings right here in this room. And we have a sure thing in the arrangements we've made. Let someone else take the risk of marketing an unknown artist."

Sibel folded her arms across her midriff. "I see this as a chance to help someone."

"Ah." Hasan had a knowing look and he wagged his finger for emphasis. "Now you've said too much."

"What do you mean?"

"You want to do this so you can have some young guy around for you to drool over."

Quicker than Hasan expected, Sibel slapped him soundly on the cheek. Startled at first, he recovered quickly and grabbed her by the wrist. "How dare you touch me in anger," he snarled.

"I see the women you spend your time with," she retorted as she jerked free of his grasp. "Every day I smell their perfume on your clothes, and you have the nerve to accuse me of infidelity?"

Hasan glared at her. "You accuse me only of the things you yourself are doing."

They stared at each other a moment, then Sibel seemed to gather her composure. "Charlotte Snider wants us to do this for him. She is good for us. She's a connection we need."

Hasan pumped his fist in frustration. "I hate this part of the business."

"I know," she said. "But it is necessary. Which is why I insist that we do it."

"Okay," he snapped. "Do whatever you want, but don't spend a lot of money on it. And don't expect some young artist to please you the way I can."

Still angry, Hasan stalked off toward the hallway, mumbling something in Turkic as he went. Before he was out of the room, Sibel turned away. That's when she noticed Frazer. Their eyes met and they both smiled.

Frazer, never wanting to miss an opportunity, stepped toward her and offered his business card. "I couldn't help but overhear you're planning an exhibition. I don't mean to pry but could you send me a notice when you set a date for the event? I'd like to come down and take a look at the work. Maybe meet the artist. Write something about it for the paper."

Sibel glanced at the card. "You work for the Times?"

"Yes," he replied. "I'm a reporter from the features section."

"And you would do an article about one of our shows?"

"I would."

Sibel nodded. "That would be good."

Chapter 19

At the FBI office, Scott Davenport followed up on Preston Cooper's direction and initiated a formal request to government agencies for records regarding the Izmirs and their gallery business. One of those requests was to the Financial Crimes Enforcement Network (FinCEN), a bureau within the US Department of the Treasury. FinCEN responded by forwarding their files to him, but the records indicated nothing suspicious on any of the three principles. However, Treasury agents, acting on their own initiative, requested updates from FinCEN field offices and promised to share them when received.

Because Treasury officials seemed interested, Davenport met with them and explained the situation further, outlining the potential international transactions that might be involved. Armed with that information, FinCEN obtained electronic access to domestic bank records for Galerie Le Meilleur and for all three Izmirs—Hasan, Ahmed, and Sibel. Likewise, the IRS provided six years of tax returns on each of those involved. All of it without obtaining a warrant and without giving notice to the account holders.

Within days, Davenport was swamped with thousands of pages of information. Rather than wading through it himself, he gave the records to a team of FBI forensic accountants and asked for a full review. Once that was completed, Davenport combined it with other information he'd obtained and reported the findings to Cooper.

"As one might expect in the art world," Davenport began, "there were wire transfers from US accounts owned by Galerie Le Meilleur to accounts at several European banks. Most of those accounts were owned by galleries and art brokers."

"Most?"

"Most, but not all. A significant number of transfers were made to a bank in Andorra. There also were transfers to US banks as well."

"Andorra." Cooper had a curious expression. "I seem to recall they pride themselves on being a safe haven for banking."

"That is correct. And over the past few years financial activity in Andorra has increased dramatically."

"Mob related?"

"FinCEN thinks they're looking for safety from increased political instability."

"So, moving money to Andorra, in and of itself, might not indicate criminal activity?"

"Correct," Davenport acknowledged.

Cooper thought a moment, then asked, "Who owned the accounts on the other end of those transfers? The accounts in Andorra that received the money. Were you able to get the names?"

"It took some arm-twisting, but they finally gave them up. All of the accounts in Andorra were in the name of Black Sea Trading Company."

"And in the US?"

"A number of transfers are for lesser amounts and appear to be for legitimate transactions. Sale and purchase of art. Those were made to a number of banks all over the country and many of them appear to be one-time transactions. But there were repeated transfers from the gallery's bank here in New York, to an account at a bank in Arizona that is only in Sibel Izmir's name."

Cooper arched an eyebrow. "A personal account?"

"Yes."

"Interesting."

"Yes, it is," Davenport said.

"Think she might be stashing some cash with the idea of leaving

Hasan?"

"Maybe," Davenport replied. "Should I look into that possibility?"

Cooper shook his head. "We'll have to wait on that. Let's stay focused on the central issue. The art business at the gallery. What about the tax returns? Has anything caught our accountants' attention?"

"Well," Davenport said slowly. "Not exactly."

"What does that mean?"

"The IRS reviewed their returns," Davenport explained. "As did our guys and accountants from FinCEN. They all acknowledge the returns appear to be straight forward in every way."

"FinCEN reviewed them, too?"

"Yes."

"And everyone thinks the returns are clean?"

"Our guys say everything fits, but they have some questions."

"About what?"

"No one found anything at all out of line," Davenport explained. "But that's just it. Nothing is out of place."

"Too clean?"

"Most people have one or two things wrong on their returns. An item reported on the wrong line or handled in a way that's not exactly correct. If the taxpayer is consistent in the way they treat it, the whole thing works out in the end and no one calls them on it."

"But the Izmirs have none of that."

"These guys are absolutely perfect."

"What happens next?"

"Our accountants are working on it."

"But not the IRS?"

"Only if we ask," Davenport said.

"They aren't curious?"

"Curious, but it's not compelling for them. Congress cut their funding too many times over the last ten years. They have fewer agents now than ever before. If we want them to get involved further, they will. Otherwise, they have bigger issues to address than this."

"Put a pin in it," Cooper said. "We may have to come back to it but let's look at the rest of the situation first. What did you find on Marcel Kirchen?"

"The State Department has a file on him from ten or fifteen years ago, but there's not much in it. Just an application for a student visa that he filed but never completed. And one or two entries into the country on tourist visas. Otherwise, nothing. The CIA says they have nothing on him, either."

"Interpol?"

Davenport grinned. "Here's where it gets a little interesting. Interpol says they have a file on him, but they won't let us see it."

Cooper was alert. "Why not?"

"Russia has a national security hold on it."

"National security?"

"That's what they said."

Cooper sat up straight. "Okay. We need to find out about that, and we need to know more about Black Sea Trading Company. Do you think FinCEN can dig out any more details on Black Sea?"

"I can go back to them and ask but—"

"No," Cooper interrupted. "Not you. Give the financial issues to a staff member. Let them research it. I want you to concentrate on Kirchen. Find out why the Russians are protecting him and what we need to do to access that Interpol file."

"Okay."

"There must be something in that file. Otherwise, no one would block it."

"Right."

"Do we have anything from the French police on him or the dead art dealer?"

"Not yet."

"Stay after them," Cooper urged. "There's more to this than we've found yet."

"I agree," Davenport said. "Something about it doesn't seem right. Do you think the man you spoke to could help us with this?"

"Who?"

"The man you spoke to. The one that started this."

"Oh," Cooper said. "Jacob Edelman."

"Yes. Do you think he could give us anything helpful?"

"He gave us information about his contact with French authorities. You have that, right?"

"Yes."

Cooper shook his head. "Then let's keep this in-house a little longer before we bring him back in."

In response to his meeting with Cooper, Davenport assigned the task of delving deeper into the finances of the Izmirs and Black Sea Trading to Susan Griffin, an FBI employee with the New York office's research staff. Like many in the office, Griffin had read newspaper articles about the Izmirs but knew nothing of Black Sea Trading. Intrigued by the name, she chose to investigate it first.

Using proprietary software created specifically to mine the databases of far-flung, multinational corporations, Griffin went deep into Black Sea's records and learned that it was owned by a company called Balkan World Services, which was incorporated in Montenegro by Giorgio Amendola, Riccardo Brega, and Paolo Fabrizi. Griffin recognized the names immediately. All three were lawyers from Italy and all three were associated with Sergei Mogilevich.

In less time than it took to read each of the names, the world as Griffin knew it came crashing down upon her head. The weight of it made her head tight and her chest heave as she struggled to take a breath.

Two years earlier, Griffin had graduated from Barnard College with a degree in history. She had hoped to attend graduate school immediately but by the time she finished her undergraduate work she was seriously in debt from student loans and excessive credit card charges.

Desperate to make money, she cast about for work in her field and found none that didn't require an advanced degree. Then a friend told her about a job opening for a researcher in the FBI's New York office. She applied for the position, passed the background check, and was hired. The job paid well but after covering rent, utilities, and service on her accumulated debt, she had little left for anything else. Attending graduate school quickly became little more than a dream.

Not long after taking the job, Griffin attended a Mets baseball game with a group of friends. Bradley Monzikova, who grew up at Brighton Beach, was with them. Griffin had known Monzikova since high school and while talking to him that day she alluded to her dire financial situation. He was sympathetic to her struggle and suggested he might know a way to help.

Over coffee that weekend, Monzikova told her he worked with a guy who was always on the lookout for information. "What kind of information?"

"Just a heads-up about things someone like you might know about?"

Griffin was uneasy. "You mean, he would want me to divulge information from the FBI?"

Monzikova shrugged. "That's a little strongly worded. All he needs is a heads-up."

"A heads-up?" She frowned. "What does that mean?"

"Notice. A phone call. A message. That's all. Let him know if the FBI is poking around in something that touches his business."

"How would I know what his business would be?"

"Look," Monzikova said, "he doesn't want access to the building or to files or anything like that. He's not asking you to plant listening devices in the office, or record conversations. He just wants to know the gist of what the FBI is doing when it relates to his interests."

"And what are his interests?"

"Ahh ..." Monzikova seemed uneasy and he looked away. "That will become ... readily apparent."

Griffin had a knowing expression. "Once I know his name, I'll know what to look for."

"Yes." Monzikova nodded his head slowly. "When you know his name, you will know what to look for."

"And he is willing to pay?"

"He pays very well. Remarkably well." Monzikova leaned forward and lowered his voice. "You will make more money than you could possibly imagine."

Griffin glanced at her coffee cup as she thought about the options. If she said yes to this offer, she was certain she would be paid well for her services. However, if she was caught passing information to someone—anyone—outside the office, her future would be compromised. Not just her future at the FBI, but her future entirely. Yet, paying her bills had become increasingly difficult and though it had only been two years since college, she was tired of the struggle.

After a moment she slowly lifted her head, looked across the table at Monzikova, and smiled. "Does this guy have a name?"

"Are you willing to work for him?"

"Yes."

"You're sure?"

"Yes."

"Once you're in, there's no going back."

"I understand."

Monzikova took a business card from his pocket and slid it across the table to her. Griffin took it from him and placed it in her purse without reading it. Later, when she was alone in her apartment, she took out the card and glanced at it. The name on the card was Sergei Mogilevich, a Russian mob boss at the heart of several ongoing FBI investigations. Monzikova was right. She knew exactly what his business interests entailed.

After acquiring information on Black Sea Trading, Griffin gathered records on Balkan World Services and the three Italian lawyers who incorporated the company. She complied all of it in a digital file and placed it in a queue for forwarding to Davenport but assigned a delivery priority that insured the files would not reach him until the following morning.

On her way home from the office that evening, Griffin stopped at a Starbucks near her apartment. Using the café's internet connection and a personal iPad, she logged into a Gmail account. In the account, she created a message that summarized her research and the direction of the FBI's investigation into Black Sea Trading and Balkan World Services, then saved the message as a draft labeled "Trading Company."

Satisfied the message addressed the major points of the FBI's interest in the matter, she logged out of the email account and ordered a cup of coffee. While she sipped the coffee, she took a burner cell phone from her purse and used it to send a text message to a phone number Monzikova had given her. The message read simply, "Email."

In Moldova, Gennady Krylov came to see Mogilevich at his home. "The FBI is asking questions about Black Sea Trading."

Mogilevich did not seem surprised. "You have heard from our contact?"

"Yes."

"What do you suggest we do about that?"

"Black Sea is a financial consolidation point. I think we should move the money in its accounts before the FBI gets its hands on it."

"But where?" Mogilevich asked. "Cyprus is no longer viable. I don't like the Cayman Islands. They aren't as private as they once were." He looked over at Krylov. "What do you suggest we do?"

Krylov smiled. "We could always bring it right back to where it is, but into a different account, under a different name."

Mogilevich looked puzzled. "The same place?"

"Run it around the world like the money guys do, moving it in and out of multiple accounts so the trail becomes too complicated to trace. Then bring it back to Andorra, but deposit it under a different name. One with no association to anyone we know."

"Not even the same lawyers?"

"Especially not the same lawyers," Krylov said.

Mogilevich grinned. "I like the way you think, but what of the people who lent us their names for the existing accounts?"

Krylov shrugged. "We do nothing."

"Nothing? They won't be curious?"

"They don't know anything about the accounts anyway. They've never checked them even once and I don't expect they ever will."

"You are sure of that?"

"Yes. And besides that, they are lawyers. They don't know much but they know enough to keep quiet. And if they are ever asked, they have a professional obligation not to answer."

"I suppose it might work."

"We have enough dead bodies for now," Krylov said. "That's what caused us this problem in the first place." His eyes narrowed in a look of anger. "If that idiot Kirchen hadn't shot all those people for nothing, no one would know we exist."

"Sooner or later, all of our people get into the same trouble."

"They make a little money," Krylov said. "Then they forget how they made it. Then they get sloppy and stupid."

Mogilevich grinned. "So, how did you and I remain above it all?"

Krylov squared his shoulders. "We are Russian," he proclaimed proudly.

"And Kirchen? What is his problem?"

Krylov scowled. "Kirchen is a German."

Mogilevich was amused. "Isn't he actually from Luxembourg?"

"It's the same thing," Krylov said. "All of them are from inferior races. The Izmirs are Turks. Kirchen is a German. That guy we had in Luxembourg before Kirchen was a German, too. All of them are inferior to the least and weakest Russian."

Mogilevich roared with laughter.

Chapter 20

Three weeks after his visit, Frazer received an invitation to Galerie Le Meilleur's exhibition of paintings by Truman Slater. The invitation reminded him of his suggestion of writing an article about the show. That was a spur of the moment idea. Something he did only as a way of meeting Sibel and talking to her. At the time, he assumed nothing would come of the offer. "Now," he whispered to himself, "I suppose I have no choice but to attend the event."

Frazer arrived at the gallery half an hour after the exhibition opened. Charlotte Snider was there, along with other dignitaries from New York's art crowd. He recognized them from the many times their pictures had appeared in the paper. Charlotte, however, seemed to be the focus of everyone's attention. Many people followed her every move and they all wanted to be wherever she was, doing whatever she did. Because of her presence, the place was packed.

From the door, Frazer made his way around the room, pretending to admire Slater's work. He understood very little of it, though he wanted to, but abstract art escaped him no matter how hard he tried to understand it. Before he'd gotten very far, though, he felt a hand against his elbow. He glanced around to see Ellen Riggs standing at his side. Riggs worked at the newspaper as Gina Wilkins' assistant. At the sight of her Frazer's heart sank into his stomach.

"Well, well," Riggs teased. "Imagine seeing you at an art show."

"Just admiring the artwork," Frazer replied.

"Right." Riggs had a sarcastic tone, reinforced by her wry smile. "You were seen, you know."

Frazer tried to appear nonchalant. He wasn't sure what she meant. "And where was that?" he asked.

"With David Anders." Riggs' smile became a knowing look. "How was lunch?"

"Tasty I suppose. I don't remember."

"Personally, I don't really care why you're here or why you met with Anders or what you're up to. But Gina is already curious about the lunch and if she finds out you were at this show, she's gonna think maybe you're working on a story that has something to do with the art section of the paper." Riggs grinned at him. "Which, as you know, is an area she guards jealously."

"Right."

"I'm just saying, if she thinks you're poaching on her domain, she isn't gonna like it—at all."

"Then I guess you'll have to make sure she doesn't find out I was here tonight."

"I'd love to help you," Riggs said. "And I have no reason to tattle. But if I'm asked, I'm not risking my job to protect you."

Frazer nodded. "Fair enough."

Even while talking to Riggs, Frazer caught Sibel's eye as she crossed the room, smiling, greeting, shaking hands, prompting interested attendees toward finalizing yet one more sale. Avoiding her, he realized, would be impossible and so he began to think of things he might say to her when the inevitable conversation occurred. He could always play along, as if he intended to write about the evening. That would work for the moment. And who knows? He might never see her again. Everything would work out right, as long as Riggs didn't find out. And as along as Gina didn't know.

Riggs continued to talk but Frazer heard only half of what she said. His eyes and his mind were fixed on Sibel and as she came closer, he excused himself abruptly and went over to where Sibel was standing. Sibel took him by the arm and guided him toward Slater. "This is the reporter I was telling you about," she explained when the three of them were together.

Frazer and Slater shook hands, then Slater said, "Thank you for coming tonight. I understand you're writing an article about us."

"Yes," Frazer replied. He cast a wary glance over his shoulder to see if Riggs overheard his comment.

"Well," Slater continued, "I hope you can help us out." They talked for a moment about not much at all, then Slater invited Frazer to visit his studio. "I'm out on Long Island now," he said. "In Springs."

"I've been there a few times," Frazer noted. "It's a beautiful area. I'd love to have a look at your studio. Maybe talk a little about how you got to where you are."

"Sure," Slater said. "Just give me a call." They exchanged business cards, then someone else caught Slater's attention. Frazer used the break to slip away and crossed the room to a table where a bartender was mixing drinks. A moment later, Scotch and water in hand, he drifted toward the art near the door, thinking he might leave soon.

As Frazer sipped from the drink, a man entered the gallery. Someone from the staff greeted him and the man gave a perfunctory response. By his accent, Frazer thought he was European. Maybe East European. Nothing odd about that. The city was filled with people from somewhere else and there were enclaves in all the boroughs where English was a foreign language. Still, something about the man caught Frazer's attention. He was different, the way foreigners are different. They look different. Sound different, act different. Not bad. Not good. Just different.

At first no one else in the gallery seemed to notice the man's presence but after a moment, Hasan Izmir appeared, moving quickly toward him. Arms wide apart. A big smile on his face. He greeted the man warmly, speaking with the loud voice of one trying to convey gladness even when it is absent. The man endured Hasan's effusive gestures, smiling politely.

Hasan leaned close and whispered something in the man's ear. The man responded with a nod, then Hasan took him by the arm, guided him toward the door, and they stepped outside to the street. As they emerged from the gallery, Hasan glanced to his left, raised his hand in the air, and waved to get someone's attention. Moments later, a car arrived and came to a stop before them. The driver stepped out, handed Hasan the keys, then the two men got in and rode away.

Frazer remained at the gallery until almost ten that evening, then caught a cab and rode back to his apartment. When he arrived, he kicked off his shoes, took a seat at the kitchen table, and placed a phone call to David Anders. "I was at Galerie Le Meilleur," he said when Anders answered.

"They had a show tonight?"

"Truman Slater."

"I saw that guy's stuff at the Frieze Art Fair. Last year, I think. Not bad, but nobody understood it."

"They understood it tonight," Frazer said.

"He sold?"

"Yeah. He sold."

"Was Hasan there?"

"For a while. Then someone came and they left together."

"Who was it?"

"I don't know. From the snippets of conversation I heard, he sounded like he might have been from Eastern Europe."

"Ahh. East Europeans." Anders seemed to understand. "That's Russian mob."

"Maybe," Frazer conceded. "But it wasn't obvious."

"Who else did you see?"

"Charlotte Snider was there."

"That's why the art sold," Anders said. "Brought a group of friends with her I imagine."

"The place was packed."

"Charlotte knows a lot of people and when she gets behind an artist, their work usually sells well."

"They were buying tonight."

"Well, look," Anders said. "There's an auction next week at Mournet's. Tuesday evening. If you're going to do an article about the Izmirs, you need to come to it. I'm sure Hasan and his wife will be there. You'll see even more of a show than you saw tonight."

"I don't know…" Frazer was hesitant. "I have a feeling this is going to cause me a lot of trouble."

"Why?" Anders asked. "Are you still worrying about Gina Wilkins?"

"Her assistant was there tonight," Frazer responded.

"Did you talk to her?"

"I didn't have much choice. She approached me. Started grilling me about being there."

"What did she say?"

"Someone saw us at lunch the other day."

The tone of Anders' voice changed. "Saw who? You're seeing Gina's assistant?"

"No," Frazer blurted. "The assistant told me someone saw you and me at lunch."

"Oh." Anders seemed unconcerned. "I go to lunch with a lot of people."

"In your world, having lunch with me might not mean much. But in my world, it means a lot."

"Why?"

"I've explained this to you before," Frazer said. "I write feature articles. Not sports. Not business. And not articles about the arts. You are a known quantity in the art world. Me, talking to you, raises all kinds of flags among our arts writers. The editors. Everyone else."

"And that has some bearing on you coming to an auction?"

"Gina knows I was at the show tonight. If she finds out I was at an auction, she'll find a way to make me tell her what I'm doing. I'll have to tell her, her editor, my editor, maybe more."

"And that will be a problem?"

"At best, they'll make me work with her."

"And, at worst?"

"They'll tell me to turn over my notes and I'll have to fight for a byline."

"Okay." Anders seemed unbothered.

"That's why I prefer to work alone."

"Well," Anders said. "To write an article about this, you have to attend an auction. I mean, all issues aside, you can't write a story about the Izmirs without seeing them at an auction."

"Right."

"And, even if nothing comes of it, you'll see a slice of New York life most people never see."

"Maybe."

"Look," Anders insisted. "Come to the auction. If it isn't as crazy as I've suggested, then you can do whatever you want about the story."

Frazer sighed. "Okay," he said. "I'll be there."

When the call ended, Frazer sat at the table and thought about the evening, his conversation with Anders, and how he could maneuver a story around Wilkins and the editors. They were sure to find out long before any article could be finished. And just as sure to confront him over it. "I can always tell them I was just looking," he said to himself. "And I can argue that I'm not looking for an art story, just a story. Something about the people. Not about the making of art. Or art itself."

And then he remembered his commitment to write something about Slater's show. Not much chance of finessing his way around anyone with that. If he wrote the article on the event, it would never get past the editors. For one thing, it was too mundane for him. It was too mundane even for Wilkins, a reporter who covered the arts. That's why she sent her assistant to the gallery instead of going there herself. And once he was outed for that article, doing anything about the Izmirs would be impossible.

After thinking a while longer, Frazer decided to make a few notes and comments on the evening, his conversation with Slater, his observations about the art, and give them to Riggs as a friendly gesture. Colleague to colleague. "Talked to Slater at the show. Here's what he said." That sort of thing. Let her run with it. If the article appeared, it would be under Riggs' name. If it didn't appear, and someone from the gallery asked, he could always say the editorial staff cut it.

A moment later, Frazer rose from the table, walked to the bedroom, and opened his laptop. While the operating software booted, he changed to house shorts and a t-shirt, then returned to the table and began preparing notes for Riggs.

Somewhere in all of that, he thought of Zoë and realized he hadn't thought of her all day. Maybe for longer than that. He checked the text messages on his phone, just to be sure, and saw that the last time he contacted her was the morning of the day before. A sinking feeling came over him as he realized he'd gone more than twenty-four hours without talking to her. He thought of texting her right then, but a glance at the screen told him the hour was late.

"It's too late now," he whispered. But he couldn't let another day pass without contacting her so, as a reminder, he sent himself an email to call her the next morning.

Despite his misgivings about writing an article on the Izmirs, Frazer went to Mournet's for the Tuesday evening auction. When he arrived, Anders was waiting in the lobby and ushered him into the gallery where the sale was set to occur. As they entered the room Frazer noticed Gina Wilkins, seated near the podium. She saw him, too, and from the expression on her face, Frazer knew she was not happy that he was there. Rather than approaching her to explain, he avoided her and stood with Anders and the dealers along the back wall.

As Anders had suggested, the Izmirs were present that evening. Not long after the session started, they began to exhibit the kind of behavior Anders had previously described. Bidding between themselves on a lot, running up the price far beyond a valuation the market would sustain, then dropping out at the last moment leaving the buyer with an over-priced item.

At first, they laughed between themselves about it, as if they were playing a game and keeping score, but the longer they went the louder their voices became. The banter between them was friendly but they were loud, exceedingly competitive, and quite disruptive. Serious collectors in the room cringed at their antics.

When the sale ended, Frazer and Anders slipped out a side door before Wilkins could accost them. They walked down the street to Johnny Galento's for dinner. "You were right about one thing," Frazer said as they made their way in that direction.

"What's that?"

"The Izmirs would make a good story."

"So, you'll write about them?"

"I don't know yet."

Anders seemed aggravated. "How long are you going to dance around this?"

"Look, I'm just trying to avoid trouble at the paper," Frazer said. "But I am intrigued by the Izmirs."

"Not sure how intriguing they are. More like aggravating as hell."

"Did you talk to Preston Cooper?"

"Yes," Anders replied. "I did."

"Has the FBI opened an investigation?"

"Cooper led me to believe they would at least take a look at it, but I haven't heard anything from him."

They had reached the restaurant and a host led them to a table near the front. When they were seated, Frazer said. "Did you see the look Wilkins gave us?"

"Not really."

"She was not happy."

"With you?"

"Yes."

"I still don't understand why it's such a big deal with you guys."

"Like I told you in the beginning," Frazer explained, "this is her turf. If I was going to do this right, I should have taken the idea to her and got her involved from the start."

"Could she be helpful?"

"I don't know." Frazer shrugged. "Maybe."

"Well," Anders said. "It's still early. You haven't written anything, yet. From what I can tell, you're barely getting started. Maybe you should involve her."

"I don't know…." Frazer's voice trailed away.

"You prefer working alone."

"Yes."

"Maybe this is one of those times when you need to work with someone else."

"Perhaps." They sat in a silence a while, then Frazer said, "What's next with the FBI?"

"We didn't really set a next with it," Anders replied. "I probably won't hear about it again unless they arrest someone. And I gotta tell you, I would like to see Hasan Izmir go down for something."

Frazer frowned. "You mean, to prison?"

"At least out of business."

"They really pissed you off." Frazer had a skeptical expression. "Are you sure there's not something else about them that's bothering you?"

"They're just bad for business," Anders groused. "Really bad. For me. For everyone."

"Well, I suppose I could take the next step with this," Frazer said.

"And what would that be?"

"I need to get inside the Izmirs' operation. Talk to someone who knows what actually happens at the gallery. Someone with firsthand information about how they do business. Do you know anyone like that?"

"Yes." Anders smiled. "I know just the person."

"You can set me up with them?"

"I'll give you a call."

Chapter 21

A few days after the auction, Frazer received a phone call from Anders. "You wanted to talk to someone about the Izmirs' business."

"Yes," Frazer replied. "Someone on the inside."

"Are you free for lunch today?"

"Yes."

"Good," Anders said. "You're having lunch with a guy named Frank Parker." The tone of his voice was more demanding than usual and Frazer was taken aback by it. Still, he had said he was interested in going further with the story and if Anders had someone for him to talk to, he felt obliged to meet with them. "Who is he?" Frazer asked.

"An art consultant," Anders said.

Frazer thought the title humorous. "What does an art consultant do?"

"He can explain what he does when you talk to him. Just meet him at Delmonico's at eleven thirty. You can ask him all about the Izmirs and their gallery. He knows the whole story."

While Anders was talking, Frazer's phone vibrated with a second call. He ignored it to jump Anders for his restaurant choice. "Delmonico's?" he roared. "Are you out of your mind? I can't afford that place." It was cheaper at lunch than dinner but, located in southern Manhattan, it was a restaurant that catered to a crowd that didn't worry about the cost of a meal.

"Listen to me," Anders responded. "Do you have room for it on a credit card?"

"Probably." Frazer didn't feel comfortable discussing that topic with him. "But——"

"Spend the money," Anders said, cutting him off. "And talk to the guy. Find out what he has to say."

"But——"

Anders cut him off again. "You wanted someone from the inside. I found you a guy from the inside. Buy him lunch at Delmonico's and listen to what he has to say."

"Will you be there?" Frazer asked, resigning himself to the inevitable.

"No," Anders said. "I think it's better if you meet him alone."

When the call with Anders ended, Frazer checked his messages and saw that the call he had ignored was from Zoë. Since the evening after Slater's show, when he remembered they'd gone all day without talking, he had made a point of texting her more often. Their messages had been cordial but when they tried to talk their conversation had been strained. Time, and the distance between them, was taking a toll. So, he called her back immediately rather than waiting until after lunch.

Zoë answered on the first ring and for the next ten minutes they talked about not much at all. It was good to hear her voice and it made him feel as though she was not that far away. But she still wanted him to give up the job at the paper in New York and come to Charleston and soon the insistence in her tone became unbearable. "I know," he said, trying to put her off. "But I'm working on this story and its starting to get interesting."

"The one about the people who live in the abandoned tunnels?" Her voice was sarcastic and patronizing.

"No," he said, doing his best to maintain his composure. "This is a different one."

"You said you were staying to write that story about the tunnels." Her voice took a hard edge.

"I know," he replied. "But—"

"Did you even write it?" There was no mistaking her anger.

"I'm almost finished." He forced himself to speak with an even tone. "Just a—"

"And now you're doing another one." She was louder and more demanding than before. "Are you ever coming to Charleston?" It was more of a statement than a question.

"I just need to do this story," he said. "That's all."

"And then the next one. And the next one after that." Her voice broke and he knew she was crying. "There will always be one more story."

Frazer glanced at his watch. "Look," he said. "I have a meeting and I need to get to it. I'll call—"

The phone went silent as Zoë ended the call without saying goodbye. He cleared the screen and slipped the phone into his pocket, then leaned back in the chair and closed his eyes. Maybe she was right. Maybe he should just end it all at the paper and head to Charleston. None of his story ideas seemed interesting anyway.

Over lunch that day, Parker listened patiently as Frazer summarized the article he hoped to write and the things he knew about the Izmirs, then asked for his help. "I'm not sure how much I can tell you about them," Parker said when Frazer finished. "But most of what you've heard about them is correct. They're crazy. The whole family."

Frazer frowned. "The family? You mean, the brother?"

Parker nodded. "Hasan. His brother. All of the cousins. All of them."

"All of them?" Frazer still was confused by the reference. "Who else is there?"

"Everyone who works at the gallery is related. Except for the artists. They have one or two young artists who aren't part of the family. And they have two employees who are from the outside. But all the rest are relatives."

"What about the artists?" Frazer asked. "Do you think they know much about what goes on at the gallery?" The purpose of talking to Parker was to get an inside view of the gallery's business operation. To find out the details. Thus far, all Parker had given him were opinions. Frazer had plenty of anecdotal information about the Izmir temperament.

"Nah," Parker replied with a dismissive gesture. "The artists don't know much. They're just artists. They come to the gallery when they have an event. Otherwise, they aren't around at all."

"Is the gallery a legitimate business?"

"They actually buy and sell art, if that's what you're asking. Most of it is of a decent quality, too. For what it is."

"And what is it?"

"It's all work from second tier European artists or American artists just getting started, but they actually make sales."

"That's the part I need to know about," Frazer said. "I need access to some hard business information. Facts. Figures. Transaction details I can cite."

"Anders told me."

"Can you help me with that?"

"One of the gallery's outside employees is the daughter of a friend. Her name is Jamie Wright."

Frazer remembered the name from his first visit to Galerie Le Meilleur. "I met her once," he said. "When I visited the gallery. Before the show."

"She could probably tell you as much about what goes on there as anyone," Parker said. "I can get you a few minutes with her."

"That would be great."

True to his word, Parker arranged for Frazer to talk to Jamie Wright. They met the next day at a bar after Jamie got off work and talked while they sipped a drink at a corner table. She remembered seeing him from before. "Actually," he said, "I've been in the gallery twice. Other than the night of Slater's show, I don't recall seeing many works by American artists."

"Galerie Le Meilleur deals almost exclusively in the secondary market for European art. We occasionally bring to auction a few paintings from established American artists, but most of the paintings come from Europe, and most of our sales are to the public through the gallery. The American art we regularly have on hand is from Sibel's emerging artists." The last reference was delivered with noticeable sarcasm.

Frazer opened a notepad and took notes while they talked. "You don't have a high opinion of those artists?" he asked.

"The artists are okay. And their work is about on par with others of their age."

"Common?"

"Yes." She nodded. "Very common."

He sensed there was more. "But what are you not telling me?"

"It seems rather obvious to most of us that she brings those artists to the gallery primarily for male companionship."

"She wants the artist. Takes the art as the cost of having them near?"

"Something like that."

"What about the other art?" Frazer asked. "Which part of Europe does it come from?"

"Most of the paintings come from France, as do most of the artists. But we've had some from the Netherlands, Italy, and Spain."

"The gallery has buyers in those countries?"

Jamie shook her head. "Sort of."

"Then how does it work?"

"Sibel and Hasan have a relationship with someone over there who buys the art and ships it to them."

"What's his name?"

Jamie looked away. "I don't know that person's name."

"Is it being purchased at auction over there?"

She shook her head again. "I don't think so. They don't pay

much for it, so I assume they have some sort of connection that gives them a price advantage. Which means they're probably buying it through a dealer or a gallery. Maybe a school for some of it."

"Some of it is student quality?"

"A little better than that, but not much."

"So, the buyer isn't buying it one or two at a time?"

"No. I've been working at the gallery for the past two years and since I've been there, it has come in large shipments. About four every year."

"So, it's sent each quarter, more or less?"

"That's exactly what it is. Every three months."

"When did the most recent shipment arrive?"

"We received one just the other day. Three crates."

"From France?"

"Yes. From Paris."

"So, three crates. That must be a number of paintings," Frazer guessed.

"Quite a few," she replied. "We're still entering them in the inventory system."

"That many?"

"The crates were large crates and the data entry is tedious. It takes a while to get them all entered."

"Any other aspects to their business?"

"Not really. Just art from Europe and then a few new artists from the United States. New York, mostly. Sibel buys paintings at some of the auctions here in the city, if she thinks she can flip them easily, but that isn't a very big part of the business."

"You mentioned the gallery represents some new artists right now. Are those the only individuals they represent?"

"Yes."

"They don't represent the artists from Europe who painted the paintings from over there that they sell in the gallery?"

"As far as I know, they don't."

"When the paintings arrive from Europe, they're arriving as inventory, not as the work of existing clients?"

"Right." Jamie nodded. "We only represent the artists I mentioned. Two guys from earlier in the year and now this new one. Slater. Those are the only people with whom the gallery has a traditional, gallery-artist relationship. And, like I said, they have some pictures leftover from artists they represented in the past, but those are ones that Sibel purchased. The artists who painted them have no connection with the gallery now."

"So, these shipments from Europe, they're all from the same person?"

"Sometimes the shipping name changes, but the transactions are always completed using the same account."

"What is that? Do you remember?"

"Parascheva."

"That's the name of the account?"

"Yes."

"Is that the name of a person or an entity? Maybe another gallery?"

Jamie shrugged. "I don't know."

"Do you handle the details for these shipments? Getting the buyer paid. That sort of thing.?"

"I usually check the crates at the loading dock, then log the paintings into the inventory system. I've only handled the payment side once. Sibel takes care of that herself."

"What happened that you handled the payments that time?"

"She couldn't be at the gallery and the payment needed to go out that day."

"For a shipment?"

"Yes."

"The gallery pays for the art electronically?"

"Yes. We pay and receive all of our invoices and bills electronically."

"You know that for a fact?"

"I've seen it. I've been told that. Sibel made a point of telling me that."

"Why?"

"I think she's proud of the way she runs the business."

"When you made those payments for the shipments, you must have entered more information than just the name. An account number, maybe?"

"Well. Yeah. I mean, the name, a bank routing number, and an account number. But I don't remember the numbers and I have no idea where the money actually goes. I just entered the information they give me."

"Did you ever see the buyer from Europe or anyone else you thought might be connected to the shipments from the European side?"

"There's a guy," she said. "I've seen him a few times, but I don't know his full name."

"You know his first name?"

Jamie glanced around, as if checking, then lowered her voice and said, "They call him Marcel. That's all I know."

"And you think he's connected to the art transactions from the European side?"

"He has an accent that sounds European to me. And he looks European. He always comes by the gallery a few days after the shipments arrive. Occasionally at other times, too, but always when the shipments arrive. Shipment arrives. A few days later, Marcel appears."

"Is he coming to check on the art?"

"I don't know what he does," Jamie replied. "I assume he comes by to make sure the paintings reached us, but he has never asked me anything and I've never seen him with Hasan or Sibel going over the inventory. Maybe he comes to make sure none of it was damaged in transit. I don't know. I saw him one evening going through one of the shipments with Hasan, as if one of them had a question about something. But I don't know."

"You've never dealt with him?"

"No." Jamie shook her head. "Hasan's the only one who deals with him. Not even Sibel talks to Marcel. And he doesn't talk to her. I mean, he seems to be cordial, but he doesn't discuss business with her."

"Yet, everyone tells me Sibel runs the business."

"Yes. She does. But she doesn't have anything to do with this guy."

"What about Hasan?"

"Hasan is around a lot. Breezes in and out. Talks loud. Shouts orders. Makes everyone feel his presence. But Sibel is the one who runs the place."

"Any possibility Marcel is the one in Europe who's buying the art?"

"From the discussions I've overheard, I don't think so. He doesn't seem like the type. Dealing in the second tier, the way they do, is a volume business. Whoever buys the art on the European end has to know precisely what they're looking for. And they have to judge it solely by appearance, not on the name or reputation of the artist. Most of the pieces at the gallery come from artists people in France don't even know. Americans who come to the gallery have never heard of them, either, but that's the key to the business. Gallery visitors think they've heard of the artists, and the paintings are priced to make them think they're getting a bargain."

"And then they buy."

Jamie smiled. "Yes. And they buy a lot of it."

"When's the last time you saw Marcel?"

"The night of the last show." A smile turned up the corners of her mouth. "The one for Truman Slater."

"You're smiling," Frazer noted. "You liked that show?"

"Yeah." She grinned.

"You like Slater."

She nodded. "I like Truman Slater." Then the smile vanished. "But so does Sibel."

"She likes Slater?"

Jamie rolled her eyes. "Sibel likes every artist she brings to the gallery. That's why she brings them in. Sometimes I think that's the only reason she's even in the business."

"To meet young artists."

"To meet young male artists," Jamie corrected.

"What does he look like?"

"Truman Slater? You were there that night. You saw him."

"Not him," Frazer replied. "Marcel. What does Marcel look like?"

"Oh," she said. "He's tall. Has dark hair. Serious eyes. Older than you. He came in the gallery that night, but only for a moment, then he and Hasan left together."

"That night? At Slater's show?"

"Yes."

That was the man Frazer saw. The one he saw while standing near the front, with the drink in his hand. "Anything else you can think of?" he asked.

"No," Jamie said. "Not really."

Frazer checked his notes, then asked, "What kind of people come to the gallery as customers?"

"Most of them seem to be tourists. People visiting the city from out of town, trolling the galleries, looking to buy the next Andy Warhol for seven hundred dollars."

Frazer smiled. "But you don't have that."

"No, we don't," she said. "The galleries around us do, but not for seven hundred dollars."

"More?"

"Way more."

"So, why do tourists come to your gallery?"

"We have art by European artists, and it's offered at a price that tourists can pay. The other galleries have better art, but not better prices. People from somewhere else come to New York, hear the names of the artists on our paintings, and think they've heard of them before. Then they check the price and see it's not too far out of their reach. So, they buy."

"Ever get any complaints?"

"From customers?"

"Yes. Or anyone?"

"Not really," Jamie said. "Most of them leave happy and we

never see them again." She paused as if remembering something else. "There was this one guy, though."

"Oh?"

"Yeah."

Frazer was intrigued. This was the kind of thing he needed. A person with a complaint who might be willing to talk. "Tell me about him."

"A guy came in the other day. Right after our latest shipment arrived. He was really upset. Said one of our paintings belonged to his family."

"What was his name?"

"Edelman. Jacob Edelman. I think your newspaper did an article on him last year. Maybe the year before. Holocaust survivor. Trying to find paintings that were stolen by the Nazis."

"We've done several of those stories. He thought you had one of his paintings?"

"Yes."

"What kind of painting?"

"He was looking for a Matisse."

Frazer raised an eyebrow. "Did you have it?"

"No." Jamie looked away, chuckling. "He thought it came to us in the latest shipment we received from Europe. Wanted to look through the paintings."

"Did you let him?"

"No." Jamie shook her head. "They would never let that happen."

"So what happened to him? How did it end?"

"Sibel came in the gallery while I was talking to him, and then Hasan came out from the back. They pretty much threw him out."

"They forced him to leave?"

"Yes."

"Has that ever happened before?"

"Not that I can recall."

Frazer checked his notes once more. "And you're sure this man's name was Jacob Edelman?"

"Yes," Jamie said. "That's his name."

As he walked home from the bar that evening, Frazer was excited. Jamie had been unable to answer all of his questions, but even so, talking to her had transformed him from reluctant reporter to interested journalist. A similar change had come to the story, too.

Whereas before, he'd seen only problems, now the story seemed to have everything—mysterious buyers in Europe, international transfers of art and money, Nazi thieves, and a Holocaust survivor searching for a long-lost art collection. All of it coalesced around the Izmirs—a family of dubious reputation—and their gallery, an enterprise that preyed on hapless visitors who came to the city for an adventure.

The story was just waiting to be written. Given half a chance, one that would write itself. Maybe already written and sitting in his computer of its own volition, waiting for Frazer to add the final touches. Might be a few more questions to ask. Perhaps a detail or two to give it that certain sense of purpose. Surely nothing he couldn't overcome. Just go back to the apartment, turn on the laptop, and get it finished. But he didn't.

Instead, Frazer returned to the apartment and fixed something to eat, then called Zoë, hoping for a civil conversation. Instead, the call went to voicemail. A moment later, she sent a text message. "At dinner. Call you later."

Two hours later, Zoë called back. "How was dinner?" he asked. He was in the bedroom when the phone rang but walked to the kitchen while they talked.

"Fine," she said.

"Where did you go?"

"Bryan Resnick was in town. He wanted to go to Barbados, so we ate there."

Frazer bristled at the mention of another man. And Barbados was an exclusive restaurant. No one went there by accident or on a whim. "You were on a date?"

"Jack, it wasn't a date." Zoë was defensive.

"Isn't he a guy you used to go out with?"

"We dated some," she conceded.

"And it was just the two of you."

"Yes."

"So, you were with a guy. Someone you used to see romantically. And you were alone at a restaurant."

"I met him there." She was firm but not argumentative. "It wasn't a date."

"Who paid?"

"He did."

"Then he walked you to your car."

"Of course."

"And he kissed you."

"Well … he wanted to."

"And?"

"I gave him my cheek instead."

"So, he tried to kiss you."

"Jack."

"And you don't think he was interested in you romantically?"

"I don't know what he was interested in. I—"

"Did he ask to see you again?"

"He's leaving tomorrow."

"So, that's a yes? He asked to see you again."

"He wants to have breakfast in the morning."

"Where?"

"I don't know. I told him I couldn't."

"You couldn't because of a schedule problem, or because you're married?"

"I told him it was good to see him and catch up, but that it wasn't right to see him again because it would only raise questions. About you. About me."

"You actually told him that?"

"Yes."

"And?"

"And what?"

"And what did he say?"

"He said, 'Oh. I didn't understand. You're here and Jack is in New York. I thought things were over.'"

"And what did you say?"

"I said things were never over between me and you." Her voice began to break but she kept going. "That I'd had enough of New York, but I would never get enough of Jack Frazer as long as I live. And that's the truth." The words came out in a sobbing rush. "Can't you come down here, Jack? Can't you?"

"As soon as I finish this story."

"This story."

"Yes."

"And not another one."

"No," he said. "Not another one."

Hearing her cry made him feel like the worst form of humanity. A real ass. The kind of man he'd promised himself never to be or become. And in truth, he hadn't meant for her to cry. It just happened, which meant he wasn't paying attention, which only made him feel worse. As if he were selfish, mean, and cruel. He apologized more than once, even though deep inside he wasn't convinced he had done anything wrong, but he felt wrong and so he braced himself and apologized, then spent the next twenty minutes putting things back together between them.

When the call ended, he sat at the table, staring at the phone, replaying the conversation in his mind. Bryan. He shook his head. "What a piece of work."

Frazer met Bryan once, at a Maybank family event. He was tall, with a muscular build and a winsome smile. The kind of guy everyone noticed when he entered a room. Especially the women. Zoë's mother seemed to fawn over him that day, which no doubt had something to do with Frazer's reaction during the phone call. But there was more to it than that. Bryan had a flaw. An obvious, glaring, obnoxious flaw. He was a first-class jerk. A self-evident fact that even

Zoë acknowledged, and which Frazer took great delight in pointing out at every opportunity.

More than an hour passed before Frazer pushed back from the table and stood. He felt a twinge of hunger but checked the clock on the microwave and was surprised by the lateness of the hour. Too late to eat. Or rather, too late to eat and sleep comfortably. The article about the Izmirs that he had started earlier that evening was calling to him from his laptop, but after the phone call with Zoë he wasn't in the mood for it. Instead, he turned out the kitchen light and made his way toward the bedroom. As he passed the table where the laptop sat, he closed the screen and switched off the reading light. Plenty of time tomorrow to work on the article. He was tired and wanted to sleep.

When Frazer arrived at the office the next morning, he sat quietly at his desk, sipping coffee, while reviewing his notes from the conversation he'd had with Jamie the day before. After reading through them once, he logged onto the newspaper's computer system and searched for information about the name "Parascheva," that Jamie had given him for the gallery transaction accounts.

After flipping through a page or two of search results, he located an article that looked promising and clicked on a link that took him to it. As the article appeared on the screen, the phone at his desk rang. He answered it to find his editor's assistant on the other end. "Mr. Gaines wants to see you," she said. Evert Gaines was the paper's features editor and Frazer's supervisor. He had no choice but to do as directed. "Okay," he said. "I'll be up there in a minute."

"Now," the assistant said, in a tone more demanding than before. She lowered her voice to a whisper. "They're all waiting for you."

All. Waiting.

That meant Gina had already complained, and Gaines already knew what he'd been doing. This might be worse than he expected. Maybe he would be joining Zoë in Charleston sooner than he thought. He thanked Gaines' assistant for the tip, then started upstairs.

Frazer arrived on the next floor to find Gina Wilkins seated outside Gaines' office. She glanced up at him as he approached. "Didn't mean to cause trouble," she said softly. "But I think you got yourself into this on your own."

"We'll see," Frazer said as he pushed the door open.

Gaines was seated at his desk, rocking the chair back and forth, waiting. Richard Norris, the arts editor, was there, too. When Frazer was inside and the office door closed, Gaines gestured in Norris's direction. "I believe you know Richard Norris."

"Yes, sir," Frazer said.

"He's our arts editor." Gaines spoke with a bitingly sarcastic tone. Frazer was used to it and ignored the tone in his voice. "We've met," he said, acknowledging Norris with a nod.

"That's good," Gaines continued. "Several of us were beginning to wonder about that."

"Yes, sir."

"I haven't seen much of you around here lately. Are you still working on that article about life in the tunnels?"

"It'll be ready tomorrow."

"That's good." Gaines had a cheesy movie actor kind of grin. "Weren't you working on something else? First surveyor of Manhattan or something like that?"

It was an earlier idea Frazer had floated. Before he got the idea for an article about the tunnels. He hadn't gotten very far with it and had meant to ask about maps for it when he was at the city records office, but he forgot. "Yes, sir," Frazer replied. "John Randel Jr. I'm still working on it."

"You wanted to collate his survey with a current map."

"Based on the iron pins he placed." Frazer was surprised Gaines remembered. "Some of them still exist. City surveyors know where they are. Find them, then do an analysis of what Manhattan used to look like in relation to what it looks like today."

"You'll need pictures."

"Yes," Frazer said. "I can get them."

"You know where they are?"

"Yes. We have some. The library and the city have the rest of what we need."

Norris looked amused. "You're doing an article about a survey?"

"Overlaying Randel's original survey with a current map, to show the things that used to exist in well-known locations."

"Such as?"

"Oh," Frazer said. "A pond in Times Square, for instance."

"Interesting."

"Yes, it is."

Gaines spoke up. "And now I hear you're working on a story about the art world, too. You're a busy man. Where do you get the time?" Frazer smiled but did not respond. Gaines kept going. "Is that true, Frazer? Are you working on an article about something to do with the arts?"

"Sort of."

"How sort of?"

"A friend suggested there might be a good story in the life of one of the dealers. Not about the art business per se, just about the dealer. Where he came from. What he's like. That sort of thing."

"Which dealer would you be writing about?" Gaines asked.

"Hasan Izmir."

"And does this friend who suggested the article have a name?"

"David Anders."

"Same guy you had lunch with the other day?"

"Yes," Frazer replied. "He gave me good tips before. I thought I ought to look around and see if there was a story in it this time, too."

"And all of this has something to do with the show you attended at Galerie Le Meilleur the other night, right?"

"I was just looking the place over," Frazer said. His voice was more defensive than he intended. "Sibel Izmir collared me and introduced me to one of her artists."

"Someone named Slater?"

"Yes."

"And you just happened to talk to him."

"Yes."

"And you just happened to agree to write a story about him, too."

"I told them I was considering it."

"You told them you would consider doing an article on an artist who had a show at an art gallery."

"Only to get through the conversation," Frazer said.

Gaines frowned. "To do what?"

"In the course of conversation, I wanted them to give me as much information as possible. So, while we were talking, I suggested I might do an article about Slater. About the show. It was something to say in conversation. But I didn't write it. I typed up my notes on the whole thing and gave them to Gina's assistant."

"That's good for the part about Slater. Very admirable of you," Gaines said. "But there's still this matter of what you're doing about the other fellow. Izmir. From where I sit, whatever story you're working on about him, or considering working on, or thinking about working on regarding him and the tip you got from David Anders falls under the responsibility of the art department."

"I don't think so," Frazer responded, "but you're the boss."

Gaines nodded his head slowly. "I'm glad you acknowledge my position."

"Yes, sir. Whatever you say goes. I never challenged that." Frazer turned to point over his shoulder. "Is Gina complaining?"

"She's protecting her turf," Gaines replied. "As you've been known to do on occasion."

"I saw her at the auction the other night. She didn't say anything, but I could see she wasn't happy."

"Well, she's not happy now either." Gaines caught Norris' eye. "You can ask Ms. Wilkins to step in here now."

Norris opened the door and held it while Gina entered. Gaines looked her with an expression that was all business. "Frazer got a lead from Anders about a story on Hasan Izmir. He's not trying to mooch off your territory, just looking for another Pulitzer, I think." Frazer was taken aback that his intentions were so obvious. Gaines kept going. "I've told him to give it up. Frazer will give you his notes and you two are going to talk through whatever he's been doing. Then you're going to write the story and make sure you give Frazer credit for his participation." He looked over at Norris. "Good enough?"

"Yes," Norris said. "I believe that'll do it."

Norris left the office. Frazer turned to leave, too, but Gaines called after him. "Next time, Jack, do this the right way and talk to Gina first, so I don't have to spend any more time on these useless meetings. Got it?"

Frazer nodded in response. "Sure thing."

Gina was waiting in the hall when Frazer came from the office. "We can talk about it after I—"

"Save it," Frazer snapped. "I'll give you the notes. You can write whatever you want."

"I'm not trying to—"

"Don't worry about it," he said. "I'm giving you my notes. I didn't get very far with it but maybe you can find something in there to write about."

They walked in silence back to Frazer's desk on the floor below and he gave her a notepad with several loose pieces of paper crammed inside. The screen on his laptop was open and as she took the notepad from him, she caught sight of the article about Parascheva that he had been reading. "What's that?" she asked, pointing to the screen.

"Nothing," he replied. "Just an article."

She stood at his desk a moment, scanning through the notes, then turned to leave. "I'll send you a draft of the article when it's ready."

Frazer didn't bother to respond.

Chapter 22

After multiple calls to the State Department, a trip to the Russian consulate, and several late-night phone calls to Europe, Scott Davenport convinced Interpol to release most of its file on Kirchen to the FBI. When it arrived at the New York office, he spent a day reading and re-reading it, then met with Preston Cooper.

"Anything in the file as interesting as we'd hoped?" Cooper asked.

"As we already knew, Interpol confirms that Kirchen is a citizen of Luxembourg," Davenport said. "But he has traveled on Russian and German passports."

"Under his own name?"

"Yes, and using at least five aliases, several of which have ties to Russian mafia figures."

"Hence the reluctance of Moscow to let us see the file."

"There's nothing definitive that connects him to criminal activity in Russia but notes in the file place him in Paris about the time the art dealer, André Crémieux, was murdered."

"Okay," Copper said. "That's a connection. Circumstantial," he acknowledged. "But a connection."

"A few days after Crémieux was murdered," Davenport continued, "Kirchen entered the Czech Republic. He was there for only a short time. Left the country the day after he arrived, but from there Interpol's trail runs cold on him. They say they don't know where he is currently located."

When Davenport had nothing further to say, Cooper looked at him in surprise. "That's it?"

"Pretty much."

"Did anyone at Interpol offer a reason for the hold on the file?"

"Nothing officially."

Cooper raised an eyebrow in a curious expression. "But unofficially?"

"The agent that I talked to said the hold was placed by an aide to a high-ranking Russian intelligence officer. They suspect it was to protect the identity of several Russian mafia dons, but no one knows that for certain."

"But some of the aliases Kirchen used are tied to the Russian mob?"

"Some of them have come up in connection with mob activity," Davenport said. "And notes in the file indicate Kirchen was a person of interest in several investigations conducted when Viktor Zubkov was the Russian prime minister."

"Back when they were trying to rid Russia of organized crime."

"Right."

"Interesting," Cooper replied. "Anything else?"

"Not really," Davenport said.

Cooper seemed puzzled. "I still don't see why Russian intelligence agents would be interested in protecting the file. I mean, the fact that they protected it is bigger than anything the file contains."

"Maybe there's more to it than Interpol knows, and the Russians just didn't want anyone to have a chance at Kirchen. Not for what was known but for what was unknown about him."

"Not a bad guess," Cooper said. "I'm guessing whoever wanted it hidden knew how extensive Kirchen's involvement really was and couldn't take the risk someone would convince him to talk. Or stumble onto something by an unguarded comment. Have you received anything back from the research staff on the trading company? Black Sea."

"Yes." Davenport looked amused.

"And something about that is funny?"

"Black Sea is a company that trades in commodities."

"Right."

"Most of that trading is in salt futures."

Cooper looked astounded. "Salt futures?"

"Yes."

"Really? Salt? Like, table salt?"

"Technically, it's sodium chloride," Davenport explained. "But salt is added to just about every food product on the market. For human consumption and for animal feed."

"So, it's a big market?"

"In every respect. Lots of mining. Lots of processing. Lots of consumption. But companies that need it for their business also need to stabilize their costs."

Cooper seemed to understand. "They trade salt futures as a way of making the price of future purchases predictable."

"Yes," Davenport said. "To lock-in those future costs at a stated price."

"Who owns the company?"

"Black Sea is owned by Balkan World Services, which owns about a dozen businesses, some of them legitimate, some of them we haven't figured out yet. As best we can determine, Balkan World was incorporated in Montenegro about ten years ago by three lawyers from Italy. The same three names pop up on all these companies." Davenport held a summary page for Cooper to see.

"The staff prepared a report?"

"Yes."

"Give it to me." Cooper gestured for the report. "I'll take a look at whatever they've written. Is someone still searching for details on all those other companies? The other ones the lawyers helped form?"

"Yes."

"Okay," Cooper said. "You stay on Kirchen. Run his aliases to the ground. See what you can find about them. Friends. Family members. Associates. Travel patterns. Places he shows up. We need the complete package on him."

Two days later, Cooper finally received a response from Paris police on their investigation into Crémieux's murder. He and Davenport sat in the conference room to discuss it. "It looks like Jacob Edelman knew what he was talking about."

"About Crémieux? That art dealer?"

"Paris police are convinced now that he was murdered, and that Marcel Kirchen had something to do with it. They've issued a warrant for Kirchen's arrest."

"Didn't Edelman think that whoever murdered Crémieux also stole a painting he was looking for?"

"The Matisse. Police in Paris think that part's right, too. They've found some documents that indicate the painting was in Crémieux's possession. And a part-time employee has given a statement that he saw it hanging at the gallery the day before Crémieux was killed."

Davenport nodded. "Just like Edelman said when you talked to him. Why did it take French authorities so long to figure this out?"

"They ran into the same roadblock we did."

"Interpol?"

"They obtained several sets of prints from Crémieux's townhouse," Cooper explained, "but they had difficulty identifying them. Most of the prints were not in the French database and when they asked Interpol, they said they didn't find a match."

"But they had the prints the whole time."

"Right," Cooper said. "Interpol matched the prints from the townhouse to Kirchen and to several of his known associates but wouldn't release the identities because of the Russian hold on Kirchen's file. All of those other suspects came with a connection to Kirchen. Interpol only gave them up to the French after they granted you access. So, good job."

"Glad it helped." Davenport looked pleased but focused on the case. "Did they give us names for those associates?"

Cooper turned the file so he could see it. "Right there," he said,

pointing to a page in the folder. Rodchenko, Senyavin and Krylov."
Cooper leaned back in his chair. "Interpol also said Kirchen was
implicated in two other murders, but never charged. One in Venice
and the other in Prague. Both victims worked in the art industry."

"Any information tying Kirchen directly to Russian organized
crime?"

"Not yet. But the French have linked several of the people whose
prints they found at the townhouse to Sergei Mogilevich, a big-time
Russian mob leader."

Davenport's eyes widened. "Think he's the one Russian intelligence was trying to protect?"

"I don't know. He's now living in Chisinau, Moldova. Exiled
there after Zubkov's crackdown on corruption."

"Ran there to avoid Zubkov. Liked it and stayed?"

"I suppose, but there's a lot about this we don't know."

"So, what do we do next?"

"If we can find Kirchen," Cooper said, "we can take him into
custody on the French warrant and hold him for return to Paris.
That will get him off the streets and give us time to question him
about the Izmirs and Edelman."

"We should check Homeland Security's system and see if we
can find him through that. They sweep up information from everywhere."

"Good idea," Cooper responded. "And ask the State Department, too."

"I'll put out an alert to everyone," Davenport said. "If he pops
up somewhere, we'll hear about it." He gestured toward the hall.
"We can go to my office and get on Homeland Security's system
right now."

"Great."

Cooper and Davenport left the conference room and walked
up the hall to Davenport's office. With little trouble, he logged into
Homeland Security's system and checked to see what they had on
Kirchen. After only a short search, he located a file. "Here he is,"
Davenport said, pointing to the screen. "He's actually in the US."

Cooper was startled. "He's here? In the United States?"

"Yes."

"When did he arrive?"

Davenport pointed to the screen. "He entered the country about four weeks ago. Came in through JFK and didn't even bother to use an alias."

"He used his own name? Marcel Kirchen?"

"Yep," Davenport said. "Gotta give him credit for being bold."

Cooper leaned over Davenport's shoulder to read the screen. "No record of him leaving, either." He stepped back, as if thinking. "Ask the State Department and ICE to flag that name and hold him if he tries to leave. Then pull together whoever you can and search the hotel guest database under his real name and all of the aliases we know."

"Any possibility he's here in New York?"

"I don't know," Cooper replied. "But if there's no indication he has crossed the border on the way out, then we should assume he could be anywhere."

Davenport seemed skeptical. "That's a big search."

"Maybe he'll make it easy for us."

"What do you mean?"

"Bad guys are just like everyone else," Cooper explained. "They get stuck on their name, whether it's the one they were given at birth or an alias they chose for themselves. They tend to stick with the ones they like. So, get the people who've been helping you on the research, grab a few more bodies, and run Kirchen's real name and his aliases through the hotel database and every other database you can find. We don't want him to leave with that warrant from France outstanding."

Chapter 23

A few days later the newspaper published a story under Gina Wilkins' byline about the Izmirs and their flamboyant lifestyle. It was long on their antics at auctions, but short on substance about their business and did little to delve into the issues that had troubled David Anders when he suggested the matter to Frazer. And it offered only a passing mention of Truman Slater and the exhibition of his work at Galerie Le Meilleur.

The morning the article was released, Anders was having breakfast with some of his fellow art dealers and serious collectors. The usual gang. The same people who had been present when Anders first suggested they attempt a coordinated approach to doing something about the Izmirs. As they ate, one of them said to Anders, "Did you see *The New York Times* this morning?"

"Saw it," Anders replied between bites. "I get the paper every morning, but I haven't read today's edition yet. Why?"

Tony Slidell said, "They have a piece in the art section about your friend Hasan Izmir."

Anders had a troubled look. "Why does everyone refer to him as my friend?"

Lloyd Davis, seated across the table, answered. "You seem so interested in him, we all thought you two were best pals." Everyone chuckled.

"And now that we've seen the article," Slidell added, "we're more convinced than ever." The chuckles became open laughter.

"Convinced of what?" Anders was in a strange mood that morning and still seemed not to realize what they were talking about.

Slidell continued. "That all this rhetoric about how bad Hasan is for the business is just a charade and that you really have his best interests at heart."

Anders rested his fork on the edge of the plate and turned to face Slidell. He had a perplexed look. Not quite angry. Not quite happy. "Tony, what in the hell are you talking about?"

"The article in this morning's paper," Slidell said. "The one you said would destroy Hasan. It's so positive, we assume now that you were kidding about it before when you said how much you disliked him."

Anders frowned. "Positive? It wasn't supposed to be positive."

"Ah," someone chided. "Now he's showing his true colors."

"Show me a copy," Anders said. "Does anyone have it with them?"

Someone handed him the arts section from the newspaper. Anders located the article and scanned through it while the others continued their banter.

"Rather flattering, I should think."

"Only adds to the Izmir mystique."

"The Turkish cachet."

"Puts another layer of bullshit on an already absurd sideshow."

Anders' frown deepened. "This isn't what they were supposed to write," he complained. "And why is Gina Wilkins' name included? It was supposed to be Jack Frazer."

In the meantime, Tom Fisher had joined them. "Well," he noted, "she is their senior arts correspondence. She wouldn't let a major piece appear in that section of the paper without her touch."

"Certainly not an article from someone outside the arts department. Frazer's a features reporter."

Anders folded the newspaper and laid it aside. "I'll get to the bottom of this," he grumbled. "I don't know what happened, but I'll get to the bottom of it."

Davis grinned at the others. "I love to watch him work his way out of things like this."

"We should put a warning sign on his back," Slidell suggested. "One of those orange triangles."

"And a message above it that says, 'Do not anger him before lunch.'"

They laughed loudly, then someone said. "We're on your side, David. Whatever side that is."

"At least you tried," Fisher said. His tone was serious and when he didn't laugh, no one else did either. "Somebody had to try. The Izmirs are ruining the business."

"I'll find out what happened with the article," Anders assured once again. "And I'll get it straightened out."

After breakfast, Anders called Frazer. "I saw the piece about the Izmirs in today's paper," he said, "but it had Gina Wilkins's name on it."

Frazer started to explain. "I tried to—"

Anders interrupted. "And it was way too soft," he said. "Nothing hard about it at all."

"If you'd let me—"

"Not really the kind of article I was hoping for. Are you going to write your own story?"

"No," Frazer replied, in a matter of fact tone. "I've been trying to tell you, this is—"

Anders blurted. "What do you mean?"

"Just that," Anders snapped. "I'm not writing a story about the Izmirs or anyone else in the—"

"Why not?" Anders was demanding. "We've been working on this for weeks."

"Look," Frazer responded, aggravated as much by Anders as by the way the article was handled. "This turned out exactly like I told you it would."

"No," Anders said. "You were supposed to do an exposé."

Frazer took a deep breath before responding. "You remember Gina saw me when we were at the auction the other night?" He spoke more calmly than he felt.

"Yes."

"The next morning, she complained to her editor," Frazer said. "Her editor complained to my editor and my editor made me give my notes to her. Just like I told you would happen."

"Well, we can't stop now." Anders sounded impertinent. A person of privilege demanding his way. Insisting, against all evidence of reality to the contrary, that events and people and things of every sort continue as he required.

"Did you just hear what I said?" Frazer was irritated. "You can do whatever you want about the article. The Izmirs. The whole business. But there's nothing else I can do."

An hour later, Sibel Izmir called Frazer to complain, too. "I thought you were doing an article about Truman Slater and the show we had the other night."

"Mrs. Izmir, I'm sorry but——"

"You made all those promises." Her voice had a sharp edge. "We had such hopes and told everyone a good report was coming."

"I'm sorry," Frazer said politely. "They took the story away from me and gave it to Gina Wilkins. Do you know her?"

"Yes. I know Gina. I've talked with her many times. But she never really writes much about us. Only those digest things she does sometimes when she runs through the schedule for the entire district. Never an article just about our gallery. She saves all of her space in the paper for the uptown galleries. That's why I wanted you to do it. You seemed interested just in us."

Frazer tried again to explain. "I'm a features writer, Mrs. Izmir. I was trying to do a feature on Slater, but they said I overstepped my boundaries. They made me give the story to Gina."

"You need to write the story we talked about," Sibel said.

"I'm sorry."

"Well I'm not," she responded. "I'll make a few calls. I know some people. I'll see what I can do about this."

Near mid-morning, Gina Wilkins came to Frazer's desk. "I don't know what happened," she said, "but my editor says your friends called to complain about that article of mine in today's paper. The one about the Izmirs."

"Don't shoot me." Frazer held up his hands in mock protest. "I had nothing to do with any of it. And for the record, I tried to warn them from the beginning this would turn out just like it did."

She found a chair, pulled it up to his desk, and took a seat. "Well, regardless, they want us to do another piece on the Izmirs."

Frazer gave her a look. "They?"

"My editor. Your editor. They think there might be more to this story than just an arts angle after all. And they don't like getting complaints from the kind of people who called them."

"Money talks."

"Something like that."

"So, what did the editors suggest?"

"They want us to see if we can find a hard news story in it."

Frazer grimaced. "I'm not too good at working with others."

"So I heard." Gina rolled her eyes. The comment stung. Frazer hadn't realized others held his preference for working alone against him. Gina kept talking. "You have developed contacts for this, and you like hard news. Ask around and see what you can find that we can use to flesh this story out."

Frazer was reluctant. "I don't think so," he said. "You wanted the story before. I gave you my notes. You write whatever it is they want."

Gina placed her hands on the desk and leaned toward him. "Our bosses want you involved. I'll work the art side of it. You work on … whatever it was you were wanting to write about before. Only, we have to produce the article together."

Frazer shook his head. "I don't like it."

"Neither do I. And obviously this wasn't my idea. But I think it's in both our interests to produce the article they want. So, let's see if we can find one for them."

Frazer imagined the conversation with Gaines that would ensue if he refused and realized there really was no way around an editor's demand. "If we were looking deeper, where would you want to begin?"

"There's a mention in your notes about something called Parascheva. You had an page on your monitor about it the other day. What is it?"

"Not what," Frazer said. "But who."

"Who?" Gina frowned. "It's a person?"

"Parascheva of the Balkans. A patron saint of the Balkan region. Romania, Moldova, that area."

"What does it have to do with the Izmirs and the gallery?"

Frazer shrugged. "I don't know."

"Then, why was it in your notes?"

Frazer leaned closer and lowered his voice. "I talked to a lady named Jamie Wright. Works at Galerie Le Meilleur. She's one of the few people who work there who's not an Izmir relative. She told me the gallery receives four shipments of art each year from Europe. It comes from various places but payment for it is always handled through an account noted in the gallery's records as Parascheva."

"That name sounds Russian." Gina had a knowing look. "Patron saint in the Russian Orthodox Church?"

"Yes."

"We should probably find out more about it. That might be the place to begin."

Frazer shook his head. "I'm not sure we want to dig too far into that part of it."

"Why not? That might lead us to exactly the kind of story we need."

"Think about it," Frazer said. "Russia. Art. Money. We won't get far down that trail without running into some ruthless characters."

"Yeah, but we can't back off a story just because it might get scary."

"We want to live, too."

"Let's go a little further with it and see what we can find."

Frazer struck a thoughtful pose. "How much do you know about the gallery, the Izmirs, Sibel, the family? That whole thing."

"Not much. Just what people say, mostly. None of the other art dealers like them. Journalists enjoy them because they're good fodder for a story. They always get noted in every publication that covers the auctions. But serious art people don't take them seriously, unless it's one of their pieces Hasan and Ahmed are bidding to an inflated price."

"Ever get a look inside to see how their business operates?"

"No," Gina replied. "Not really."

"You say not really a lot. What are you not telling me?"

"Nothing." Gina glanced away. "I've been to their gallery, but not many more times than you and I don't even know anyone who works there. You know more about that than I do."

"But you've covered them before, right?"

"I did a piece on one of their new artists earlier this year. They don't have many, but they usually have two. I think with Slater they actually have three right now. James Sedaris and Paul Stone are there, too. Robert Capriati was one of their guys for a while. I did a story on him two years ago, before he got popular and moved to a bigger gallery uptown. That's about all I know."

Gina moved to stand, as if to leave, but Frazer stopped her. "What about those artists?" he asked. "Sedaris or Stone. Think either of them might be helpful?"

"Maybe, but I'm not sure they know any more about what goes on down there than we do. They mostly just show up for exhibitions and spend the rest of their time working on new pieces. Why? What are you thinking?"

"We need to find out what goes on at that gallery and I'm thinking those artists would be a safe place to begin. Safer than trying to delve into the Russian angle. Not much chance a couple of artists are going to shoot at us. Do you have addresses for them?"

"Yes," she said. "I think so. You want to interview them?"

"We should do it together," Frazer replied.

"When do you want to see them?"

Frazer scooted back his chair and stood. "What about now?"

Frazer and Gina chose to begin their collaboration by interviewing James Sedaris. They took a taxi from the office and rode to his apartment, a second floor two-bedroom on Milton Street in Greenpoint, just across the East River from Manhattan. They knocked on the door and Sedaris answered but when they went inside, they found Paul Stone was there, too. Gina knew them both and they seemed glad to see her. "We read your article in today's paper," Stone said as he drifted toward them from across the room.

Gina smiled politely. "I hope you liked it."

"Would have been better if it was about us," Sedaris noted.

"But we were glad for the gallery to get the exposure," Stone offered quickly. "A rising tide lifts all boats, you know."

An easel stood in the corner opposite the door with three tables clustered around it. The tabletops were cluttered with tubes of paint, brushes, and an assortment of rags, palette knives, and other things an artist might accumulate. An unfinished painting rested on the easel, and the whole place smelled of turpentine.

In the corner diagonally across the room there was a second easel, also surrounded by tables with brushes and tubes of paint. Like the first one, this easel held an unfinished painting. This one not as far along as the other.

A sofa and two chairs with a coffee table between them occupied the space in the center of the room. Recent copies of *Art News* lay on the table, along with a week-old edition of *The New Yorker* and pages from the day's *The New York Times*.

Sedaris guided them toward the chairs. "Have a seat," he said. Stone dropped onto the sofa and Sedaris took a spot beside him. As they settled into place, Stone instinctively rested his hand atop

Sedaris' thigh. Frazer and Gina took the chairs.

"We were wondering what you could tell us about the Izmirs," Gina began.

"Oh." Sedaris looked surprised. "Is there a problem?"

"He means with the article," Stone added. "Did you get some pushback from Sibel?"

"Sibel runs the place, you know," Sedaris said. "If anyone was going to cause a problem, she'd be the one."

Stone shook his head. "I don't think so. Not her."

Sedaris turned to look at him. "You don't? Then who?"

"If anyone was going to cause a problem it would be Hasan."

Sedaris gave a dramatic shudder. "Ugh. That man gives me the creeps."

Frazer spoke up. "Hasan was a problem for you?"

"He didn't like us," Stone replied.

"You had some trouble with him?"

"No. He had trouble with us." Stone gestured between them. "He was very uncomfortable when he found out we were … together."

"Oh." Frazer realized what they were saying and shifted positions uncomfortably in his chair.

"But that's okay." Stone leaned over and kissed Sedaris on the cheek. "We know who we are."

Gina smiled. "You said Sibel runs the business."

"Yes," Sedaris said. "She looks after the details. When Hasan is there, he acts like he's in charge."

Stone jumped in. "And she lets him. Have to preserve that fragile masculine image, you know."

"Yes," Sedaris acknowledged. "She's very careful to protect his image as the boss."

"But she's the one in charge," Stone said.

Gina nodded. "You didn't have any problems with her?"

Sedaris and Stone exchanged glances, then a grin came over both. "Well," Stone said. "She wasn't upset by our relationship as such."

Sedaris had a knowing look. "She just didn't realize we weren't attracted to her when she brought us into the gallery."

Gina nodded again. "She thought you were young, handsome men and—"

"We are young, handsome, men," Sedaris said proudly. "She just didn't realize we are gay."

Frazer spoke up. "She had other ideas for you."

"Exactly," Sedaris said. "And we found out later, that's what she does. Brings in young male artists because they're young and male."

"Gives them lots of support."

"Then seduces them."

"From what we heard," Stone said, "the seduction hasn't required much effort."

"And it's always with men."

"No women."

"They've never represented any female artists."

Frazer asked, "How did she find you? How did you end up at her gallery?"

"Ed Kushner recommended me," Sedaris answered.

"She saw me at a fair," Stone offered. "Asked if I was interested in working with a gallery. I said sure. I mean, who wouldn't?"

"Then we met each other when we got there. I think she took me because Kushner said so, but she took Stone because she wanted his body." Sedaris snuggled closer to Stone. "He has a great body."

"Did either of you see anyone suspicious at the gallery? Any activity that made you think something else might be going on there."

"Not really," Sedaris said slowly.

Stone's face brightened with interest. "Was there? Was something else going on?"

"That's what we're asking about," Frazer said.

Gina spoke up. "What about a guy named Marcel? Ever hear of someone by that name."

"Oh." Sedaris leaned back and his eyes turned dark. "Marcel."

"We never knew his last name," Stone offered. "I don't think we wanted to."

"You didn't like him?"

"I didn't," Sedaris offered. "He gave me the creeps. Just like Hasan."

"He was a little creepy," Stone acknowledged. "But he was a hunk."

Sedaris looked over at him. "You really had the hots for that guy."

"At first." Stone took Sedaris' hand. "But then I saw you without your shirt."

"Doesn't stop you from drooling over that guy every day."

Stone's cheeks glowed. He gave Frazer an embarrassed look and explained, "I took a couple of pictures of Marcel when he wasn't paying attention. Just something to have for … my own enjoyment. He didn't like it, but I did it anyway."

Pictures. Just the kind of thing Frazer was hoping for. "Do you still have the pictures?" he asked.

"Yes," Stone replied. "Of course. That was the point of taking them."

"Think we could have a look at them?"

"Sure." Stone pushed himself up from the sofa and walked to the bedroom. He returned a moment later with four photos and handed them to Frazer. After a quick glance, Frazer handed them to Gina. "This is the guy I saw at the show."

Sedaris seemed surprised. "You were at our show?"

"No," Frazer said. "The gallery had a show for Truman Slater a few nights ago."

Sedaris and Stone giggled. "We just love him."

"Slater?"

"Yes."

"And with him around," Stone added, "we don't have to worry about Sibel harassing us."

Gina seemed to understand. "She likes him?"

"Oh, my. Yes," Sedaris gushed.

"Before he came to the gallery," Stone offered, "she kept telling us we should go straight. But now, she spends all her time with him."

"And leaves us alone."

Frazer gestured to the photos. "Think we could take one of these with us?"

"Sure," Stone replied. "Take all of them. I have the digital files. I can make as many as I want."

They talked a while longer, then Frazer and Gina left. As they walked down the steps from the apartment Frazer said, "At least we have a photo."

"What do we do with it?"

"I don't know. We don't even know the guy's last name."

They reached the street and came to a stop on the sidewalk. Gina looked over at him. "Anyone else we can talk to?"

"Jamie Wright mentioned someone named Jacob Edelman. He came to the gallery looking for a painting. A Matisse."

"We ran an article or two about him."

"Do you know him?"

"Yes." Gina nodded. "I've talked to him a few times. Nice guy. Holocaust survivor. Nazis stole the family art collection during the war. He's spent all his life trying to recover it." She looked up at Frazer. "Do you want to talk to him?"

"I think we should. Jamie said he was really upset the day he came in there. He thought one of his paintings was included in the gallery's latest shipment. Do you know where he lives?"

"I have an address for him." Gina checked the contacts list on her phone and found the address. "He lives in Manhattan. Not too far from the office."

"Good." Frazer opened the Ride-Along app on his phone to schedule a ride for them. "Let's talk to him and find out what he has to say."

Chapter 24

From Greenpoint, Frazer and Gina rode back to Manhattan. They reached Edelman's apartment late in the afternoon and knocked on the door. After a moment, the door opened and Anne Meltzer, Edelman's granddaughter, appeared. They identified themselves as reporters, then Frazer said, "We were looking for Jacob Edelman and wondered if we might talk to him a moment."

Anne glanced at them suspiciously. "Is he expecting you?"

"Probably not."

Edelman appeared in the hallway. "Let them in," he said.

Anne stepped aside to let Frazer and Gina enter. While they followed Edelman into the living room, Anne closed the door, then joined them. Edelman took a seat in a chair near the window, looking dejected and in foul humor. "What does The New York Times want with me?"

Anne gestured to chairs positioned across from him and caught Gina's eye. "I remember you. You know my grandfather, don't you?"

"We've met a few times."

"Then you know he's trying to locate one of the pieces of art that the Nazis took from his parents. A work by Matisse. And he's convinced the painting is at Galerie Le Meilleur in Chelsea."

"I'm sitting right here," Edelman said in a flat, affectless voice. "You don't have to talk about me like I'm not present." He looked over at Gina. "And I know it's there. It arrived at the gallery in a shipment from France. Three crates of their second-rate art, with one Matisse hidden among them. My Matisse." He looked over at Anne. "Our Matisse." They exchanged glances, then Edelman continued. "They have our painting, and no one seems to be able to do anything about it. Not even the federal government can get it. They can tax your cat, but they can't seize one single painting." Tears came to his eyes. "They're no better than the Nazis."

Anne patted his knee and looked over at them. "He's really upset. Maybe you should come back another time."

"No," Edelman said with a wave. "Let them stay. They can get it raw, just like I feel."

"Tell us about the painting," Frazer said.

Edelman began slowly, speaking in a gruff voice at first before warming to them as he talked through the story—how his father acquired the painting from Matisse's wife, Amélie, after she left the artist. It had hung in their apartment many years, then the Nazis came and took it along with many others. He vowed to get them all back and tracked the Matisse to a gallery owned by André Crémieux in Paris. Before he could take possession of it, Crémieux was murdered, and then the painting went missing again.

"All of this is documented, of course," Edelman said. "I'm not making it up."

"You have records?"

"I have boxes and boxes of records."

"Of the missing Matisse?"

Edelman looked over at Anne. "Could you get the papers we have from Paris. They're on my desk."

Anne disappeared down the hall and returned with a file folder. She handed it to Gina. Edelman pointed to the file. "That is the information we received from the French Ministry of Culture."

Gina glanced through the pages until she came to a shipping document and saw the name, Marcel Kirchen. She handed the paper to Frazer and pointed to the name. His eyes opened wider. Edelman caught the look. "Did you find something interesting in there?"

"This name," Frazer said. He leaned forward and handed the

document to Edelman. "Marcel Kirchen. What do you know about him?"

Edelman sat up straight. "Would either of you care for coffee?"

They moved from the living room to the kitchen. Anne made a pot of coffee and Edelman kept talking while they waited for it to brew. When it was ready, they sat at the kitchen table and sipped coffee while Edelman told them about his relationship with Jean-Louis Ferro and the details of tracking the three crates from Paris to London to New York. He gave them copies of the information Ferro sent him and while they studied those documents, he went to the bedroom he used as a study and brought back boxes of documents. Records from his father's business. Old family photographs. Pages and pages he had accumulated in his search for the family paintings.

Edelman seemed happy to talk. Even relieved, that someone would listen to the full account of what he'd experienced. He recounted the story again that he'd given them before—the painting, the Nazis, finding all the other pieces from the collection except one. Tracking the Matisse to Crémieux, only to have it stolen again. And this time, with someone else dead instead of all the members of Edelman's family.

Frazer and Gina let him talk, afraid that if they interrupted or stopped him, they might miss something important. After three cups of coffee, they had filled their notepads and were writing on copier paper taken from the tray of Edelman's printer. Then Edelman showed them a picture of the painting. "This is the Matisse. *Woman With Table and Vase*." He handed it to them, a color photograph printed at the apartment.

Gina studied it a moment, then passed it to Frazer who looked at it and offered it back to Edelman, who refused to take it. "You can keep it," he said. "I have plenty of copies. I give them to everyone I meet. Maybe it will help you."

The sun was all but gone when Frazer and Gina finally came from Edelman's apartment and walked up the hallway to the elevator. As they rode to the lobby, Frazer said, "This is more than a single article."

"More than a series of articles," Gina replied.

"Where do we begin?"

"Take your pick," she said. "Germans. The war. Death camps. Murder in Paris."

"I'll flip you for the first draft."

"No," she said. "I did the last one. You take this one. You write the draft. I'll do the revisions."

"Do you think our editors will go for a series?"

"I don't know, but this was your idea, so you get to ask."

He chuckled. "Okay. I'll see how the first draft goes, but we're not ready to write."

"What more is there to do? We don't have a way to get further inside the business."

Frazer was thinking of Cooper and the FBI. "Let me make a few calls," he said. "Check on a few things."

She studied him a moment, as if trying to determine what he was up to, then said, "Okay. But nothing illegal."

"Sure," he said with a smile. "Nothing illegal."

When they reached the street, Frazer turned in the direction of the office. Gina hesitated, then gestured over her shoulder. "I'm headed this way."

"What's in that direction?"

"The subway."

"It's only a few blocks to the office," he said.

"It's late," Gina responded. "I'm done for the day."

"You're headed home?"

She frowned. "Don't you have a wife?"

"Yeah."

"Wouldn't she like to see you once in a while?"

"Probably." He had a solemn expression. "But not tonight."

"Well, I have things to do at home," Gina said. "I'll see you tomorrow." And as an afterthought she said, "Eat dinner before you work on this any more."

"Sure thing."

As Frazer walked up the street, he thought of all that Edelman told them and replayed the conversation in his mind, but every few steps his thoughts drifted to Gina. The softness of her smile. Her eyes, clear and bright. Her hair, a color of brown he had never noticed, cut short like a man but slightly longer on top and combed away from her forehead in a swoosh that made her seem younger than she really was. And the sound of her voice. Warm. Soothing. Inviting. The kind of voice that made one say things they'd not intended to say, not meant to say. As if behind the voice was someone who could be trusted with things kept secret. Deep secrets. Things hidden from the beginning.

Frazer had never worked with her before, but he had seen her in the office and he heard about her from others. Opinionated, they said. Exacting. Demanding. A friend at the paper described her once as "that lady from *Devil Wears Prada*, only with less heart." But she wasn't like that at all. At least, not with him. And not so far.

Gina had been considerate and professional with him. Witty, engaging, even compassionate, with those they interviewed. And she hadn't asked stupid or meaningless questions. Nothing shallow, boring, or inconsequential, which Frazer hated. Nothing petty or rude or needling, either. The facts. That's all she seemed to want. Not in a heartless way, but in a way that seemed driven by a superior intellect. She was sharp and, beyond the way she looked when she smiled, that was what drew him to her.

He had wanted to have dinner with her and intended to suggest it as they made their return to the office. Now, in retrospect, the abruptness of her departure left him wondering if she had sensed his intention and cut things off deliberately to avoid him. Perhaps not to avoid him, but to avoid a moment not strictly related to work. It was more than that, though.

They had worked well together all day. Back and forth. The two artists. Edelman and his granddaughter. An idea becoming a story becoming something bigger. Maybe much bigger. They talked. Considered. Evaluated. Then, for some reason, a wall went up. Everything else had gone well between them. Something about the moment when he would have asked about dinner put her off.

No. He shook his head. Not put her off. It didn't put her off to be with him but saying yes to him would lead to something she didn't want him to know. Would force her to reveal something about herself she didn't want to show.

"Now I'm really curious," he said to himself.

With dinner in Gina's company no longer an option, Frazer decided to forgo the office and return home. He could work from the apartment. Sort through his notes. Prepare summaries of their interviews. Create a timeline of the events. Maybe make a list of other people to interview.

At the next corner, he turned in the direction of the apartment and forced his thoughts back to Edelman. Nothing good could come from thinking of Gina. Besides, dinner with her was the same as Zoë having dinner with Bryan Resnick, which had seemed so unreasonable and unnecessary just a few nights earlier.

There had been more to his anger than just Zoë having dinner with a guy, he knew that. Resnick was a favorite of Zoë's mother. Frazer was not. But he felt guilty just the same and remembering their phone call and all that he had said, and now all that he was thinking about Gina, sent waves of guilt over him. Piling up and crashing down, over and over. The way he had accused and berated her. The tone of his voice. Biting. Cutting.

Before he reached the apartment, Frazer took his phone from his pocket and typed a text message to Zoë, entering it with his thumbs while holding the phone with both hands as he walked. Twice he had to jump aside to avoid a collision with an oncoming pedestrian and once he banged his shoulder against a pole. He went three steps past the apartment entrance before he finished, finally stopping in the center of the sidewalk to type the last words and hit the button to send it. The doorman laughed at him, but Frazer was determined to send the message and assuage the condemnation that seemed so real. He wasn't interested in anyone other than Zoë. Not like that. It's just … Gina was so damned interesting. And he liked interesting people.

Chapter 25

The next morning, Frazer was at the office early and called Preston Cooper on his personal cell phone, hoping to find out something new about the Izmirs. The call, however, went to voicemail and Frazer left a message.

Not long after that, Gina appeared and took a seat in the chair beside his desk. "Have you been here all night?"

"No," he replied. "I got here early."

"I talked to Richard Norris. He liked our idea of doing a series. Thought we could base it on our interviews, as long as the articles are stories and not just filling space."

"I never merely fill space," Frazer said. Though he knew reporters who insisted on appearing in the paper, regardless of whether they had something to report.

"And," she continued, "he wants us to talk to someone at Galerie Le Meilleur and give them an opportunity to respond before we publish."

"I already talked to Jamie Wright."

"I think he means someone in authority."

"From what we know right now, that would be Sibel."

Gina nodded. "And, since you've talked to her already, you can be the one to give her a call and set up an interview." She smiled playfully. "We should get that done today if we can."

"Okay, but you're going with me."

"Wouldn't miss it."

She stood and turned to leave but he called after her. "There's one more."

She came back. "One more?"

"One more person."

"Oh?"

"When I was at the gallery for the show, Truman Slater invited me to his studio."

"And you think we should talk to him?"

"We have some good information," Frazer said. "But it's just a start. We need more. He might give us something that would help."

"You're right about that. Where is his studio?"

"Long Island."

Her shoulders sagged and she gave him a look. "Where on Long Island?"

"Springs."

"That's a long way out."

"Just about at the end."

Gina thought for a moment, then said, "Let's talk to Sibel and decide after that."

Frazer called Truman Slater but was unable to reach him. He left a message and phoned Galerie Le Meilleur to arrange an appointment with Sibel. She agreed to see them later that morning.

Sibel was waiting in the main gallery room when they arrived and at first seemed glad to have them. From her responses, it was apparent she thought they had come to follow up on their conversation from the night of Slater's show and in response to the phone calls she made about Gina's article. Everything was going well, until Frazer asked about Jacob Edelman.

At the mention of his name, Sibel's face went cold. "I thought you were going to write about Slater, not some crazy Jew looking for a piece of art that maybe never existed in the first place."

Gina showed her a picture of the painting. "This is the one he's talking about." Sibel glanced at the photo. Gina noticed the look in her eye. "You've seen it?"

"No." Sibel shook her head. "I have never seen that painting." She turned away. "I am not even sure it is a Matisse."

"What about this man?" Frazer showed her a picture of Kirchen. "What can you tell us about him?"

Sibel glanced at the photo and was visibly shaken but denied knowing him. "Is this some kind of interrogation?"

"Just trying to fill in some missing information. Are you sure you've never seen him?"

"What do you mean? Are you accusing me of lying?"

Frazer pointed to the photo. "This man was here the night of Slater's show."

"You do not know that."

"Yes, I do," Frazer replied. "I saw him. Your husband saw him. In fact, your husband left with him."

"I cannot answer any more of your questions." Sibel turned toward the door and gestured. "You must—"

Gina spoke up. "Tell us about Slater."

"What about him?"

"You did a show for him. How did you find him?"

"He was with Raymond Wyatt. Raymond is a good man, but he doesn't know much about art. Not willing to invest in an artist. Just wants to sell the easy things." She looked at Frazer. "Truman invited you to his studio. He thought you would have come there by now."

"We plan to talk to him."

"I hope not about all this Jew business," she snarled. "About his art."

Gina spoke up again. "So, you found him at Raymond Wyatt's studio."

"Truman worked for him, first. Preparing the walls of his gallery. Hanging new pictures. Then Raymond gave him a few shows, but Truman needed some help. A little nudge. Charlotte Snider took him in hand and then brought him to me."

"Show us some of his work," Gina suggested.

"Many of his things are in the back." Sibel's mood lightened and she smiled as she led them to the opposite side of the room. "But we have some of his pieces over here." She took them to a painting hanging near the entrance. "He was just another starving artist languishing in obscurity. Then we put him on the walls of our gallery, did a showing, and now his work is selling well." Her eyes seemed more alive than ever.

"I understand he came here from Montana."

"Yes. A good western man," she beamed. "With an eye for space and color." Sibel looked over at Frazer. "You have the address for him?"

"Yes."

"Good. You should see him at his studio and write that article you promised."

After a few more questions, Frazer and Gina left the gallery. As they walked away, Gina glanced in his direction. "How many articles did you promise them?"

"I was just trying to get them to talk."

She popped him with a backhand to the chest. "Just because you won a Pulitzer doesn't give you the right to run over me."

He laughed. "I never wrote the piece."

"Yeah, well, you shouldn't have promised them a piece of my section."

"I was trying to write about Hasan Izmir from a broader perspective. Hoping to find a story about the business, not about the art."

"Did you call Slater about coming to his studio?"

"Had to leave a message."

"Follow up with him and set an appointment."

"I plan to."

They walked in silence to the next block but as they crossed the street Gina said, "She was lying about that painting."

"I know. Sedaris and Stone were right about her, too. She's obviously interested in more from Slater than his paintings."

"Think it goes beyond an affair?"

"You mean, like romance? Love? Fleeing New York in the dark and living on the run?"

She frowned. "On the run? What are you talking about?"

"They're from Turkey. Do you really think her husband would let her run off with a white guy from Montana without a serious fight?"

"Never thought about it like that."

"I bet Hasan Izmir would."

"He might. Maybe we can figure some of this out when we see Slater."

When Frazer and Gina were gone, Sibel went to look for Hasan. She found him in the office, seated at his desk. He glanced up as she entered the room. Her presence seemed to aggravate him. "I'm busy," he growled. "What do you want?"

"Two reporters were just here."

Hasan shrugged. "What of it? I'm busy."

"They came to talk about an article for Truman Slater."

"What smalltime rag are they with?"

"The New York Times." She said it in a weighted voice.

He stopped what he was doing and looked up at her. "Really?"

"Yes." Sibel had a serious tone. "Really."

"That's a good thing," he said. "Why do you look troubled?"

"They were also asking about Jacob Edelman."

His eyes narrowed. "That crazy Jew?"

"I think they're working on an article about him, too."

Hasan gave her an angry scowl. "I told you this wasn't going to work." He pointed at her for emphasis. "Having those young, unknown artists was a big mistake."

"The young artists aren't the problem," she snarled.

"Then what?" He had a demanding tone. "What are you blaming me for this time?"

"The reporters had a photograph of the Matisse."

Hasan leaned back in his chair and threw up his hands in a gesture of frustration. "That damn painting …." His voice trailed off and he sat staring blankly before saying, "We need to get rid of it."

"It's already gone."

Hasan was stricken. "I didn't mean literally. That's a million-dollar painting! What happened to it?"

"Relax," she said. "It's safe."

"You took it?"

"I moved it."

"Where? Where did you put it?"

"I hid it."

"Where? Tell me."

"No."

"No?"

"I'm not telling you where it is."

"Why not?"

"Because you'll do something with it."

Hasan was even angrier than before. "That's why you took it?" he shouted. "Because you don't trust me?"

"I don't trust you," Sibel said. "I don't trust Edelman. And I don't trust those reporters."

"If you don't——"

"Wait," Sibel interrupted. "There's one more thing."

"What?"

"They have a photograph of Marcel Kirchen."

Hasan had a blank expression. "They?"

"The reporters. And they know his name."

Hasan struck the desktop with his fist. "This is not good."

"This is not good for any of us."

"We must tell him at once," he said. "We have no choice." He reached for the phone but Sibel grabbed his hand and pinned it against the desktop, leaning against it with all her weight. "I don't think that is a good idea," she said.

"Why not? If they find out we knew and didn't tell them, they will blame us for whatever happens."

"Like I told you before." Sibel's voice was calm, but steeled, firm, and unwavering. "Marcel Kirchen is crazy. He has already killed two people that we know of. He probably killed the art dealer in Paris that Edelman was yelling about. And no one can say there aren't more bodies lying in his wake."

"I don't think we can keep quiet about this."

"One of the reporters was here the night we did the show for Truman Slater."

Hasan slid his hand free of her. "So?" he shrugged. "What is the importance of that?"

"He saw you leaving with Marcel."

"Damn it, Sibel," he shouted. "Those shows of yours are nothing but trouble. Trouble! Trouble! Trouble! When will you ever listen to me?"

"You walked out the front door with him," she countered coolly. "Did you think no one would notice?"

He gave an angry sigh. "What do you suggest we do?"

"The first thing we should do is stop looking out for their interests and start looking out for our own."

"What are you talking about?"

"I'm saying, if a reporter has this photograph of Marcel, who else has one?"

"You mean like the police?"

Sibel nodded. "The New York police. The FBI. The French police. This city is full of cameras. Paris is, too. And if the authorities come after Marcel, our arrangement will fall apart. And then we will have even bigger problems."

Hasan whispered, "Mogilevich."

"He will drop all of this at our feet."

"They were supposed to take care of everything." Hasan folded his arms on the desktop for a pillow and rested his head against them. "They didn't think about the cameras," he muttered.

Sibel had a questioning frown. "Who was supposed to take care of what?"

"His contacts with the Russians."

Sibel moved a chair near the desk and took a seat. "Kirchen has contacts with the Russians?" This was a complication of which she was unaware.

"No," Hasan replied. "Not him. Mogilevich."

"And how were these intelligence contacts going to help?"

"They placed a hold on Kirchen's file with Interpol. Mogilevich said with a hold in place, no one would ever find out he was involved."

"Who told you this?"

"Marcel."

Sibel shook her head. "Whatever they did, it didn't work. A reporter from The New York Times has his picture."

Hasan raised his head and looked over at her. "Let me think about this for a while. In the meantime, keep your mouth shut." He pointed at her with a jab of his finger. "Not a word to anyone, you hear me?"

"I hear you."

Sibel rose from the chair and walked down the hall to her own office. She held herself upright and walked with grace and self-assurance. Inside, though, she was shaken, afraid, and angry. Hasan was supposed to handle Marcel. That was part of the arrangement. She ran the gallery business. He took care of the European connections. None of this was ever supposed to touch her. Now, it seemed to be unraveling and her safety was in jeopardy.

Fear and panic swept over her in waves, but she forced it aside. This was no time to give in. If she was to survive the calamity she knew was coming, she would need options. And for that, she needed money. Lots of money. Hasan could offer her no protection like money could. With it, she could relocate. Acquire a new identity. Disappear.

Using a laptop at her desk, she logged into the gallery's New York bank account and checked the balance. Then, with only a few keystrokes, she entered an order transferring a hundred thousand dollars to an account she had established at a bank in Arizona. "If he goes down," she mumbled, "I am not waiting around here to die. When they come for us, they will find only him."

Chapter 26

Friday morning, Frazer took his car from the parking deck at the apartment and drove to the office. Gina was waiting for him out front. He brought the car to a stop by the curb and waited while she got in.

From the office in Manhattan, they took the Midtown Tunnel to Brooklyn, then picked up the Long Island Expressway, and settled in for a ride to the eastern end. They filled the time reviewing details from the interviews they'd conducted thus far, and by making small talk, which Frazer didn't care for but endured as a gesture of politeness.

Two hours later, they reached Riverhead and stopped for an early lunch at Farm Country Kitchen, a restaurant on Main Street. Located in a nineteenth century dwelling, on the south side of the street, it overlooked the Peconic River. Frazer and Gina were seated at a table near the window. They ordered coffee and a light meal.

At first, the view of the river kept them occupied while they waited for their food, but the silence became uncomfortable and finally Gina said, "All I know about you is that you came from California and you can work a story to death." She smiled at him. "What got you interested in being a reporter?"

Frazer had hoped to avoid the topic. It always seemed to mundane and expected. But he found no way to deflect her question so he offered a response in increments, hoping the waiter would arrive to interrupt before he'd gone very far. "I grew up in California," he noted, "but I went to school in North Carolina."

"Oh. Where?"

"Wake Forest."

"A Baptist school," she said.

"Sort of." From the expression on her face, Frazer thought she might divert the inquiry into a discussion of the school and the way its ethos and culture deviated from standard Baptist mores, but she was not deterred. "Is that what brought you there?" she asked. "The Baptist history of the place?"

"No. My grandfather had been a professor there."

"What subject did he teach?"

"English."

"And he got you interested in journalism." She said it as a statement, not a question.

"No." Frazer shook his head. "That was something I picked up from a teacher in high school."

"Okay." She gave him a look that asked for more and took a sip of coffee while she waited for him to continue.

"We had this English teacher," Frazer said. "A guy named Bob Glidden. He was still stuck in the '70s when I had him for class and he made us read *Fear And Loathing In Las Vegas*."

"Hunter Thompson."

"That got me started. When I finished that, I read—"

"Let me guess," Gina said. "*Catcher in the Rye*."

Frazer shook his head. "I read that one, eventually. But that's not what I read next."

"What was that?"

"*The Best and Brightest*."

"Halberstam."

"Right."

"There are still a lot of people at the paper who knew him."

"I'm sure."

"So, that got you started. What happened next?"

Despite his distaste for the topic, he enjoyed talking to Gina and he liked it when she smiled. "Not long after I read that book," he continued, "our local newspaper fired one of its reporters for doing a series on migrant workers and the farmers who took advantage of their illegal status."

"Wait." She frowned. "They let him do the articles, then they fired him for it?"

"They didn't like the response they got from the farmers." Frazer had an ironic smile. "So, they forced the guy out. After that, I was hooked."

"The reporter got fired and you decided to become a journalist?"

"Yeah. I figured if reporting the truth meant that a guy could get fired for doing it, I was all in." He took a sip of coffee. "What about you? What brought you to the life?"

"Well, it was nothing like that." She gazed wistfully out the window. "I wanted to be an artist."

"That makes sense."

"But I had no ability to do representational art. And I wasn't able to conceptualize abstract art."

A puzzled expression wrinkled his forehead. "I thought that was the whole thing about abstract art. That it had no concept."

"Most people see it that way, but abstract art is far from random. Pollock, Rothko, Motherwell. They were very intentional about the way they painted and the images they created."

"Really?"

She nodded. "Their work was planned from the beginning. They left room in the process for spontaneity, but they had a pretty good idea of where a painting was going before they picked up a brush."

"I think Pollock lived around here somewhere."

"Yes," she said. "Just up the road from where we're going."

"But there are other forms of art besides painting. Sculpture. Drawing. Did you try any of that?"

"Only in school." She gazed out the window again, in the direction of the river, but the cloud in her eyes suggested she was looking much farther than that. "It was more than just not being able to paint," she said. "I painted, but I couldn't say anything with it. I drew, but I couldn't say anything with that, either. The result just never had meaning."

"But you could write."

"Yes." She looked over at him. "I could always write, and I could write about the things I tried to paint with much greater clarity, with a much more authentic voice, than I could ever get onto the canvas."

"So, how did you make the change? What pushed you out of the studio?"

"I kept a journal about what I was doing and one day I read some of my entries. That's when I realized I was a much better writer than artist. So, I began writing about art and artists, instead of painting. Created a few essays. Showed them around. Magazine editors liked what I did and after a few articles I wrote a book. And that—"

"You've written a book?" His eyes were wide and he spoke with genuine enthusiasm.

"Yes." She smiled at his reaction. "I wrote one and have another in progress."

"A book that was published."

"Yes." Her smile broadened. "That was the point."

"Wow. I didn't know that."

"The articles and that first book got me noticed by editors at the paper. They offered me a job and I took it."

Long before they reached that point in the conversation, the look in Gina's eyes and the curious nature of her smile had captured his attention. Her hair caught his eye, too, and that drew his attention to the smooth skin of her neck. He knew better than to think of those things and did his best to avoid it. Diverted his eyes to the food on his plate. The typeface on the menu. The birds floating on the water outside the window. Anything to distract his mind from her and from the guilt he felt every time his mind wandered. He was married. Zoë was waiting in South Carolina. He shouldn't allow himself to think like that. But sometimes, he found it impossible to avoid and this was one of those times.

After lunch, Frazer and Gina continued eastward, driving along the lower shore of Great Peconic Bay. On the far side of East Hampton, they turned left onto Old Stone Highway, catching it at the southern end, then proceeding north. Just past St. Peter's Chapel, Frazer caught sight of the house number. "There," he said, pointing.

"Where?" Gina looked bewildered. "I don't see it."

"On that mailbox."

"Which one?"

"The gray one with a splash of red."

The mailbox sat atop a post, just beyond the entrance to a gravel driveway. Frazer slowed the car, then made the turn. He lifted his foot from the pedal and let the car idle to a stop beside a white two-story wood frame house that sat back from the road in the middle of a one-acre lot. The house had clapboard siding and a porch on three sides.

Beyond the end of the drive were two buildings. One directly behind the house and the other at the end of the gravel. Past them was an overgrown fence and beyond the fence, between the trees of a wooded grove, Frazer caught a glimpse of sunlight shimmering off the surface of Napeague Bay.

Nearer the house, a large oak stood at the front, its branches bare from the long winter. Two more were in back, the trunks blocked from view by the house, but the branches towered over it nonetheless. Frazer watched a moment as they swayed against a brilliantly blue late-winter sky.

Gina looked around. "Is he renting this?"

"I don't know, but I doubt it."

"Me, too. I don't think he could afford it. I couldn't."

As Frazer and Gina came from the car, a door opened on the side of the building at the end of the drive and Slater appeared. He was dressed in blue jeans and a white t-shirt over which was draped an apron that had splatters of paint down the front.

It took a moment for Slater to recognize them but when he did, he called to them. "Glad you made it."

Frazer grinned. "That building is your studio?"

"Yes."

Frazer introduced Gina, then Slater took them into the studio. "I saw the article about Hasan Izmir," he said as he closed the door behind them. "You mentioned the show but there wasn't much in there about me. I'd kinda hoped for more. Sibel did, too."

Gina spoke up. "We're doing another one that will dig a little deeper."

"That's why we've come to see you," Frazer added.

"And here I thought you'd come for the art," Slater quipped. He gestured to several canvases hanging on the wall opposite the door. "These are my latest works in progress."

A canvas lay across the center of the room, occupying most of the floor. Gina made her way around it and examined the cavasses on the wall. As she did, Frazer asked, "What do you know about the Izmirs?"

"Not much. He and his wife sell art. Most of it seems to come from Europe, other than mine and a few others. A lot of it is from France. Second tier stuff."

"Are they selling much of yours?"

"Yeah." Slater seemed self-conscious. His eyes darted away. "One or two a month, which is way better than I was doing before."

"You were with Raymond Wyatt?"

"I worked there, just doing odd jobs, and convinced them to take me on."

"So, how did you get in at Galerie Le Meilleur."

"Well." Slater grinned. "I'm a good artist."

"No one's doubting that," Gina said. "But most people can't just walk up to a gallery and say, do a show for me. They're brought in by someone else. Who brought you in?"

"Charlotte Snider."

Gina knew that but feigned a look of surprise. "How'd you meet her?"

"She was at my last show with Raymond Wyatt. The art didn't sell very well that night and Wyatt threw me out. The discussion got pretty loud. Charlotte heard us talking and came to see me later."

Frazer had a questioning look. "Came to see you?"

"At my apartment."

"Why?"

"Said she got some of her best artists from the ones Wyatt threw out of his gallery." Slater gestured broadly. "This is her place."

"She lets you stay here?"

"Yeah."

"You're from Montana," Gina said. "How'd you get interested in art instead of ranching?"

"My father asks the same question."

"He has a ranch?"

"Yes."

"You didn't want to do that?"

"I guess art is something I was born with. When we used to work on the ranch, everyone else saw cows and wide-open spaces. I saw shapes and colors. The way the light reflects off the mountains at sunset. The way it looks on the water in the pond in the morning at dawn. How the light rays shoot up from behind a cloud."

"Interesting education."

"Yes, it was."

Frazer spoke up. "How well do you get along with Hasan Izmir?"

Slater shrugged. "All right, I guess. I don't see him much. Most of my contact is with Sibel."

"You get along with her?"

"Yeah." Slater nodded quickly. "Sibel is nice."

Frazer showed him a picture of Marcel. "Have you ever seen this guy?"

Slater glanced at the photo. "I saw him the night of the show. He was at the gallery. Never talked to him. Didn't stay long. Hasan seemed to know who he was. They left together."

Frazer showed him a picture of the Matisse. "Have you ever seen this painting?"

"*Woman With Table and Vase*." Slater spoke with an admiring tone. "I've never seen it. Read an article about it once. Stolen by the Nazis during World War II. Some people say it was destroyed in a fire near the end of the war. I'm not sure it still exists." He handed the photo back to Frazer. "Why do you ask?"

"You've never seen it at Galerie Le Meilleur?"

"No." Slater looked surprised. "Was it there?"

"That's one of the things we're trying to confirm."

They talked about the art in the studio, then Slater led them to the house, and they went inside. Frazer liked the house but was bewildered by the art. To him, it was only swirls and lines and colors, with no meaning or connection. Except for two that caught his eye in the back hallway. He stared at them while Gina took over the interview. Something about them—the colors, the flow of the lines perhaps—reminded him of the beach at Oxnard. He'd spent a summer up there when he was seventeen. One of those summers. When everything was great, and it all clicked in place.

After a while, Frazer heard Gina and Slater talking and found them in the kitchen, standing near a door that led to the porch. As he entered the room, he noticed a sweater that was draped over the back of a chair. Slater caught the look in his eye. "Sibel left that," he said. "The last time she came out."

"She's been out here to see you?" Frazer asked.

"Yes."

"How often?"

Slater shrugged. "A few times."

"More than once?"

"Yeah. I suppose. What difference does it make?"

"More than three?"

Slater frowned. "I don't know. Why do you care?" He had a defensive tone.

Frazer had a knowing smile. "You two are ... involved?"

Slater's cheeks turned noticeably pink. "Look, I don't know what you're trying to imply but—"

"She has been known to become romantically involved with her young artists."

Slater shoved his hands in his pockets. "I've heard those stories, but this isn't that."

"What is it?"

"I don't know what it is, but it's not that."

The afternoon was getting late and the mood was tense. Gina gave Frazer a nod indicating it was time for them to go. She opened the door to emphasize the point and stepped out to the porch.

"I'm not trying to be difficult," Frazer said. "I'm just trying to understand the situation."

"I thought you were writing an article about my art, not my love life."

"I am, but I like to understand the full picture before I write."

They shook hands and Frazer followed Gina to the car. As Frazer steered the car from the driveway onto the road, he glanced over at her. "Any doubt about whether they're having an affair?"

"Never a question in my mind, but if that's all we came here for, we wasted our time."

"You think we wasted our time?"

"He talked a lot but I'm not sure we ever got much out of him. If we're writing a bigger story, it was a long way out here just to look at his art."

"He told us about Charlotte Snider," Frazer said. "That's something we didn't know before."

"And now I suppose you'll want to talk to her."

"Do you know where she lives?"

"Yeah," Gina said with a nod. "I've been to her apartment a couple of times." She slid low in the seat and closed her eyes. "I'll call her and find out if we can see her."

Chapter 27

While Frazer and Gina talked with Truman Slater at the house on Long Island, researchers at the FBI office in Manhattan met with Scott Davenport and reported the results of their work in the hotel reservation database. Derek Lancaster, who was in charge of the research team, led the discussion. "We began with the domestic database and found four people in the US with hotel reservations under the name Marcel Kirchen. A worldwide search—"

"Four people?" Davenport interrupted.

"Yes."

"With the same name?"

"We were surprised, too," Lancaster said.

"That's an unusual name," Davenport continued. "I didn't think there would be even two in the entire country. What are the odds there are four?"

Olivia Freeland, a member of Lancaster's staff, spoke up. "They could be the same person."

Davenport scowled. "All four of them?"

"Yes," Freeland replied. "Most online reservation systems allow a person to make multiple reservations. Under the same name and even for the same nights."

Davenport looked back at Lancaster. "You couldn't distinguish their identities from the reservation details?"

"It's possible," Lancaster replied. "But we had a lot of data to

THE ART DEALER'S WIFE

sort through. Getting deep enough into the files to confirm their identities would take a while. We thought you wanted a quick and dirty result."

"Yes," Davenport said. "Quick and dirty is a start."

"Where are these reservations? What city?"

"One in Detroit. One in Jacksonville, Florida. And two here in the city."

Davenport's mouth fell open. "Two?"

"Yes."

"Right here in the city."

Lancaster smiled. "Right here in Manhattan."

"And they are in the hotel now? Today?"

Lancaster nodded. "Both of them have checked in. Can't say if they are physically present at this moment, but both have checked in. One for a two-day stay. The other is booked for four."

"What hotels?"

"One is registered at the Biltmore Hotel on Madison Avenue. The other is at the Commodore on Forty-Second Street."

Davenport was startled. "You're sure of this?"

"That's what the system says."

"I only ask because they are about to get a visit."

"I understand."

"We need to move on this." Davenport stood abruptly and turned toward the door to leave the room.

Lancaster called after him. "Do you want us to continue our search?"

Davenport paused with a hand on the doorknob. "No," he said. "But give me something with the address and room number for both locations."

Lancaster handed him a printout. "This has the information on it," he said.

Davenport glanced at the document, then stepped into the hallway. "Good work," he called. "Email me this file."

❖ ❖ ❖

Document in hand, Davenport bounded up the stairs to the next floor and hurried toward Cooper's office. An assistant seated out front stopped them. "He's in a meeting," she said.

"This can't wait."

"Don't—"

Davenport ignored her and opened the door. Cooper was startled by his sudden appearance. "We're in the middle of something."

Davenport glanced to the right and saw three people sitting in the office. "This can't wait," he said.

Cooper excused himself from the meeting and followed Davenport into the hall. "This better be good," he said.

"Two people are registered at Manhattan hotels under the name Marcel Kirchen."

Cooper frowned. "You're kidding me."

"Not at all." Davenport handed him the printout. "One at the Biltmore, the other at the Commodore."

Cooper scanned over the printout, then handed it back to Davenport. "Assemble two teams. Alert SWAT. Get the mobile command unit ready. We'll need to hit both locations at the same time."

"Are you going with us?"

"Yes," Cooper replied. "I'll need a few minutes to get out of this meeting, but I'll join you downstairs."

"Which hotel do you want?"

"I'll take the Biltmore," Cooper replied. "Get moving." He turned back to the office, then paused. "Make sure everyone knows we need Kirchen alive."

While Cooper and Davenport prepared their teams for the hotel operation, Susan Griffin, a member of the FBI research staff, placed her iPad in an oversized purse and stepped away from her desk for a break. Rather than remaining in the building, as was the normal routine, she took the elevator downstairs, crossed the lobby to the street, and walked up the block to the Starbucks café.

Using the iPad and the café's Wi-Fi service, Griffin logged into the email account she used before and created a new email. This one read, "They have Marcel's file and picture and are searching for him to detain him on the French warrant. They are closing on his hotel location." She saved the message in the drafts file and exited the program, then she used her smart phone to send a text message to the phone number she obtained from Bradley Monzikova. The text read, "Email." Then, to make certain they understood the urgency of the moment, she added, "Hotel room is hot."

After sending the message, Griffin ordered a latte and took a seat at a table by the window. She sipped coffee and gazed at the pedestrians on the sidewalk outside. Gradually, individual faces faded from view, becoming a stream of people flowing by her position. Her eyes remained on the street, but her mind was on the operation, the things she knew from the FBI's files, and the risk she was taking by divulging that information.

How long would Mogilevich require her to do this? Would he ever release her? And how long could she continue to tip him to FBI activity without getting caught? The FBI had some of the most sophisticated surveillance technology in the world. Proprietary software developed solely for the purpose of discovering activity just like hers. Perhaps not quite as thorough as the NSA, but better than most and they were not above turning it on their own employees. In fact, scrutiny of FBI employees was one of the bureau's largest internal programs.

No sooner had she thought that than she remembered her own situation. Money from Mogilevich had all but retired her student debt with plenty left over in her budget to afford the things she enjoyed. Clothes. Movies. Meals at nice restaurants. Even a trip to Los Angeles. She had been careful. She had avoided buying big-ticket items. No new apartment. No car. Nothing that would attract attention. But the extra money was addictive. The luxury it afforded. The ease of lifestyle. That was something she didn't want to do without and right then, leaking information to Mogilevich was her only means of obtaining those things. Without his money, she would be back to scrimping from paycheck to paycheck, barely getting by.

Doing it was bad. She recognized that. A breach of her contract. A breach of the oath they made her sign when she accepted the job. Made her sign it two or three times in the process. But it wasn't like she was betraying state secrets. The FBI wasn't the military. She wasn't giving away launch codes or troop positions or selling guns from the national stockpile. Nothing she disclosed to Mogilevich put anyone's life in danger. There was no risk to anyone. Just one friend telling another friend about her day ... sort of.

While Griffin was at the coffee shop, Cooper arrived on a side street near the Biltmore Hotel. He parked the car at the curb and walked to the corner where an FBI mobile command center was parked alongside the hotel. As discreetly as possible, he opened the rear door and stepped inside.

A technician, who was seated at a console to the left, glanced in his direction. "Everyone is in place, sir."

"Good." Cooper put on a headset and gave the order. "Okay," he said. "We need him alive." He ran through a final checklist with his agents, then gave the order and set the operation in motion. Instantly, the team took control of the hotel exits, sealing the occupants inside.

Once they were in place and the access points were secured, two agents approached the front desk, explained the situation to the manager, and asked for assistance in entering the room rented to Marcel Kirchen. After an argument that cost the agents valuable time, the clerk agreed to help.

When they arrived outside Kirchen's room, the agents were joined by members of an FBI SWAT team that entered from the kitchen and rode to the floor in a service elevator. They assembled outside Kirchen's hotel room and waited while the clerk opened the door, then they pushed aside the clerk and rushed inside.

Cooper listened from the command unit as the team filled the hotel room. He heard their excited voices. The clatter of armed men taking control. Then an agent said, "The room is secure but the suspect is not here."

"Any indication it's the guy we want?"

"Not sure. The name matches hotel records, but we haven't confirmed his identity yet."

"Get someone on that right away."

"Copy that."

"Anything of note in the room?"

"We have a laptop and his personal effects," the agent said.

"Bag everything," Cooper said. "And get a crime scene unit in there to process the site."

"If we take anything, he'll know we were here."

At that point, Cooper realized any hope of anonymity was lost. The only option was to get whatever they could from the room and move on. "We'll sit on the hotel entrances," Cooper said. "Maybe we can grab him when he arrives. Before he realizes we've been there."

"Very well."

"Process the scene and make sure you bring that laptop back with you. I want our technical staff to examine it today."

A few blocks away, Davenport led the second team of agents into the Commodore Hotel in a raid much like the one conducted at the Biltmore. When the room was secured, Davenport reported to the mobile command center. "We found a man in here," he said. "His ID shows him as Marcel Kirchen, but he doesn't fit the description we received from Paris."

"Bring him in anyway," Cooper replied. "I'll meet you at the office. We need to talk to him."

Once the scenes of both raids were secured, Cooper placed control of the details in the hands of agents on the scene and drove back to the office. When he arrived, Davenport was waiting for him.

"We have our guy from the hotel in an interview room," Davenport said.

"Have you to talked to him?"

Davenport nodded. "He says he's a stockbroker from Milwaukee, returning from a trip to China. He stopped over in the city to spend a few days at his employer's headquarters."

"Does anyone there vouch for him?"

"Yeah. People at the office confirm what he told us. And he has a stack of receipts from Beijing, Shanghai, and two or three other places."

"Did you check his passport?"

Davenport handed him the passport. Cooper flipped through the pages. "He was in China when the murder in Paris occurred."

Davenport shrugged. "Looks that way."

Cooper gave him the passport. "Let him go."

"Are you sure?"

"He's not the guy." Cooper turned to leave the room. "Let him go. We'll have to find Kirchen another way. Maybe he'll show up at the Biltmore tonight."

An hour later, Marcel Kirchen approached the Biltmore Hotel from a side street. Half a block from the corner, he felt the phone in his pocket vibrate. He glanced at the screen and saw a message that read, "FBI." He returned the phone to his pocket and scanned the street up ahead, all the way to the corner.

A man sat on a bench at the bus stop. Another stood on the opposite side of the street, waiting for the traffic signal to change. A large gray van was parked alongside the hotel. It had dual tires on the back and opaque windows in the rear doors. He couldn't be certain, but it appeared to be a command center like several he'd encountered in the past.

Rather than risk being swept up in something, Kirchen turned away and walked calmly in the opposite direction. Two blocks later, he ducked into a café and took a seat near the back. Using his smartphone, he logged into the same email account used by Susan Griffin and saw a new message had been saved in the draft file. He read it, then added a message in response asking for assistance. When the message was complete, he saved the email and bought a cup of coffee. He returned to the table with it and sipped from the cup while he waited.

A few minutes later, Kirchen checked the email account again and saw a new message had been added. This one contained an address for an apartment in Brooklyn. He took the coffee with him, left the café, and walked up the street toward the nearest subway station. As he made his way in that direction, he tossed the cup in a garbage can, then began disassembling the phone. The battery went in the next trashcan, the case in the one after that. As he started down the steps to the subway platform, only the SIM card remained. He placed it in his pocket, passed through the turnstile, and boarded a train to Brooklyn.

Thirty minutes later, he arrived at an apartment building on Bay Parkway in Bensonhurst, a Brooklyn neighborhood known for its ethnic enclaves. This one was home to a large Chinese community. Kirchen climbed the steps to the second floor and made his way to an apartment that overlooked the street on the front side. He felt along the ledge above the door for a key, found it, and went inside.

In the bathroom, he took the SIM card from his pocket, broke it in half, and flushed the pieces down the toilet. He flushed the toilet twice, just to be sure the pieces were gone, then went to the kitchen and found a six-pack of beer in the refrigerator. He opened one and sipped it while he walked to the living room. There, he flopped onto the sofa, turned on the television, and surfed the channels, hoping to find a newscast that might indicate the nature of whatever was happening at the hotel.

In Chisinau, Gennady Krylov made the drive up to Mogilevich's house for yet another meeting about Kirchen. They had met many times to discuss him and each time Mogilevich had decided at the last moment to give him a reprieve. This time Krylov hoped things would turn out differently. This time, he hoped, Mogilevich would give the order to end the son-of-a-bitch and let him carry it out.

They sat opposite each other in the room with the large windows and commanding view of the city. Krylov would have enjoyed the view, and a stout drink, but he had business to attend to first. "We received a message from our contact in New York," Krylov said. "The FBI knows about the French warrant and they are searching for Kirchen to detain him on it."

"Do they know where he is?"

"Yes," Krylov said. "They are in his hotel room right now. Even as we speak."

Mogilevich looked concerned. "Did they capture him?"

"No." Krylov shook his head. "We received the message in time to warn him. He is at the safe house."

"He should have been there all along."

"We tried to tell him."

"I suppose he insisted on having his freedom."

Krylov shrugged. "He likes his women."

"How did the FBI find him? Something must have set them off. What pointed them toward him?"

"I don't know for certain but look at this." Krylov showed him Gina Wilkin's article in *The New York Times* about the Izmirs. Mogilevich glanced at it and shook his head in disgust. "If not the FBI, then the reporters." He tossed the paper on the table. "These arts people leave a trail even the idiots can follow."

"It's the wife," Krylov said. "She's the one who wanted the article."

Mogilevich frowned. "She knows the nature of our business, yes?"

"Yes."

"You are certain someone explained it to her?"

"Yes."

"Then what was she doing talking to a reporter?" Mogilevich's voice was loud and he gestured in anger with both hands. "Is she stupid? Is she insane? I thought she was supposed to be the smart one."

"She thought it would be good for their business. And, she met an artist."

Mogilevich rolled his eyes. "That again?"

"I'm afraid so."

"Are they having an affair?"

Krylov held up his smartphone as if offering it to Mogilevich. "Would you like to hear her in the act?"

"No." Mogilevich had an anguished look and he shook his head vigorously. "Having sex is one thing. Listening to someone else have sex is not good."

Krylov smiled. "I agree."

Mogilevich stared out the window a moment, then said, "Does the husband know about this? This business between his wife and the artist? Does the husband know?"

"I don't think so. He's too busy with the young girls to notice."

Mogilevich's forehead wrinkled in a frown. "Young girls?"

"Yes."

"How young?"

"Very young."

"Teenagers?"

Krylov shrugged. "Some of them."

Mogilevich looked over at him. "Younger?"

"Occasionally."

"Where does he get them?"

Krylov answered with a knowing look.

Mogilevich's eyes opened wide. "Kirchen?"

"Yes."

"Damn it." Mogilevich face turned red and the veins in his neck throbbed. He trafficked in women. Sold them into the sex trade. In Europe. In the US. Anywhere they wanted women, he would supply them. But even he had limits, and this was one of them. No minors. "How many times have I said, 'No teenagers.'" He glared at Krylov as if awaiting a response. Krylov knew better than to speak. "You

bang a broad," Mogilevich continued, "you might get an angry husband, but that kind of anger is directed at her, not you. But if you
bang a minor, you're banging somebody's kid and the anger for that
comes right back to you. And when it comes to one of you guys, it
causes me trouble. How many times have I explained that?"

Krylov raised his hands in a defensive posture. "Don't look at
me. I stick to women my own age."

Mogilevich insisted. "How many times?"

"Many times."

"Damn right. Many times, I have explained it. Many times to
Kirchen. No minors." Mogilevich turned back to the window. He
stood with his feet apart and his arms folded across his chest which
heaved now from the shouting and gesturing. After a moment he
said, in a low voice, "We should have ended our relationship with
Kirchen after that trouble in Venice."

Krylov felt elated. "I couldn't agree more," he said.

"Get over there." Mogilevich sighed. "Find Kirchen and clean
up this mess."

"Yes, sir." Krylov was relieved to receive the order. He'd wanted
to take out Kirchen for months. Almost did it on his own when they
were in Paris.

"I can't believe I get myself into these situations," Mogilevich
muttered. "He kills and now we have to kill to straighten things out."
He looked over at Krylov again. "Take care of it."

"Yes, sir. Our usual people?"

"No." Mogilevich shook his head. "Bring in some fresh faces.
All of the old ones know Kirchen too well. And he knows them. Use
your discretion. Only get it done."

"Very well." Krylov stood. "I'll leave right away."

"Just make sure this is tied off tightly. Neatly. Cleanly. I want as
few loose ends as possible."

"Yes, sir."

Krylov turned to leave but Mogilevich called after him. "And
make sure you retrieve my artwork."

Krylov paused, a puzzled look on his face. "Artwork?"

"I want that Matisse. It's costing me a bundle now. I might as well have it hanging in my house. And all the others, too."

"The others?"

"We did business before the Izmirs. We'll do business after them."

Chapter 28

Saturday morning, Frazer was at the office early. He came there under the guise of working on the article—that's what he told himself when he took a shower and dressed and he repeated it to himself again while he waited at the shop on the corner for an extra-large coffee. And he said it as he walked the rest of the way to the office and while he rode the elevator up from the lobby. Said it in his mind, though not out loud. "Going to the office to work on the article. That's all. That's what I'm doing. The article."

But inside he knew the real motivation had nothing to do with the article or work or anything else. The real motivation for getting out of bed early on Saturday and coming to the office was the possibility that he might see Gina. She wasn't known at the paper for being one of the regular Saturday morning crowd. That moniker was reserved for young reporters and a few committed veterans. But sometimes she made an appearance and Frazer hoped that morning would be one of those occasions.

When the elevator doors opened, he expected to see only a few people scattered about the floor. The usuals. Hammond at the station near the stairwell—she even came in on Sundays. Davies, who sat at a desk in the corner to the left, was often there. As was Conrad Barber, whose cubicle was the only one with anything protruding above the divider. Frazer was surprised to find the place alive with reporters scurrying about, calling to each other from across the room, shouting into their phones, and otherwise consumed by frenetic activity. He looked over at Hammond. "What's going on?"

"FBI raid yesterday," Hammond said.

"I heard something about it on the news last night. Why all the attention?"

Hammond shrugged. "Nothing else happening this weekend, I guess."

"Must be more to it than that."

"Somebody has a source who indicates there's a Russian mob angle. Something about a stockbroker and questionable transactions. Maybe connections to the White House. I don't know." Hammond gestured to the room. "They seem excited about it."

Frazer continued to his desk, logged onto the system, and checked his email, then made the rounds in an effort to find out what was going on. Twenty minutes later, he was back at his desk knowing nothing more than what Hammond had told him when he arrived. He took out his notes from the interviews he and Gina had conducted and began sorting through them, incorporating ideas and references into the article he'd begun earlier in the week.

Trolling the office had taken his mind off Gina for a moment and he thought of Zoë. They had exchanged text messages earlier in the day and talked by phone before he left the apartment, but as he worked deeper into the interview notes, he heard Gina's voice speaking to him from the interviews. The way she talked. The tone of her voice. The cadence of her speech. Before long, thoughts of Zoë had vanished, and his mind held only images of Gina. Her eyes. Her smile ... the shape of her buttocks ... the—

Just then, a familiar voice spoke to him. "Don't you have a life?" At first, he thought it was only his imagination and for an instant he wondered if he should get up, move around again, go for a walk, find out more about the story everyone seemed to be working on, to get his mind on something else. Then he caught a scent in the air and looked up to see Gina standing just a few feet away. He smiled at her. "Fancy seeing you here on a Saturday." It was a cliché, but it was the best he could do right then. He couldn't really tell her the things he'd been thinking.

She took a seat in the chair beside the desk. "You spend too much time here."

"And look who's talking," he replied. "You're here."

"It's Saturday."

"What of it?"

"You have a wife. Isn't this a day most people spend with their family?"

He had a questioning look. "Why do you keep asking me about that?"

"I don't keep asking you."

"You asked me the same thing yesterday."

"Well, if I do ask, it's because you spend a lot of time at the office."

"That's what she said."

"Who?"

"Zoë."

"Your wife?"

"Yes."

"And what is she saying this morning?"

When he didn't answer immediately, Gina gave him a look. "Jack. What's going on?"

Finally, he said, "She left a few weeks ago."

"Left?"

"Went to her mother's house in South Carolina."

Her shoulders sagged. "I'm sorry."

"Me, too."

"You should go see her. Bring her back."

He shook his head. "I don't think she wants to be brought back."

"I'm thinking she probably does."

"Not to New York."

"Oh. The city was too much?"

"Something like that."

"All the more reason to go see her."

"If I go down there, she'll want me to take a job in Charleston and stay."

"And you don't want to do that?"

"There's not much to write about down there."

"But she's your wife. Isn't she more important than your job?"

"I suppose."

Gina had a disapproving look. "You suppose?"

"Well, I don't mean it like that, exactly."

Her look deepened. "Exactly?"

"What I do is more than a job. At least, it is to me. This is who I am."

She leaned back in the chair. "Then you've got worse problems than just your marriage."

"What's that supposed to mean?"

"If your values are tied up in this job," Gina said. "If this is your identity and the most important thing in your life, you've got a wrong view of life."

"Maybe so." He wanted to change the subject. "Are you married?"

"No," she said, and her eyes darted away as if she had something to hide.

"Why not?"

"We wanted to at first, but it wasn't legal back then, so we put it off. And now we don't really need it."

At first, he didn't understand, and a frown wrinkled his forehead. "Wasn't legal? What are you talking about?"

She gave him a knowing look. He thought for a moment and when it dawned on him what she meant, his jaw dropped and his eyes widened. "You're kidding?"

"No," she said. "I'm not."

"You're just saying that," he scoffed.

"Why would I say it if it wasn't true?"

"Because we had a good time together yesterday," he smirked. "And you think I'm interested in you and you're afraid I might be thinking about not going back with my wife so I can keep seeing you."

She smiled. "We did have a good time yesterday."

"Yes, we did."

"But that's not it. I'm in a relationship with a wonderful woman and not interested in a man so let's leave it at that." She stood to leave. "I'm going home. You should, too."

He sat up straight. "But you just got here."

"I've been here a while. I only came down here to see if you were here."

"For what?"

"To tell you that I talked to Charlotte Snider. We can see her Monday."

"Why not now?" He didn't want her to go. Not yet. "We could get a taxi."

"She's not that kind of person."

He was puzzled. "Not what kind of person?"

"Not the kind you can just show up and interview. We'll see her Monday morning." She turned again to leave and he called after her. "Wait a minute," he said. "I'll ride down in the elevator with you."

Frazer logged out of the system, gathered his things, and came from his chair at the desk. They walked together to the elevator, then started down to the lobby. Alone for the ride, he looked over at her. "So, all this time, you've been living with your partner and I didn't know it?"

"Imagine that," she snarked. "Just like normal people."

"I didn't mean it like that."

"How did you mean it?"

"I'm just surprised. That's all."

"Surprised? Now you think I'm going to hell?"

"I didn't mean it like that."

"Then like what?"

"I don't know. You see someone. You think you know them. Then you find out you don't. That's all. It was about me. Not about you."

"You don't have an opinion?"

"You can live with whomever you want to. I was just surprised."

THE ART DEALER'S WIFE

She grinned. "You liked me yesterday. Do you still like me today?"

"Yeah," he said, suddenly self-conscious.

"But not like that."

"Like what?"

"Yesterday, you liked me as a woman. Today, you like me as a colleague."

"More than a colleague."

"Like a sister."

He made a sour face. "No." He shook his head. "Not a sister."

She laughed. "Why the look? Bad experience with a sister?"

"No. It's just a sister is someone—"

"You have no hope of going further with." The elevator came to a stop and the bell rang as the doors opened to the lobby. "Saved by the bell," she said. "Literally."

They crossed the lobby together and stepped out to the sidewalk. "Look," he said. "Do you want to have lunch?"

"Maybe Monday," she said. "After we talk to Charlotte."

Gina started down the street and he watched until she disappeared in a cluster of pedestrians at the corner, then he turned in the opposite direction and started toward the apartment. And just like that, thoughts of being with her evaporated. When he tried to think of her again, there was nothing. No meaning. No significance. Only the malaise of a void where the fantasies had been. But the void demanded filling and before he reached the next corner an overwhelming sense of guilt rushed in to fill it.

Since lunch the day before, at the restaurant, he'd been thinking of her. Thinking of far more than just the sound of her voice or the look in her eye, and the realization of what that meant landed on him like a heavy weight, pressing against him from all sides. How could he have been so stupid? So disloyal. So naïve. His cheeks warmed with a sense of embarrassment. The lobes of his ears grew hot just thinking about how he had deceived himself.

Zoë was everything he'd ever wanted in a woman and being married to her was the greatest thing that ever happened to him. He knew it. He'd always known it. And he'd never once entertained the notion of leaving her. Not actually. But with her gone and him with Gina all day on Long Island, he had come to the edge. To the brink. At least to a place where he could see the edge. To a place where he could entertain the notion.

And now he knew there was nothing for him on the other side. In the course of a single conversation, it had all been snatched away. Hours and hours of dreaming. Hours and hours of wondering. Then with a snap, it was gone.

Whatever meaning and significance he had in life, it wasn't with Gina or anyone else. It was with Zoë. Beautiful, wonderful Zoë. The love of his life. The point of his life. The source of everything important to him was bound up in her. He'd known it before. Years before. When they were first together. But he'd forgotten it until right then. That very moment. How did it come to this? To thinking of someone else. Of entertaining even so much as a thought that anyone could replace her.

By the time he reached Forty-Fifth Street he had worked over the feelings of guilt and moved on in his mind, combing through all the usual topics for something to break the malaise. To restore the sense of purpose, meaning, significance. To put the spring back in his step. He thought of the article he and Gina were trying to write. About the Izmirs and their gallery business. The art. The Matisse. Edelman. And Slater. But did it mean anything? Or was it just one more article? Columns of words to fill the space on a newspaper page. Content for a website. A blog.

Seemingly from nowhere, snippets of his conversation with Gina from the day before flitted through his mind. Hunter Thompson's book *Fear and Loathing in Las Vegas*. Yes. Hunter Thompson. That started it. Then David Halberstam and the Vietnam War. The Nixon era. Those were the days. When stories mattered. He wanted to write stories that mattered, too. Stories on topics that mattered, with a perspective that mattered. He wanted to see through the clutter and spin to get to the heart of the issue. To avoid being duped by one side or the other.

As he crossed Fiftieth Street, he realized he was going the wrong way but he kept on walking and at Fifty-Ninth Street he came to Central Park. He took a seat on a bench near the park entrance and remembered how much Zoë enjoyed sitting there, watching the world go by. Zoë. The thought of her made him smile.

He remembered the first time he saw her. The touch of her hand against his. The smell of her hair, her neck. Her lips against his. The guilt he'd felt before was gone, replaced by sadness, and sadness quickly became longing. For the first time since she left, he genuinely missed her and wanted her beside him. To see her. To hear her voice. He reached in his pocket for his cell phone.

Chapter 29

Monday morning, Frazer and Gina visited Charlotte Snider at her apartment. They began with questions about Sibel and Hasan Izmir.

Charlotte appeared cautious. "Why do you think I know anything about them?"

"I attended Slater's showing at Galerie Le Meilleur," Frazer said. "You were there."

Gina spoke up. "Truman Slater says you convinced the gallery to take him as a client."

Charlotte looked over at Gina. "You've talked to Slater?"

"Yes."

Frazer spoke up. "And we know that you didn't just cold call the gallery about him. You know them or you wouldn't have taken Slater to them."

Charlotte nodded. "I know Sibel. Why are you interested in her and Hasan?"

"I've seen them at an auction," Frazer replied. "They're rather unconventional in their approach."

"They're colorful," Gina added. "Seemed like there might be a good story in it."

"Your paper has done articles about them before," Charlotte said. "This is something different." She gave them a curious look. Then her eyes brightened, and she turned to Frazer. "You're friends with David Anders. I've seen you around."

"Yes." He had a sheepish look. "I know him."

"He gave you that 'they're doing something illegal' routine."

Frazer was surprised she knew Anders well enough to make that comment. "Are they? Doing something illegal?"

Charlotte shrugged her shoulders. "I don't know and neither does Anders. But I do know why he's angry."

"Why's that?"

"Because Hasan outbid him on a Pierre Bonnard painting at an auction last year. Anders has been angry about it ever since."

"Pierre Bonnard?"

"French Symbolist," Gina offered. "But I'm wondering why someone would get mad over being outbid on a Bonnard. They come up for sale quite often."

"It wasn't the Bonnard itself. You know how it is. People keep score. Who's up. Who's down. Who got outbid. Who couldn't keep going. And, probably the significant thing for Anders, people notice the point at which a bidder is forced to drop out."

"They saw him as financially weak."

"Or so he thinks." Charlotte folded her arms across her chest. "Hasan pays outrageous prices for art sometimes and he sometimes buys things just because he can. I've seen him bid the price way over market and drop out just to leave someone holding it at a ridiculous price. That kind of thing makes people mad, but he has the money to pay. And he pays when he's the one caught by his own game."

"So, it's not fraudulent or illegal?" Frazer asked.

Charlotte shook her head. "Just infuriatingly arrogant."

"Is that what happened with Anders?"

"Yes. And Anders has been looking for a way to get back ever since."

Gina spoke up. "Sibel says she discovered Slater."

"Yes. I suppose. Among the gallery owners." Charlotte had a sly smile. "But that has a double meaning for her."

Frazer understood. "You think she's having an affair with Slater?"

"I'm sure you've heard others talk about her relationship with young artists."

"And you think that's what she's doing with Slater?"

"I try not to mind other people's business."

"Do you think that would damage Slater's career if he was?"

"If she was having an affair with him?"

"Yes."

Charlotte smiled. "No one really cares about that except who-ever represents him next."

"So," Gina said, "you found him and took him to Sibel?"

"Yes."

"How did that happen?"

"He did a show with Raymond Wyatt. Actually, did several, but his art didn't sell well. None of it sold at the last show. Wyatt told him to find another place. I thought Slater's work was incomplete but good. He seemed like a guy with potential, so I gave him the use of my house on Long Island. Convinced Sibel to take a look at his work. She liked what she saw. Gave him a show. She's been working with him since."

"She seemed rather enthusiastic about him."

"Yeah."

Frazer was skeptical. "And you just did this out of the goodness of your heart?"

"I help people for the joy of helping them. I buy art for many reasons but always with an eye for value." She pointed to a paint-ing that was hanging on the wall. "That one over there is a Robert Capriati. I found him at the same place I found Slater."

"He was with Raymond Wyatt?"

"In the beginning. Then Wyatt ran him off and I took him to Galerie Le Meilleur. Sibel loved him."

"In more ways than one," Frazer noted.

"Like I said," Charlotte responded. "That was their business. Back then, Capriati was unknown. I bought that painting for a thou-sand dollars. Now, his work sells for seven hundred fifty to a million dollars."

Gina changed the subject. "What do you know about Jacob

Edelman?"

"Everyone knows Jacob."

"Tell us about him."

"He's a good guy. Totally obsessed with the past. I mean, the family had a terrible ordeal with the Nazis. He hasn't been able to get past it."

"Have you worked with him?"

"Only in an attempt to buy from him. He has a great art collection. He showed it to me once. I tried to get him to sell. Said he wanted to leave it to his grandchildren. Too many memories for him to part with any of it."

Frazer showed her a picture of the Matisse. "Have you ever seen this painting?"

"No. Where is it?"

"Jacob Edelman says it was included in a shipment that Galerie Le Meilleur received recently."

Charlotte demurred. "I wouldn't know about that. You'd have to ask Sibel or Hasan."

"Do you think Edelman is mistaken?"

"Jacob Edelman is one of the most well-connected private citizens you'll ever meet. He's been working on recovering his family's art for a long time and everywhere he goes he meets people and makes friends. He knows people on every continent. Influential people. People who can make things happen. And, he's as honest as anyone alive. So, if he says that painting is there, I wouldn't bet against him."

Frazer showed her a picture of Marcel. "Do you recognize this man?"

"I don't think so." She looked away. "Who is he?"

"Have you ever seen him around Galerie Le Meilleur? Perhaps with Hasan?"

"I don't think so." She avoided the picture.

"Are you sure?"

"Yes. I'm sure." Charlotte checked her watch. "Is this going to take much longer? I have an appointment."

"Is there anyone besides Sibel or Hasan who knows about the gallery's business practices?"

"The only other person down there that I know is Jamie Wright."

"Okay," Gina said. "We appreciate your time."

"Wish I could be more helpful."

Frazer and Gina left the apartment and took the elevator to the street. They were joined for the ride down by another tenant, but when they reached the lobby, Frazer said, "Why do people keep lying to us about Marcel?"

"Who lied to us?"

"She did."

"Yeah." Gina grinned. "She seemed to know more than she was saying."

"And Slater did, too."

"You saw him," Gina noted. "Notice anything about him that would make you react that way?"

"He looked like a Wise Guy."

She grinned. "You mean, mafia?"

"I mean, if you see pictures of those guys, they have a look."

"And this guy Marcel had that look?"

"Yes. I wouldn't want to provoke him."

"Then I guess that's the answer."

"What?"

"They don't want to talk about him because they don't want him to find out they talked about him."

"Because then he would be provoked."

"Right. If we're going to get something in the weekend edition, we need to get busy."

"We don't have enough for the piece I had wanted to write about the gallery."

"You mean, the piece David Anders wanted you to write about the gallery."

"But we could write about Edelman and take a swipe at them."

"Get me a draft and I'll take a look at it." She sounded skeptical. "But I'm not sure we want to just 'take a swipe at them.'"

Using information collected from their interviews, Frazer and Gina prepared an elaborate and detailed article about Jacob Edelman and his quest for the missing Matisse. The article included Edelman's account of the Nazis seizing the family art collection, his quest to locate and retrieve the missing pieces, and the murder of André Crémieux, the art dealer in Paris. It discussed the trail that led Edelman to Galerie Le Meilleur in Chelsea, his confrontation with Sibel and Hasan Izmir, and their refusal to permit him to inspect the gallery's paintings.

One of the more explosive topics was the article's discussion of supposed money laundering schemes using art, art galleries, and art auctions as conduits for moving money generated by illicit means from continent to continent. An initial installment in a proposed series, the article teased a coming report about a mysterious figure known as Marcel Kirchen, alleged to have connections to the Russian mafia. The article included a photograph of Kirchen with a credit for Sedaris and Stone.

As might be expected, publication of the article set off a media storm in the art world, replete with angry denials, blistering phone calls, and threats of legal action. Gina was upset by the negative reaction and raised the issue with Frazer. He smiled in response. "This is great."

"Great? You think all of these accusations are great?"

"Free publicity," he said.

"That whole 'any publicity is good publicity' thing is overdone. It's not always good publicity when they're telling you how bad and malicious your work is."

Frazer was unmoved. "Relax," he said. "It'll never come to anything."

"How can you be so sure?"

"Because lawsuits involve depositions. Depositions are freewheeling events with questions ranging far and wide. And it requires both sides to produce documents and disclose details no one wants to make public. If they sued us, we could find out anything we want to know."

She raised an eyebrow. "Sounds like you've had experience with it."

"A few times, but don't worry." He gave a dismissive gesture. "This will never come to that."

"Why not?"

"Because somewhere in the process, a lawyer will point out to them the full extent of the disclosure they'd be forced to make and that will be the end of it."

On Wednesday morning, David Anders had breakfast at Tom's Restaurant, a diner on Broadway near Columbia University. He was seated in a booth on the side near the street and as he ate, he re-read the article about Edelman. Before he reached the third paragraph, Tony Slidell, an art dealer, joined him and took a seat on the opposite side of the table.

"Still reading that article?" Slidell said.

"It's a good piece."

"That's the one you wanted?"

Anders took a sip of coffee. "Close," he said as he set the cup on its saucer. "Better than the other one."

"I think it had the opposite effect from what you intended."

Anders frowned. "What do you mean?"

"You were trying to put the Izmirs out of business."

"Maybe," Anders said.

"I hear the Izmirs are covered up with business."

Anders had heard the same thing from others but did his best to appear unshaken. "Who told you that?"

"Some of the guys. They say foot traffic to the gallery has doubled."

"You shouldn't believe everything you hear."

Alex Rollins, another dealer, slid onto the bench next to Slidell. He pointed to the newspaper. "Got that article memorized yet?" He leaned over to Slidell. "He's been reading it every day since it came out. Over and over. All the time."

A waitress appeared with a cup and an urn of coffee. She poured a coffee for Rollins and Slidell. When she was gone, Slidell said, "This is a serious problem for us. This could be a big deal, and not in a good way."

Rollins gave him a look. "What are you talking about?"

"If the feds go after this, they won't stop with the Izmirs. They will look into everyone. It could kill the gallery business. Maybe even the whole deal."

Anders nodded. "You think it's that big?"

"This is just the sort of thing the feds like to dig into. A full-blown investigation. Interviews. Subpoenas." Slidell tapped the paper for emphasis. "Think about it. A subpoena for all of your records for the last five years. Every check. Every invoice. Every receipt."

"Doesn't matter to me," Rollins said. "I got nothing older than three years."

"They'll want copies."

"It's all in boxes in a warehouse," Rollins replied. "They want copies, they have to pay for them."

"An investigation would be just the beginning," Slidell said. "When the federal government gets interested, it regulates, and when it regulates, it destroys."

"Well," Rollins responded. "It's our own fault. We should have done something about Hasan and his brother ourselves. A long time ago."

Anders spoke up. "Even if they investigate, I don't think it'll be that big of a deal. Cash transactions have to be reported. Even for galleries."

"Yes," Slidell said, "but that's for transactions originating in the US. The transactions they're talking about in that article didn't originate here. They originated in Europe. Existing regulations wouldn't reach that."

"It's an ingenious idea," Rollins noted. "If they're actually doing it. I don't know whether they're doing it. The article doesn't really say. It just suggests. But it's the kind of thing we should have thought of ourselves."

Lloyd Davis, another dealer, arrived. He nudged Anders and gestured for him to slide over. Anders moved his plate and newspaper down the table, to the end next to the window. Davis looked over at Rollins. "What are you blathering about today?"

Rollins scowled. "I never blather."

"We were discussing the article," Slidell offered.

"Article?" Davis looked interested. "The one about the Izmirs?"

"Rollins was telling us how we should have thought about using art as a money laundering tool."

"I did think of it," Davis replied.

"Right," Anders said. He had a skeptical tone. "You thought of it."

"I did," Davis insisted. "But I was too scared to try it. And I don't know any criminals who need to move money around like that."

"Wouldn't have to be criminals," Rollins suggested. "Anyone with money invested overseas could use it to bring their profits back here."

"I'm not sure about that." Anders enjoyed talking to them but sometimes they took things too far. "I don't think that would work. Unless you lied on your tax return. They ask about foreign income on the form."

"You could buy art in Europe," Davis suggested, "then ship the art back to the US and hold it until you needed some cash."

"I don't think you can get it through Customs without lying," Slidell noted.

"You wouldn't have to lie," Anders said.

"You could get it through without lying," Slidell conceded. "But unless you lied about the value, you'd have to pay a duty on it. I mean, assuming we're talking about real art."

"Are you sure?"

"I think I'm right on that."

"But this isn't a straight transaction. They're talking about converting hot Euros to artwork."

Davis chuckled. "Hot Euros?"

"Drug money."

"The cartels don't care about lying to Customs."

"Look," Anders explained. "The article's talking about people who use their drug money to buy art in Europe or wherever. Then send the artwork here. Galleries pay them with a check or a transfer through a legitimate bank account. That converts the drug money into legitimate deposits in legitimate accounts. That's all they want. They don't care about tax returns. When the gallery gives them a check or wire transfer for the proceeds, money from a drug dealer in Milan—cash—is suddenly in the legitimate system without any red flags."

"It's brilliant," Rollins said. "From that point of view."

"All it takes is an art dealer on the foreign side willing to accept satchels of cash for his paintings."

"We should have thought of that a long time ago."

"I did," Davis said.

Chapter 30

That night, a young woman approached Hasan Izmir at a bar in Manhattan. She leaned against him and suggested they go somewhere else. Hasan was eager, thinking she meant a back room, which was how things normally occurred. Instead, she took him by the hand and led him outside to a car behind the building.

As they approached, the driver stepped out and opened the rear door. Hasan looked inside and found Marcel Kirchen seated in back. "Get in," Kirchen ordered.

The girl disappeared as Hasan made his way to the opposite side of the car and crawled onto the back seat. As he closed the door, the car started forward. He looked around, startled and more than a little concerned. "Where are we going?" His eyes were wide and there was a note of distress in his voice.

Kirchen ignored him and showed him the newspaper. "Did you see this?" The paper was open to the article about the gallery. He gestured with it to get Hasan's attention. "Look at it. Did you read it?"

Hasan glanced at the newspaper. "That article did wonders for our business," he said. Being hustled from the bar by a woman and now seated in the car with Kirchen made him nervous. He glanced out the back window to check their location. "Where are we going?" he asked once more. And again, Kirchen ignored his concern. "This article is not doing wonders for me," he said. "How did they get my name?"

"I don't know."

"And my picture?"

Hasan pointed to the credits. "It looks like Sedaris and Stone gave it to them."

"Who is that?"

"A couple of artists we're showing at the gallery."

Kirchen's forehead wrinkled. "Those two gay guys?"

"Yes."

"I told you that part of your business was a problem."

"I know, but it couldn't be helped."

"What do you mean?"

"Sibel."

"Your wife?"

"She likes them."

Kirchen raised an eyebrow. "She likes them?"

"Not like that. They're gay, you know that. We can't very well have a gallery without having artists."

"I've tried to explain to you many times," Kirchen implored. "You don't need a gallery. We give you plenty of paintings. You can sell everything at auction."

"It doesn't work like that," Hasan replied.

"Why not?"

"Most of the art you send us won't sell at high enough prices to interest an auction house."

"I don't understand."

"I know."

"But I do understand this." Kirchen pointed to the paper. "They have a photograph of me. That is bad for everyone. People are asking too many questions that shouldn't be asked."

"We're selling lots of paintings, though."

Kirchen shook his head. "Doesn't matter. It's not good. Reporters asking questions about your business, articles in the newspaper about murders in Paris. It's not good. You must stop this."

"That's your line of work. I just sell art."

"My line of work?"

"You know. Fixing things. Isn't that what you do?"

Kirchen shook his head in disbelief. "Now you are the one who does not understand. My way is too…messy for this."

"Since when did that matter?"

"Mogilevich frowns on that sort of thing these days."

"So what are you saying?"

"I'm saying you have to get your wife under control."

"My wife?"

"Yes. Your wife."

"What's she got to do with this?"

"Look," Kirchen said. "They quote her right there." He pointed to the article again. "She talked to reporters." He pointed again. "And her boyfriend. Look right here. Truman Slater. He's quoted in the article. Did you know about him? Did you know she is having an affair with him?"

Hasan glanced at the paper. "Don't worry about that. It's not—"

"Don't worry?" Kirchen's voice was louder still. "Your wife is having sex with another man. What kind of husband lets his wife have sex with another man? People I know would end this for both of them."

"It's not a problem."

"It is a problem." Kirchen's frustration was evident. "This man. This Truman Slater. He is a liability."

"Look," Hasan said. "The gallery was Sibel's idea. Taking on young artists as clients was her idea. She's only trying to—"

"That's what I am talking about!" Kirchen shouted. "She is the key! Stop her and our troubles go away. Your troubles go away. Stop her."

"And how do I do that?"

"Explain things to her in a way she will understand."

"We don't have that kind of relationship."

"You are her husband. I am sure you can talk to her about this in a convincing manner."

Hasan shook his head. "I don't know that I can."

Kirchen sighed. "Then let me make this as plain as I know how. You can do it, or I'll have to."

Hasan's eyes widened. "Mogilevich sent you?"

"I have not heard from Mogilevich on this," Kirchen replied. "Not yet. And that is what I am trying to prevent. For both our sakes. When he speaks, it will be too late us. We must settle this matter now."

The car arrived back at the parking lot behind the bar where they began in Manhattan. As it came to a stop, Hasan reached for the door handle. "There is one more thing," Kirchen said. He looked over at Hasan and their eyes met. "Where is my painting?"

"Which one?"

"You know which one," Kirchen replied. "The Matisse."

"It is safe."

"It was not in the safe at your gallery."

"You have been in the safe?"

"I am Kirchen," he said with a smirk. "I know everything."

"Then you should know that your painting is safe."

"I want it."

"I will arrange to have it delivered to you."

"See that you do."

Hasan opened the car door and stepped out, then waited while it drove away. As it turned the corner and disappeared from sight, he started toward the rear entrance to the bar. The things Kirchen had said were troubling, but Hasan was not overwhelmed by them. If Mogilevich had not issued an order, there still was time to prevent a disaster. "Plenty of time," he mumbled.

But such troubles he had. Kirchen or Mogilevich. Sibel or Slater. Life or death. Surely no one had ever borne the kind of burdens he endured. Perhaps the girl who had approached him could help. A smile came to him. She was nice. Not quite as young as he liked, but nice just the same. Maybe she could make him forget his troubles.

Late that evening, Hasan came from the bar and drove home to the apartment he shared with Sibel. She was in the bedroom when he arrived, seated in a chair near the window, reading a book. He went to the closet door and removed his jacket.

"Kirchen came to see me," he grumbled.

Sibel's eyes widened. "Kirchen is here?" She did not like him. If he was in the city it could mean only one thing: trouble.

"He is upset about all the attention the newspaper article is attracting."

"He should be happy," she replied. "Business is better than ever."

"I agree. But that is the problem."

She set aside the book she had been reading. "We sell their art and that is a problem?"

"This article is attracting too much attention. The business is attracting too much attention. These people do not operate in the legitimate world. They do not like to be seen or heard or known."

"Then let Kirchen come over here and run the business and see what he can do without customers."

"He particularly doesn't like seeing his photograph in the newspaper!" Hasan shouted.

Sibel ignored his anger. "We're supposed to sell paintings. Attention is part of the business of selling. No attention, no sales. It's that simple."

"They don't like it," Hasan snapped.

"Then what would they have us do?"

"What they really want is for us to close the gallery and sell the art at auctions."

"Close the gallery?" Sibel was exasperated. "They know nothing about the art business."

"I tried to tell him that."

"Then you should try again."

"I tried!" he shouted. "But the attention is too much. And this business with you and Truman Slater is a liability."

Sibel's eyes narrowed. "Kirchen mentioned Slater?"

"Yes."

"Mentioned him by name?"

"He knows what we do, Sibel." Hasan jabbed his finger at her. "He knows what you do."

"And what about you and those girls?" She spoke in a haughty, accusing tone. "Did he say anything about that?"

"That?" Hasan was dismissive. "That's nothing. Just a man having a little fun."

"And you don't think anyone notices how young they are?"

Hasan seethed. "Shut up."

"And the way you and Ahmed behave like idiots at the auctions." Sibel's voice was strident and growing louder. "Ever think about how much attention that attracts? Huh? Think no one notices you then?"

"Shut up," he repeated.

"Shut up? You put on a show, with those girls on your arm, call attention to yourself in a thousand ways, then come in here and tell me the gallery is getting too much coverage in the press. That I should close our business and take the advice of stupid people. That I should shut up and do as I'm told." She was out of the chair and standing inches from him. "You want me to shut up? Well how about you shut up!"

They stood inches apart, glaring at each other, then Hasan took a step back. "It's not just the gallery." He lowered his voice. "The questions those reporters asked about Paris. About Jacob Edelman. About the missing Matisse. And the photograph of Kirchen." He threw his hands up in a gesture of frustration. "You are going to get us both killed."

"That article was written by the reporters," she said. "Not me. They are the ones who wrote that stuff. They are the ones who tracked down the photo. It didn't come from me."

"And you are the one who talked to them," Hasan retorted. "You and that artist boyfriend you've been sleeping with."

"How dare you talk to me like that?" She stepped closer again and raised her hand. "You with your teenage whores and—"

WHAP!

Before she could react, Hassan slapped her in the face. The force of the blow knocked her backwards. She stumbled against a chair and fell to the floor. He glowered over her. "Shut up about what I do! Just put an end to all of it now!"

Hasan turned away, stormed out of the apartment, and slammed the door behind him. Sibel lay on the floor, crying, but only for a moment. When she was sure he was gone, she pushed herself up, grabbed her purse, and headed downstairs. Despite the late hour, she had no intention of being there when he returned.

Chapter 31

At two in the morning, Truman Slater was awakened by a knock on the door. He checked his watch for the time, then checked his phone to make sure. A knock on the door at that hour could mean only trouble. He came from the bed, slipped on his pants, and went to the window. Sibel Izmir's car was parked in the driveway.

Slater hurried downstairs and opened the front door, ready to take her in his arms, to kiss her madly, to run his hands over her body, but when he saw her, he froze at the sight of her cheek, bruised and swollen. He winced at the sight of it. "Who did this?"

"Don't worry about it." She stepped toward him. "It is nothing." He backed away, holding her at bay with his hands on her shoulder. "Who did this?" he insisted. She turned her head away. Slater pressed the issue. "Hasan hit you? Did Hasan do this?" Sibel nodded in response.

Slater turned away to get a shirt. "I'll kill the son of a bitch," he growled.

With one hand, Sibel grabbed him by the arm. "No," she pleaded. "Stay here." She used her free hand to turn him toward her and he spun around to face her. "He can't do this to you and get away with it," Slater fumed. "I won't let him."

"Shh." She pulled him close and lowered her voice. "Leave it alone."

"It's too much to let it go." Already Slater's resolve was weakening. "I have to do something."

She placed her lips near his ear. "Never mind about him." She placed the lobe of his ear between her teeth. "Just stay here with me."

Sibel continued to kiss his ear, then worked her way down to his neck. Slater was unresponsive at first but as she moved from his neck to his chest, he ran his fingers through her hair. She raised her head and pressed her lips against his. "Make me forget everything." Her voice was low and husky. "Make me forget everything but you."

Slater kissed her deeply while he backed her toward the sofa, then eased her onto the cushions. She grabbed him by the shoulders and pulled him onto her.

Sometime later, there was a knock at the door. Slater opened his eyes to find it was morning. The sun was up and streaming through the windows. He was lying naked on the sofa with Sibel, their arms and legs entangled. Her soft breasts pressed against his chest. Her skin was damp and tacky.

Sibel's eyes were open, too, and wide. She looked straight at him. "Who is that?" she whispered. Slater moved her arm aside and climbed over her to see. She rolled onto her back. "Is it him?" Her voice trembled.

Slater put on his pants and stepped to the window. A car was parked in the driveway. He recognized it at once. "It's Charlotte Snider," he said. She was standing near the porch railing, hands on hips, waiting impatiently. A sense of embarrassment came over him, like the time when he was seventeen and his mother walked in on him with Simone. They weren't naked but well on their way to being.

Sibel must have felt the same. "Oh no," she gasped. "Charlotte can't see me like this." She came from the sofa, grabbed her clothes, and hurried upstairs.

When she was out of the room, Slater unlocked the door and opened it while putting on his shirt. "Hey." He smiled sheepishly.

"Didn't expect to see you today."

Charlotte glanced past him. "That's Sibel's car in the driveway, isn't it?"

He ignored the question and opened the door wider. "Come on in."

"I know she's here," Charlotte said. "Hasan called me, looking for her."

Slater spoke over his shoulder. "You want some coffee? I was just about to put some on." He closed the door and turned to cross the room, that's when he realized she noticed the rumpled cushions on the sofa. "Sorry about the mess."

"This isn't going to work," Charlotte said, pointing to the sofa.

"What isn't going to work?"

"You and Sibel. How many times has she been out here?"

Slater continued to ignore her questions and made his way toward the kitchen. "I haven't had breakfast yet. Do you want an egg with that coffee?"

"Sibel!" Charlotte shouted up the stairs. "You might as well come down here. I know you're up there."

Slater continued to the kitchen and started a pot of coffee. Charlotte followed. "She and Hasan had a fight last night." Charlotte cut her eyes at him. "But I'm sure you know that already." She took a seat at the kitchen table. "You should know—" A noise from upstairs interrupted. She glanced at him with a questioning look. "Sibel really is up there, isn't she?"

Slater's shoulders sagged. "Yes," he said, reluctantly. "She's really up there."

Charlotte fixed her eyes on him. "This isn't the first time, either, is it?"

"No."

Charlotte stared at him. "Are you crazy? How many times has she been out here?"

"You know." He shrugged. "It's just one of those things." Sibel had been there many times since that first day she came with Charlotte, but he had no intention of telling her. Especially not now. Not after the way she reacted.

Her eyes were wide and her mouth open. "Just one of those things?" When he didn't respond she came from the chair, grabbed him by the arm, and guided him toward the back door. "Come with me."

Outside, she hustled him across the yard to the studio and when they were inside with the door closed she said, "Listen to me. You don't understand what you're doing. You are jeopardizing everything you've worked for."

Slater leaned against a work bench. "Hasan hit her."

"Hit who?"

"Sibel."

Charlotte looked alarmed. "Why?"

"I don't know. I haven't gotten to that part of the story yet."

She stared at him a moment, then shook her head. "Never mind about that. Whatever happened is between them. You have to let them solve that."

"I think we're beyond that."

"No," Charlotte snapped. "You don't understand. Hasan Izmir is a dangerous guy."

Slater frowned. "A dangerous guy?"

"Yes," she insisted. "He's a dangerous man." She took him by the shoulders and looked him in the eye. "Do you understand me?"

"I've seen him a few times." Slater shrugged free of her grasp. "I think I could take him."

"No. You can't. Believe me. You can't. And even if you could, you wouldn't want to."

Slater was puzzled. "You think I can't handle myself?"

"It's not him that's the problem. It's the people he's working with."

"What do you mean?"

"Hasan has friends," Charlotte said. "Russian friends. You don't want to mess with this."

Slater felt confused. "Russian friends? What does that mean?"

"You know exactly what it means," Charlotte insisted. "These are the kind of people who think of murder as a useful problem-solving technique."

"How do you know this?"

"I just do."

"She told you?"

"Who?"

"Sibel. She told you this?"

Charlotte shook her head. "Did you read the newspaper article that came out last weekend?"

"The one about that guy looking for his family's art?"

"Yes."

"I read it. What about it?"

"That article included a picture of a man identified as Marcel Kirchen."

"I saw it." Slater shrugged. "So what?"

"That man has ties to all sorts of people. People you go to bed at night hoping never to meet."

"So, what are you saying? I should just drop whatever I feel for Sibel and be glad to be alive?"

"Yes." Charlotte nodded her head vigorously. "That is exactly what I'm saying. Paint art. Sell art. But leave sex with Sibel out of the equation. And do absolutely nothing to draw the attention of Hasan or Ahmed Izmir."

The warning seemed earnest enough, but Slater was curious. "If they're so bad," he said, "why did you take me to them in the first place?"

"Because I know Sibel and I knew if she saw your work, she would take you as a client. You needed a place immediately and I knew she'd take you quickly. I just didn't think she would take things with you to this level this fast."

Slater grinned. "It did happen rather quickly."

"And it needs to end just as quickly, too."

"Or what?"

"Or you'll both end up dead."

Charlotte left without talking to Sibel, which Slater found curious, but when she was gone, he went back inside the house. Sibel was waiting for him in the kitchen. "Where's Charlotte?"

"She's gone."

"What did she want?"

"I'm not sure. She came here looking for you, I think."

"I didn't want to talk to her."

"Why not?"

"She would just tell me I shouldn't be here." Sibel looked over at him. "Is that what she said?"

"Yes."

"What else did she say?"

"That it's dangerous for us to be together."

Sibel looked worried. "Why did she say that? Has she seen Hasan?"

"He called her to find out where you are."

"Did she tell him?"

"I don't think so." The coffee was made and Slater poured himself a cup. "She thinks Hasan has dangerous friends. That you and he are in business with the Russian mafia."

Sibel slipped her arm in his and guided him toward the living room. "No one in the art world likes Hasan or Ahmed. Not even Charlotte."

"Did Hasan hit you because of me?"

She pointed to the sofa. "Sit next to me."

"No." He moved his arm from hers. "Tell me. Did he hit you because of me?"

Sibel took a seat on the sofa and patted a spot next to her. "Sit here beside me."

Slater stood a few feet away and took a sip of coffee from the cup he held. She was ignoring his question and he meant to have an answer. "Tell me why Charlotte thinks my life is in danger with you here."

"Okay." Sibel sighed. "It's a bit of a story."

"I have plenty of time."

Sibel leaned back on the sofa. "We used to be in the real estate business. Hasan, Ahmed, a few others. They were all partners. Made money. Lots of money. We had a good life. One night, a friend took us to an art auction. Introduced us to people. Many people. People who were wealthy and influential and we'd only known before from things we'd read about in the newspaper. Hasan loved it. So, the next week we went back. Then he started buying and before long, we were part of the regular crowd. A few years later, when we got out of the real estate business, we took a trip to Europe. Attended an art fair. Saw many artists. By then we had a sizeable collection and knew many people in the art business. So, we decided to open a gallery. Not long after that, a man we met in Venice approached us about selling art for him. Our gallery was new. We thought it was good for business."

"What was this man's name?"

She waved him off with a gesture. "It doesn't matter. He's dead now." She continued. "We thought the paintings we were selling for him were from his private collection. Turns out, they were actually owned by Sergei Mogilevich." She paused. "Do you know that name?"

"No." Slater shook his head.

"Good. You don't want to know him." She kept going. "The next year, this person from Venice, the dealer, sent us three crates of paintings. They were respectable pieces of art and we knew how to sell them, so we did well. I thought it was just art. I didn't know it was owned by drug dealers."

Slater set the coffee cup aside. "Drug dealers?"

"Yes."

"And you didn't know that?"

"Not at first. Hasan told me later. I just knew at the time they didn't seem like the art type."

"American drug dealers?"

"Europeans. That's when I learned that Sergei Mogilevich was a member of the Russian mob and that those first crates of paintings had belonged to him."

Slater slumped into a chair. "This can't be good."

"He is a very powerful man."

"And he was buying art?"

"He was buying it in Europe with cash. Sending it here and selling it."

"Money laundering?"

She nodded. "By the time we finished with those first three crates, we were hooked on the money."

"But you know they are using the art to launder drug money."

"That is what Hasan told me."

"So, people who come into the gallery have no idea what they are buying? No idea that it has a connection to the European drug trade?"

"These are works by newer artists, but they're European artists and they have names that sound important. So, they sell in the market but not at prices so high as to attract attention. Mostly a hundred thousand and below."

"And the people you deal with are from Russia?"

"I only know one man. Marcel Kirchen. But I don't actually deal with him. Hasan deals with him. When Hasan told me what he was doing, I said you can do it if you want but you're dealing with him. Not me. I don't want anything to do with him."

"Why not?"

"He's bad. The man in Venice we first met who is now dead, Marcel is the one who killed him."

"How much of this does Charlotte know?"

"Most of it."

Slater was startled. "How does Charlotte know about this?"

"She saw Marcel at the gallery one day and overheard bits of conversation and put it together that way. She's very smart."

"She was in the gallery that much?"

"She's been there since the beginning."

"Does she own some of the art from Europe?"

"Oh, yes," Sibel said. "She is a big buyer and she's made money on the things she bought from us. She spends time with galleries up the street who sell similar pieces from American artists, but I don't think she has made as much from them as she has from us."

"How did you get to know her?"

Sibel's eyes darted away. "Like I said, she's a good customer."

Slater shook his head again. "There's more to it than that. How do you know her?"

"She comes to the—"

"No," he snapped. "I know when you're not telling me everything. How does Charlotte know about this?"

Sibel sighed. "Charlotte used to be married to Hasan's cousin."

Slater's mouth fell open. "His cousin?"

"Yes."

"What happened?"

"He was just like Hasan, always running round with the ladies. She came home and caught him in bed with the neighbor's teenage daughter. They divorced but she agreed to keep quiet in exchange for everything they owned. That's how she has enough money to live the way she does." Sibel patted a spot on the sofa again. "Sit here with me now."

Reluctantly, Slater took a seat next to her and she turned toward him. "That was my life before." She draped her leg over his. "But I don't want that life anymore. I want out. And I want you."

Slater frowned. "Out?"

"Out of the business and out of the marriage." Tears filled her eyes. "He hit me. What kind of man would do that to his wife?"

"I don't know."

"Neither do I. And I don't want to spend another minute trying to figure it out. We can leave today. Right now. Just you and me. Go someplace new. Someplace where no one knows us. I have money."

Slater leaned away. "But we would always be looking over our shoulder. Wondering when he would find us."

She pulled him closer and rested her head on his shoulder.

"Maybe there is another way."

"What do you mean?"

"I know things."

Slater twisted from under her and moved to one side, facing her. "What are you talking about?"

"There are people who would be interested in hearing what I have to say."

"You mean criminals? The Russians?"

"No. I mean the police. The authorities. If they knew what I know, they would send Hasan and Ahmed to prison for a long time."

Slater was skeptical about how much she actually knew and whether she would go through with such a plan. From what he knew about it, this sort of thing required a clean, immediate break with everyone and everything one had ever known. A friend of a friend had known someone who did that. It sounded brutal. Sibel had been with Hasan a long time and, by her own admission, the lifestyle they'd enjoyed was addictive. He wasn't sure she understood all of that. "You would testify against your own husband?" he asked.

"If it got me away from him and the chance to be with you, then yes, I would. They have witness protection programs, don't they? I've read about it. They will resettle you in a new place if you help them."

"That's the FBI," Slater said. "They're the ones who have witness protection."

Getting her away from Hasan was one thing. Going with her into a witness protection program was quite another. From what he knew, people who did that left not just their friends and family behind, but everything about their former life. And for him, that meant leaving behind painting. His art was an extension of himself. An identifier almost as distinct as a fingerprint. Perhaps more so. He had spent all of his life finding his voice as an artist. Being with her would mean giving that up and he felt hollow inside at the thought of it.

"Then I would go to the FBI," she said.

"But you'd have to tell them everything and you'd be gambling that they would actually do something with what you told them."

"As long as they get us away from here, that's all that matters."

"It's not just Hasan you have to worry about. All those people in Europe you deal with would be after you to."

She had a questioning expression. "But how would they know it was me?"

"If you testified in court——"

She blurted, "In court?"

"Yes. You'd have to sit in the courtroom and tell a jury about it."

"I don't care." She leaned toward him, wrapped her arms around him, and pressed her face against his chest. "I don't care what it takes. I would tell the world if it would get me away from him. Do you think the FBI would be interested?"

"I don't know."

"Would you go with me?"

"To the FBI office?"

"Into the witness protection program."

His eyes were wide in a look of concern, but with her head against his chest she couldn't see his face, so he said, "Sure. I'll go with you to talk to them, but we can't go tonight."

She looked up at him. "Why not?"

"We need to arrange for you to talk to the FBI first and find out if they are interested."

"How do we do that?"

"We need someone to talk to the FBI for you."

"How is that better than me talking to them myself?"

"A lawyer or someone like that could talk to them for you. That way, if they aren't interested, you could always deny that you said anything."

She was already shaking her head. "No lawyers. All the lawyers I know work for us. And they tell Hasan everything I say." She sat up. "Do you know someone who could help?"

"No." He shook his head. "Not in New York."

"But you could help me find someone?"

"Are you sure you're serious about this?"

"Yes." She had a determined look. "I'm serious."

"It's not the kind of thing where you can start, then wake up the next day and change your mind. Once you start, you have to go all the way through with it."

"If we are together, that will be enough." She kissed him. "Find someone to help us with it. I'm ready to talk." She kissed him again. "And then we can be together forever." She slid her hands beneath his shirt and pushed it off over his head, then leaned against him, this time pressing him down onto the sofa.

Chapter 32

In the afternoon, a Learjet with Gennady Krylov aboard landed at Teterboro Airport in New Jersey, just across the Hudson River from Manhattan. The plane taxied to a stop inside a private hangar and when the door opened, Krylov stepped out carrying a leather overnight bag with his left hand. Tariel Kumarin was waiting and escorted him to a black SUV that was parked nearby. Krylov got in back and placed the bag on the seat beside him.

As the rear door closed, Nikolay Ivanov, the driver, glanced up. Their eyes met in the rearview mirror. "You had a good flight?"

"Yes," Krylov said. He was cordial but impatient. "We must get moving. There is little time to waste."

Kumarin was seated in front. As they drove away from the hanger, he turned sideways in the seat to talk. "Your message was rather cryptic," he said. "We are glad to assist, but what exactly do you need us to do?"

Krylov leaned forward. "I need information about the people we discussed."

"The art dealer and his wife?"

"Yes. And the boyfriend—Slater. Also the two reporters."

Kumarin frowned. "Jack Frazer and Gina Wilkins?"

"Yes."

Kumarin hesitated. Krylov looked over at him. "Is that a problem?"

"They were not on the list."

Krylov jabbed in with his index finger. "They are now. Is that a problem?"

"No," Kumarin said. "No problem at all. We have people who can take care of the information side."

Krylov was not convinced. "We will need access to email accounts, phone calls, text messages, whatever we can get for every-one involved."

"They can do that." Kumarin seemed confident but Krylov had been gamed before.

"I understand this artist is a hot property right now."

"His paintings are selling well."

"We still need him. If she has talked to anyone about us, it will be him." Krylov looked over at Kumarin. "Your people don't mind being involved with something like this for someone like that, do you? If you do, just tell me and I'll get someone else." The look in his eyes and tone of his voice made the offer a threat.

"No. No," Ivanov said. "It's not a problem at all. He may be popular, but he is not out of reach for our people."

Krylov looked over at Ivanov. "The logistical issue is getting the artwork out of the country. Can your crew handle that?"

"That will not be a problem," Ivanov replied. "They are ready to go when you give the word."

"You have a plan for it?"

"A single painting, right?"

"No," Krylov said. "All of it."

"All of it? All of what?"

"Everything in the gallery."

"You want us to move all of it? Tonight?"

"It all belongs to my boss. He wants his property returned." Kry-lov scooted closer and propped on the back of the front seat. "I'm getting the feeling that you two don't know what you're doing."

"We know very well what we are doing," Ivanov said. "We were told there would be a single painting. Now you are telling us there will be many."

"I'm sensing you don't know what to do."

"Crate it, take it from the gallery," Ivanov said. "Then we haul it to the docks in Brooklyn."

Krylov was troubled. "You are certain that will work? We don't need to fly it out?"

"Our order was to send the Matisse anonymously. We arranged to do that. Flying it requires the shipment to clear Customs which requires documents we don't have."

"A ship is better," Kumarin added.

Krylov was still unconvinced. "US authorities upgraded port security after September 11. Some of our people have had trouble with ships."

Ivanov grinned. "If you know someone, it's not as secure as they think."

"And you know someone?"

"We have people who can get anything through the gate."

"Even crates full?"

"Yes."

"What about the paperwork for that? Doesn't it require documentation?"

"This will arrive at the port with stamps and seals affixed. As if it came pre-approved for Customs."

"That won't work at the airport?"

"No contacts there."

"And a ship?"

"Already set. When we're ready to go, a ship will be waiting to take whatever we bring it."

"Even crates?"

"Even crates."

Krylov remained skeptical even then. He had worked with American crews before and they were anything but reliable. These two had European names, but they'd both grown up in the United States. He was certain they were as American as anyone, which in his mind meant worthless. But he didn't care much about this part of the mission. They had been recruited through channels and vetted by Mogilevich's American contacts. If the paintings never arrived in Moldova, it would be on them and those who vouched for their integrity. Krylov had something else to do that was more important to him. He leaned back in the seat, closed his eyes, and thought about that for the remainder of the ride.

Before long, the SUV turned into the driveway at a house in Bound Brook, New Jersey. When it came to a stop, Krylov opened the door. "Meet me tonight. You know the location?"

"Yes," Kumarin replied. "We know it well."

"Don't be late and don't stand me up." Krylov didn't wait for a response. He stepped from the SUV, closed the car door behind him, and started toward the house. When he looked back, the SUV was gone.

Krylov took a nap that afternoon but a few hours after arriving at the house, he was rested and ready to address the real reason he'd come to the United States—to deal with Marcel Kirchen once and for all. Despite the tedious nature of the discussion he'd had with Kumarin and Ivanov on the ride from the airport, this part of the plan was simple. Find Kirchen and kill him. Far from worrying over it or obsessing about each step, Krylov looked forward to it with the anticipation of one receiving a gift. That German bastard was finally getting what he had coming to him for a long time, and Krylov was the one who would deliver it. He had difficulty recalling anything in his life that had made him happier.

An hour or two after dark, Krylov came from the house in Bound Brook and walked out to a garage at the end of the driveway. A car was parked inside. It was gassed and ready to go. Krylov got in behind the steering wheel, started the engine, and backed the car to the street.

From the house, he drove toward Brooklyn. He'd been there many times and knew the way by heart. With little difficulty, he located Kirchen at the apartment on Bay Parkway in Bensonhurst.

Kirchen was surprised to see him.

"Relax," Krylov said as he stepped inside the apartment. "I'm here to bring you back."

Kirchen frowned. "Bring me back? To where?"

"Mogilevich is worried about you. We have a plane waiting in New Jersey."

"I'm not interested in going anywhere. And certainly not with you."

"Not with me?" Krylov feigned offense. "Why the hostility?"

"We both know you don't really like me."

"And you don't like me," Krylov responded. "So, we're even. But you don't get a choice in the matter. You can't stay here. Not after the FBI raided your hotel room."

"You know that for certain? They were in my hotel room?"

"You haven't heard?"

"Heard what? I have heard nothing. I have been sitting here all this time, waiting, and I have heard nothing."

"They have your laptop and everything else that was in your room."

Kirchen still seemed unconvinced. "I don't think Mogilevich said anything about me. And I don't think he sent you. This is all your idea."

"Call him," Krylov said. "Ask him yourself."

Kirchen turned away. "You know we can't talk with him on the phone."

"Then I suggest you get moving."

"And where do you plan to take me?"

"Moldova. To Mogilevich's house. Where you'll be safe. Really safe."

Kirchen turned in his direction. "Moldova?" A questioning frown wrinkled his forehead. His eyes seemed alive with energy.

"Where did you think we were going?"

"And what does he intend to do with me when I arrive? Kill me?"

"If he was going to kill you, he would do it here," Krylov replied.

"Where else would he want you? Certainly not back in that shack you call home in Luxembourg."

"You followed me that day." Kirchen smiled. "To Luxembourg."

"You left us hanging out to dry."

"You would have taken the money."

"Not a chance," Krylov said.

"No?"

"I value my life too much to treat Mogilevich that way."

"And that's the reason I don't think he sent you. He was offended that I took the Matisse and kept the money. He would like to see me dead."

"He would like to see a lot of things, but the last thing he wants is for the FBI to get their hands on you. And you don't want that either. Now, get moving. If we wait much longer, we'll both be stuck here."

Kirchen turned toward the bedroom. "What about the Matisse? It's the only painting that was worth anything out of that last shipment."

"Hasan knows what to do. And if not, Sibel will tell him."

"Sibel," Kirchen scoffed. "She's banging another of her young artists again." He shook his head. "Sometimes I think she has lost her mind." He looked over at Krylov again. "And to think we were certain she was the smart one."

"Everyone has their weakness," Krylov said. "And yours is wasting time. If we get out now, we can always come back. If we stay, we won't be able to leave under any circumstance." Krylov gave him a push. "So, get your shit together. Quickly. We're leaving."

Kirchen went to the bedroom, opened a dresser drawer, and began stuffing clothes into a duffel bag. Krylov heard him and stepped to the doorway. "You don't need everything."

"Why not?

"We can buy clothes when we get to Moldova. Just the essentials. Let's go. We don't have time to argue anymore." Krylov sighed. "If you really want this stuff, someone will send it to you later. The FBI is coming. We have to go."

Kirchen zipped the duffel bag closed, brushed past Krylov, and started toward the door. Krylov followed. When they were in the hallway outside the apartment, Kirchen turned in the direction of the elevator. Krylov took him by the shoulder and spun him in the opposite direction. "Too many security cameras down there. We'll take the stairs."

"The staircase leads to the outside," Kirchen warned. "An alarm will sound if we open the door."

"No." Krylov shook his head. "It won't."

"What makes you so sure?"

Krylov smiled. "Because I know things."

When they reached the bottom of the stairway, Krylov pushed open the door. No alarm sounded and he led the way toward the car he'd driven from New Jersey. Kirchen followed a few feet behind, but Krylov noticed. If Kirchen bolted, he would have to kill him right then and there. That would not be good. So, he stopped and waited a moment while Kirchen came alongside him.

Krylov smiled, doing his best to keep Kirchen under control. "In less than an hour, we will be at the airport in New Jersey and on our way out of here."

"You're going back with me?"

"I'm sure not staying around here." Krylov laughed. "Too much attention on us here."

From the apartment, they drove south on Bay Parkway. Kirchen glanced around, nervously checking the route. "Why are we going this way? We should be on the highway in the opposite direction."

"Relax," Krylov said. "We have to make a little detour."

"You said you had a plane waiting in New Jersey."

"I do. But we gotta make a stop before then."

"I thought you were in a hurry."

"We are, but we still have to make this stop. I gotta pick up something before I leave."

"I don't like it."

"We'll take Belt Parkway around to Staten Island," Krylov explained. "And go up on the other side. Won't take long."

When they reached Belt Parkway, they continued past it and

drove along the edge of Gravesend Bay. It was a pleasant drive, with the bay on the left and the park on the right. Thinking of what was about to happen made it even more pleasant for Kirchen. His heart rate quickened with anticipation and his palms were sweaty. The moment was at hand and he found it difficult to contain his enthusiasm.

The car traveled at an idle but Krylov had to ride the brake to keep it under control. Kirchen noticed. "What's the matter with your car?" He sounded nervous and Kirchen realized he could easily open the door and jump out.

"The engine is running fast," Krylov said.

"They should maintain it better."

"It's an old car," Krylov said.

"Where did you get it?"

This was good. He was talking. Keep him distracted just a little longer. A few more meters. Not far now. He knew the exact spot. Beyond the security camera angles. Hidden from view to those who might be walking in the park. "Actually," Krylov said with a sheepish grin. "I think it's stolen."

Kirchen's eyes were wide. "Stolen? Are you out of your mind? We never use stolen vehicles over here. All the numbers. Everything on it is traceable."

"Relax," Krylov soothed. "It's not traceable."

"There is no such thing."

"Believe me," Krylov said. "No one will ever connect me to this car."

They were at the spot and he took an automatic pistol from the pocket of the door, pointed it at Kirchen, and shot him in the head. Brains and blood splattered against the car window. Kirchen slumped against the door and Krylov shot him twice more, just to be sure. Then he pointed the car toward the bay, opened the door, and rolled out from the driver's side onto the ground.

The car continued off the pavement, across the grass, and plunged into the bay. It made a splash when it hit the water, but in no time at all sank beneath the surface and disappeared from sight.

Krylov didn't wait to see it, though. He picked himself up from the grass, tucked the pistol in the waistband of his pants, and pulled his jacket over it, then walked into the park.

The black SUV was parked near a picnic area. Ivanov was behind the steering wheel and Kumarin was seated on the passenger side. Krylov made his way to them and got in the back. When he was inside, they drove away.

"Any trouble?" Kumarin asked.

"None at all," Krylov replied. His hands trembled and his heart pounded. Kirchen was dead. A problem was solved, and many future problems averted. It was exhilarating and he would have enjoyed reveling in the moment, but they had work to do and there was no time to relax. "We have a lot of work to do," he said. "We should get to it."

Chapter 33

The next morning, Slater awakened to find Sibel was gone. She'd been lying next to him as they drifted off to sleep the night before. Her leg over his. An arm across his chest. His hand on her thigh. Now, her side of the bed was empty, and the sheets were cool.

At first, he was worried that she had changed her mind. Given up on being with him. Gone back to Hasan. The thought of it, though, brought an unexpected sense of relief that surprised him and left him genuinely energized, but it was short-lived. For in the next second that sense of elation was buried beneath a wave of guilt.

True, his life would be much easier to manage if he simply stayed where he was, doing the things he was doing, but he wasn't like that. He was taught from childhood to follow through. To do what he said he would do. He said he would go with her, and that's what he meant to do.

Still, the nagging question wouldn't quite go away. He was an artist. Could he ever be himself without painting? Could he enjoy life, even life with Sibel, without it?

The longer he lay in bed, the more his mind raced from one thing to the next. Instead of changing her mind and leaving him, maybe something else had happened. She awakened in the night, went downstairs, and Hasan was waiting for her. Stepped out from the corner of the room. Grabbed her from behind. Held his hand over her mouth to muffle her voice. Dragged her to the car. Forced her to leave with him.

Drugged her with chloroform. Threw her over his shoulder. Carried her to the car. Dumped in the trunk. Drove away.

Nah. Slater dismissed each thought as it came to him. There would have been a noise. He would have heard it. Chloroform had a sweet smell. Very different from the odor of the house. He would notice it. And anyway, if Hasan was as dangerous and connected as Charlotte suggested, someone would have come upstairs to settle things with him. A bullet to his head or a knife to his throat.

Or would they? Maybe they were—

"This is no good," Slater said to himself. "I need to get up." He propped on his elbows and glanced around the room.

Sunlight through the windows told him it still was early. Perhaps eight at most but not past nine. He listened for the sounds from outside and heard a car go by on the road in front of the house. But only one. It might not even be eight yet.

Then his gaze fell on the dresser and he saw Sibel's makeup bag sitting in front of the mirror, where she'd placed it the day before. A sense of certainty came over him and he collapsed onto the pillow. She never went far without that makeup bag and the sight of it in the bedroom was a relief.

"She's probably downstairs," he said to himself. "Lying on the sofa. Or in the kitchen preparing breakfast for us." He rolled out of bed, pulled on his pants, and made his way to the staircase, then started downstairs taking each step with a slow, jaunty plop. When he reached the bottom, he paused and glanced around. Looking. Listening.

Light from outside reached the front windows at a low, winter angle. Soft and subdued, it gave the room a cold gray hue. And the room was quiet. Too quiet and too still for anyone else to be present.

After a moment, Slater came from the staircase and started toward the kitchen, but as he turned toward the sofa, he noticed a painting propped on a chair near the wall to the left. The painting wasn't his and it hadn't been there the night before, but he recognized it at once as the Matisse the reporters had asked about a few days earlier. They'd shown him a picture of it and told him the name. *"Woman With Table and Vase,"* he whispered.

The painting was in a gold-colored frame that was simple yet elegant and of a variety common to the museums or the better galleries. A slip of pink paper, folded in half, was wedged between the frame and canvas. Slater pulled the paper free, unfolded it and found a note that read, "Hide this in a safe place. We can use it to start our new life together."

Tears filled Slater's eyes and a pained smile came to him. Sibel hadn't abandoned him. She hadn't vanished in the night or been taken by Hasan. She had remembered. All that she had said. All that she had promised. She remembered every word. And she meant to follow through. To do the things she had said she would do—leave Hasan, make a new life in a place with him. A life in a place where no one knew their story, and no one cared.

Slater wiped his eyes and studied the painting. The vivid colors. The bold brushstrokes. The vigorous style. That's how the books described Matisse's technique. Rigorous. Slater had tried to paint like him once. Earlier. When he still was in love with the smell of the oils and the mystique of the artist's life. Before the newness of studio life had dulled his enthusiasm and the sameness of an everyday malaise had overtaken it. Before Charlotte found him and set him right.

Charlotte. His eyes opened wide in a look of realization. Charlotte? Not Sibel? No. It must be … But he knew the truth. Sibel had given him a place to show his work but it was Charlotte who sorted out his style and pointed him toward a form that let him paint the way he wanted to paint. The way he always knew he could. Maybe one day, if he stayed with it, he could be as famous as Matisse. His paintings in all the museums. Collected by all the collectors. Sought after by—

Could he really give it up? He was on the cusp of something wonderful. "Two somethings," he said aloud. A lifetime of romance and a romantic lifetime. But they were leading him in opposite directions. Forcing him to choose. The woman who captured his heart or the career that had become his heart. It seemed he could not have them both and as he stared at the painting, he knew he would be forced to choose between them.

The Matisse was a magnificent painting and Slater knew from its appearing in his living room that many of the things Sibel had said about Hasan and their business were true. The art. The money laundering. The nefarious nature of their European connections. He also knew the painting was likely stolen by the Nazis, just as the reporters had suggested. "Everything worth having has been stolen by someone," he said to himself. "At some point." Works of art perhaps most of all. It sounded like a platitude. A justification. Perhaps. But it also was true. Generally. Many of the greats had been stolen or otherwise come under the shadow of a suspicious provenance.

After admiring it a moment longer, Slater took the painting upstairs and hid it behind a suitcase in the bedroom closet. While he was up there, he finished dressing and when he came downstairs, he brewed a pot of coffee, then sat at the kitchen table and drank it as he thought about what he should do next. Phoning Sibel was an obvious choice, but his calls went straight to voicemail. He drank more coffee and thought about following his normal routine. Wait to see what happened. Who turned up. What events transpired through the day. He could walk over to the studio and paint. Two canvases tacked to the wall needed his attention. A third was unrolled and lying on the floor, waiting for him to begin, but it seemed a pointless exercise. Art, at least the kind he created, required emotion and right then, all of his emotion was wrapped up in Sibel. Wondering. Thinking. Where could she be?

As he finished his fourth cup of coffee, Slater considered again Sibel's request that he help locate someone at the FBI. He'd promised to do so, then quickly regretted the decision but after a day with her in bed, he wasn't sure he regretted it at all. Nor was he sure he would regret the loss of a career, if it meant being with her the way they were together the day before. She was a wonderful woman. Physically. Emotionally. Absorbing and giving. Devouring him completely while radiating an image of himself back to himself in the most rapturously fulfilling experience he'd ever known.

How could Hasan treat her so poorly? How could he yell at her? Strike her in anger? Accuse her. She was the most fascinating woman he had ever known. Ever talked to. Ever touched. Ever felt. Surely there was a downside to her. Everyone had at least as many negatives as positives. As many things going for them as against. As many irritating quirks as invigorating qualities. But try as he might to see the bad in her, Slater found only the best. He wondered if it always would be that way. Surely not. Yet he could not conceive of a day when he, too, would be angry with her for no reason other than that she was Sibel. Though he thought that day must surely come, he couldn't see it. Not then. Maybe one day. Sometime. Maybe. But not then.

When he'd drunk all the coffee, Slater decided that, regardless of his ultimate choice about Sibel or art, he must take the next step and that step was to find someone at the FBI who was in a position to help. And for that, he knew only one place to begin: Charlotte Snider. She was his point of contact with New York. The one person he knew who had access to anyone in the city. Literally, anyone. From the mayor to the street sweeper. They all took her calls. She was the only one who could help and he found her number in the contacts list on his phone, then thought better of it.

This wasn't something he could discuss on the phone. Could put it out there for anyone to hear. Anyone to see. Anyone to find. This was a topic he needed to discuss with her in person. Face-to-face. Eye-to-eye.

The drive from the house on Long Island into the city took about two hours and when Slater reached Charlotte's apartment, he found she was preparing to go out. "I have someplace to be," she said. "What brings you here today?"

"Sibel."

"Oh."

"I need to talk to you about something."

"Okay." Charlotte stepped aside to let him enter, then closed the door behind him. "What is this about?"

"We talked the other night."

"We?"

"Sibel and I."

"And?"

"She wants to leave Hasan."

Charlotte frowned. "Leave him?"

"Yes."

She had a wary look. "And marry you?"

"I don't think she mentioned marriage," Slater replied. "But she wants to be with me."

"Was she serious?"

"I believe so."

"This is moving rather fast, isn't it?"

"Yes," he replied. "I suppose it is."

"As I told you before, Hasan and his brother are dangerous." Charlotte took a seat in the living room. "They have serious ties to the Russian mafia."

Slater took a seat across from her. "Sibel says if the police knew what Hasan and his brother were doing they would arrest them."

"I'm sure they would."

"She wants to talk."

"Talk?"

"To the FBI."

Charlotte's eyes opened wide. "She told you this?"

"Yes."

"And you're certain of it."

"Yes. Why?"

"She's mentioned it to me before," Charlotte said. "But I never thought she was serious about it."

"I think she is now."

"She would have to go into witness protection."

"I know."

"You would never see her again."

"She wants me to go with her."

"You can't." Charlotte shook her head. "If you do that, you would have to leave everything behind."

"I realize that."

"You could never paint another picture in your life."

Slater nodded grimly. "I know."

"Every picture you paint comes from inside you. You leave a piece of yourself on every canvas. If you painted even one painting, you'd be putting up a billboard telling people where you were."

"But if I don't go with her," Slater responded, "I'll never see her again. And when Hasan finds out what we've been doing, it won't be good for me anyway. Even if I stay behind."

She had a knowing expression. "Hasan already knows what you've been doing."

Slater frowned. "How do you know that?"

"I've told you before, I know Sibel and I know Hasan. You aren't the first."

"What do you mean?"

"Why do you think she takes on new artists?"

Slater shrugged. "Because she likes the arts. It's something she thinks she can make money at."

"Maybe. But she also likes the artists."

"That can't be a bad thing."

"It's the way she likes the artists."

Slater knew what she meant. He'd heard the stories about Sibel. Someone had told him. He couldn't remember who. Maybe it was Charlotte herself. Still, he didn't like hearing it now. Not from her. Not in the midst of their plans. "Why are you telling me this?" he asked.

"Because you are seriously considering throwing away your life to go away with her and you ought to know before you do that she is always going to be looking for the next guy."

Despite what he knew, the statement made Slater angry. "I can't believe you would say such a thing," he retorted. "This is Sibel you're talking about. She thinks you're her friend and here you are talking about her as if she's some common whore. She's brave. She's determined. She wants to talk. She could lose her life for it, but she wants to talk and tell the truth and put everything else behind her. Behind us. Behind all of it."

"Yeah." Charlotte seemed unconvinced. "She wants to start a new life, but if you are part of it you will lose yours in the process. Maybe not your physical life, but your art, your creativity, your identity. You will lose the soul of the man you've been every day until now. Art is who you are. It's all you've ever been. It's all you are right now. And you would lose every bit of it, and you will never get any of it back."

Slater knew she was right but he didn't want to accept it. "You're just saying that so I'll stay here and keep painting and you can make money off me."

"I can't believe you'd say that to me," Charlotte replied. "I've never made a secret of my business interest in you. But I've never asked you to give up your life for it, either. In fact, I've gone out of my way to give you the life and career you said you wanted. The life you left Montana to find."

Slater regretted what he'd said. His shoulders slumped and his countenance softened and he looked over at her. "She really went after other guys like she's gone after me?"

"Ask Robert Capriati," Charlotte replied. "He'll tell you what it was like."

"I'm not sure I have time for—"

"His studio is on Grand Street," she said, cutting him off. "In Williamsburg. A few blocks off the river. Here, I'll give you the address." She stood, crossed the room to a small table near the window and opened a drawer. A notepad was there and she scribbled the address on it, then tore off the page and handed it to him. When he hesitated to take it, she insisted. "At least talk to him. He'll tell you what it was like."

Slater took the note from her and shoved it in his pocket. "Do you know anyone at the FBI that she could talk to?"

"I don't think you want to do this. And I don't think she does either. Not really."

"Charlotte, I'm not talking about a final decision. Just an option. Do you know someone? Maybe someone you could call for her?"

Charlotte sighed. "Yes. I know a few people."

"Good." Slater stood. "Could you make a call? Find out who she would need to talk to?"

"I suppose. If it means that much to you."

"It does," Slater said. "But don't talk to her about it and don't try to talk her out of it. Whether I go with her or not, she at least needs to make her own decision about it." He turned to leave. "Make the call. Tell me what you find out and I'll let her know."

When Slater was gone, Charlotte phoned David Anders. "Meet me at Blue Hill," she said."

He seemed reluctant. "What is this about?"

"If I could talk over the phone, I wouldn't ask you to meet me."

"When?"

"Ten minutes," she said, and abruptly ended the call.

Charlotte was waiting at Blue Hill, a restaurant on Washington Place in Greenwich Village, when Anders arrived twenty minutes later. "You're late," she said as he took a seat across from her.

"I was in the middle of something." He had a defensive tone. "What's this about?"

"You know someone at the FBI, don't you?"

Anders was evasive. "What makes you say that?"

"You were the source behind that article in the paper last week. The one about Edelman and the Izmirs."

The remark seemed to unsettle Anders. "Who told you that?" he asked.

"Never mind who told me. I need a name at the FBI."

"For what?"

"I know someone who might want to talk to them."

Anders arched an eyebrow in a curious expression. "Might?"

She gave a dismissive gesture. "You know how these things work. I need a name. Someone I can call."

"What's this about?"

Charlotte lowered her voice. "Your favorite art dealer."

Anders looked puzzled. "Judd Horton?"

Charlotte leaned forward. "Hasan Izmir," she whispered.

Anders' eyes widened. "Someone on the inside wants to talk?"

"Yes."

"Do I know them?"

"I can't say any more than that. But if this person talked, they would need protection. That would be a condition of talking."

"Okay."

"Can you call someone? Get us a name? See if the FBI would be interested?"

"Yes." Anders nodded. "Of course."

"Good. You call them, see if they're interested, then call me back and I'll contact the person on my end. And Anders, do us both a favor. Don't tell anyone else about this."

"Sure."

"I'm serious." Charlotte stood. "No reporters. Not a word to those dealers you hang out with. This could put us all in danger."

"I understand."

Charlotte left the table.

Anders remained at the table after Charlotte left the restaurant and telephoned Preston Cooper, the FBI agent he talked to before. "We need to talk," he said when Cooper answered the call.

Cooper sounded distracted. "I don't have time right now."

"Yes," Anders insisted. "You do."

"What's this about?"

Anders borrowed Charlotte's response. "If I could tell you that," he said, "I wouldn't need to meet in person."

"Okay. Where?"

"There's a Dunkin' Donuts right across Broadway from your office."

"I'll need twenty minutes," Cooper replied.

"I'll be waiting."

When the call ended, Anders left Blue Hill and walked over to Broadway. He was seated at the end of the counter in Dunkin' Donuts when Preston Cooper arrived. Cooper took a seat on the stool next to him. "What's so important it couldn't wait?" he asked.

"I have been approached by someone on behalf of a person inside Galerie Le Meilleur. This person wants to talk."

"Someone on the inside at the gallery wants to talk to me?"

"They want to talk to someone who can give them protection."

"I'm willing to listen," Cooper replied. "But I can't guarantee anything."

"They say they'll need protection before they talk."

"That's not how this works. We'll have to hear what they have to say first, then decide if we can do it."

"They say it's a condition for their cooperation."

"I can get them into witness protection," Cooper assured, "but not for just any information. It has to be something we can use. Something substantial."

Anders shook his head. "I don't know if that'll be enough."

"That's all I can do. I can't promise it ahead of time, but if the information is substantive—and by that I mean if it takes us into the heart of a case, and if the threat to them is real—we can take care of it."

"All right. I'll tell them and get back to you."

As Anders came from the café, he called Charlotte Snider. "Where are you?"

"Houston Street," Charlotte replied. "Coming up Broadway."

"In your car?"

"Yes. Why?"

"Meet me at Lafayette Street and Jersey. By the Mulberry Street library. Find a spot for your car and I'll meet you there."

"When?"

"Now."

Anders made his way to the library and was seated on a bench out front near the bus stop when Charlotte arrived. She parked in a lot near the center of the next block. Anders came to her car and got in on the passenger side. "I talked to someone," he said.

"That was fast."

"You said you needed to know."

"I do," Charlotte replied. "What did they say?"

"He can get your person into witness protection, but he can't guarantee it upfront. It depends on the information this person gives." Anders looked over at her. "Now tell me, who are we talking about?"

"I ... I can't say. Not yet."

"It would be easier to set this up if I knew."

"It has to be this way."

"Well ..." Anders seemed dissatisfied, but he kept going. "Okay. You talk to your person and get back with me, then, if they're still interested, I'll set up a meeting with my guy at the FBI."

"Just like that?"

"Just like that. These things aren't that complicated, once you decide to do it."

"And that's all we have to do? I call them, then call you?"

"You call your person, then call me and let me know if they're still interested," Anders explained once more. "I'll call my guy at the FBI. They'll take it from there. We'll be out of it. Is that a problem?"

"No," Charlotte replied. "But it seems to be happening fast."

"It has to happen fast if it's going to work."

Anders got out of the car and Charlotte drove away. As he walked up the street, he called Jack Frazer. "Somebody at Galerie Le Meilleur is ready to talk."

"Who is it?"

"I can't say but it's someone with intimate knowledge of whatever they've been doing and apparently they've been doing a lot."

Chapter 34

Frazer was seated at his desk in the office when he took the phone call from Anders. After the conversation ended, he went upstairs to find Gina. "The FBI has a witness who wants to talk," he said.

"About?"

"Galerie Le Meilleur. The Izmirs. They have someone on the inside."

Gina seemed unexcited. "That's good," she said. "Have any idea who it is or what they want to say?"

"No," Anders replied. "But it doesn't matter."

She looked up at him with a puzzled expression. "What do you mean by that?"

"This is a great chance for us to break this story."

"What story?"

"The story we're writing about the Izmirs."

"It would be great if we had a story." She shook her head slowly. "But we don't have it yet."

"Sure we do," he insisted. "We can write about the investigation and use what we know so far. We can say the FBI is investigating and a witness has come forward."

"Did you talk to someone at the FBI about this?"

"No."

"And did your source tell you the FBI was investigating?"

"Well ... no. Not exactly."

"So, you want to write an article that leads with 'a source says something about a witness,' and maybe adds a mention that 'the FBI are apparently investigating' and then dump everything else we know or think we know into it."

Frazer grinned. "Yeah. That's what I'm talking about."

The corners of her mouth turned down in a disapproving expression. "Jack, doing a story like that would be absolutely reckless of us. We don't know who it is or anything about what that person might say or even if the FBI is investigating this."

"But we would be ahead of everyone else," Frazer said. "And we would be first."

"You need to calm down and slow down."

"Why are you against this?"

"Breaking a story is a good thing. But there's one thing we have to have in order to do that."

"And what's that?"

"A story."

"I'm telling you, we have a story. We write about the FBI investigation. Report about them having a witness from inside that wants to talk. And then we dump in everything we've learned so far."

"This person who told you about the witness, does that person work for the FBI?"

"No, but——"

"Then you don't have a source."

"I do have——"

"Not at this newspaper," she snapped. "What you're talking about is bush league. It's the very reason legitimate news outlets get slammed as producing fake news. You want a story, get multiple sources and write about it from a position of substance and authority. Not conjecture and innuendo. We get enough of that crap on talk shows and cable channels."

"I don't——"

"And one more thing," Gina interrupted. "We can't do this kind of story without bringing in the Metro desk."

"Metro?" Frazer shook his head with a disapproving look. "We can't bring them into it. Why would we need them?"

"Because they have people who cover the courts, city hall, the FBI. They know the people and how the system works. And, they have sources."

"We have sources."

"We need someone to fill in the details from the FBI perspective. Someone who might be able to confirm whether the FBI is even conducting an investigation of the Izmirs."

Frazer sighed. "Metro will just mess it all up."

"This is how we do it," Gina explained. "This isn't the 1970s and you're not Hunter Thompson. We don't go it alone. We bring in the people we need, and we do the story right."

"Great," Frazer groaned. "And everyone gets credit."

"Yes," she said. "Everyone gets credit."

Suddenly, he thought of Cooper. Frazer's eyes opened wide in a look of realization. "Then wait." He gestured with both hands. "Give me a chance."

"For what?"

"I know someone who can help."

Gina gave an offhand shrug of his shoulder. "Talk to whomever you want. Take all the time you need. But if we do this story now, with what we have, we're using Metro to help and we're not writing about 'maybe, might, and could' conjecture."

"Okay." Frazer backed away from her desk. "Just let me talk to my guy. I'll find out the details."

Frazer hurried to his desk downstairs and phoned Preston Cooper. The call went straight to voice mail, but he didn't leave a message. Instead, he grabbed his jacket and started toward the elevator. It was late in the afternoon. Cooper was probably at home already. If he wouldn't answer his phone, Frazer would go straight to Cooper's apartment. It was only a quick taxi ride away.

The sky was growing dark when Frazer arrived outside Cooper's apartment building. He came from the taxi and made his way upstairs. With each step, though, he had second thoughts. Maybe this wasn't such a good idea after all. It seemed like a good idea when he was at the office. In the heat of the moment after talking to Gina, he thought it was the thing to do. But now that he was in the building, maybe he should forget the whole thing. Leave now and try to reach Cooper by phone tomorrow. But he didn't stop, and in no time at all, Frazer was standing at Cooper's door. Instead of leaving, he rang the doorbell and waited.

A moment later, the door opened, and Cooper's wife appeared. "Hello, Jack." She had a friendly smile. "I didn't expect to see you today."

"I was wondering if Preston had a moment."

"I'm sure he does," she replied. "Come on in and I'll get him."

As Frazer entered the apartment, Cooper appeared in the hall behind her. He seemed troubled by Frazer's visit. "A little unusual for you to make house calls, isn't it?"

"Yeah," Frazer said. "Maybe this wasn't such a great idea after all."

"Well, you're here now. So, what was so important it couldn't wait?"

"We've been working on a story about the Izmirs."

Cooper shook his head. "I can't comment on that."

"You remember, I'm the one who set you up with Anders."

"And I appreciate it, but I can't talk to you about it."

"We're trying to get ahead of everyone on this and—"

Cooper took Frazer by the shoulder and moved him toward the door. "I really can't talk to you. And I don't appreciate you barging in here like this."

Frazer shrugged free of Cooper's grasp. "I hear you have a witness. Someone from the gallery who's on the inside. Someone who can tell you exactly what they've been doing."

Cooper reached past him and opened the door. "Get out," he demanded.

"Can you at least give me an interview first? Before you give the story to someone else?"

Cooper shoved Frazer into the hall. "Tell whoever you get your information from that they can keep quiet or suffer the consequences. And if you come back here again without an invitation, I'll arrest you."

"But I only—"

Cooper slammed the door shut and Frazer was alone in the hall. Inside he felt as though this was the stupidest thing he'd ever done.

That evening, Charlotte Snider drove to the house on Long Island to talk with Truman Slater, hoping to make him realize the enormity of his decision regarding Sibel. She parked the car in the driveway and walked up the steps to the porch. Through the window, she saw Slater seated at the kitchen table. She tapped on the pane and at the sound of it, he glanced in her direction, then started toward her.

As Slater came from the kitchen and crossed the living room, Charlotte moved toward the door. A moment later, he opened the door and she stepped inside.

Charlotte took a seat on the sofa. Slater sat in a chair opposite her. He looked at her expectantly. "You talked to someone?"

"Yes," she replied. "I talked to a friend who knows someone."

"What did you find out?"

"If Sibel wants to talk, the FBI is willing to listen."

"And they'll take us into witness protection?"

"They won't guarantee protection until they hear what Sibel has to say."

He looked concerned. "Did you tell them her name?"

"No," she replied. "I didn't think I was supposed to."

Slater seemed relieved. "You weren't. We have to keep this as safe as possible for her. But I guess if we told them her name, they might be able to give a more definite answer. Maybe even guarantee protection."

"I doubt it," Charlotte replied. "If I told them her name, I think they might have expressed greater interest, but I don't think they would have guaranteed any more than they've already said."

"Okay. I'll tell her."

Charlotte leaned forward. "Truman, this is a big step."

"I know."

"A lot has happened for you in these last few months."

"Yeah."

"You're discovering yourself at a new level. Your paintings are selling. You're getting lots of attention."

"I know."

"This is everything you wanted. You've worked all your life for this."

"I know that, too."

"Do you really love her?"

Slater looked away. "I ... I don't know. I mean, when it comes right down to it, what is love? You know? What is it? What does it mean to love someone? We have a great time together. My art has gotten a lot better since I've been with her." He looked at her with an ironic smile. "The sex is certainly good."

Charlotte averted her gaze from him. "I don't need to know about that."

"I'm just saying."

She turned back to him. "Well, look. These are the things you ought to be asking yourself. Before you go through with this and throw everything away, you ought to know whether you love her or not. Is she more important than your art?"

"I can't say."

"You need to be certain about that. If you do this, if you go with her, you'll never be able to paint again."

"You told me that before."

"And I'm telling you again now. This is important. And it's not about the value of the paintings I've bought from you, or anything else. This is far more important than any of that."

Slater had an accusing expression. "Why didn't you tell me you were married to Hasan's cousin?"

The question caught Charlotte by surprise. She settled back on the sofa and crossed her arms. "That was a long time ago."

"Not that long. You aren't that old."

"It feels like a long time."

"What was his name?"

"Selim."

"Selim Izmir?"

"No. Selim Tanyu. His friends called him Kem."

"Why?"

"It was short for his first name. Kemal. Kemal Selim Tanyu."

"You refer to him in the past tense. What happened to him?"

"He was in the wrong place at the wrong time."

"Where?"

She wanted to change the subject. "It doesn't matter. We don't need to talk about that."

"He's dead?"

"Yes."

"Do you miss him?"

"Sometimes."

"When?"

She glanced around the room. "Usually, when I come out here."

"Why?"

"We bought this house together. It was our getaway from the city." A smile turned up the corners of her mouth. "He loved this place."

"So, what happened to him?"

"He went to Venice on a trip for Hasan. Something went wrong. One of the men they work with shot someone. Others shot back. Selim was in the way. He got hit."

"He died in Italy?"

"Yes."

"And that's why you told me the people Hasan knows are dangerous people."

She looked over at him. "They are very dangerous."

"Do you think Selim's death was an accident?"

"I have my doubts."

"Did you ever try to find out?"

Charlotte shook her head. "I don't want to know any more than I already do. I prefer to leave it alone."

"So why do you keep working with them? Why not just move on and never see Hasan or Sibel again?"

"I've asked myself that many times and I don't know the answer. It doesn't make sense, but I like Sibel, in spite of herself, in spite of what has happened, and they have some good pieces for sale."

"But you know who they are and yet you continue to do business with them."

"Life only has to make sense in a novel."

"Yet, here you are telling me I shouldn't associate with her."

"No," Charlotte replied. "I'm telling you that you should think about what that association means and the price you will have to pay. The sex might be good, but if that's all you have with her it won't be enough to hold you when it's ten o'clock at night and your heart is begging to express itself on a canvas and you have to keep saying no. Sex won't satisfy that craving."

They sat in silence a moment, then she said, "Did you talk to Robert?"

Slater looked at her blankly. "Robert?"

"Capriati. The artist I—"

"Oh. No."

"You should talk to him before you decide about Sibel."

"Yeah. I suppose so. Can I just call him on the phone?"

"No one would talk to you on the phone about this. You have to go see him. Do you still have his address?"

"Yeah." He felt in the pocket of his pants. "I have it. I can just show up?"

"Yes," Charlotte assured. "And if he has a problem with it, tell him to call me."

Late that night, posing as members of the cleaning crew, six of Nikolay Ivanov's men entered the New York Times building. Cleaning tools and rags in hand, they wandered through the offices until they located a desk with a computer terminal that was logged onto the newspaper's internal system. Using it as an access point, they scrolled through the email accounts for Frazer and Gina and tagged the files with a program that allowed them to see account activity in real time from a remote location.

In Chelsea, others loyal to Ivanov entered Hasan and Sibel's apartment building and tapped their phone lines. Using that tap, they accessed devices in their apartment that were logged onto the Internet and downloaded the user logs.

When they finished at the apartment, the crew did the same at Galerie Le Meilleur. While at the gallery, they also tested the alarm system, mapped the position of security cameras, and noted vulnerable entry points.

While those men were occupied, Darren Brenner, another of Ivanov's associates, rode to the house on Long Island. He passed it once, noting the location of the windows and doors, then went around to a road that took him behind the house. He parked the car at the edge of a wooded area, then switched off the lights and engine. From the glovebox, he took a small card reader and shoved it in his pocket, then stepped from the car, eased the door shut, and made his way into the woods.

A few minutes later, Brenner emerged at a spot that afforded a clear view of the backside of the house. From his location, he watched the lights go on downstairs and caught a glimpse of Slater in the kitchen. After a while, the lights went out downstairs and came on in a bedroom upstairs. They burned a while but finally, only a light in the bathroom remained.

From the activity he'd observed, Brenner concluded Slater was alone in the house and most likely upstairs in bed. Probably asleep.

He waited a while longer, just to be sure, then came from the woods, walked to the back of the house, and jimmied open the door.

Stepping as quietly as possible, he slowly worked his way through the kitchen to the living room. Slater's paintings lined the walls in both rooms and more were propped along the wall beneath them, but he saw nothing of note among them.

As expected, he found Slater asleep in bed upstairs. His pants hung from the bed frame at the foot of the bed. His shoes were on the floor beside it. A shirt lay in the floor. Along the wall opposite the door there was a dresser and on it was a cell phone.

Brenner made his way to the dresser, picked up the cell phone, and retreated to the hall. He took a seat at the top of the stairs and removed the card reader from his pocket. Using a pocketknife, he popped out the SIM card from Slater's phone and inserted the card into a slot at the end of the reader. He placed an empty SIM card in a slot on the side of the device and pressed a button that cloned Slater's SIM card to the empty one.

When he was done, Slater returned the original SIM to Slater's phone, then placed the reader and the SIM card copy in his pocket. He listened a moment to make sure Slater still was asleep and when he heard nothing suspicious, he returned Slater's phone to its place on the dresser.

With his work in the house complete, Brenner made his way downstairs and left the house through the back door. He retraced his path across the yard to the woods and stepped into the shadows. He waited there a few minutes, to make sure he was not followed, then continued to the opposite side of the woods where the car was parked.

In the car, he removed a cell phone from the glove box and inserted the copied SIM card into the phone, then turned on the phone and checked for a dial tone. Satisfied all was in order, he placed the phone on the seat beside him, stowed the card reader in the glovebox, and cranked the engine.

Three hours later, Brenner arrived at the house in Bound Brook. Inside, he found Krylov seated at the kitchen table, sipping from a water glass that was half full of whiskey. A bottle sat on the table. Krylov looked over at him as he entered the room and their eyes met for the first time. Krylov smiled. "Did you know that to be labeled bourbon in the United States, whiskey must be made from a grain mixture that is at least fifty-one percent corn?" He gestured to the bottle and Brenner noticed the Jack Daniel's label.

"No," Brenner replied. "I didn't know that."

"And." Krylov took a drunken pause. "In addition to that." He paused again. "It must be aged in new, charred-oak barrels. New, mind you. Not used."

"That's interesting."

"I'm sure it must make the barrel makers happy."

"No doubt." Brenner took a seat across from Krylov. "It seems to be doing a good job making you happy, too."

"Oh, it is," Krylov replied. "But you have to drink quite a lot of it."

"Not as strong as you're used to?"

Krylov smiled broadly. "Unlike fine Russian vodka, American Bourbon whiskey cannot be distilled any greater than eighty percent alcohol."

"Looks like you're getting the full eighty percent from that bottle."

Krylov admired the drink in his hand a moment, then emptied the glass in one gulp. He set the glass on the table and looked over at Brenner with a surprisingly serious expression. "Were you successful?"

"Very much so," Brenner replied. He took the cell phone from his pocket and placed it on the table. "That is now a clone of the artist's phone." He tapped it softly with his index finger for emphasis. "If this phone rings, just listen. Don't talk."

"Right."

"Any calls the artist receives, will ring on that phone."

"Good." Krylov placed the phone in his pocket, then filled the glass half full with bourbon. "Care for a drink?"

"No," Brenner replied. "I still have to drive home."

Krylov took a sip and smiled. "Be careful."

Chapter 35

A little before eleven the next morning, Charlotte picked up Sibel Izmir from the parking lot behind Galerie Le Meilleur and drove her across town to Bobby Van's Steakhouse on East Fifty-Fourth Street. Sibel was quiet that morning and Charlotte didn't attempt to engage her in conversation as they drove away.

Two blocks from the restaurant, though, Charlotte steered the car to the curb and brought it to a stop, then looked over at Sibel. "Are you sure you're okay with this?"

"Yes," Sibel said with a nod. "I'm just nervous."

"That's to be expected."

"This is new for me, you know." Sibel gripped the door handle with one hand. "I've never turned against my husband before. I've never turned against anyone before."

"The thing you should be asking is whether it's the right thing."

"Do you think it's the right thing?"

"That's not for me to say," Charlotte replied. "We both know what Hasan is like. We both know what he's doing."

Sibel nodded her head nervously. "And we both know you'd never do this, no matter what."

"I was never in this situation."

Sibel cut her eyes at Charlotte in an accusing way. "You think Kem wasn't part of it?"

"I'm not saying that. I'm saying, I never got to this place with him."

"And what place is that?"

"Look, Sibel." Charlotte's voice was stern. "I know you're nervous. I know this is unsettling. But don't pick a fight with me because you're upset. If you don't want to do it, tell me and I'll take you right back to the gallery."

"Sorry," Sibel said meekly. "It's just, one minute it feels right and the next minute it feels wrong."

"I'm sure it does."

Charlotte faced forward in the seat, put the car in gear, and steered it into traffic. Two blocks later, they arrived at Bobby Van's. An attendant helped them from the car, then parked it for them while they made their way toward the restaurant entrance.

Inside, Charlotte surveyed the dining room from the entryway and noticed two men seated at a table midway to the kitchen door. One of them was David Anders. The other was a man she'd never seen before but assumed was an FBI agent. Anders caught her eye. Charlotte turned to Sibel. "I believe you know David Anders?"

"Yes."

"You see him at that table?"

Sibel glanced across the room. "Yes," she said. "Who is that with him?"

"That man is an FBI agent."

"What do I do? Just walk up to the table and introduce myself?"

"The restrooms are located through a door in the corner to the left. Do you see it?"

"Yes," Sibel said. "I see it."

"Walk back there and go through that door. The man at the table will follow you and take you out through the kitchen."

"Just like that?"

"Just like that."

Sibel looked worried. "Are you sure it's safe?"

"As safe as it can be."

"I'm scared."

"I know." Charlotte forced a smile. "I'm a little shaken myself but that man with Anders is the one you want to talk to."

"Okay."

Anders turned in Charlotte's direction and gave her a look. She turned to Sibel. "It's time," she said. "They're ready for you."

Sibel looked over at her. "I love you like a sister."

"And I love you," Charlotte replied. "Now go. Do what you came here to do." She watched as Sibel turned away, squared her shoulders, and walked through the dining room at a deliberate, measured pace. The same pace, the same elegant gait Charlotte remembered from the thousand other times she'd seen Sibel take control of a room merely by the force of her presence. A lump formed in her throat at the sight of it, but she swallowed hard and watched as Sibel pushed open the door to the restrooms and disappeared from sight. Before the door closed behind her, the man who had been seated at the table with Anders caught up to her and followed her through. And then the door closed behind them, and they were gone.

Half an hour later, Susan Griffin was seated at her cubicle in the FBI building when she noticed Preston Cooper go past in a hurry. He returned a moment later with Scott Davenport in tow. Both men seemed excited and Griffin watched as they made their way to the elevator. Lights above the elevator door indicated they were traveling upstairs. Griffin assumed they were going to the floor where Cooper's office was located.

Griffin remained at her desk a while longer, then, with a notepad for a prop, she walked over to the elevator and rode upstairs. When the elevator doors opened, she glanced to the left but saw nothing of interest, so she started down the hall to the right. She moved slowly, checking each open room as if searching for someone, which she was.

Finally, Griffin came to an assistant seated at a workstation a few doors from Cooper's office. The assistant's name was Mary. Griffin had seen her around but hadn't bothered to remember her last name. She did, however, remember that Mary enjoyed listening to alternative music, which was odd given her otherwise plain and unassuming demeanor.

Griffin did her best to appear legitimate. "Did Scott Davenport come up here?"

Mary nodded. "Do you need him?"

"I don't want to interrupt," Griffin replied. "I'm working on a project with him and was going to ask him a question earlier, but he went by my desk so fast I couldn't stop him."

"He's been doing that a lot lately." Mary scooted back from her desk. "Want me to get him for you?"

"No." Griffin waved her off. "I don't want to interrupt if he's in a meeting. It's not that important."

"He's in with Mr. Cooper. They're talking to someone."

Someone scurried past Griffin with an armful of documents. She moved to get out of their way. "Looks like you're into something big up here today," she said. "What's going on?"

"They brought in a witness."

"Oh?" Griffin gave her a look of surprise. "For what?"

"Something to do with an art gallery," Mary said. "Apparently they think it's some kind of scam. Money laundering. Something like that."

Griffin feigned a perplexed expression. "Galerie Le Meilleur?"

Now Mary looked surprised. "How did you know?"

"I've been working on that case."

"You must have done some good work." Mary smiled. "I hear whoever they brought in is the focus of that investigation."

"A focus," Griffin corrected. "We're looking at more than one person."

"Rather big stuff," Mary continued. "They've been working on a search warrant application this morning, in addition to everything else."

"For the gallery?"

Mary nodded. "The US Attorney has been in here a couple of times already."

"I didn't hear about that." It was true. Griffin hadn't heard and this was just the sort of thing she wanted to know. "What are they searching for?"

"I'm not sure. I suppose whatever they can find that has something to do with that case."

"That's what Scott's meeting with Cooper about?"

"Yes."

Griffin feigned concern. "I'm right in the middle of this and I didn't know about it."

"It's all happening rather fast."

They talked a while longer, then Griffin returned to her desk. It was early still, almost half an hour before her usual lunch, but the matter of the warrant seemed urgent. If Cooper searched the gallery, he would find documents and names and no telling what else. She had to tell someone. She had to act.

Rather than waiting for her scheduled lunchtime, Griffin took her purse from the desk, rode the elevator downstairs to the lobby, and left the building. Once outside, she walked up the block to Starbucks on the corner. The clerk seemed to recognize her and greeted her with a smile. She ordered a cup of coffee and waited impatiently while it was prepared, then made her way to a table in back and took a seat.

When she was settled in place, Griffin reached inside her purse for the iPad, then realized she'd been in a hurry that morning and left it at home. A sense of frustration came over her. She preferred the iPad to her smartphone. It was easier to use and seemed more secure. And it allowed her to send documents easily. But she had no choice. This couldn't wait. If Cooper searched the gallery before she warned anyone, she would be in trouble.

Griffin took a sip of coffee, then used her phone and sent a text to the number she used before, the one obtained from Bradley Monzikova at the beginning of her involvement. The message read, "Gallery warrant pending."

❖ ❖ ❖

Gennady Krylov lay across the bed in the house at Bound Brook where he'd been staying. His head throbbed with a hangover from the bourbon he consumed the night before and he did his best to remain still and quiet.

Killing Kirchen felt good and right. It had to be done. But killing anyone, even someone as aggravating and troublesome as that damn German was upsetting for him, especially when the killing was messy. Kirchen's head exploded against the car window on the passenger side and the image of it was stuck in Krylov's mind, just as the gray matter from his head stuck to the window. And the blood. Red, thick blood. All over that side of the car. Dumping it in the bay was a relief but it didn't erase the image. Bourbon was supposed to do that but it was taking more and more these days.

As he lay there, trying not to move, Krylov's phone vibrated. He wanted to throw it against the wall and silence it forever but instead he checked the screen and saw he had received a message. He opened it and read, "Warrant. Move the art."

It took a moment for the meaning to sink in, but gradually Krylov realized the FBI was about to search Galerie Le Meilleur. If they searched the gallery, they would seize documents and information related to the many transactions Mogilevich had been involved with. Not directly, but close enough to cause a problem. They might even find a document or two bearing his name.

More important for Krylov's immediate concern, a search of the gallery by the FBI would mean the place would be occupied by federal agents. Their presence would prevent him from removing the remaining paintings from the gallery, particularly the Matisse, which was one of the things he was sent to do.

Ignoring the throbbing in his head, Krylov pushed himself to a sitting position on the edge of the bed and sent a reply to the text that read, "Notify Hasan." He then called Kumarin. "Are your guys ready?"

"Almost," Kumarin replied. "Why?"

"We have less time than we thought."

"How much time do we have?"

"We have to go now."

"Now?" Kumarin sounded upset

"Right now," Krylov replied. "Get your guys and the truck and meet me here at the house. We'll go together."

"I can't—"

"Just do it," Krylov shouted.

"Okay," Kumarin answered. "We're on our way."

When the call ended, Krylov forced himself up from the bed, put on his jacket, and made his way downstairs. He took a soft drink from the refrigerator in the kitchen and sipped from it as he made his way to the front room where he stood by the window, watching as traffic passed by on the road out front.

Twenty minutes later, the truck turned into the driveway and came to a stop beside the house. Krylov went out to meet it. As he made his way toward it, he noticed Kumarin was seated in the cab with only one other member of his crew.

Krylov yanked open the door on the passenger side and glared up at Kumarin. "Where is everyone else?"

"They're coming in the SUV." Kumarin pointed toward the street. "There wasn't enough room in here for all of them."

Krylov hauled himself up to the passenger seat. The crewman moved to the middle. "I wanted us to go together," Krylov grumbled. "So we wouldn't be hanging around waiting for the others to arrive."

"They're right there." Kumarin gestured over his shoulder. Krylov glanced in that direction and saw the SUV waiting. He slammed the door shut and slumped against it. "Let's go," he said. "We can argue about this later." Kumarin backed the truck into the yard to turn it around, then drove to the street and started on the way. The SUV followed.

Chapter 36

An hour later, Krylov and the crew arrived at Galerie Le Meilleur. Kumarin backed the truck to the loading dock and when it came to a stop, Krylov got out. He entered the building through the service doors and made his way to the safe room where the paintings were stored. Jamie Wright was there and initially refused to give them access but Krylov phoned Hasan who told her to do it. She opened the room, then retreated to the main exhibition room. As she left, Ahmed Izmir arrived. "What is this?" he demanded.

"Kirchen sent us," Krylov replied.

Ahmed looked perplexed. "Kirchen? What does Kirchen have to do with us?"

Krylov chuckled. "Good answer." He took Ahmed by the shoulders and turned him toward the hall. "If you don't mind," he said kindly, "we have work to do. You should join that lady out front."

"Not until you tell——"

Krylov interrupted. "Your brother can answer all your questions."

Just then, Hasan entered from the loading dock behind them. He glared at Krylov but remained silent and motioned for Ahmed to follow him. They walked together up the hall and disappeared.

Meanwhile, Kumarin and his crew went to work removing artwork from the safe room. They counted it, listed it on an inventory document, then crated it for shipment using the same wooden crates from the recent shipment that Krylov had helped orchestrate from France.

When the crates were full and all of the art had been accounted for, Kumarin and his men used a forklift and began placing the crates inside the cargo area of the truck. Krylov checked the inventory once more. "Did you see a painting by Matisse."

Kumarin frowned. "He is an artist?"

"Yes. He is an artist." Krylov found it impossible that Kumarin wouldn't know the name. "There was supposed to be a painting by him in this lot. It's a picture of a woman with a table and a vase. Did you see it?"

Kumarin shrugged. "I have no idea who painted any of them." He pointed to the list. "Whatever we found is listed on that notepad you are holding."

Krylov checked the list once more, then walked up to the exhibition room in search of Jamie Wright. He found her standing near the window and asked about the Matisse. She denied knowing anything about it. "Where's Hasan?" Krylov asked.

"He's gone," Jamie replied.

"And Ahmed?"

"He's gone, too," she said. "They left together. Do you want me to call them?"

"No," Krylov answered. "There isn't time now. I will deal with them later." He walked back to the loading dock and discovered the crates with the paintings were gone, as were the men who'd helped load them. Only Kumarin remained. He stood near the truck with the door closed and locked.

"Do you have documents for this load?" Kumarin asked.

Krylov was puzzled. "Everything is loaded already?" He assumed the process would take longer.

"Yes," Kumarin replied. "Everything is loaded, but we need papers for it."

Krylov retrieved an envelope from the desk in Hasan's office and brought it to Kumarin. "Papers," he said, and he slapped the envelope against the palm of Kumarin's outstretched hand.

"Good." Kumarin turned to get into the cab of the truck. "Now we can leave."

"Wait," Krylov barked.

Kumarin halted abruptly and turned to face him. "Wait? For what?

"I want to see the crates," Krylov said. "Open the door."

A frown wrinkled Kumarin's forehead. "You don't trust me?"

"I don't trust anyone. Open the door."

Kumarin unlocked the cargo door and raised it all the way up. Krylov took a crowbar from a workbench in the loading area and gestured with it toward the truck. "Get in there with me."

Kumarin looked worried. "Why? You think I might lock you in there and drive away?"

"The thought occurred to me," Krylov said, "but I need you to help me get the lids open on the crates."

"What for?"

"I want to see inside."

With Kumarin helping, Krylov pried open all three boxes, moving the lids far enough to see the contents. Assured that the crates held all of the paintings taken from the gallery, and equally certain the painting by Matisse was not among them, he replaced the lids and banged them tight with the backside of the bar.

When they were finished, Krylov looked over at Kumarin. "Here's what you must never do," he said. "You must never assume that everything is going well. If I send you to do a job like this on your own, I want you to check the crates. And if you get distracted, as I was just now about that painting, then you must make your own people—people who hold your life in their hands—you must make them show you they are worthy of your trust even when you question it."

Kumarin nodded. "Okay."

"Otherwise," Krylov continued. "One day, a new man will join the crew, and you will think nothing of it, and he will kill you. Understand?"

"I understand."

"Good. Now let's get these crates to the docks. Brooklyn?"

"Yes. In Brooklyn. I have connections."

With Kumarin at the steering wheel, they drove from the gallery in Chelsea to the docks in Brooklyn. When they arrived at the gate, a guard stopped them but when he saw Kumarin in the cab, he stepped aside and waved them through.

"Friend of yours?" Krylov asked.

"Relative," Kumarin replied.

At the Customs screening station, Kumarin handed an officer the documents for the load. The papers indicated the contents of the crates had been pre-approved for Customs. The officer acknowledged that status and directed them to an area where the truck was x-rayed by a mobile scanner. When the scan was complete, an officer on the ground waved them past.

Krylov looked over at Kumarin. "That is it?"

"Yes," Kumarin replied. "That is it."

"How is that possible?"

"They know from the documents that we are supposed to be carrying art. So, that is what they are checking for. That and explosives."

"And you don't try to hide the contents."

"No. We don't have a bomb so trying to hide the cargo would only bring unnecessary attention. The best way to get a shipment past US Customs is to give them what they want. Fill out the forms properly. Check the correct boxes. Don't try to pass off a load as something it could never be."

"So, we said it was art on the papers, we have art in the crates, and they can see that from their scanning equipment."

"Right," Kumarin said. "We let them do their job and their scanner confirms what we said. The images look like art. They were checking for art. That is all they want to know."

"And no bombs."

"Right. They're mostly worried about bombs. Nuclear devices. Stowaways. They don't look at the cargo to see if it is precisely what the documents claim it to be. The papers say artwork. The scan fits the pattern for artwork. They're good. We're good."

Krylov was optimistic. "Where is this ship you mentioned?"

Kumarin pointed to the right. "It is over there." He steered the truck along the docks to a Russian freighter that was being loaded with roll-on roll-off freight—a ship with an opening designed to accept trucks and trailers driven directly onto it.

A man near the rear of the ship directed them forward. Kumarin pointed the truck in that direction and eased it into the hold of ship. The man shouted as they passed, "Someone will show you where to park it."

They drove the truck deep inside the ship and parked the truck behind a trailer truck already in place. Krylov climbed from the cab and waited for Kumarin to join him. As they walked back to the entrance, Krylov said, "How will they get the truck off on the other side?"

"The keys are in the ignition," Kumarin said. "Someone will drive it off."

Krylov had never heard of such a thing, but he was impressed by the ease of the process and made a mental note to remember it for future shipments.

While the crates were being loaded onto the Russian freighter at the Brooklyn facility, Preston Cooper and Scott Davenport arrived at Galerie Le Meilleur with a team of FBI agents. New York policemen were on hand for extra manpower. They sealed the building perimeter and cordoned off the streets, front and back.

Armed with a search warrant, Cooper and Davenport entered the gallery through the front door. Cooper noticed the paintings hanging on the wall. They appeared undisturbed and he was confident they would find what they were after.

Jamie Wright stood at the counter near the back wall of the main room. Startled by their presence, she raised her hands above her head as Cooper came toward her and FBI agents filled the room.

"We're with the FBI," Cooper announced. "We have a warrant to search the premises."

"There's no one here but me," Jamie said. Her voice quavered.

Cooper took the warrant from the inside pocket of his jacket. "This is a search warrant," he said. "It allows us to search the building and seize evidence." He handed the document to her.

Jamie lowered her hands and took the document from him. "Sibel and Hasan aren't here," she said. "Neither is Ahmed."

"That's okay," Cooper replied with a smile. "You're here and we have a warrant. That's all we need."

Davenport and the other agents had disappeared down the hall that led to the loading dock. Cooper remained up front in the main exhibition room. He glanced around the room at the art on the walls. "Interesting pieces." He stepped closer to those nearest where he stood and saw a placard that noted the artist's name. "Truman Slater," he said. "That's a popular name these days."

"We are the official dealer for his work," Jamie explained. "We have—"

Davenport interrupted as he burst into the room. "It's all gone," he blurted. His eyes were wide and he had a worried look.

Cooper frowned. "What do you mean?"

"The only thing left is what you see on the walls out here." Davenport gestured to the room. "Everything else we thought was here is gone."

"And the Matisse?"

Davenport shook his head. "No sign of it."

Cooper turned to Jamie. "What do you know about this?"

"Some men were here earlier today. They loaded everything from the back into a truck and took it away."

"When?"

"I don't know. Not long. They haven't been gone long."

"Where were they going?"

She shrugged. "I don't know."

"Do you know who they were?"

Jamie shook her head. "I've never seen them before."

"Was Hasan here with them?"

"He arrived just after they got here, but he and Ahmed left while the men loaded the truck."

"Ahmed was here, too?"

"Yes. He arrived about the time they did."

"Did he know who those men were?"

"No. I don't think so. Hasan seemed to know, but Ahmed was upset. I don't think he knew who they were."

"All right." Cooper turned to Davenport. "We need to find Hasan and Ahmed. Bring both of them in for questioning." While Davenport passed the assignment to one of the agents, Cooper turned back to Jamie. "I assume you have security cameras that cover the building."

"We have cameras." She nodded. "But I don't know how much they caught."

"Were they operational?"

"I assume so," she said. "The system is supposed to operate all the time."

"Who is in charge of it?"

"Sibel usually takes care of it. She usually takes care of everything."

"Sibel Izmir?"

"Yes. She's Hasan's wife."

"Where are the monitors for the cameras?"

"In Sibel's office."

"Show me."

Jamie led Cooper and Davenport to Sibel's office and pointed to a panel of monitors mounted on the wall to the left. "That's the monitors for the system," she said. "The server is in there." She pointed to a cabinet in the corner. "Images upload to the cloud but I don't know the password for it."

"We need copies of whatever the system recorded."

"I'll have to call a technician to get it. How far back do you want?"

Cooper thought a moment, then said, "You know what, we need

the entire system." He glanced over at Davenport. "Get our people in here. This is a crime scene. I want our people to go through this security system, the computers, the files. Have them to go through everything in the building and glean whatever information they can find that might tell us what went on here today and what this gallery is actually doing."

"That'll take a while," Davenport said.

"We have all the time we need," Cooper replied. "Put out a bolo on the two brothers. Hasan and Ahmed. And make sure Marcel Kirchen is still on the list." He looked at Jamie. "Do you know Marcel Kirchen?"

Jamie nodded. "I know who he is."

"Was he the one who took the art?"

"No," she replied. "Kirchen wasn't here. I've seen Kirchen before, but I've never seen the men who came today."

Davenport spoke up. "And you just let them take the art?"

"No," Jamie retorted. "I didn't know them, and I refused to let them in, but they called Hasan and he told me to let them in the room. So, I unlocked the safe room where we keep the art and got out of the way."

"Okay," Cooper said. "Thank you for your help. Someone will take a statement from you." He gestured to one of the other agents and they escorted her from the room. When she was gone, Cooper looked over at Davenport. "Hasan and the others knew we were coming." His voice was firm and his look intense.

Davenport scowled. "Someone tipped them off."

"And if they had as many paintings as Edelman claims," Cooper noted, "they had a lot to move."

"To get that many paintings out of here this morning, they would have had to know about our search almost as soon as we did."

"That's what bothers me most," Cooper agreed. "Whoever tipped them off is working for us."

"What can we do about it?"

"Maybe not much. I'll see if the NSA can sift through their information. They scoop up everything. They might be able to tell us something about our leak. And maybe about where the truck went."

Davenport looked perplexed. "Isn't that illegal?"

"Spying on criminals? I thought that was what we do."

"Whatever happened here today is a domestic issue," Davenport noted. "The NSA is barred from listening to US citizens."

Cooper gave him a look. "We don't know if the people who did this were US citizens."

"They were on US soil."

Cooper nodded. "NSA listens to everything. We need to know what they heard whether we can use it or not."

"It would be easier to do it that way," Davenport acknowledged, "but if they share their information with us, I don't think it or anything that results from it will hold up in court."

"I'm not worried about making a case that will hold up in court," Cooper argued. "If we have a mole in our operation, we have bigger problems than the court."

"Bigger than enforcing the law?"

"This is about the integrity of the Bureau," Cooper said.

"And you would ignore the law to protect the Bureau?"

"Not ignore it," Cooper replied. "Just squeeze it a little."

Chapter 37

While events transpired in the city, Truman Slater was alone at the house on Long Island. Lonesome. Frustrated. Surely Sibel must be talking to someone. It was all arranged. Charlotte had helped. He knew that much. But the silence. He hadn't been ready for the silence of Sibel not being there.

After a while, he left the house and walked out to the studio. He picked up a can of paint and a brush and tried to paint, but it was no use. The emotion he'd come to rely on wasn't there. He tried again but it was no different so he laid the brush on the table and set the paint can beside it, then walked outside.

The sun was bright and the sky clear and he shielded his eyes against the glare. The day seemed pointless without her to share it. Pointless. Deflated. Listless. He glanced to the left and saw the car parked at the end of the driveway. He could go for a drive. Let the windows down and cruise along the water with the wind blowing through his hair. A drive. That might—

Suddenly it occurred to him that he didn't have to stay out there by himself. He could drive into the city. Find Sibel. Talk to her. Find out what happened and what she planned and when they could be together.

In just a few strides, Slater was at the car and got in behind the steering wheel. Moments later, he backed the car onto the grass, turned it around, and drove out to the road.

Two hours later, Slater was in Chelsea and only two blocks from Galerie Le Meilleur. He slowed the car and searched both sides of the street for a parking space but found none. As he approached the gallery, though, he saw half a dozen parking spaces were empty. He started toward them, then noticed the crime scene tape and a patrolman out front. The patrolman motioned for him to keep moving and Slater continued down the block.

From the gallery, he drove over to the apartment building where Hasan and Sibel lived. He wanted to park the car and go inside to knock on their door, but police cars were parked up and down the block. Agents in suits with jackets that identified them as FBI agents were going in and out. A van was parked among the patrol cars and some of the agents were placing boxes inside it through the rear doors.

Once again, Slater kept going and eventually came to Broadway. He turned south and took it toward the tip of Manhattan, intending to drive down to Battery Park. The traffic signal at Delancey Street caught him and as he waited for the light to change he saw the towers of Williamsburg Bridge off to the left. That reminded him of Charlotte's suggestion that he talk to Robert Capriati about Sibel. He didn't want to. He preferred to talk to Sibel herself. But she wasn't available and he wasn't sure if she ever would be and suddenly he was curious about the nature of her relationship with Capriati. Had they really been involved? Were they lovers? Really lovers? In love with each other in the maddeningly passionate way that he felt for her and she felt for him. Or where they merely partners for sexual activity? Benefits or commitment. That's what he wanted to know.

When the traffic signal turned green, Slater was in the wrong lane to make a left turn so he continued down Broadway, then made the block and came back to Delancey Street. He followed Delancey onto the Williamsburg Bridge. The off-ramp on the Brooklyn side dropped him onto Roebling Street and he brought the car to a stop in front of a bagel shop a few blocks away.

With the car idling, he dug a wadded piece of paper from his pocket that held Robert Capriati's address. The building where he lived was on Driggs Avenue. He drove in that direction and located it with little difficulty. Instead of going inside immediately, though, he parked in an open spot across the street and sat there, staring at the building and thinking.

He didn't need Robert Capriati to tell him about Sibel. He knew her better than Capriati ever did. Better than anyone. "I just need to know where she is. Capriati doesn't know anything about that." The only person who did, was Charlotte Snider

After a few minutes, Slater put the car in gear and drove back to the Williamsburg Bridge. He crossed into Manhattan and parked outside Charlotte's apartment. A few minutes later, he knocked on her door. When she opened the door, Slater pushed his way past her.

"Where is Sibel?" he demanded.

Charlotte closed the door. "I don't know where she is and I don't appreciate you forcing your way in here."

"I'm not forcing my way into anything," Slater replied. "I'm just trying to find her. I've looked everywhere and I don't know where she is."

"Truman." Charlotte spoke with a parental tone. "This is how it works. People who talk go into protection. No one they knew before ever sees them again. It's brutal, but apparently it works."

"She was supposed to take me with her."

"You were really going with her?"

"Yes." He looked over at her and sighed. "I don't know."

"Then maybe it's better this way."

"What do you mean?"

"You have your art. You have …"

"No," he snapped. "I want her. I didn't know it before, but I know it now. I want her."

"Are you sure?"

"Yes," he said. "I'm sure." Once again, though, he looked away. "I think so."

Charlotte rubbed his shoulder. "I know this is difficult."

"She was everything to me. She wouldn't just leave like this. They must be holding her somewhere. They weren't supposed to arrest her." He glared at her. "Did you let them arrest her?"

"Don't be ridiculous. Did you ever think maybe she wanted to go without you?"

"You mean she was just using me?" Charlotte just looked at him. He shook his head. "She would never do that. She loved me."

"Talk to Robert Capriati."

Slater was angry. "I don't need to talk to him." He turned toward the door. "I'm going down there to the FBI and make them let me see her."

Charlotte grabbed his arm. "Don't. It'll only make things worse. They know what they're doing."

"But she loves me," Slater insisted. "I know it. She wants to be with me and they're not letting her."

"Talk to Capriati. Talk to him right now. I'm sure he's in his studio."

"I don't give a damn about Robert Capriati. I want Sibel."

Slater opened the door and stormed from the apartment. He walked downstairs, made his way to his car and got in. Frustrated. Angry. Sad. He rested his head against the steering wheel. "She would never treat me like this." He began to cry. "I just know she wouldn't."

From Charlotte's apartment in Manhattan, Slater drove back across the Williamsburg Bridge and located Capriati's studio again. This time, he parked the car, went inside, and knocked on the door. When Capriati saw him, his face lit up. "You're Truman Slater." He said it with genuine excitement and a broad smile. "I've heard good things about you."

Slater was caught off guard by Capriati's brash friendliness. "I don't think we've met."

"No." Capriati stepped aside and gestured for him to enter. "But we have now. Come in." Slater stepped inside and Capriati closed the door. "You don't look so good," he said. "Is something wrong?"

Slater ignored the question and glanced around the room. It was a big space with a high ceiling and there were lots of large canvases. Half a dozen with paintings in progress. "You work on a large scale," he noted.

"Yes," Capriati replied. "Big pictures. Big space. Lots of things going at once. That's the way I like it. Big ideas."

"Big ideas?"

"That's the key."

Slater pointed to a canvas on an easel. A painting of a man standing alone in a vast field. "The isolation of man against the enormity of nature?"

Capriati had a puzzled frown. "The what?"

"The big idea," Slater elaborated. "Isolation of man. Man alone against the backdrop of nature's enormity. Frustration of attempted change."

"Oh." Capriati grinned. "I don't mean that kind of big idea," he explained. "I mean, ideas like, 'brown won't sell well unless you contrast it with something bright.'" He moved closer to the painting. "So here we have the field." He pointed to indicate while he talked. "A wheat field. Wheat. Grass. Whatever. But it's lightened some from what it is in nature, so it isn't too dark on the canvas. And then the trees on the side are green. The sky is blue. His shirt is red. Draws the viewer's eye to the center of the painting. Emotes a pleasant sense of home."

Slater nodded. "So, by idea you mean concept. Design. Intention."

Capriati smiled. "Find something that sells and work variations of it until it stops selling."

Slater glanced around the room once more and noted that all the paintings seemed to follow this general color scheme, regardless of the content. "They taught you that at that California art school?" He knew a little about Capriati. More than he cared to acknowledge.

"Yes. The color part," Capriati replied. "You're a California man, too, aren't you?"

"Montana."

"Montana," Capriati observed. "The real West."

"It's definitely real," Slater said.

"Did you come here for something? I seem to remember Charlotte Snider mentioned you might stop by."

"I wanted to ask you about Sibel Izmir."

"Ah. Yes." Capriati leaned against a table. "You're at her gallery now. I noticed your paintings are selling quite well. Getting some buzz from the Times."

"A little."

"Any publicity, as long as they spell your name correctly?"

"I suppose."

"But that's not the part you're asking about."

"No." Slater shook his head. "Not that part."

Capriati grinned. "She got to you, too, I see."

Slater didn't like the comment and his forehead wrinkled in an angry frown. "What does that mean?"

Capriati pushed up from the table and walked over to a refrigerator at the opposite corner. "You want a beer?"

"Sure," Slater said. The guy might be a jerk but right then, a cold beer would taste good. Capriati took a bottle from the refrigerator and handed it to him, then took one for himself. After a sip or two, Capriati said, "When Charlotte Snider convinced Sibel to take my paintings, I thought she took them because she was interested in my art. Turns out, that was only a cover."

"A cover?

"A story to tell Hasan, if he asked. I'm not sure he ever asked. Maybe it was a story she told to herself." Capriati shrugged. "I don't know. All I know is, she got me in bed and the paintings started to sell and I was happy." Once again, Slater was angered by Capriati's comments, and by his cavalier attitude, but he said nothing. Capriati seemed to understand. "I know how you feel. I was angry when Haddon had this same talk with me."

Slater was puzzled. "Haddon?"

"Calder Haddon. The guy before me."

Haddon was an artist who came to New York from Michigan.

He was enormously talented as a representational artist. Landscapes, mostly. Then, right when his art was taking off and everyone who saw it wanted to buy it, he was killed in an accident on the Long Island Expressway. But Slater did not know he had once been represented by Sibel. "She sold Haddon's art?"

"Sold his art and took him to bed. Just like with me. And now with you."

"What about the other two guys? The ones who are there now."

"Stone and Sedaris?"

"What about them?"

"What happened with them? As far as I can tell, she didn't dump them for me."

Capriati grinned again. "They're gay."

Slater was surprised. "Gay?"

"You didn't know?"

"I never thought about it."

"They didn't know each other until she brought them to the gallery. Now they live together. I can't remember where. Decent artists, by the way. Much more commercial than your stuff."

Once again, Slater ignored Capriati's attitude. "So, if you were seeing her back then, why aren't you seeing her now?"

"She dumped me for Stone."

"But you said he's gay?"

"She didn't know it at the time any more than you did until I told you. She saw Stone at an art show or fair or something. Took a liking to him. Then she suggested I had matured to a point that I needed to move on to the next level. You know, the 'I'm concerned for your future' story. Which was right. I was ready to move uptown. But that's not why she pushed me out. She wanted Stone."

"And then she found out he was gay."

"Yes. So, she moved on to Sedaris. Then she found out they were partners."

"How do you know this?"

"After she found out they were gay, she came over here wanting to get back together with me. I was established at another gallery and selling at a totally different level. I also was seeing someone and had no interest in her, professionally or otherwise."

"How did she take it?"

"Not too well at first. But not long after that, she brought you into the picture."

"She didn't find me. Charlotte Snider took me to her."

"Which I thought was odd when I heard about it. They've never had three new artists at one time at that gallery, then I saw you at a showing and realized why she took you on."

Slater nodded. "For the sex."

"It was obvious. Handsome guy. Young."

"And not for the art."

"Well, the art had to be good enough to sell. Which it is. So, I guess, for her, the art is extra. For you, it's the other way around."

"I suppose."

"Look, man, whatever it takes. Right? You gotta sell to live and you're selling well and living right. So, enjoy."

After talking to Capriati, Slater drove to the house on Long Island. He entered through the back door and came to the kitchen where he found a bottle of whiskey in the cabinet. It was half full and he poured himself a drink in a water glass, then had another. After gulping down a third while standing at the sink, he took the bottle and glass and moved to the living room where he flopped onto a chair and stared out the window while he finished off the rest that was in the bottle.

When the first bottle was empty, he went back to the kitchen, tossed the empty into the trash can, and searched through the cabinet again. He was drunk, inebriated, intoxicated, perhaps as never before, and his body swayed from side to side as he stared at items on the shelf, trying to remember what he was looking for.

After a moment, he remembered and found a bottle of Scotch near where the whiskey had been. He removed the top and filled the water glass half full, then topped it off with ginger ale from the refrigerator. Thoroughly inebriated, he spilled Scotch on his pants in the process and sloshed some on the floor. And then he began talking to himself.

"So, you were seeing Capriati before me."

"Yes, you were," he shouted in response. "Don't start lying to me now. I know things. I've talked to people and I know things now."

"No!" He shouted again and swatted with his free hand as if attempting to elude Sibel's touch. "You can't cover this up with sex now. Not this time. I know your secret. You weren't interested in my art. You were just interested in sex." He grinned. "I thought I was banging you. But all the while, it was you banging me." He swayed to one side, caught himself, and braced against the counter. "We're both whores." His speech was slurred. "But I wasn't one before I met you. You made me a whore. Your whore."

"No," he said, still answering himself. "No need to deny it. I enjoyed it. But you made me that way. Haddon. Capriati. Me." He swallowed more from the glass. "Who else have you been sleeping with?" He leaned forward, as if looking at her closely. "Tell me that much. Who else have you been sleeping with?"

Slater poured more Scotch and ginger ale into the glass, then took a gulp. "Well somebody ought to put an end to it. It's not right. You can't go around hurting people like that. I loved you. Maybe they didn't. Capriati didn't seem to mind you being with someone else. But I do. I mind. I loved you. You hurt me, and now I want to hurt you!"

He dropped onto a chair at the kitchen table. "I want to hurt you, but I can't." He started to cry. "You're off with the FBI and I can't get to you. Probably banging the agents by now. You have them and I'm left with nothing. Nothing. Except that old Matisse."

"Just me and Mr. Matisse." Suddenly his eyes brightened. "Maybe I should bring old Mr. Matisse down here and let him join the conversation. See what he thinks about the whores we've become."

From the kitchen, Slater staggered through the living room to the staircase and hauled himself up to the second floor. In the bedroom closet, he tossed the suitcases aside and lifted out the Matisse. "There you are," he said. "Been hiding in the dark all this time."

Using the banister for support, Slater stumbled downstairs with the painting in one hand and the other for support, but instead of propping the painting on a chair where he'd first found it, he carried through the kitchen, picked up the bottle of Scotch on the way, and walked out to the studio. He set the painting on an empty easel that stood in the corner and paused to take a drink from the bottle. "You slut," he snarled at the Matisse. "She's made you a whore just like herself!" He took another swig from the bottle. "Well, we're gonna fix that right now."

Slater pried the lid from a can of red house paint, snatched a brush from the table, and dipped it in the paint. With a flick of his wrist toward the Matisse, he sent a glob of paint sailing through the air. It splattered across the woman on the canvas.

"Yeah," he grinned. "That's you Sibel. Sitting at the table with your precious vase. And I did it. I splattered paint all over you." He repeated the motion, then did it again. And again. Working himself into a frenzy, he moved the painting from the easel, laid it on the floor, and stood over it, drizzling paint on it like Jackson Pollock.

After a while, he changed to blue but didn't like the appearance. "Too damn patriotic," he growled. Using a wide brush, he smoothed out the paint, completely covering the canvas, and started over.

For the next several hours, Slater drizzled, splashed, and poured paint onto the canvas of the painting by Matisse. It felt cathartic and he kept going, applying more and more paint. "Look at you now," he said, mimicking Charlotte's voice this time. "You've become Jackson Pollock. Or is it Roy Lichtenstein?" He squatted and drew the word "Pow!" in a word bubble across the painting in comic strip letters. "Or maybe I'm just me," he said as he stood and continued to throw paint at the canvas. "Finally finding myself after finding myself in Sibel and losing myself in her. Here I am, standing on the opposite side."

By then, the Matisse was unrecognizable except for the frame and even it was covered with paint. Whatever it had been before, it now was an abstract painting. Anyone else would have been horrified but Slater, still fired by the bottle and a half he'd consumed, was captivated by the shapes and images that formed in the splotches of color and the bold brush strokes that seemed to leap up at him from the painting.

Inspired by what he saw, he unrolled a fresh canvas, spread it flat on the floor, and began painting in earnest, continuing with the same energy using bold stokes of color from a wide brush. In a few hours, he finished the canvas and tacked it to the wall, then started another.

Finally, as the gray light of dawn glowed through the studio window, he collapsed on the floor exhausted and spent. He folded his arms together and rested his head on them as a pillow. "Just a little rest," he said softly. "Just a little while and I'll get up and paint some more." But soon, he was fast asleep right there on the studio floor.

Chapter 38

That afternoon, Gina appeared at Frazer's desk. "I received a call from someone working with the Metro section. The police pulled a car from Gravesend Bay with a body inside. They're saying the body is Marcel Kirchen."

Frazer raised an eyebrow in response. "When did they find him?"

"Just now. Call went out less than ten minutes ago."

"Gravesend is pretty big," Frazer noted. "Where are they?"

"Across from Bensonhurst Park." Gina motioned for him to follow. "Come on. We'll take my car."

When Frazer and Gina arrived at the scene, they found the street blocked with equipment. The car rested on the grass between Shore Parkway and the water. Evidence technicians from the police department and the FBI were examining it. An ambulance was parked nearby with a stretcher behind it. A body bag lay on the stretcher. From the look of it, a body was inside.

Gina followed Frazer as they picked their way through a maze of police officers and first responders. When they reached the ambulance, he looked over at a medical officer. "Can we see the face?"

The officer unzipped the body bag and the head appeared. Gina grimaced. "It looks like him."

Frazer flipped through the pictures on his phone to a scan of the photo they received from Sedaris and Stone. He checked it against the body for comparison, just to be sure.

While he was doing that, Preston Cooper appeared at his side. Cooper noticed the image on the screen. "Where'd you get that?"

"A source," Frazer replied.

"What source?"

"A confidential source." Frazer gestured to the body. "That looks like a hit, doesn't it? Two shots to the head. Professional?"

"Yeah," Cooper replied. "But don't quote me on it."

"What can I quote you on?"

"No comment."

"That's your quote?"

"Yeah."

"Listen, about the other night," Frazer said. "I was out of line. I shouldn't have come to see you at home like that."

"You were out of line," Cooper responded. "But apology accepted."

Frazer turned back to the body. "What do you know about Marcel Kirchen?"

"Probably not as much as you," Cooper said. "Ties to the Russian mafia. Probably working from a country in the Balkans."

"His name came up regarding several shipments of art," Frazer said. "From France to Hasan Izmir's gallery. Have you found any documents about that?"

"Why do you think we would have anything on that?"

"Everyone knows you searched his hotel room the other day," Frazer replied.

"And you searched the gallery," Gina noted. "And Hasan's apartment."

"We can't comment on that right now," Cooper said.

"But you're investigating the possibility. Ties to the Russian mob. The Balkans."

"Don't quote me," Cooper said.

"Unnamed source close to the investigation?"

Cooper looked over at him. "You never give up do you?"

"Neither do you."

Cooper sighed. "Unnamed sources."

"Good."

After a moment, Cooper looked over at him. "My wife received a call from Zoë the other day."

"Yeah?"

"You didn't tell me she left."

Frazer shrugged. "Not much to tell."

"What's the problem?"

"She doesn't like New York."

"And you do."

"I like doing stories like this." Frazer gestured to the body once more. "There's not much of this in South Carolina."

They stood there in silence, watching while officials from the medical examiner's office closed the body bag and loaded it into the ambulance. As the ambulance drove slowly away, car doors closed behind them and Gina nudged Frazer. "Metro's here," she said.

Frazer turned in that direction. "I guess they'll want the story."

"Probably."

"They can write theirs," he said. "We can write ours."

"Maybe," Gina responded. "But the paper usually doesn't like that approach. Easier to understand if you include all of the angles in a single piece."

Brandon Cutler, the senior Metro writer, appeared at Gina's side. "I told them to call you," he said. "Glad you made it. What do we have?"

"Car went in the bay," Gina explained. "Passenger in the car took two shots to the head."

"Execution and body disposal?"

"Looks like it."

"Who has the lead?"

"I think the FBI is in charge," Frazer said. Cooper had moved over to the car and was talking to the evidence technicians. Frazer pointed to him. "That's him over there. Preston Cooper."

Cutler nodded. "I know Preston. But I meant, which of us has the lead?"

"You guys had the tip," Gina replied.

"Are they still thinking this is Marcel Kirchen?"

"It's him," Frazer answered. "We checked the body against his picture."

"You have a picture?"

"Yes."

"Well," Cutler said. "If the dead guy really is Marcel Kirchen, then you two have been in this story since long before now."

Gina smiled. "So, what do you think?"

"We'll use our sources and keep up with the legal side of it," Cutler said. "You keep doing what you're doing. You two can write the article but give us credit. Fair enough?"

"Fair enough," Gina replied.

"But we gotta make the deadline tonight with something," Cutler added. "Everyone will be reporting on it. We have to be in tomorrow's paper with it."

Cutler walked over to Cooper and Gina glanced at Frazer. "That wasn't so bad, was it?"

"As long as he sticks to it."

She jabbed him with an elbow. "He's a professional. He'll do what he said."

"He's a reporter," Frazer replied. "He wants a story same as us."

That evening, Gennady Krylov waited by a dumpster in an alley behind an apartment building in lower Manhattan, where Hasan Izmir met for sex with women procured through a pimp that catered to men with demented tastes. Most of the women were underage. Trafficked here from Eastern Europe. The thought of what Hasan was doing upstairs made Krylov sick. Since coming to work for Mogilevich, Krylov had killed dozens of people. Maybe more. He lost count along the way. And he had stolen millions of dollars in property and cash, some of it from people who were left in abject poverty. But he never once dealt in drugs and he never dealt in minors. The flesh trade, perhaps. Minors, never. He had his limits.

Hasan, it seemed, had no such scruples.

In a little while there was a clatter from above and Krylov looked up to see Hasan climbing out a window from the second floor. His feet were heavy on the rungs and the metal vibrated loudly with each move as he slowly descended the fire escape. When at last he reached the ground, Hasan started toward a car that was parked nearby. Krylov came from his place by the dumpster and moved quietly behind him.

As Hasan opened the driver's door of the car, Krylov struck him with a forearm to the back and shoved him into the car. Hasan scraped his head against the door frame, but sprawled across the seat and console. "Hey!" he protested. "What are you—" He fell silent when he saw it was Krylov.

"Move over," Krylov ordered and he gave Hasan another shove to push him into the passenger seat. Hasan glared at him. "What are you doing?"

Krylov ignored him and got in behind the steering wheel, then closed the door and pressed a button on the armrest, locking all four doors at once. Krylov held out his hand. "Give me the key," he said.

"To what?"

"The car."

Hasan handed him the key and Krylov started the engine. Hasan glanced over at him. "Did you get all of the paintings?"

"All but the ones out front," Krylov replied.

"Why did you leave them?"

"So things would appear normal from the street. Plus, we didn't want to risk being seen by having everybody in that part of the building."

"Well, I better get my money."

"Your money." Krylov smirked as he put the car in gear. "You have more things to worry about than money."

"I'm entitled to the profit I would have made on all those paintings."

Krylov steered the car down the alley to the street. "You work at the pleasure of Sergei Mogilevich," he said. "Just like the rest of us.

You are entitled to whatever he says you get."

"My deal was with Marcel Kirchen," Hasan argued. "Where is he?"

At the street, Krylov turned the car to the left and blended into traffic. "He couldn't make it."

"I haven't seen him in a few days."

Krylov looked over at him. "You know, you're lucky to still be alive."

"Why?" Hasan chuckled. "Is somebody after me?"

Krylov had a serious expression. "Everyone's after you."

"No one is after me," Hasan scoffed. "Why are you still here? Shouldn't you be gone by now?"

"In due time."

"What do you want with me?"

"I want the Matisse."

Hasan looked nervous. "Matisse? What Matisse? We don't deal in paintings like that. If you want something like that you have to see one of the galleries uptown."

"It was sent with the last shipment, but it wasn't in your gallery when we went there." Krylov turned the car onto Dover Street and brought it to a stop beneath the Brooklyn Bridge. The street was dark and deserted. "How do you know what was in the shipment?" Hasan glanced around warily. "What are we doing here?"

Krylov insisted, "I want that Matisse. Where is it?"

"I don't know."

"We both know you're lying. I'm not leaving until I find it. Where is it?"

"I'm telling you; I don't have it."

"Well, maybe I can help you remember where you put it." Krylov unlocked the car and came from the front seat, then started around to the passenger side. As he did, Hasan threw open the door and bolted in the opposite direction. Krylov quickly caught up to him, grabbed him by the collar, and dragged him back to the car. "Now, I'll give you one last chance." His eyes were intent, and his voice steeled. "Where is the Matisse?"

"I don't know anything about it."

Whap! Krylov struck Hasan on the jaw with his fist.

Hasan slumped against the fender of the car and slid to the pavement. His eyes were glassy and his muscles limp. Krylov stood over him and struck him again. With just a few blows, Hasan was bloodied and nearly unconscious. Krylov pinned him against the tire with a foot against his chest and Hasan gasped. "The last time I saw the painting," he said, finally, "my wife had it. I don't know what she did with it. I don't know where it is. But she had it. Not me. Honest. That's all I know."

"Okay." Krylov nodded. "I believe you."

"Good." Hasan smiled through bloody lips. "Can I go home now?"

"Yeah," Krylov said. "You can go home." With practiced ease, he drew a pistol from the waistband of his trousers, pointed it at Hasan, and shot him in the head. Twice.

Chapter 39

The next morning, Frazer was late arriving at the office. He found Gina waiting for him as he collapsed in the chair at his desk. "What time did you finally leave last night?" she asked.

"We beat the deadline with the story," Frazer replied. "Then Cutler wanted to go out for a beer."

She grinned. "So, I'm guessing one led to another."

"Yeah."

She had a knowing look. "And it was really late by the time you got home."

"Yeah." Frazer rubbed the back of his neck. "Why?"

"We received a call. The police found another body."

"Who is it?"

"Hasan Izmir."

"Wow." Frazer's eyes opened wide. "I didn't see that coming, but I guess we should have."

"I suppose."

"Where's the body?"

"At the morgue."

"And they're sure it's him?"

"Yes."

"Do you think we ought to go down there? Find someone to talk to?"

She shook her head. "I don't think so. It's just a body in the morgue now. No one there will know anything."

"Okay."

"But." Her expression turned somber. "We have another situation."

"What's that?"

"Richard Norris called me into his office first thing this morning." Norris was the editor for the arts section of the paper and Gina's supervisor. "Gaines was there, too," she added. Gaines was the features editor, to whom Frazer reported.

"That doesn't sound good."

"They wanted you there," she said, "but no one could find you. I told them you worked late on the Kirchen story."

"Thanks for covering for me. What did they want?"

"They're giving Metro the lead on this story."

Frazer nodded. "I figured that might be coming."

She looked curious. "Why?"

"Something Cutler said made me think it would happen." Frazer folded his arms together on the desk, leaned forward, and rested his head atop them. "So, what do you think this means?" he asked.

"They think Metro has better sources and the story isn't about art anymore. And it's not the kind of story features covers, either."

"No," Frazer said. "I mean the bodies. The dead people. First Kirchen and now Hasan. What does it mean?"

"I don't know," she shrugged. "It's not really our worry now."

"They didn't say we were out of it completely, did they?"

"No. But I think we've contributed about as much as we can. I don't know what more I have to give."

Frazer turned his head to the side and looked over at her. "Do you think Sibel will be next?"

"Well." Gina took a seat in the chair at the end of the desk. "If that tip you received about someone on the inside wanting to talk to the FBI was correct, she could be the one. She's definitely on the inside."

"In which case," Frazer noted, "they would put her in some kind of protective custody."

"Has your guy at the FBI confirmed whether anyone came forward?"

"No. And I don't think he will." Frazer hadn't told her what happened when he tried to see Cooper at his apartment.

"Any possibility she's on Long Island with Slater?"

"Maybe." Frazer sat up straight. "I assumed that if anyone talked it would be Jamie Wright."

"Not a bad assumption," Gina conceded. "She's not a family member. And apparently she knows a lot about whatever's been happening at the gallery."

"She knows more than she's said so far, too."

"Maybe you should talk to her and find out," Gina suggested.

"Okay." He ran his hands over his face in a tired gesture. "That's a good idea. Maybe I can tell from her reaction whether she's cooperating or not."

"Just remember," Gina cautioned. "Metro has control of the story now, so whatever we find we have to share with them."

Gina stood to leave, and Frazer walked with her as far as the coffee machine. He returned to his desk with a cup in hand and sipped from it while he checked his notes for Jamie's phone number.

Jamie answered Frazer's call on the second ring and after re-introducing himself, he reminded her of their previous conversation. She seemed receptive to a conversation so he asked if she knew Kirchen was dead.

"Not until I read the paper this morning," she replied.

"Have the police or the FBI talked to you?"

"About Kirchen?"

"Yes."

Suddenly she seemed reluctant. "I ... Can we do this in person?"

"Sure."

"I really don't want to talk about it over the phone."

"No problem," Frazer said. They arranged a time to meet later that morning at a coffee shop on the East Side. Frazer went there alone.

"So," he said after they were seated at a table. "As I was saying, has the FBI or the police brought you in for questioning?"

"Not about Kirchen. I talked to them the other day when they came to the gallery."

"You talked to them at the gallery?"

"Yes. And then they had me come to their office and give them a formal statement, but I haven't talked to them since then. I don't think they would need me for anything else. They took all the gallery's records, so they know as much as I do now."

"Have you seen Sibel?"

"Recently?"

"Right."

She shook her head. "Not since before the FBI searched the gallery."

"Do you know where she is?"

"No."

"Where do you think she might be?"

"That's a good question. I think she was spending a lot of time with Truman Slater. But from what I hear, no one's seen or heard from her since before everything started happening."

"You mean, since before the FBI searched the gallery?"

"Yes."

Frazer paused to take a sip of coffee, then said, "The police found another body this morning."

Jamie looked worried. "Who is it? Sibel?"

"No," Frazer said. "It's not Sibel. They think it's Hasan."

Jamie was nervous. "Two people?"

"Yes."

"Two people connected to the gallery."

"I know. It's scary."

"Damn right it's scary. I'm connected to that gallery. If they were killed, am I next?"

"I don't think—"

Jamie stood. "I'm sorry but I'm not talking anymore."

"But wait," Frazer said. "I just want to—"

"No." She cut him off with a wave of her hand and she backed away from the table. "I'm done." Then she hurried from the café and was gone.

Frazer left shortly after her and took a taxi back to the office. When he arrived, he went looking for Gina and found her at her desk. "I talked to Jamie Wright," he said.

"Was she helpful?"

"She's not their witness."

"You're sure of that?"

"Yes. She only found out Kirchen was dead from reading the article. And she didn't know Hasan was dead."

"And you were able to talk to her."

"Exactly," Frazer agreed. "If she was the key witness on a case like this, with two people dead, she'd be unreachable now. They would have her in custody."

"So, that leaves Sibel."

"Yes. Assuming they actually have someone who is cooperating with them."

"There's also Ahmed. The brother."

"Yes." Frazer had forgotten about him. "But I'm not sure how much he knows or how helpful he could be. Hasan and Sibel seem to be the important ones."

"And if Sibel is their inside source," Gina added, "she would have wanted immunity before she talked."

"Right," Frazer said.

"Which leaves only Slater." Frazer nodded. Gina asked, "Do you want to talk to him?"

"I think we should. And maybe Edelman, too."

"Edelman can't help us with the gallery."

"So, we talk to Slater."

Chapter 40

Meanwhile, Preston Cooper came to Davenport's office. "We need to talk." He closed the door and took a seat. Davenport had been working all morning with documents from the gallery, but he put them aside and looked over at Cooper. "Okay," he said. "What's up?"

"NYPD just called. They have Hasan Izmir's body at the morgue."

Davenport leaned back in his chair. "That changes everything."

"I know."

"What happened?"

"They don't know all of the details yet," Cooper said. "A delivery man found him this morning."

"Where?"

"Lying beside his car on Dover Street."

"Dover Street?" Davenport had a perplexed expression. "That's beneath the Brooklyn Bridge."

"Right."

"They found him this morning and they're just now calling us?"

Cooper shrugged. "It took a while to identify the body. And then a while longer before they realized who they had."

"How did he die?

"Two shots to the head."

Davenport arched an eyebrow. "Two to the head?"

"Yeah." Cooper nodded. "The same way Kirchen died."

"Shouldn't we send someone over there to find out what they know?"

"We will," Cooper said. "But we've got something bigger we need to address."

Davenport frowned. "What's bigger than this?"

"What I'm going to tell you can't leave this room. Understood?"

"Sure."

"The NSA has intercepted a number of text messages from a phone in Manhattan to a phone number in Moldova."

Davenport looked surprised. "Moldova?"

"At least one of those text messages was sent just a few hours before we served the warrant at the gallery."

"Our leak."

"Yes."

"Who is it?"

"Susan Griffin."

Davenport looked deflated. "Griffin?"

"I know. She had access to almost everything."

"I brought her into this case."

"I know."

Davenport's eyes opened wide. "Do you think I had something to do with it?"

"No," Cooper assured. "Not at all. But she was so deep into our case, everyone's worried now about Sibel."

"Have you told Sibel's protective detail about this?"

"I just came from a meeting with them. They were my first call."

"Yeah. We can't let anything happen to her. She's the whole case now."

"Exactly."

"And they're certain Griffin's the leak?"

"Yes," Cooper replied. "Do you know where she is? She didn't come in today."

Davenport shrugged. "Home, I guess. I didn't know she wasn't here."

"So, you don't know why she didn't show up for work?"

"No."

"We need to locate her and pick her up."

"She's been with us a while. Not a long time, but long enough." Davenport shook his head. "I find it hard to believe she had anything to do with this. Could this be someone ghosting her phone?"

"A clone?"

"Yes."

"I suppose anything is possible," Cooper said, "but we have to find her first. Then we can get to the bottom of it."

"If she was an informant, she might have told them about Sibel."

"She might be next."

Davenport stood and took his pistol from a drawer. "Let's go get her. Two people connected to this case are dead already. If she's involved, she can help us make this case, but she could also be next on somebody's list."

"If she's involved," Cooper said sternly, "she can go to prison."

"Yeah. But not until after we nail Hasan Izmir's accomplices."

Cooper stood but held up his hand to stop him. "I think you should stay here."

"Why?"

"She worked for you on this case. Like you said, you brought her in. We need to do this right."

"You think something's going on between us?"

"You seem rather interested in her."

Davenport smiled. "I like her, but we never did anything."

"All the same. Stay here. Call your friends at FinCEN. Get them to check Sibel's accounts in Arizona."

"You think something happened with them?"

"I don't want to get played. By her or anyone else."

"Okay." Davenport returned his pistol to the desk drawer. "I'll give them a call."

"We also need to find out what kind of outside contact Sibel has had since we took her into custody. Call them and see what you can find out about that."

Cooper reached for the door. Davenport called after him. "I'd like to be there when you pick up Griffin. I brought her onto the team. I'd like to take her down."

Cooper turned back to face him. "And I would like for you stay here and do what I told you." He spoke with an authoritative tone. "I'll find Griffin. You find out what Sibel's been up to with her bank accounts and who she has seen since we talked to her last. Without Hasan, she's all we have right now to unravel the rest of the details."

Two hours later, Cooper and three additional agents arrived at Susan Griffin's apartment. They sealed off access to the floor, then Cooper knocked on the door. When there was no answer, Cooper kicked open the door and went inside.

The apartment was furnished and clothes were hanging in the closet, but Griffin wasn't there. As Cooper and the agents searched for an indication where she might be, Cooper's phone rang with a call from Davenport.

"Griffin is booked on a flight Toronto out of LaGuardia," Davenport said. "The plane leaves in an hour."

"Have airport police detain her," Cooper said. "She can't get on that flight."

Cooper left an agent behind to secure the apartment and inventory its contents, then took the other two and hurried to the airport.

When they arrived they found Griffin locked in a room off the TSA sector near the passenger screening checkpoint. Cooper went in to see her but before he could speak, she said, "You have to help me."

"Help you? I have to arrest you."

"Because of the text messages?"

"What were you thinking?"

"Look they came to me and—"

Cooper cut her off. "Stop right there. Don't say another word. I have to take you into custody. You're under arrest. You have the right to remain silent—"

"I don't care about that," she said. "I know my rights. I'll tell you what I did, but you have to protect me."

"Against what?"

"Against the people I sent those texts to."

"Who was it?"

"Sergei Mogilevich."

Cooper took a seat. "You dealt with him directly?"

"No. I never met him or dealt with him at all."

"Then how did you get hooked up with him?"

"I have a friend. I've known him since high school. He found out I needed money and said he had a way to help. All I had to do was alert someone whenever something came up about Mogilevich. Didn't have to be anything big. Just, whenever his name came up, I should let them know."

"Let your friend know?"

"I don't know who it was. He gave me a number and I sent a text message."

"And they sent you money?"

"Yes."

Cooper had a pained expression. "Why did you do it?"

She looked away. "Debt."

"Gambling?"

"No." She shook her head. "School loans. It was overwhelming."

"You should have told us when you were approached."

"I know."

"What did you tell them?"

"Like I said, I told them when we were working on something that had to do with Mogilevich. And I shared research with them."

"Files?"

"Research files. Not case files," she said. "And I never shaped the research. I didn't falsify my work. I played it straight up, but when I saw something that I thought they would be interested in, I told them about it."

"I'll need the name of your contact."

"I need protection. This is Mogilevich. His people are ruthless."

"We can't promise anything until we get you down to the office and debrief you."

"If I talk, and you send me to jail, I'll be dead before the end of the month."

"We need to get you a lawyer and do this right." Cooper stood. "Come on. I have to cuff you."

Griffin stood and Cooper placed her wrists in handcuffs, then he led her out the door and into the corridor.

When Cooper returned to the FBI building, he placed Griffin in a holding cell, then went to his office. Davenport was waiting when he arrived. "Did you have any trouble bringing her in?" he asked.

"No trouble at all," Cooper said. He took a seat behind the desk. "Other than the ride from her apartment to the airport, everything went smoothly. What did you find out about Sibel and Hasan? Was that body under the bridge really him?"

"Yes," Davenport replied. He took a seat on the opposite side of the desk. "It's Hasan Izmir. He took two shots to the head. Just like Kirchen."

"Anything else from the scene?"

"They lifted a fingerprint from the car."

"Whose is it?"

"Gennady Krylov."

Cooper frowned. "That name doesn't sound familiar. Do we know him?"

"We have him in our files as Yuri Turgenov, but it looks like that's an alias."

"What do we know about him?"

"He's an enforcer for the Russian mob."

"Mogilevich?"

"Yes."

Cooper smiled. "This case just keeps going and going. What did

THE ART DEALER'S WIFE

you find out about Sibel's bank account?"

"FinCEN confirms transfers from the gallery accounts to her account in Arizona the day before we executed the search warrant. But she's cleaned them out."

"When?"

"Two days after we debriefed her."

"What did she do with it?"

"They don't know yet."

"If she hid the money, she would've had help."

"Right. Our people are checking on that."

"Has she had contact with anyone?"

"I asked the detail. They didn't think she'd had contact with anyone but they were going to check on it and get back to us."

"Do we even know where she is?"

"They have her in a safe house somewhere in the city, but we're not supposed to contact the protectee directly."

"She may be the bureau's protectee, but she's our witness. Will they let us meet with her?"

"They'll give us all the access we want, but they don't like it."

"Will they bring her to us, or do we have to go to her?"

"The guy I talked to seemed to think that we could see her at the location where they currently have her."

"If we do that, won't they have to move her?"

"If they bring her in and we talk to her here, they'll move her to a new location anyway."

"She won't go back to the same place?"

"No," Davenport answered. "If she sees us at all, she's going to a new site. So rather than bring her here and then move her, they say we can come there and they'll move her to a new place after we talk to her."

"This safe house, it's not a permanent location, right?"

"Right. They knew we will need to talk to her as we build our case. So, she's somewhere around here. They just don't want to tell us where."

"When can we see her?"

"I asked to see her as soon as possible. They're going to confirm everything and get back to me. But we need to be ready to go as soon as they let us know."

"Okay." Cooper stood. "Come on. We need to talk to Susan Griffin."

Chapter 41

ater that afternoon, Frazer and Gina arrived at the house on
Long Island where Truman Slater lived. Frazer parked the car in
the driveway, and they made their way to the porch. When repeated
knocks on the door brought no response, they walked to the building
behind the house that Slater used as a studio. The found him there,
drizzling paint on a canvas that lay on the floor. Paint can and rag in
one hand, a brush in the other.

Unlike his previous paintings, this one had broad swaths of bright
colors with vivid contrast that added a sense of urgency, energy, and
tension missing in his previous work. The difference was obvious.

At first Slater seemed not to notice them and neither Frazer nor
Gina spoke, their attention, instead, captured by the work at Slater's
feet. But as they entered and light from the open door fell across the
room, he looked up at them. His eyes flashed with anger or excitement, Frazer couldn't determine which, then he recognized them.
"Oh." He stood up straight and squared his shoulders. "I wasn't
expecting to see you today."

Frazer pointed to the canvas. "That looks different from your
other pieces."

"It *is* different," Slater said, with a proud smile.

Frazer walked slowly around the canvas, looking, assessing,
admiring. After a moment, though, he glanced around the room
and noticed a framed painting resting on an easel a few feet away.

Images on the painting were very much like those on the canvas that lay on the floor. He pointed to the picture. "Are you copying that?"

"No," Slater replied. "Not really. That's just my inspiration."

Frazer looked at the framed painting a moment longer. "Who did this?" he asked.

"I did," Slater answered.

Gina came around to where Frazer was standing and took a closer look at the painting. "I like this," she said. "Bold strokes. Lots of paint. Nice choice of color."

"I was angry," Slater admitted. "That's why it looks different."

"Painting, not thinking?"

"I guess. With the other things I did before," Slater said, "I had to search for emotion. With that one, the emotion was just … there."

Frazer glanced back at him with a smile. "What were you angry about?"

"Sibel."

Frazer turned to face him fully. "Is she here?"

"No." Slater shook his head. "She's gone."

"Where?"

Slater shrugged. "I don't know. That's what I was angry about."

"She left and didn't tell you?"

"Something like that."

Frazer knew there was more to it—and he suspected he already knew what it was, that Sibel had agreed to cooperate with the FBI and was in protective custody—but he was careful in coaxing Slater to talk about it. "You heard Kirchen is dead?"

"Yes." Slater wiped the handle of his brush with the rag. "And I understand Hasan is, too."

"Yes." Frazer nodded. "How did you hear about him? Are they reporting it on the news already?"

"Charlotte told me."

Gina frowned. "How does she know? They only found him this morning."

Slater smirked. "Charlotte knows everything."

Frazer glanced back at the framed painting once more. This

time he noticed details he'd missed before, and splotches of paint on the frame. He pointed to them. "You did this one with the canvas already framed?"

"Not by design." Slater had a sheepish grin. "Though maybe I should try that again." Frazer waited for him to continue. Slater seemed uncomfortable. Almost embarrassed. "Actually," he said slowly, "that is the Matisse you asked me about earlier."

Frazer's eyes were wide, and his mouth dropped open. Before he could speak, Gina blurted, "The Matisse? You painted over a Matisse?" Her sense of incredulity was obvious in the tone and volume of her voice. "A Matisse?"

Slater blushed. "Yeah," he said. "Kinda crazy, huh?"

"Kinda?" Gina was beside herself.

Frazer shook his head in disbelief. "Why did you do that?"

"I woke up one morning and Sibel was gone." Slater pointed to the picture. "I found that sitting on a chair in the living room with a note from her asking me to hold onto it. So, I hid it in the house and then I went looking for her."

"Sibel?"

"Yeah. But I couldn't find her in the obvious places. So, I went to see Charlotte and a few other people and after talking to them I realized she was gone. And gone without me."

"She left?"

"Yeah."

"Where did she go?"

Slater turned away. "I'm not sure I can talk much about it."

Gina spoke up. "She's cooperating with the FBI." It was a statement of the obvious, not a question.

Slater looked over at her. "You know about that?"

"We heard a rumor," Frazer offered.

"Lots of rumors out there," Slater said. He offered it in a half-hearted manner, as a way of covering for the fact that he had just confirmed the truth of whatever rumor they had heard.

"It's not difficult to figure it out," Gina said. "Hasan's dead. And Kirchen's dead. We talked to Jamie Wright. With two people dead, if she was a key witness, she would be in custody now. But she's not."

"That leaves only you, Ahmed, and Sibel who know anything about the gallery's business. Ahmed was a minor player and you're standing right here. It's rather obvious Sibel is cooperating with the investigation."

They stood in silence a moment, then finally Slater said, "That's why she's gone."

"She's under FBI protection?"

"Yeah."

"Do you know where they have her?"

"If I did, I would have gone to her as soon as I found out."

"Have you heard from her?"

"Not a word." Slater had an anguished look. "She said we'd go together, and I guess I would have gone with her, but she didn't give me the chance. Came out to the house. Stayed a while. Next morning, she was gone. Left that picture behind. When I couldn't find her, I started drinking." He gestured toward the framed picture. "That's what happened."

Gina sighed in disbelief. "You painted over a Matisse," she said again, this time in a whisper.

"I feel bad about doing it like that," Slater said. "But it set me free. I mean, I was so mad I just started slinging paint at it." Slater chuckled. "Threw the brush at it at one point. Then I saw the form and shape of what I had done. And the beauty of it. It was like a whole new me opened up." He sighed. "I'm not sure I would undo it, even if I could."

"There's only one problem with that," Gina said.

Slater glanced at her. "What's that?"

"The painting isn't yours."

"I know. It's Sibel's but I don't—"

"No." Gina cut him off. "It's not hers either."

Slater had a puzzled look. "Whose is it?"

"It belongs to Jacob Edelman."

Slater's expression turned serious. "Well ... I guess that would be a problem, wouldn't it?"

THE ART DEALER'S WIFE

"Yes," Gina replied. "That would be a problem."

"A conservator could probably fix it," Frazer suggested. "But I imagine it would cost a lot to do it." He glanced at Slater. "Do you know anyone who could fix it?"

"Not really," Slater replied. "I suppose it's possible to fix it. They do all kinds of things to old paintings now and find things beneath the layers. But I don't know anyone who does that. Charlotte probably does."

"I know someone," Gina offered. "But he's not cheap."

Slater's shoulders slumped and he had a deflated look. "I hate to get rid of it. That painting is the reason I found myself as a painter. I've been trying to do that all my life." He pointed to the Matisse once more. "Painting that took me there."

"Edelman's been on a quest, too," Frazer said.

"Yeah?"

"A quest to find that painting," Gina said. "It's one of the last pieces in his family's collection."

"You told me before."

Gina told him again. "It's been missing since the Nazis stole it and now it's here and it's ... that."

Slater seemed suddenly resolute. "Then maybe we should talk to him. See if we can work something out."

Frazer raised an eyebrow. "Do you think that's wise?"

"What do you mean?"

"Well, technically, you destroyed a valuable piece of property that belonged to him."

"And technically, I didn't know it was his," Slater responded. "I thought it belonged to Sibel."

All three stood there in silence a moment, then Slater said, "If we don't talk to him, it'll bother me the rest of my life." He wiped his hands on the rag he'd been holding, then tossed it aside. "Let's find out what he has to say. Either of you know where he lives?"

"Yes," Gina said. "We know where he lives."

Frazer was hesitant. "We're just gonna show up with the painting?"

"It won't make much difference," Slater said. "If he's been looking for this painting that long, and if it means that much to him, he's going to be shocked when he sees it no matter how much advanced notice he has."

"But now?"

"I don't want to spend a lot time worrying about it." Slater took the painting from the easel. "One of you get the door. Let's do this now, before I change my mind."

Darkness had fallen by the time Frazer and Gina arrived with Slater at Jacob Edelman's apartment. Anne, his granddaughter, answered the door when they knocked. She knew Frazer and Gina from before but seemed troubled by Slater's presence. Still, she held the door for them while they entered. Slater carried the picture.

When they were inside, Anne said, "I assume you're here to see my grandfather."

"Yes," Frazer replied. "Is he available."

"He's in here," and she led them into the living room.

Edelman was seated in a chair by the window. His daughter, Diane was on the sofa. Edelman turned from the window to face them as they entered. He gasped when he saw the painting. "The frame," he whispered. His jaw quivered and he covered his hand with his mouth as tears formed in his eyes.

Diane was alarmed by his reaction and scooted forward on the sofa to reach his knee with her hand. "Papa," she said. "What's the matter? Do you know these people?"

Slater held the painting with the back showing. Edelman pointed to it. "That is my father's writing."

Frazer turned to look and for the first time noticed written on the back were the words "Amélie Matisse," written in black. Across from it was a printed label. It was faded and tattered at the edges but clearly visible and read, "Galerie Paul Guillaume, Paris."

"The name?" Frazer asked, pointing.

"Yes. Amélie Matisse. I told you about her before."

"I assume from your reaction," Frazer continued, "that you know what this is."

"The Matisse," Edelman whispered. "Turn it around and let me see."

"The Matisse?" Diane was indignant. "How can you tell? You haven't even seen it yet."

"I would know that painting anywhere. Turn it around and show it to me."

"Before we do that, you need to know—there's a problem."

"A problem?" Edelman looked up at Frazer. "What's happened to it?"

"Oh, stop it!" Diane shouted. "You're upsetting him terribly."

Edelman held out his hand in a gesture. "Shh," he said.

Slater spoke up. "The problem is all my fault," he said. "This is what happened to your painting." He turned the painting around and Edelman sagged against the chair. His eyes were wide in a look of shock. Slater continued. "Sibel Izmir brought this to my house about a week ago. You probably don't know her, but she—"

"He knows her all too well," Anne interjected.

"She brought it to me and wanted me to hide it for her," Slater said. "She'd been having trouble with her husband and I thought I was doing her a favor. I didn't know it was yours. Sibel and—"

"Why did she bring it to you?" Diane demanded.

"They represent my art."

"The Izmirs?"

"Yes." Slater looked uncomfortable. "And ... Sibel and I were ... seeing each other."

"Seeing each other." Diane folded her arms across her chest. "You were having an affair with her." She said it in self-righteous tone.

"Yes," Slater acknowledged. "We were having an affair. But she dumped me, and I got mad. Then I got drunk. Lost my head. Got the picture out thinking it was hers."

"But you knew it wasn't," Diane insisted. "If you knew Sibel you knew she never dealt in art like this. Certainly, you knew that much."

"If I'd been sober, I would have probably thought about it that way but by the time I got the picture out of the closet, I'd already drunk a bottle and half of liquor and I wasn't thinking anymore. So, in an act of revenge against her, I started painting—"

Edelman gasped. Diane interrupted again. "This is too upsetting for him. Daddy you need to—"

"Hush." Edelman spoke sharply this time. His eyes were bright and he focused on Slater. "I just now realized who you are. You're an artist."

"Yes."

"I've seen your work. At the gallery. Izmir's gallery."

"Yes, sir," Slater said. "That's what I was saying. They represent me."

"You're Truman Slater."

"Yes, sir. I'm Truman Slater and I've come to apologize and tell you I'll do whatever you want me to do to make this right."

Diane spoke harshly. "You're damn right you'll—"

"Hush, Diane," Edelman said, with disdain this time. He looked back to Slater. "A friend of mine has one of your pieces. He had it appraised the other day for fifty thousand dollars."

"I didn't know that." Slater appeared surprised. "Who did your friend buy it from?"

"The Izmir's gallery, I presume. He was surprised by the valuation, too. I don't think he paid anywhere near that much for it."

"I will say this," Slater offered, "painting over your picture—the rage and passion that I felt when I was doing it—somehow it set me free. I'm not the painter I was before that. I've found a style I've been searching for all my life."

Diane pointed to her father. "He's been searching for that painting all his life, too. A lot longer than you've been searching for your so-called style. And you'll be paying—"

Edelman stood, grasped Diane by the shoulders, and guided her into the chair where he'd been sitting. "Stay right there and don't open your mouth again until we're finished." With her in place, he turned back to Slater. "My father purchased that painting from Henri Matisse's ex-wife while they were still in Paris, a year before the Germans arrived. The purchase was handled by a dealer, but he was buying it from Matisse's wife. It was special to my parents mostly because of the occasion. I think it was their wedding anniversary. I figured it up once and as best I could determine, he paid the equivalent of about three thousand dollars for it, which was a good bit of money back then."

Diane remained seated in the chair but blurted out, "It's worth—"

"Diane." Edelman cut her off with a sharp word, then looked over at Slater and the others. "Forgive my daughter," he said calmly. "She's sometimes given to inappropriate outbursts."

"So, what will it take to put this right?" Slater asked. "I can take it to a conservator and see if he can remove the paint from it and restore it to its original appearance. It's a lengthy process but I'm sure they could remove most of it and get it back like it was."

"Oh, my. No," Edelman said. "That would never do."

Slater looked confused. "Excuse me? I don't understand."

"I've seen your other art," Edelman said. "It's good, but it's not like this." He looked admiringly at the painting. "This is extraordinary."

Slater tried to be casual about it. "Like I said, I found myself as an artist while doing that to your Matisse."

"My father acquired many pieces," Edelman said. The tension was gone, and he was in full lecture mode. Explaining himself. His family. Their history. Topics on which he loved to expound. "Most of the works he acquired are quite valuable now, but he didn't know they'd be valuable when he bought them. He just bought them because he liked them. In the case of Matisse, there was a bit less uncertainty but still, he was not as popular then as he is now. And there was a war on. Germany was at the gate." He paused for a moment and no one else dared speak. Then he said, "I'm thinking maybe we should do this." He looked Slater in the eye. "You give me back this painting—the one with the Matisse beneath the surface." He pointed. "And give me two more in this same vein, and of about the same size, then we'll call it even."

Slater looked as if he might faint. "You're sure?"

Frazer wanted to stick something in Slater's mouth to keep him from saying anything else. Such an incredible display of grace. Of dignity. Of generosity and support for a young artist. And dare one say, an example of forgiveness none of them was likely to see again. All Slater needed do was say thank you and leave.

"Yes," Edelman replied. "I'm sure. Quite sure." He took the painting gently from Slater's grasp and held it at arm's length, admiring it. His eyes filled with tears, but he blinked them away. "My father would be so proud." He indicated for Diane to move and she came from the chair. He set the painting in her place, stepped back, and draped an arm over Slater's shoulder. "One day, you will be twice as famous as Matisse and when that happens, I shall have three of your paintings in my collection. And I'll have the Matisse, too, though no one except me will see it when they look at that canvas." He beamed with joy that seemed to light the entire room.

Frazer, Gina, and Slater left Edelman's apartment and walked back to the car together. All the way there, Slater kept saying, "Wow. I never thought that would happen."

Finally, Gina asked, "What did you think was going to happen?"

"I thought he might agree to let me have it fixed and maybe agree to not sue me for damaging it, but I never thought this would happen."

"It was an amazing outcome," Frazer acknowledged. "Totally unexpected."

When they reached the car, Frazer looked over at Gina, "I can drop you at the office or your apartment."

"We have to take Slater home."

"I'll take him home. No need for you to go all the way out there again."

"Okay. That would be great.

Slater spoke up. "I'll take the train to East Hampton. I have a friend there who'll give me a ride to the house."

"Are you sure?"

"Yeah," Slater said. "It's not a problem. I've done it before."

Frazer and Gina said goodbye to him, then watched as he walked to the corner and started down the steps to the subway station. As he moved out of sight, Gina said, "This will make a great story."

"Yeah, about that." There was a note of hesitancy in Frazer's voice.

"What's the matter?"

"I don't think we should write it," he said.

Gina frowned. "You mean not at all."

"Yeah."

"As in, don't do it ourselves. Don't give it to someone else?"

"Right." Frazer nodded. "Just let it go."

"But why? A story like this could easily make the short-list for a Pulitzer. Trial. Tribulation. Redemption."

"Three people with a connection to that painting are already dead."

"Three?"

"Kirchen, Izmir, and the dealer in Paris Edelman told us about at the beginning."

"And Edelman's father," Gina added. "If you want to go back that far."

"I'm a little concerned about what might happen if we write an article that says what happened to the painting. We'd be disclosing to the world the location of the painting and the name of the person who has it. The world and whoever killed Kirchen and Hasan."

"You mean the person who killed Hasan and Kirchen might come looking for Edelman?"

"Or Slater. Or you. Or me, for that matter." Frazer shoved his hands in his pockets. "I don't think we should do anything with the story. Just keep quiet. Let it go." A grin lifted Gina's cheeks. He saw the look. "What? What are you thinking?"

"The Jack Frazer I knew before never would have suggested

something like this."

"I just think—"

"No," she interrupted. "You've changed."

"It just seems like the right thing to do."

"Okay," Gina agreed. "We won't do a story about Edelman and the painting. We'll let Metro run the follow up on Hasan and talk about Sibel with the FBI. And that will be that."

"Good."

They got in the car and Frazer started the engine. As they started forward, Gina asked, "Do you have an idea for your next story?"

"No," Frazer replied. "I'm taking some time off."

"Oh?" Gina sounded surprised. "When did you decide to do that?"

"The other day. I told them when we were finished with this story, I needed to take a break. They're giving me three weeks."

"What are you gonna do with the time?"

"I thought I might drive down to South Carolina and see if Zoë still wants me."

"Excellent idea." Gina said it with a burst of genuine enthusiasm. She whacked him hard on the back to emphasize the point. "Best idea you've had since we started working together."

"You think?"

"Took you long enough to figure it out."

"I'm a slow learner."

"How long will it take to drive to Charleston?"

"Fourteen hours, if I don't stop often."

"I hear it's a beautiful drive along the coast.

"Yeah," he replied. "It is."

Chapter 42

The next morning, Gennady Krylov was asleep in bed at the house in Bound Brook when the ring of a cell phone awakened him. Groggy and confused, he groped on the floor for his pants, found them, and took his phone from a pocket. A check of the phone's screen showed nothing, but still the ringing continued.

More awake than at first, he realized the noise was from the cloned cell phone he'd received from Darren Brenner. Krylov took it from the nightstand, swung around to a sitting position on the edge of the bed, and waited for the ringing to stop. As soon as it did, he pressed a button to listen.

"Come get me," a voice said.

It was the voice of a woman but husky and low, and unmistakably that of Sibel Izmir. Krylov had heard her just that way, always in the morning, just after she awakened, when they'd been together for the night. She came to their assignations, full of passion and energy, her voice bright and clear. Who gives a damn what Hasan Izmir thinks, she would say. I would see you every night if you were here. But as the sun came up and dawn appeared after a night of sweaty romance in a seedy Brooklyn motel or a house she sometimes rented for them on Staten Island, the energy would be gone and her voice would be low, husky, full of worry. I must go, she would say. Hasan will find us and then what would he do. She always said it as a statement, too, never a question. What would he do. Krylov laughed each time. He wouldn't do anything, he assured her. But the pattern was the same with her each time. Passion. Sex. Worry. Then two days later, passion all over again.

A second voice on the call responded. "Where are you?"

This was the voice of a man. Younger, but not too young. A bit timid and unsure. Krylov assumed it was the artist, Truman Slater, though they had never met.

"I'm at an apartment in Manhattan," Sibel said. Still with the whisper. "I did what we said. I found someone to talk to."

So, it was true. Sibel was cooperating with the FBI. Krylov had heard from others that she had done this, but he was willing to give her the benefit of the doubt and leave without addressing her situation. Hasan was awful to her. He hit her sometimes and then he went for his dalliances with those minors. The things he did to them were not right and Krylov had been willing to put the rumors about Sibel aside and let the matter with her go, as an act of penance for those girls, but now, after hearing her on the phone, he had no choice. She had to be dealt with. Killing Hasan had been a pleasure. The thought of killing Sibel made him sad.

"Don't they have people protecting you?" Slater asked.

"Yes," she replied. "But I can get away from them."

"How?"

"They are moving me later. I'll have a chance then. Come get me."

"When?"

"Soon. You must come now to be ready. I will give you the location. Will you come get me?"

"Okay."

"Good. Bring the painting with you."

"I ... don't have it anymore." There was hesitancy in Slater's voice, as if he knew he was telling her something she wouldn't like. A tone that anticipated a negative response.

"Don't have it?" Sibel was angry.

Krylov listened and grinned, covering his mouth to suppress a laugh and prevent making a noise they might hear. He'd been the object of that voice, too.

"What do you mean you don't have it?" she continued.

"I don't have it. It's gone."

"How can you not have it?" She was all but shouting. "I told you to keep it for me. I was counting on you keeping it." This was the bossy, indignant, defiant Sibel. The one who insisted on having things her own way. The Sibel her young lover probably had never encountered.

"I painted over it." Damn, Krylov thought, he ruined a million-dollar painting.

Slater spoke with a matter of fact tone. Almost defiant. As if something had changed between them. The balance of interest had shifted and in spite of his reaction to what Slater had done, Krylov sensed a shift between them, too.

"Are you stupid?" Sibel railed.

"No," Slater said coldly. "I'm not stupid. You left me. You never came back. I know you don't intend for us to be together."

"We could go now if you had the painting." She tried to soften her tone, but he wasn't having it.

"Well, I don't have it," he said. "So there."

The call ended abruptly and Krylov, still seated on the edge of the bed, pressed a button to disconnect his phone. When the screen was clear, he laughed out loud. Sibel was such a manipulator. She tried to manipulate him. Tried to convince him, more than once, to take her to Europe with him. That she would leave Hasan and they could be together for the rest of their lives. It was funny to hear her and know she had told someone else the same thing.

Using his own cell phone, Krylov called Brenner and explained the situation. "Can you trace the number that she called from?"

"Not a trace. You have to do that while the call is ongoing. But I can find the phone she used if she still has it turned on. What's the number?"

Krylov gave him the number, then Brenner said, "Sit tight. I'll call you back."

A few minutes later the phone rang. It was Brenner. "She made the call from a burner phone. It's near the corner of Thirty Fourth Street and Dyer Avenue. There's an apartment building on the corner. I think she must be in there, but I don't know which apartment."

"You can't give me an exact address?"

"No."

"Whose phone is it?"

"There isn't a name associated with it," Brenner said.

"But you're sure the phone is at that location."

"Yes. It's there right now."

Krylov ended the call and thought about how to use the information he'd learned from Brenner and from Sibel's conversation. Sibel had told Slater to come get her, and he had refused. He could call her back and pretend to be Slater, but as quickly as he thought of it, he realized that wouldn't work. He could never disguise his accent enough to make the call believable. And besides, Sibel knew his voice. And then he thought about using that to his advantage.

He could call her up. Tell her he knew she was with the FBI and he was coming to get her. But if she probably knew Kirchen was dead and if she was with the FBI, she probably knew Hasan was dead, too. And if she knew all of that, she would suspect that he was responsible for it. She knew the kind of jobs he did for Mogilevich. Eliminating loose ends. Cleanup jobs. Just like this one. Which meant she would be too scared to go with him and might even disclose the call to the FBI.

Then he thought of sending a text message. He could send her a text as if it came from her artist boyfriend. Make it like he thought about what she said and was willing to help her. That might work. She might go for that. And if she didn't, she would just respond in anger. Slater might see the texts and realize his phone was compromised, but at this point, that wouldn't matter. And that's what he did.

Krylov used the cloned phone and sent a text to the number Sibel had called from. It read, "Okay. I'll help. Tell me where to meet you."

"If I'm meeting you, we're leaving together."

"Okay."

"And bring that painting. We can get someone to fix it."

"Good. When?"

"I'll text you when they move me."

"Wow!" Krylov shouted. "That worked better than I ever thought it would." He dressed quickly, backed the car from the garage, and started toward the city.

An hour later, Krylov crossed from New Jersey into Manhattan through the Holland Tunnel and emerged on Canal Street. From there, he made his way north on Sixth Avenue, followed it up to Thirty-Fourth Street, and located the apartment building at Dyer Avenue.

After making the block twice, Krylov saw that the building had only one usable access point: the front door that faced Thirty-Fourth Street. There was a service entrance from the rear, off Thirty-Fifth Street, but using it would require Sibel and her detail to cross half a block of open courtyard that lay behind the building. Krylov was certain the FBI would opt for the more direct front entrance where they could park a vehicle within a few feet of the door and shield her with agents for the few steps it took to cross the sidewalk to the curb.

With that in mind, Krylov found a parking spot in the next block of Thirty-Fourth Street that gave him a view of the apartment building entrance. It wasn't the best setup. If he had more time, he might have chosen another location—the courthouse, or the FBI building, or some other opportunity that might emerge—but he didn't have time for that. He'd killed two people. If Sibel talked, she would tell them about him, eventually. They would be looking for him now and it wouldn't be long before they were closing on him. He had to finish this and get out of the country quickly. This was the best chance for doing that.

An hour later, the cloned cell phone received a text message. "Dyer Avenue. Now."

Krylov sat up straight and scanned the sidewalk at the corner.

Alert. Apprehensive. He didn't want to miss her. Just then, the door opened and Sibel emerged alone from the building entrance. She ran to the corner, then started up Dyer. Krylov started the car, shot across the oncoming traffic, and turned up the Dyer behind her. He came alongside her and honked the car horn. His head was turned to the left so she couldn't see his face. A moment later, he felt the car door open and heard her drop onto the front seat. The car started forward as she slammed the door closed. He looked over at her and smiled. "Hello, Sibel. Expecting someone else."

"What are you doing?"

"Giving you a lift."

"How did you know?" When Krylov laughed in response, she reached for the door handle. "Let me out."

Dyer Avenue led directly into the Lincoln Tunnel approach and Krylov pressed the accelerator. The car sped up, making it impossible for Sibel to jump out. Less than a minute later, they were speeding through the tunnel on their way to New Jersey.

"You were talking to the FBI?"

"I had to get away from Hasan."

"Hasan is dead. Didn't they tell you that?"

"Yes. But he wasn't when I contacted them."

"What have you told them?"

"Not much."

"You told them about me."

"No. I didn't say a word about you."

"Then what did you tell them?"

"I told them about the art."

"You gave them Mogilevich?"

"I had to give them something. Otherwise, they wouldn't put me in protection, which was the whole point."

"What point?"

"To get away from Hasan."

"Why not just leave?"

"I wanted him to pay."

"To pay?"

"I wanted him in jail."

"And now he is in the grave."

"He wasn't when I went to them."

"This is not good," he said.

She moved closer to him on the seat and touched his shoulder with her hand. "But it could be good," she said. "It could be like all those times we had before. Do you remember the last time?"

"That was before your artist boyfriend came along."

"He is nothing to me. Just something to fill the time."

"Is that what you told him?"

"Why do you care what I told him?"

Thirty minutes later, Krylov and Sibel arrived at Teterboro Airport in New Jersey. Krylov steered the car around the perimeter of the field to a hanger. He parked it on the far side of the building. "Come on," he said as he came from the driver's side. "You can't stay here." She came out of the car and started toward him, then hesitated when she reached the front fender. "Where are we going?"

"Someplace safe for us both."

"Both?"

"If you're in FBI custody, you've probably confessed to crimes already. That's how they get their teeth in you. And if that's true, then I committed a crime by giving you a lift." He gestured with a sense of urgency. "Come on. We haven't much time. They'll be onto us soon."

Krylov led the way into the hangar. A business jet was parked there with the door open and the stairs down. He waited for her to catch up, then followed her up the stairs and into the plane. "But where are we going?" she asked once more.

"It's a surprise," Krylov said.

When they reached the top step and Sibel was inside the plane, he pressed a button that retracted the steps, then pulled the door closed and latched it. The engines started immediately and in just a few minutes they taxied onto the runway.

Sibel took a seat over the wing. Krylov took a seat across the aisle. That should have been a clue, but she seemed not to notice. She tightened her seatbelt and closed her eyes. He imagined that she was thinking how things had worked out well for her. She'd thought the young artist was coming for her. That they would have a life on the run. And here she was, on a plane bound for … somewhere.

Krylov glanced out the window in time to see the last of the city disappear beneath them. Soon, they would be over the water and in an hour, they would pass well beyond US airspace. The plane would descend to an altitude below a thousand feet, where cabin pressurization wasn't necessary. Then he would finish his business with Sibel and dump her body for the sharks. All traces of her would be gone before morning and he would be safely in Moldova.

Epilogue

Frazer had meant to leave the city the morning after they returned the painting to Edelman, but events of that day left him too excited to relax and when he finally did get to sleep, he slept deeply. He didn't awaken until almost noon the following day.

Rather than rush off right then, he took his time with packing and closing things up in the apartment. Placing subscriptions and services on hold, forwarding the mail, that sort of thing. Late that afternoon, just before dark, the car was loaded, and he set out for South Carolina. He thought he should surprise Zoë, so he didn't bother to tell her he was on the way.

From New York, he followed the interstate as far as Wilmington, Delaware. Traffic wasn't heavy and he would have reached Charleston before sunrise had he continued on that way, but instead of staying with that route, he moved over to the coast. It was almost midnight when he reached Norfolk.

By the time he reached Wilmington, North Carolina, the sky in the east was turning gray. Sunrise wasn't far off. He took a nap in the parking lot of a convenience store in Leland and didn't awaken until ten that morning.

Two hours later, he stopped in Myrtle Beach long enough to buy a hamburger, then ate it while he drove. Half an hour later, he called Zoë.

"Is something wrong?" she asked. "You sound different."

"Yeah," he said. "Something's very wrong."

"What is it?" The alarm in her voice was more pronounced. "What's the matter?"

"Once you get past New Jersey, you can't find a decent bagel or burger on this highway."

"What are you talking about? Where are you?" Alarm was turning to worry. "You sound like you're in the car."

"I am somewhere south of Murrells Inlet."

"In South Carolina?" She said it with a spontaneous rush of emotion.

"Yes," he said calmly. "In South Carolina. Do you know a good place where I could stop in Charleston?" He heard the sound of her crying and it made him feel good that his surprise had worked, but bad that she was in tears. "You are still in Charleston, aren't you?"

"Yes," she sobbed. "I'm still here."

"Good. I'll see you in a little while."

"Are you coming to stay?" The old question wouldn't go away.

"They gave me three weeks to decide. We can talk about that when I get there. But whatever we do, we have to do it together."

When the call ended, Frazer tossed the phone on the seat beside him and glanced out the window. It was nice down there, he admitted. Warmer weather. Interesting countryside. Pine trees with palmettos beneath them. A coastal breeze that blew one way in the morning and another in the evening, he couldn't remember which. The Old South lurking in the background added a hint of mystery that no one seemed to discuss but everyone seemed ready to fight about. A paradox. A conundrum that only someone from the outside could see but only someone from the inside could fully appreciate. The pride. The arrogance. The pain and misery. And no one to—

Just then, the phone rang. He glanced at the screen and saw the call was from Gina. His first instinct was to answer it and he reached for the phone with this right hand, but as he moved his thumb toward the button to connect the call, he hesitated.

Other fiction works by Joe Hilley

Sober Justice

Double Take

Electric Beach

Night Rain

The Deposition

What the Red Moon Knows

The Legend of Dell Briggers

For more information, please visit www.JoeHilley.com.